harpsong

Oklahoma Stories & Storytellers

Teresa Miller, Series Editor

Also by Rilla Askew:

Strange Business (New York, 1992)
The Mercy Seat (New York, 1997)
Fire in Beulah (New York, 2001)

harpsong

Rilla Askew

University of Oklahoma Press : Norman

This is a work of fiction. Names, characters, places, and incidents are either the product of the author's imagination or are used fictitiously, and any resemblance to actual events or persons, living or dead, is entirely coincidental.

Cover photo courtesy Library of Congress. Title page, first deepsong, and last deepsong photos by Dixie Ezekiel.

LIBRARY OF CONGRESS CATALOGING-IN-PUBLICATION DATA

Askew, Rilla.
    Harpsong / Rilla Askew.
        p. cm. — (The Oklahoma stories & storytellers series ; v. 1)
    ISBN 978-0-8061-3823-7 (hardcover : alk. paper) ISBN 978-0-8061-3928-9 (paper)
    1. Folk singers—Fiction. 2. Oklahoma—Fiction. I. Title.
    PS3551.S545H37 2007
    813'.54—dc22

                                                2006028955

Harpsong is Volume 1 in the Oklahoma Stories & Storytellers series.

The paper in this book meets the guidelines for permanence and durability of the Committee on Production Guidelines for Book Longevity of the Council on Library Resources, Inc. ∞

3 4 5 6 7 8 9 10

For Paul

this is always

Acknowledgments

My gratitude to the Civitella Ranieri Center for providing me with a writing fellowship at the castle in Umbertide, Italy, where I did important work on this book, and to my fellow "fellini" for their artistic support. Special thanks to Guillermo Martinez for spying the harp in San Sepulcro and to Vivan Sundaram for staying behind to help me get it. I'd like to thank Sue Weissinger at the No Man's Land Museum in Goodwell, Oklahoma, who generously opened the museum for me on a day it was closed so that I might view the exhibits and do research. My affectionate thanks to the Amherst posse, Martine Bellen, and Teresa Miller for their help, and a very special thank you to my close friends and fellow travelers Constance Squires and Steve Garrison for their insight, wisdom, and willingness to read these words again and again.

harpsong

the sound is deepsong. only the earth hears it now, the little spirits in the trees, the hills and box canyons. the singer dreamed it awake through long nights on a bed of stones, blew it across limestone bluffs, falling away in the timber. the sound is fading now with his harp's cry, hollowed back in the hills, but the echo remains. the stones tell their version, the blackgums theirs. the dogwoods, the bois d'arcs, the waters.

the people, of course, only tell what they know.

Part One

folksay
1907–1932

Folks say he was born the same year the state was, 1907, but you won't find a public record to prove that, or deny it. Some say he was first cousin to Tom Joad and second-cousin-once-removed to Pretty Boy Floyd's family in Sallisaw—except the Joads weren't real Okies, they were a made-up clan, and it is certain that the Floyds never claimed him. You'll even hear it told from time to time that he was kin to our most famous favorite son, Will Rogers, but that's just a tall tale. To be honest, the Oklahoma son Harlan Singer favored most was the one from Okemah, but we disowned that Okemah boy on account of he was a communist they say, and anyhow, Singer had vanished in the hills by the time Woody Guthrie began to make a reputation.

Some people believe he grew up in the coal mining district, on account of what happened later at McAlester, but the fact of the matter is, Harlan Singer came from the Cherokee hill country, and to this day, depending on how far back in the bo-jacks you go, you'll hear all kind of stories: his mama was an antlered doe with a scream like a Cooper's hawk. He was whelped by a she-wolf and weaned on panther milk. He could walk across the Verdigris in seven steps, limber as a cottonmouth, loud as a crow, he gobbled his deathsong a dozen times and lived a dozen and one times to sing about it. Some say he was a descendent of old-time Cherokee outlaws, Ned Christie or Henry Starr, but the folks around Sallisaw will tell you very well that his mama was a lunatic white woman who went by the name Jones.

She arrived in town on the Kansas City Southern in 1909, and folks figured she'd come from somewhere up north, or east across the border. The boy was a knee-baby then, not quite able to talk, dark all over as his mama was light, and she carried him with her while she roamed the muddy streets in her widow-weeds, trailing a long black veil, though the town believed in its soul she'd never once been married. She said things a woman ought never say outloud, such as the boy had been conceived in her virginity. She began to take him with her, walking or getting wagon rides, deep into the hills where none but the old fullbloods lived, and so we knew she hadn't come from elsewhere at all, and everybody knew why the boy was dark, and we believed we understood his lineage. She would stay gone a week or a month, but she always came back, living hand-to-mouth on the charity of the town, though it irked people that she didn't somehow seem to know it. And then, after years, she got to speaking in tongues, not just at church but anywhere she went. At first we thought she was talking Cherokee, and then we knew she wasn't. So folks wrote up a petition for the sheriff to put her on a train and ride her to Vinita and lock her in the crazy house, but he never got the chance. She set the boy on the Church of Christ steps one morning and went up towards Tahlequah, and before anybody knew it she'd jumped off a bluff into the Illinois. The river didn't turn her loose for seven days, till she rolled up on a sandbar somewhere below Cookson. That was when the boy was nine.

He lit out to the hills the same day they laid his mama's blue body in a pauper's grave, and he roamed from Baron Fork to Webbers Falls, Wild Horse Mountain to Sparrow Hawk, and all through the Brushy Mountains. After a while he disappeared from people's minds. We thought he'd gone to live with the fullbloods around Marble City, until certain things began to come up missing, such as eggs from the henhouse and milk from the porch, pies in a window, shirts from the line. He'd learned to thieve from being on his own they say, but it was just to keep his young self alive, and sometimes you'd find a wildflower in that thieved egg's place, or a bunch of hickory nuts, or a hollowed out gourd—useless things, but he was trying to pay his way. And then he got religion at a brush arbor meeting near Muldrow one August, and the boy quit his thieving.

He came in from the hills and stayed in the old shack in back of Reverend Letbetter's house, and we gave him the same charity we'd given his mother, though he didn't seem to know it any better than she did. We called him Willie Jones, and sometimes for a joke, and because he was so small, Wee Willie Jonesy. He took to hanging around the Sallisaw barber shop, he'd sweep the floor, run errands for a penny or a dime, whatever somebody might give him. He was an eager boy, pretty as a girl, with black curly hair and skin that was the wrong color to match his eyes, but people tolerated him. He was quick and amiable and he learned to play a Jew's harp and a comb with a cigarette paper on it, until somebody gave him a harmonica—a French harp we called it, or mouth harp, but a twenty-five-cent harmonica is what it was—and that's when he began to correct people about his name. No, ma'am, he'd say. No, sir, that's not my name. My name is Harlan Singer.

He'd blow his harp in front of the Rexall Drug with his cap turned upside down on the walk, and if he wore his grin a little too cocky to suit and if he jig-danced a little too wild, well, we forgave that, on account of we knew his history. If we had a loose nickel we'd be sure to toss it in, to see if he would come up with a new song. Some folks said he went down into colored town to learn his songs, but others said he was awful clever on that harp, he might could have made them up himself. And then about the time he got good and grown and sharp enough to start showing something for himself, he turned up gone.

Well, we didn't think much about it. We had other worries on our mind. Banks were failing, crops were lost, there was heat and drought and plagues of berry blight, boll weevils in the fields, walkingsticks on the walls, and nobody had any money. By the time we came to know anything about him again it was 1932 and the whole country was in a mighty trouble. That's when folks began to come to town swearing they'd seen Willie Jones in Muskogee or Tahlequah or Paradise Hill. He showed up in the town of Vardis one sweltery July morn, limping along Main Street with a little possum-haired gal in tow, the both of them swallered in clothes too big to be right and the gal wearing britches to boot, and he proceeded to set her to wait in front of the mercantile while he went across the street and robbed the Farmers Bank, and all he used, the people say, was a smile and a feedsack and a very polite note, and a six-gun pointed toward the ceiling. Later we heard that gun didn't have any bullets. Folks cheered when he stepped out of the bank tossing paper dollars by the handfuls in the dusty dirt. We'd come to expect that, on account of that's how Pretty Boy Floyd had always done, or so we'd heard, though Pretty Boy never did hit the bank at Vardis. But Harlan Singer surely did, and by Christmas that year he had a name far and wide, in our part of the country anyway, and nobody could remember him ever being called anything but Singer.

So the people thought he was going to copy himself after some of our more famous bank robbers. The same folks who believed he'd got his songs from colored town were the very ones declaring up and down that we had ourselves a new-minted copycat Pretty Boy. Folks predicted Singer would turn up in Red Oak—that was an easy bank to rob—or Earlsboro, where the oil money still was, or Kinta or Quinton or Crowder.

One morning a little boy in new overalls showed up in Vardis toting a brown parcel tied around with string, addressed to Mr. Oliver Teasley, Sole Owner and Proprietor of the First Farmers & Merchants State Bank of Vardis, Oklahoma. Mr. Teasley took one look at that box and blanched pale as a toad-belly. He made the boy carry it outside and set it in the middle of Main Street, and then Mr. Teasley, who wielded considerable power in the town, had the mayor stop all the passing traffic, and then he went back in the bank and got inside the vault while the mayor fired his double-barreled shotgun from a hundred paces at that paper-wrapped box. The box didn't do anything. The mayor reloaded and blasted it again. The box hopped around every time the mayor blasted it, but then it would just settle down and sit still, mocking everybody.

We watched it an hour or two, hoping it would blow up or do something interesting, but along towards noon Mayor Mayfield, who hated being made a fool, stomped right out in the street and tore the shredded butcher paper off.

Inside, in a tattered, shot-riddled tin box, was most of the money Harlan Singer had taken in the first place from Mr. Teasley's bank—what amount, that is, folks hadn't stuffed in their pockets between the time Singer flung it out of the sack and Teasley finally got up the nerve to come chasing outside in his suspenders hollering for somebody to catch the long-gone robber. Of course, those greenbacks were shot all to pieces now and weren't fit to be of use to anybody, and when the mayor went to look for the little boy, he was gone, and nobody could remember seeing him before that day or since, but the point is, Harlan Singer gave back the money. So then we knew he still had his religion. That kindly surprised us.

People said, Well, he aims to rob from the rich and give to the poor. That's how our folk heroes have always done, and that's also what Jesus taught, idn't it? More or less? Singer don't intend to make a career of robbing small town banks, we said. Too many working folks' money sits in the little town banks. He'll go right out in bright daylight and rob a big city bank, a *rich* man's bank, an oil-company or a government or a utilities-type bank—that's how you rob from the rich to give to the poor, and that's what Harlan Singer aims to do. He'll be doing it here any day now. Just watch him.

Sharon

That's me and him standing at the side of the road outside Joplin, Missouri. To look at it you wouldn't know where it was, would you? Dirt road, bare trees, it could be anywhere, Arkansas or Mississippi, these Oklahoma hills even, where we came from. You wouldn't know what year either, but I can tell you. 1935. I believe it was March maybe. The trees were just fixing to bud. The lady that took it posed us to look like that, like we were hitchhiking, which we weren't, though we did do a lot of hitching. We rode the rails too, especially at first. That valise in the dirt wasn't ours. Me and Harlan used a rucksack. The lady drove us in her car to that spot and got that valise out of her turtlehull and set it on the ground between us before she took the picture. It's the only picture ever taken of me and Harlan, so far as I know.

I didn't know about that one, or I didn't know it was a public picture, till I ran across it in a postcard rack in Tahlequah way up after the end of the war. I about fainted. I felt like I was watching an old dream come alive in front of my face. I bought it so quick, like somebody might snatch it, but for the life of me I couldn't recollect when it was taken. My hat there's what caused me to finally remember. I'd found that cloth hat in a bar ditch near Joplin and lost it to the wind outside McAlester, so I knew right when the picture had to have been taken, and then I remembered the lady.

She came and picked us out of all the other folks camped under that railroad overpass, she walked right past women and their little kids and men with sores on their feet, which, if she meant to be taking pictures of poor people, like she said, you'd think she might have picked one of them. We were sitting in the shade underneath a girder, Harlan wasn't playing his harp or anything, but that lady made a beeline right for us, and really, I don't know why, unless it was just because my husband was so pretty. He didn't like anybody to say it, of course, he acted like that was such an embarrassment, but you'd seldom catch him smiling with his mouth open to show where his tooth was broke. See it there? She caught him with his lips open. You can't tell if he's grinning or squinting, but Harlan kept his lips shut tight over that chipped tooth most the time, except when he was singing or talking.

I cherish this picture anyway, even if it does feel like the lady stole it. She didn't really, I guess. She told us what she was doing, and we stood right there, still as still, while she took our picture with a big black box camera. It wasn't like she snuck around. She drove us back to the camp after and dropped us off, we never saw or heard from her again. Come to find out, she put that picture in a book along with a bunch of others. I didn't know you could do that, take somebody's picture and put it in a book or on a postcard and never ask them. But she paid us two dollars and a half, or she didn't call it pay, she just gave it to us, said, "Here, get y'all something to eat." We left for Oklahoma the next morning.

There's another thing about this picture. I was with child then. I didn't know it at the time, or my mind didn't, but if you look at my face, staring off at the side of the road like that, you can see how I'm looking inward and outward at the same time, so some part of me must have known. So really, if I think about it, this is the only picture in existence of me and Ronnie and his daddy. That's another reason I love it. I don't care if a hundred thousand people see it, this picture is mine. My own and only, now. Oh, people act like they know everything, they tell all sorts of stories, don't none of them know the real truth. They don't. Me here, Sharon, his wife. I'm the one that knows Harlan.

I was fourteen years old the first time I laid eyes on him. He come walking out the road from Cookson on a hot May morning the week after school was out, 1931. It was a Saturday. My daddy was gone preaching. I was supposed to be sweeping the yard but what I was doing mostly was watching for Marie Tingle. She was a neighbor girl who sold Cloverine salve and delivered our *GRIT* once a week, and she rode an old white dray horse that mudged along slow as cream rising. I'd drag that shoemake broom through the dirt, weave a pattern out to the yard fence, and then I'd stand a while, looking. I aimed to be the first one at the gate when Marie got there, because if Mama saw her first, she'd come grab that magazine and put it away till we got the work done. Then she'd go off by herself to read the story, and the day would be half gone before I'd get my chance to read the next chapter. The *GRIT* ran a love story that went week to week, I was real anxious to find out what came next, I remember.

I seen him coming, I thought at first it was only the dust stirring, and then I thought it was a drunkard lolling, he had that rolling slap-footed gait, you know. I forgot all about Marie Tingle. I dropped the broom and ran up on the porch hollering, "Mama! Mama!" All five kids came tumbling out the door, and Mama right behind them. The dogs were barking a racket. Harlan kept coming along, he stopped outside the fence and said howdy, and then he stood there, peering up at us, smiling. Mama called the dogs off, they slunk back under the house, and after that it was just the sound of the locusts. Well, nobody was surprised to see a stranger in the road in those days, even if you lived a mile out from town, like we did, but Mama gawked at Harlan the way a calf looks at a new gate. He was all dressed up like he was set to go someplace. Believe me there wasn't anywhere to go around Cookson, Oklahoma, that would justify a tie and a snap-brim hat, but that's not what Mama was staring at anyway. She was looking at his face.

Oh, I can't describe it, you can see for yourself. What that picture don't show though is the color of his eyes, they were the prettiest light green. It don't show how smooth his skin was, just practically like he was covered in doeskin. You can't even see how long and black his eyelashes were, or how they curled up. *Pretty.* I'll bet that was the very word in my mama's mind. It was sure enough in mine. He asked for a drink of water, and Mama said, "Sharon, honey, go draw him some water."

I blinked at her. My mama never called me honey. She motioned for him to come inside the fence and have a seat on the busted crate in the shade of an old bo'dark tree we had in the yard there. I felt Harlan's eyes on me, I went to the well and drew the bucket, handed him the dipper. We were only a few feet from each other, out in the bright sun—he didn't go to the shade and he didn't sit down—but I wouldn't glance at him any more until I got back on the porch. His hat was pushed to the back of his head. He thanked Mama for the water, commented on the heat and so forth, but he kept flicking his eyes my direction. Mama stepped to the porch ledge, hoisted Ellie Renee on her hip, said, "I suppose you're hunting a handout." She didn't appear nearly as suspicious as the words sounded.

"No, ma'am," Harlan said, "don't reckon I am. Wouldn't mind if you had a little job of work a fellow could do, though."

"What kind?" Mama said. I turned my whole head to stare at her. I'd never heard her say anything to a hobo but move on down the road.

"Any kind, ma'am. I can do about anything on a place needs doing."

"I ain't got any money to pay you."

Harlan laughed. "Ain't nobody got any money, near as I can tell. No place I been."

"Where-all have you been?" Mama asked. She was shading her eyes with her free hand, but I saw her slip her other hand back to smooth her hair behind her ears.

"All over the country, ma'am." Harlan cut his eyes at me. "Here to California and back," he said. "Down to Texas, east as far as Georgia. Hadn't been to Washington, D.C., yet, but I'm goin'. Maybe in Washington somebody's got some money."

"Sounds like you been doing some hard traveling."

"I have that, ma'am."

"Well," Mama said. The yard got so quiet, except for the insects. Even the twins were hushed, staring out from behind Mama's skirt, Leonard had his fist wrapped in the cotton, sucking it in his mouth. I could see the baby moving up and down with Mama's breathing. She was about two then, I guess, Ellie Renee. She was the blondest of any of us, had the finest hair, it feathered out in wisps all around her head like little fish fins. Mama kept reaching up to wipe her dirty cheek, rubbing over and over till Ellie started squirming, and then whining, and finally squalling, and then it wasn't quiet no more.

Mama said over Ellie's squalls, "You might bust me up some stovewood if you want. I could probably feed you a bite. The ax is yonder." She nodded at the double-bitted chopping ax stuck in the tree stump.

"Ma'am, if I could get that bite to eat first, I could sure work better. I'll even sing you a song for a bonus. Singer's my name anyhow, like the sewing machine. I don't sew but I do-si-do every chance I get." Harlan folded his arms and cut a gawky little square-dance step in the yard. Mama tried to frown, but her face wouldn't let her.

"Well. Come on then," she said.

Harlan started across the yard, and I saw it again, how awkward he walked. Ellie kept squalling in Mama's arms. Harlan stopped, whipped a harmonica out of his pocket and ran a trill up and down. The baby hushed and stared. The other kids peeked out from behind Mama's skirt, the busted ladderback, the old canning crate, where they were all hiding.

"Have a seat," Mama said. Harlan ran one last trill, moved to sit on the steps. "Sharon," Mama said, "go fix Mr. Singer a plate."

Well, there wasn't a plate of anything in our house to fix, only cold biscuits left over from breakfast, which me and Mama both knew, but that wasn't what had me caught. I was watching Harlan, how he held onto the banister while he swung himself down. His left leg flopped to the side like he couldn't control it. My stomach dropped. The only person I knew with a leg that wouldn't work right was the mail carrier Max Stunke, and that was because his was wooden. I thought that was what was wrong with Harlan's.

"Sharon Earlene," Mama said, "go in the house and fix Mr. Singer a plate of biscuits."

I slammed in the house and poured about a pint of sorghum on those cold biscuits, and you know sorghum molasses was just nearly liquid gold to me, even if our daddy did own a sorghum mill and got paid with syrup for grinding other folks' cane. Seemed to me like I just never could get enough of it. But I slathered those three biscuits like a punishment, like I was going to punish the stranger on the porch with too much of the thing I loved best, because in those few minutes he'd went from being perfect to awkward to one-legged. That's what I thought.

I came back outside. Harlan had his harp making every kind of sound in the world, a train and a laying hen and a hoot owl and a jaybird, and the kids were jumping up and down and clapping, and the rooster was all puffed up on the chopping stump, crowing, and even Mama was leaning against a porch post, smiling. I set the plate on the top step and Harlan turned to me. He still had his lips wrapped around the harmonica, but he kept his eyes on my face. He nodded. My stomach went hot, my chest runny, like syrup on the stove, melted and running down. I forgot all about his crippled leg. I mean that. It was like I couldn't see it anymore, even when he stood up afterwhile and went slap-footed across the yard to split a few licks of kindling.

When Daddy came home Monday afternoon, me and Mama were doing the wash on the back porch. We heard the team and wagon, the kids shouting, we neither one looked at each other. Mama wrung out Daddy's second overalls, handed them to me to put on the line. I didn't watch her wipe her palms on her apron, but I felt it, how she raised a hand to smooth her hair. I was still standing by the clothesline when she stepped off the porch and went around the side of the house.

Mama was shading her eyes on the porch steps when I got to the front. Daddy was yonder by the barn, trying to unhitch the team one-handed. He had the baby in his left arm, a twin hanging off the back of each leg. James and Talmadge were shooting each other dead in the flatbed. Mama hollered, "You, Leonard! Leora Jane! Let your daddy alone! Talmadge Ray, I'm going to cut a switch to you two in a minute. Y'all quit that and help your daddy get them horses in the barn!"

Daddy glanced at Mama, but he went on unhitching, and when the boys led the horses off, he reached in the bed for a sack of flour and hoisted it to his shoulder, started toward the house. To look at him you wouldn't know he was a preacher, not on a regular day like that. In the Sunday pulpit he'd have on his brown suit, his head would be bare, he'd be wearing a tie and a white shirt. When he wasn't preaching, though, he wore overalls and a straw hat, same as any farming man.

Oh, you know my daddy was an itinerant pastor. He traveled around to a half dozen different communities all over Cherokee County. He'd preach Sunday mornings at Welling, Sunday nights at Peggs, trade off to different churches the next week, and that's not even counting baptisms and revivals. If we'd had a car he could have stayed home more, but seemed to me like only townfolks had cars, or anyhow we didn't, and every Saturday morning he'd drive off in the wagon and stay gone till Monday, and all he did it for was the love of God and whatever little bit of cornmeal or chickens the people could give him. The rest of the time he cropped shares, shoed horses, ground sorghum, anything he could think of to earn a nickel or trade for what we couldn't grow ourselves. But Daddy's heart was in the ministry. If he could've just preached full time and still fed us, that's all he would've done. Mama blamed him for it though. Not for the preaching, of course, but for leaving her alone to take care of things, for having to do so much farm work herself and us never having any money. She mouthed at him about that all the time.

Daddy started up the steps, stopped with one foot on the bottom. "Why, hello, Sissy," he said. He'd seen me standing around at the side of the porch. "You ain't got a hidey for your old daddy?" There was a flickering moment then, I looked up at Mama, and then Daddy did, and then Harlan came ambling around the corner from the back of the house with the hoe laid across his shoulder. After that, everybody's eyes were on Harlan. That's how it always was, no matter where he turned up.

"Howdy," Harlan said.

Mama said, "Earl, this fellow here's going to help plant the cotton."

Well, we'd never had any help planting cotton, chopping it, picking it, nothing. Cotton was your cash crop and there was little enough profit to begin with, and the landlord Mr. Casper was owed a third of that. Plus, the ground was broke already, Daddy'd busted it with the cultivator a week ago. The real work wasn't set to start till it was time to chop the cotton, and that wouldn't be for another month. I figured for sure Daddy was going to say, Move on down the road, mister, but he only stared at Harlan a minute, drew his chin in, nodded real slow. Then he continued on up the steps, carried that hundred-pound sack of Clara Bell flour in the house.

At supper that night I kept my head bowed after Daddy finished the blessing. My daddy was the type of man, he never spoke harsh to anybody, but he could look at you from deep in his brown eyes, you'd feel like it was God looking—or not God. Jesus. The Man of Sorrows. Like every sorry thought in your sorry sinful mind was known to him, it hurt him so bad he didn't want to talk about it. I was afraid he could read the nervy thoughts I had about Harlan, so I ate with my eyes on the table until I heard Daddy's voice saying he'd decided to take a job at the bank in Vardis. Well, that made me look up. My daddy had never worked a public job in his life.

"When, Earl?" Mama said. "How much are they paying?"

"I'll have to let him know. We haven't spoke yet about the money."

Mama's forehead got that line in it, her mouth set, but she didn't say anything.

"These runs are getting bad," Daddy said. "Mr. Teasley's real anxious about the situation."

"Bank runs?" Mama said. "In Vardis?"

"I don't know," Daddy said, and then he asked Talmadge to pass him the butter.

Now, I didn't particularly know what a bank run was, and Vardis might as well have been in Texas for how often we ever went there, but I figured President Hoover must have something to do with it. Folks were always talking about the banks and Hoover, the banks and Hoover, like Herbert Hoover was the cause of all the banking trouble in the world. There weren't any banks in Cookson, and even if there'd been one, we didn't have any money to go in it, and I didn't know anybody who did. Anyway I just felt relieved. Daddy wasn't paying attention to me or Harlan, his gaze was on Mama. I got up my grit then and glanced over. Harlan smiled and winked at me. I ducked my head quick, my face hot. I don't think I heard another word Mama and Daddy said the whole rest of supper.

While I cleared the table Harlan took out his harp and began to play old-timey hymns for my daddy. That's how he would do. Harlan just had a feel in his heart for what a person wanted to hear, he'd be playing it before you even knew it was what you wanted. Before Daddy got home Harlan played jigs and hornpipes for us after supper, the kids would bounce in their chairs and my mama would laugh. But that evening he played church music and my daddy sat at the table with his eyes closed, listening like he was praying. Next morning Daddy rode one of the horses over to Mr. Casper's to use the telephone, and he didn't come home till almost dark. Mr. Teasley drove right up from Vardis that morning and got him. After that, Daddy laid out the work for us at breakfast each day and left the house before daylight to walk in to Cookson, where Mr. Teasley picked him up in his Buick. Mr. Teasley drove nineteen miles every morning to get him and brought him back again in the evenings, that's how fierce he wanted my daddy to work for him, and none of us questioned why.

It's strange, looking back, to see how it all meshed together. Any one part could have been left out, everything would've gone different. Daddy had met Mr. Teasley coming out of the Vardis mercantile one Saturday, and that was the same Saturday morning Harlan walked up in our yard. Mr. Teasley begged Daddy to come to work for him, and that was right at a time when Mama had been on Daddy real hard about no money and him gone three Sundays a month leaving her to work a farm with one lazy grown daughter and five young ones too little to help. And my daddy was bad to put the fleece out, you know, he liked to have him a sign to tell him God's will in any matter. So when he came home and found Harlan with the hoe over his shoulder and his hymn-playing harp, Daddy must have felt like God was giving him the go-ahead to take that outside job, and he did take it, and Harlan stayed to plant the cotton. Daddy was glad, I guess, because he knew me and Mama couldn't do all the field work and the inside work both without him there through the week to help us, and Mama was glad too, at least in the beginning, or she acted like she was. She made dessert every night for supper. And me, I was really glad, but I kept it a secret.

Harlan sparked me the first time a couple mornings later, right out in the truckpatch in back of the house. That's how bold he was. He was supposed to be in the field, of course, it was mid-morning already. Daddy had been gone to Vardis for hours. I looked up from my hoeing and seen him coming, my breath caught a fist in my chest. He was still far enough away and he was walking so slow you almost couldn't detect that little slap in his gait. I was praying he wouldn't come over. It was a real sweltery morning, all I could think about was the sweat on my face and under my arms.

Harlan started calling from way off at the edge of the corn, "Sharrrrron! Sharon Singer!"

I got so flustered. I hacked at the weeds around the potatoes, acting like I didn't hear it, even to myself. He came and stood outside the double strand of bobwire Daddy'd put up to keep the cows out.

"Man alive," Harlan said, "that plantin's thirsty work."

I shot him a look. Planting cotton wasn't hard. All you had to do was walk the furrows behind the team.

"Where's a fella supposed to find a drink of water in these parts?" Harlan said.

I could see he was sweating too, his white shirt soaked through. "If you'd just waited," I said, "they'd have brought you the bucket before noon."

"Who would? You?"

"No," I said. "That's the twins' job."

"Well, see," Harlan said, "that's what I was afraid of. You spoilt me that first morning. If it's not you bringing me water, I'd as soon go on and die of thirst."

I dipped my head so my hat covered my face. It was Daddy's hat, really, tied on with string. I wouldn't put on my bonnet that morning to go to the garden, I thought a poke bonnet was too old-fashioned, made you look like an old woman. Isn't that funny? Me worried about looking like an old woman at fourteen. I didn't want him to see how red my face was, which I knew, because that's how it felt.

"What you got there, a copperhead?"

I was chopping the weeds fast, making my way down the row. "I've got work to do," I said. "You'd better get to work too. If my daddy catches you sluffing off you'll wish he hadn't."

"What's your old daddy going to do?"

"Kick your lazy self off this farm."

Harlan laughed. "He's not going to do that."

"You just hide and watch," I said.

But the truth is, I was scared. I'd been hoping that if Harlan worked really hard maybe Daddy would keep him, but I could tell already Harlan wasn't any too work brittle. I figured for sure Daddy was going to come home one of these evenings and see how little work had got done and send Harlan packing. I turned and started chopping another row. "That cotton's not going to run out there and plant itself," I said.

"It won't?" He was sidling along the wire, following me. "Why, Miss Sharon Earlene, didn't you know there's a place where the bitterweed don't grow and the cotton plants itself? Picks itself too, jumps its own self right in the sack."

I snapped back over my shoulder, "Not here it don't!"

"Well, just naturally a place like that ain't in Okla*hom*a. It's far, far away," he said, his voice dreamy. "This land where the cottonseeds hop their own selves in the ground and the green plants pop up in a minute and dance around. You haven't got to chop it neither, they tell me. There's no such of a thing as a weed in this place. Come autumn, they say the cotton's blooming far as your eye can wander, pretty and white as popcorn, man alive, the bolls just itching to jump off the plants."

"Who told you that?"

"Ohhh, an old prophet fella I used to know."

I snorted, turned to start another row. I could feel him following. Sweat was running down, my eyes were stinging, I had to let go the hoe with one hand to wipe my forehead. I glanced back at the house in case Mama was watching but I didn't see anyone, only the baby playing with her spoons in the dirt yard.

"Know where it is?"

"Where what is?" I said.

"The land where weeds don't grow and the water tastes like cherry wine?"

I knew I oughten to answer, and I didn't, really, but I guess I shook my head.

"Why, it's in California!" Harlan laughed, like it was a big joke. "That's how the song goes, innit?" he said. He pulled his harp out of his pants pocket. "That's where I'm fixing to carry you, Miss Sharon Earlene, one of these sunny mornings."

I glanced at the house again. "What'd you do," I said to change the subject, "leave them horses standing loose in the field?"

For an answer he went to playing that old Jimmie Rodgers song about going to California where the water tastes like wine.

I worked on down the row, the tops of the potato plants flying as much as the weeds.

He called out, "I been meaning to ask you something! How'd you get so pretty?"

I stopped. I knew he was mocking me.

"You're the prettiest thing I seen since Christmas."

"Shut up," I whispered.

"How'd you get to be out here in these old blackgum hills?" He was talking soft now, not calling it out, because I'd quit moving away. "How is it I been hunting all over creation, and you were here all the time, getting growed up right under me? You reckon God likes a good joke?"

"Shut up," I said.

"I been to Tipton." He kept coming, walking slow along the wire. "I been to Pampa, Amarillo, Georgia, I been all over God's green and dusty country, you were here all the time, the prettiest girl in the world, standing in her daddy's yard."

"Shut up!" My chest was burning, I wasn't anything but knob-kneed and meatless, my hair hung straight down, we couldn't afford any Toni home permanents, my ears stuck out through my hair, it was so fine and thin, it wasn't yellow like the baby's, it wasn't reddish like Mama's, it was just plain ashy-brown, and I couldn't think anything but he was making fun of me. I felt like I hated him, except I was too ashamed.

Harlan said, "Reckon I'm going to have to start believing in the Almighty again."

That threw me. I stared at the potato plants. It'd never occurred to me there could be such a thing as *not* believing. That'd be like not believing in sky or wind or water.

"What else could it be but a miracle of the Lord that you were standing in the yard when I walked up the road?" His voice was so quiet. "Otherwise I might've walked right on past. What would have happened then?"

I kept looking at the ground. There was a soft tumping sound, his foot in the dust as he came along the fence.

"What would've happened if I never met you?" he whispered. He was only a few feet away, just on the other side of the wire. I heard him plain. Then all I could hear was the sound of the oak trees, the locusts crying in the oak trees, and way off by the pond, Belle calling her calf. Harlan kept on not saying anything.

After a long time, I answered, "Well." I still had my head down.

He started blowing the saddest, most beautiful sliding minor tune on his harp.

To this day I can't name what that song was. I heard him play a lot of mournful songs through the years, but I never heard that same one again. He made it up in that moment. He thought there was a chance he wasn't going to get me, see, and he was telling me in the music what would happen to him if he didn't. I raised up finally. He stopped playing, lowered the harp, smiled with his lips closed. My insides were ringing, my chest was making its own song alongside Harlan's, because I knew that what I'd heard him calling from far off was real. I knew he meant me to marry him. And I knew that I would.

He climbed over the bobwire, he had to lean on a post to swing his leg over. He came straight across the rows to where I was standing, took the hoe from me and let it fall on the ground. He went to try to kiss me, but our hats bumped. I pulled away. I was so sweaty. He took his hat off, bent his face again

I just . . . it was such a surprise. I'd never felt anything like it. I'd practiced kissing my arm under the covers at night, but this was nothing like it. His mouth was so soft. I could taste the salt. Then he reached under my chin with two fingers, touched the base of my throat, where the blood beats, said, "Sharon Earlene Singer." He put his hat on, turned and limped off. The soft dirt in the garden made it harder for him to walk.

It wasn't until I picked up my hoe and turned to finish the row that I saw Mama standing way across in the backyard, looking my direction. She was too far away for me to see what her face said. I was hoping she'd just then come out the door. I said to myself, She's fixing to light into me for lolling around when I'm supposed to be working. I started chopping a fury, like there really could've been a snake in the potato plants. I just wanted to believe it, you know, that she didn't see me and Harlan. Out of the corner of my eye I watched her bend over and lift the baby. She started toward me.

"Hi, Sissy," the baby said, from where she was riding on Mama's hip. "Hi, Sissy." The closer they got, the more she said it, trying to get me to answer. "Hi, Sissy."

I was on the far side of the patch then, back toward the cornfield, acting like I didn't expect anything, I just kept hoeing. Mama hiked her skirt and stepped over the wire, coming toward me.

"Hi, Sissy. *Hi.*"

I raised up, said hi, finally, to hush her. Mama didn't look mad or pursemouthed or anything, just smooth and blank. The baby started in with her next favorite word after hi and no. "C'mon. Come on, Sissy. C'mon." She was still saying c'mon when Mama reached me and took the hoe out of my hand and dropped it, like Harlan did, and then she slapped the fire out of me. Everything was quiet until Ellie Renee let out a long wail. After that, I could hear her squalling while Mama carried her back to the house, but I couldn't see her, I had my hands up over my face.

deepsong

on his back, in the thicket, staring straight up at the
winks of stars between the leaves, the singer remembers
    her in the yard, her hand on the brushbroom, her eyes big,
    how he'd been coming along the lane, thinking nothing, trying
only to lift the one foot and set it down, trying not to scuff, not to drag
dust, the lameness new then, coming along the lane from braggs, from
muskogee, from lawton, where he'd sipped the jake in the dark boxcar,
the old man's hand on his arm, the old voice saying, don't, son.
    how he'd been so careful, hearing nothing, walking, coming home,
when he saw her in the yard her hand on the brushbroom her eyes
big. how she'd dropped the broom as if it scalded her, and the sumac
puffed a spit of dust while she skittered onto the porch, hid behind the
cedarpost, a young bandit coon, her silverish hair and tiny hands, her
sloping nose and little mouth, and in her light face, the eyes, dark and
large as mulberries.
    how his chest lifted then, the numbness fell away, how the
tenderness swelled in him, and he'd longed to pick up a horseapple, an
osage orange from the ground beneath the bois d'arc, and offer it to her,
a gift.
    how he'd coveted her,
    as she hid behind the cedarpost, watching, while he talked to her
mama, how he'd known even then he would steal her, like the brown
henhouse eggs, the cooling pies from the windows.
    how the only reason it took him so long was that he couldn't think
what to leave behind in her place.

Sharon

The next Sunday was the third Sunday of the month, the one Daddy stayed home and preached at Cookson. It was peculiar, him gone in the daytime that whole week and then home on Sunday, but I was glad, because Harlan rode in the back of the wagon with me and the kids while Mama sat up front in the spring seat beside Daddy. She'd never told Daddy about me and Harlan in the truckpatch—I would've known if she did, I'd have seen it in Daddy's features—but she watched me like a hawk now, and when Harlan played his harp after supper Mama didn't smile anymore. She would make me get up and go start the dishes, carry the slops out or something. Riding to church beside Daddy, though, Mama didn't turn around, and I felt like I could meet Harlan's eyes if I wanted. He had on his tie and his snap-brim hat, of course, and his white shirt still damp from last night's washing. Even across the flatbed I could smell the soap on him. Every time I looked up, he was watching me. His eyes were so bright in the May sunlight, burning right through me, and I'd meet them a minute, but then I'd have to turn my head.

Driving along, Daddy started singing "Power in the Blood," not loud, just under his breath, but Harlan took out his harmonica and started to play, and Daddy sang louder, and after a while Mama started singing. *"Would you be free from the bur-den of sin? There's pow'r in the blood, pow'r in the blood. Would you o'er e-vil a vic-to-ry win?"* And the kids joined in, shouting out the words. *"There is power! power! wonder-working power! In the blooood! of the Laaamb! There is power! power! wonder-working power! In the pre-cious blood of the Lamb!"*

By the time we got to Cookson there was a kind of high giddiness in all of us, and Daddy was wound up to a fine pitch to preach. My daddy was a gentle man, you know, at home he was a lot easier to get along with than Mama, but he could really preach hellfire when he wanted. That morning he took Revelation for his text, the part about the liars and abominators being cast into the lake that burns with fire and brimstone, and I'm telling you, my daddy's voice thundered all over that sanctuary. He shook the windows, he rattled the rafters, he painted the flames till you saw them licking, heard them crackling, saw the sinner's skin splitting open, pink and blackening, like a pig on a spit. "That's e-*ter*-nity brethren! Forever and ever without end!" Believe me, if you weren't washed in the blood already, you sure knew you better get to it. Our little Cookson Free Will Baptist was just a small congregation, we only had about thirty members, but there were three decisions made that morning—two rededications and one profession of faith—and it was mostly on account of Daddy's preaching, I know, but I think it was also partly on account of Harlan.

At the end of the sermon Mama slipped out of the pew like always and went to the piano to play the invitation, and Harlan pulled out his harp and played along with her, "I Surrender All," right there from the fourth pew where we sat with my little brothers and sisters. The sound was soft, barely loud enough to be heard under Mama's playing and Daddy's praying, but it changed the air in that churchhouse. You could feel the spirit moving, the music pulling, nudging. I felt like I wanted to step out in the aisle and go forward, and I'd been saved already eight years. I had to grip my hands on the pew back in front of me. I was praying too, but what I was praying for was Daddy to hurry up and finish. Which he did finally and stood at the back of the church and everybody passed by and shook his hand, said that was a mighty fine sermon, Brother Earl, mighty fine, and went out in the hot sunlight smiling, and it was like that high giddiness had spread from my family to the whole congregation.

Daddy was in a really good mood at Sunday dinner, he blessed everything from the cottonseeds in the ground to the food to the nourishment of our bodies, and Mama gave everybody extra helpings of cobbler, but the biggest one she saved for Harlan. I couldn't tell whether that made me glad or not. The kids were hanging all over him, begging him to make the rooster sound, make the robin, make the train whistle blow. Harlan sat at the table, smiling in his white shirt, his teeth so white in his tan face, his tie loose, and he went from hymns to train sounds to cowboy songs and back again without stopping. I cleaned up the dishes and went out to the porch and sat on the canning crate till it was time to get ready to go to prayer meeting.

Next day Harlan came and found me in the yard where I was throwing out scratch to the chickens. He tried to kiss me again, but I wouldn't let him. I knew Mama might be watching out the kitchen window, but that was only partly why. Truth is, I think I was mad at him for paying so much attention to my family. I jerked away and flounced toward the house barefooted. I stepped on an old stob sticking up in the yard and cut my foot bad, and I didn't even yelp. I just kept walking. I didn't want to show anything, I had a kind of pride about it. And the week just went on like that. Evenings, Harlan played music for my folks after supper, he'd tell jokes, tease the kids, sometimes he talked Scripture with my daddy. Days, he'd pretend to do a little work in the mornings, but then before long he'd come looking for me, he'd find me in the truckpatch, the barn, the henhouse gathering eggs, wherever I was working. I'd pretend not to listen when he talked about how the oak trees never die in California, how you can pluck an orange or a peach right off a branch and eat it for breakfast and the palm trees grow as tall as church steeples. He'd always go to kiss me and I'd always act like I was going to push him away. But every day Harlan got bolder.

And then one night Daddy didn't come home to supper. The Vardis bank closed at two, of course, and even after Daddy waited around for Mr. Teasley to count all his money, still, he'd be home by the time I went out to do the milking. Mama didn't say a word at the table, not even to nag our manners. I watched her face, pinched and still. I thought Daddy not being home had something to do with me and Harlan. I was afraid Mama had seen us kissing out back of the smokehouse that morning. Harlan was quiet too, his eyes upon Mama. He didn't make one joke. Talmadge kept pestering him. "Ain't you going to play us nothing, Mr. Singer?" Harlan sawed out a quick hoedown finally, and then quit. He laid his harp on the table.

Mama said, "Mr. Casper come by this afternoon." It was hard to tell who she was talking to. She was spooning up the vinegar pie, making huge helpings. "Oh, these bank runs just worry me to death," she said. She set a bowl in front of Harlan. "They had one at Sallisaw this morning. The bank closed, locked all the doors and about caused a riot." Mama got quiet a minute, then she said, "Mr. Casper thinks somebody might've got shot."

My throat shut. Talmadge squeaked out the very words I was thinking: "Is something going to happen to Daddy? They're not going to hurt him, are they?"

Mama said, "Well, no. I don't reckon." But her voice sounded scared.

"Do they run people over with their cars?" Talmadge said.

"No, son," Harlan said, leaning forward real quick, his voice light. "That's not what they mean by a bank run." He picked up his harp, ran a couple of glad licks. "I seen one of them runs at Little Rock last year, I hate to say it, but it's a pretty poor affair. Lots of folks standing in line looking desperate, is all. You don't want to spend too much time at one. Boring enough to curl your hair." He ran his fist across the top of his head. "Look what happened to me." James Arnold laughed, but Talmadge was still frowning. "Aw, just think a minute, son," Harlan said. "Out of all the men hunting a job of work in two counties, old Oliver Teasley hired your daddy. How come is that?"

Talmadge shook his head he didn't know, and James Arnold, who copied every move Talmadge made, did the same.

Harlan winked at them. "Take me," he said, "I been looking for work for about fifty years, I'd a been pleased if the bankers'd hired me. But they knew better, on account of, one, I can't count worth a nickel, and, two, I'm the type of a fella who's liable to start throwing punches if folks come in to get their money. Whereas, your daddy's only got to gaze head-on at a man and the fella will just naturally think twice on any subject."

Talmadge looked up at Mama. "Is that right?"

Mama said yes, but she still had her worried look.

"Why's it wrong for people to come get their money?" Talmadge said.

"It's not wrong," Harlan said. "The bankers just don't like folks to do it all at once."

"How come?"

"Oh, that's a question an uncountable fella like me couldn't answer."

"Is my Daddy beating up the people that want their money?"

"Good Lord, no. Did you ever see your daddy beat anybody?"

"No, sir."

"Well, then," Harlan said.

"How come *you* would?"

"Now wait a minute, did I say that?"

Talmadge nodded, but he didn't seem too sure.

"I believe what I said was I'd start throwing punches. Well, now, that's why the bankers won't hire me, see. It's them bankers I'd go to hit when I seen they didn't want to give the people back their money."

Talmadge appeared relieved, but he glanced at Mama to see if what he felt was all right.

"Let me tell you something, mister," Harlan said, "don't you be giving me your million dollars to count and make change, no sir. You wasn't planning on doing that, was you?" Talmadge shook his head. "That's good," Harlan said. "That's mighty good. Because I'd be bound to make a mistake and exchange you a ten for a twenty, then we'd both be mad. I promise you I can't cipher worth a durn. Can you cipher?" Talmadge nodded. "Can you count?" Talmadge and James Arnold both nodded. Leonard piped up, "I can! I can! I'm good at numbers!" And Leora cried, "Me too!" and Ellie Renee went to saying, "Me too! Mama! Me too!" and the boys laughed. Harlan played a little square-dance tune then. After a while he quit blowing, kept the rhythm thumping with his palm on the table while he called out in singsong something like *I can't ci-pher and I can't count! / I can't ride and I can't mount! / But I'll raise you a ruck-us, low'r you a hoe! / Dance you a jig and skin you a doe! / Han-dy with a hammer, ruth-less with a cup, / slay you any var-mint you can rustle up!* Or words to that effect. I can't recollect all the words Harlan sang, but I could always tell when he was making them up instead of remembering them, on account of the bright look he'd get on his face. He wasn't singing then though, he was calling the words the way a square-dance caller calls the figures, and I kept looking to the door. I was afraid Daddy would come in and see that Harlan had the kids dancing. They were all every one jig-dancing while me and Mama cleared the table.

That was one worry I could have just as well saved myself, because it was long after dark before Daddy got home. Harlan had headed out to the barn to sleep a while ago, the kids were all in bed. Me and Mama'd been sitting at the table for hours, not saying anything, while she did the mending. I watched her turning the collar on Daddy's white preaching shirt, snipping the threads to unhook it so she could stitch it back on the other way where the frays wouldn't show. That was just right before we heard Daddy's step on the porch. Mama's head flew up, he came through the door and she leaped from her chair half across the room, threw her arms around him, then she jumped back away so fast he could've been a hot stove. Mama stood in the middle of the dining room floor rubbing her palm down the front of her apron, rubbing it again and again down her thigh under the apron, same way she'd rubbed Ellie's dirty face on the porch that morning. Like she was trying to rub a spot of dirt off her skin under her clothes.

"Here, Earl, set down here," she said. "I'll pour the coffee." She glanced at me. "Sharon, go get in the bed."

Daddy sat down at the table like he was too tired to move. At the same time, though, he was agitated, he kept stuttering his fingers along the oilcloth, tracing a circle around the butter crock. You'd have to know him, how slow and deliberate he was by nature, to know how awful that was to see. When Mama set his plate in front of him, he went right to eating, he didn't bow his head. I'd never seen my daddy put a bite of food in his mouth without asking the blessing, not even out in the field when I'd bring him his lunch bucket.

"Go on now, Sis," Mama said.

I slipped around the corner to the front room and waited to hear Mama tell my daddy she'd seen me kissing Harlan. That's how guilt does a person, you know it? Makes you think your own sin is all anybody else has got on their mind. The whole country was falling apart, all I was worried about was if Daddy would look at me with his eyes, turn around and send Harlan away. I thought everything in the world was about me and Harlan. When Daddy began to sob at the table the sound was so unfamiliar, so ragged and choky, at first I thought he was laughing. When I realized it was my daddy crying, my insides felt like they wanted to fall to the floor. My ears were roaring, the healed cut place on the bottom of my foot started hurting. I pressed my back against the wall. My foot throbbed like there was a beating heart in it. Daddy's voice caught and he choked out some words. "She was so tiny, Catherine," he said. "I just stood in the cage. I couldn't do anything. What could I do?" And then he started sobbing again.

What it was—I pieced this together later—the news about the Sallisaw run had gotten around fast, and the folks in Vardis began to collect at the Farmers Bank right after, but instead of closing the doors, the way the Sallisaw bank did, Mr. Teasley kept his bank open. He set my daddy up in the teller's cage and told him to count out people's money in one dollar bills, a dollar a minute, he said, slow, slow, slow. And that's what Daddy'd been doing, all morning and on into the afternoon, with people lined up out the door onto Main Street. That way, everybody thought they were going to get their money back, see, they believed Mr. Teasley's bank wasn't going to fail. Oliver Teasley was a shrewd man. My daddy had preached revivals at Vardis, the people there all knew him, they respected him, they trusted him, a Christian man and a farmer, like themselves, and Mr. Teasley figured, rightly, that if it was Brother Earl Thompson at the cashier's window, folks wouldn't get rowdy, they wouldn't try to agitate or put pressure on him to hurry up and hand over their money, and that's how come Daddy to be in the teller's cage when that woman walked in with her dead baby girl.

I don't know if it's true the baby died because the woman couldn't get her money out of the bank to pay the doctor, that's just what she screamed at my daddy. Probably there was more to the story. I never heard of a doctor who wouldn't treat a sick baby, you'd just pay them however you could. When the twins got the mumps Mama paid Doctor Booth with a box of quilt scraps, I remember. But the thing is, my daddy believed her. He believed to his soul he'd killed that child by counting so slow. Oliver Teasley stayed in the back office, he let my daddy be the one to face that poor woman weeping over her dead baby, and all the people standing in line, watching. So patient. So quiet. That's what Daddy kept saying. When you hear about bank runs, you think folks were yelling and shoving, but what the people in Vardis did was stand and be patient, looking desperate, I guess, the way Harlan said.

Mama seemed to already know about it, that's another strange thing. Because Daddy wasn't telling it to her, you know, he was grieving it, in his soul, he was groaning. He kept saying, "Her wrist wasn't as big around as my finger, Catherine. Her little legs were so bowed." The groans coming out of his chest were terrible to hear, and the caught sobs were worse.

I looked around the corner. Daddy's head was in his hands. Mama was standing behind him, her palm was on the back of his neck. I hardly ever saw them touch each other, or I can't remember seeing it, only that one night, and yet that's the picture of them I'll carry with me till I meet them on the other side, I guess. Daddy was in his preaching suit. His shoulders were shaking. Mama's hair was smoothed back behind her ears. Her face was wet.

Daddy walked out to the barn next morning and hitched up the cultivator. He didn't go back to work for Oliver Teasley. There was something different about him, though, from that time on. He'd turned...doubtful somehow. And tenderhearted. And stiff. All at the same time. Seemed like the more Daddy doubted, the sterner he got, and the sterner he got, the more he doubted—not his faith, oh no, he doubted himself. And then, he'd get so emotional besides, he would choke up when he asked the blessing, or if he tried to talk about something decent, like a neighbor walking miles to help out a neighbor, anything like that. His feelings showed to a degree I'd never seen before, and yet he kept his face stiff as a brush. He got even quieter, he turned inward, and the more Daddy turned inward, the more Mama turned outward. She bossed us worse than ever, she griped and raged, you couldn't keep her satisfied no matter what you tried. It was me she took it out on most though. I couldn't do a thing to suit her. And Harlan, she acted like he was invisible. She quit making dessert, never gave him the best helping. At supper she'd sit at the far end of table.

Months later, clinging to a catwalk beside Harlan with the nightwind blowing and the train sounds roaring and the little pricks of stars passing slow overhead, I thought to myself, Our lives got set the night Daddy came home broken. Probably it isn't true, because Harlan was who he was and the whole country was going to pieces anyhow, but I do know one thing: I never dreamed I'd have to leave Cherokee County when I settled my heart on marrying Harlan Singer. I don't know what I thought we'd do. Just live at the house until we could find us a place, I guess. Raise a few pigs, crop shares, live poor as Job's turkey, same as everybody else. I'd quit worrying about Daddy sending Harlan away, not so long as Harlan kept playing hymns after supper, I knew he wouldn't. Those hymns brought my daddy a kind of peace, and that was the only peace you'd see in his face in all those days. But when Harlan slipped in the barn one evening while I was milking and said we had to leave, I didn't argue. I knew it was true.

This was, oh, I'm going to say three weeks after Daddy quit working for Teasley. The cotton was up good, I remember, and Daddy had set Harlan to whitewashing the house. The milk stream hitting the pail must have covered the sound of Harlan coming, because the first I knew he was there was when I felt his fingers on the back of my neck. I jumped a little, shrugged him off. I still had to act like I didn't care one way or the other if he came around. I thought if he knew how much I loved him, he'd quit me. I was afraid if I gave in even a little bit I'd keep on giving till there was nothing left, he'd toss me off like a used tater sack. Harlan touched me again, oh, that could make me shiver, any time he brushed my neck.

"Quit," I said, and pulled hard on Belle's teats.

"How about you fix yourself up a little traveling bag this evening."

I stopped right then, shoved back on the T-stool and stood up.

"We'll leave out in the morning," he said. The sun slanting through the barn slats lit up his skin that pretty amber color. The hay dust floating around him was like gold dust sifting in stripes in the air. I couldn't make out anything by the set of his features.

"Leave?" I said finally.

He smiled, except his eyes weren't smiling. He took off his hat. His hair lay close to his head in tight little black ringlets, shining in that slash of sunlight. He went to kiss me. I put my hand up. "Did he fire you?"

"Not him," Harlan said.

"What then?" But I knew already. It wasn't Daddy. It was Mama.

I'd been seeing it, how her lips clamped thinner every day, how she'd get up and go in the other room any time Harlan came in the house. How she'd scold the kids to hurry up and eat, and then she'd clear the table herself and clash around in the kitchen while Harlan played Daddy's hymns. She'd been waiting for him when he came in at daylight that morning, he said. Harlan had started coon hunting at night with a mixed-blood Cherokee he knew, a fella from upriver named Calm Bledsoe. They were selling the hides two for a quarter to a trader from Fort Smith. That's how we were saving our marrying money. Harlan said he'd seen Mama by the yard fence as soon as he came up the road, but he just kept walking. She caught him at the barn door, told him he'd better get gone off our property by noon or she'd have Mr. Casper phone the sheriff. What Harlan didn't let on till long months later was how she cussed him when she said it. How she threatened him with Daddy's shotgun.

"I'll be at the gate at daybreak," Harlan whispered. He kissed me, touched my throat, went out the door. I heard a meadowlark trilling in the hayfield, another one answered by the fencerow, it was getting late, Mama would be waiting on me to set the table. The main thing I remember thinking is, How am I going to sit there and not have us-fixing-to-leave show all over my face?

Whether it showed or not, I couldn't say, but my mama's eyes never left me a second, grace to pudding, I could feel them on me while I stared at the beans on my plate. She said, "That boy took off this morning, finally. Good riddance."

"What boy?" Talmadge said.

Mama didn't answer.

"Where's Mr. Singer?" Talmadge said.

"Never mind. Sit up to the table, now. Leonard Lee, quit your smacking, I'll smack you in a minute. Jimmy, hand that bowl to your daddy. Look out, son, you're spilling."

It was quiet then for the rest of supper, or I mean the little ones were chattering, they didn't know, but neither Daddy nor Mama said anything except maybe pass the cornbread. I didn't see what their faces said. I couldn't look up. After everybody scattered and I'd started to clear the table, Mama came behind me and whispered, "He's banished out of here, Sissy." That was the first she'd ever said it out loud, that she knew about me and Harlan. "You hear?" Mama said.

I nodded.

"You see him skulking around," Mama said, "you'd better come tell us."

I nodded again, stacking plates. She followed me to the kitchen. The whole time I was dipping water from the reservoir for the dishes, scraping scraps in the bucket, she was trailing behind me, talking low: "Your daddy and me's agreed, Sharon. He's a drifter. He's lazy, he's no account, I rue the day I ever let him come in this yard. He hadn't done a thing since he's been here but hang around you like a bitch dog in heat."

My face flared hot like she'd slapped me. I sprinkled soap flakes in the dishpan, swished up the suds.

"I'd better not see him," Mama said and turned and went to the front of the house. I kept looking over my shoulder to see if she'd come back while I wrapped the leftover cornbread in a clean page I peeled out of the *Grit* I'd plucked from the burn trash. I would have liked to put sorghum on it too, but that would've made a mess. I tucked the slab of cornbread in my apron.

I heard him scratching at the screen before daylight. I slid from the bed where I slept with the twins and went to the window. He was motioning in the yard for me to come on. I hadn't slept a drop, and from the looks of him I don't think he had either. I mouthed the words, "Wait till I come out to milk," thinking we could slip away from the barn. But Mama heard me—maybe she didn't sleep all night either—and then it wasn't any time before Daddy was up and we were all fighting. Harlan came on in the house, everybody was talking loud. I stood my ground. I'm proud of that. I mean, I didn't actually say anything, but I went and got dressed and put on my saddle shoes, came and stood next to Harlan. I'd remembered to take the cornbread from my apron but I forgot all about the traveling bag I'd fixed under the bed. It wasn't anything but a little makeshift bindle, it had my one change of clothes and an extra pair of anklets and underwear in it, and my Bible, and the twenty-eight cents I had saved from swiping eggs at the henhouse and selling them to Mr. Stratton in town. But I forgot it.

Mama followed us across the linoleum, out onto the porch, her voice wheeling like a jaybird's. "You knew better than to show your face on this place again!" That was to Harlan. And then to me: "You'll starve and your babies'll starve. Don't be whining back here with your tail between your legs expecting us to feed you!" And then to Daddy: "This is what comes of you worrying about the souls of worthless heathens all over Cherokee County instead of the souls and bellies of your own children!"

We were standing in the yard then, even the little ones. The dew hadn't burnt off yet. Ellie Renee was bawling on Mama's hip, Mama would whip around from one of us to the other, Harlan to me to Daddy, back around again. Mostly it was to Daddy, though, she laid into him the worst, got right up in his face, said him being gone all the time and not giving us regular church-raising was how come me to turn out so *immoral*. Said if I'd went to church more than once a month when he preached at Cookson I'd have turned out decent instead of a hussy and shameless and *immoral*.

Harlan got so mad at that word, his face crimped like a fist, he stood with his hat pushed back, he was opening and closing his right hand, opening and closing it, like he wanted to hit something. If it'd been Daddy saying that, I believe Harlan would've hit him, but Harlan wasn't going to raise his hand to a woman. Daddy either, he just stood there, letting Mama rant. Me, I didn't get mad, I got—oh, I don't know how to say it. *Apologetic*. That's how I felt. I watched my daddy's face lined and cracked like the dirt in the yard and Mama spitting right in it, saying awful things about him and me and Harlan, and I wanted to say, I'm sorry, I'm *sorry*! Harlan didn't give me no chance for sorry, though. He took me by the wrist and walked me on out the yard gate.

We waited an hour on the gravel road beside the river outside Cookson. I was burning up hot, I was hungry, more than anything, I was scared. Harlan broke the cornbread in half and we ate it, and then I was thirsty on top of everything else. I wouldn't drink the Illinois water though, it was running too slow. I kept looking towards town to see if anybody I knew would see me. Cookson is gone now, did you know it? They've got this place here they call Cookson, but it's not really. The real town is drowned. There's no river now, they took the bridge down, it's all under water. Lake Tenkiller they call it. My hometown is a ghost town in a watery grave in a dry land. I dream about it sometimes.

Harlan kept playing music, as if that could fix things, or he'd blow those clacky rhythms, make the train whistle disappear down the tracks. Finally a milk truck stopped and we got a ride to Pettit. After that we rode in a Model A with a drygoods salesman, we bounced around in the empty bed of a wood hauler's truck, ended up in a flatbed wagon with a Creek family, it was way up late in the afternoon by then. The man stopped at a house near Fort Gibson and let his family out, his wife and an old woman and seven or eight kids, and then Harlan gave the man four bits to carry us on into Muskogee. I knew we couldn't afford to be giving that money away, and it seemed to me like we would have done better to wait for a car or a truck to come by making thirty or forty miles an hour, but I didn't say anything. Harlan was propped on the seat beside that Indian man playing strange songs I never heard of all the way to Muskogee. By the time we got there it was coming on dark.

Muskogee, Oklahoma. My, I thought that was the biggest town God ever made. Six months later I'd seen Kansas City, Dallas, Saint Louis, but I don't think anything could ever compare with how grand Muskogee, Oklahoma, looked to my eyes that night. The downtown stores were finer than anything I'd ever seen—which isn't saying much, I know, the only place of any size I'd ever been to was Tahlequah. We rode right down the main street towards the courthouse, the store windows were all lit up, and they had such pretty things in them. I didn't know what kind of people lived in Muskogee that they had money to pay for fancy men's Stetsons and women's tailored suitdresses and high heel shoes and silk hats. The courthouse was closed when we got there, of course, which I knew already it would be, because the stores were. We climbed down anyway, and Harlan said good-bye to that Creek man like they were old friends, like he could hardly bear to part from him. The man gave him a bag of tobacco, and Harlan didn't even smoke then.

I said, "Well? What now?" I was worried about where we were going to sleep, or probably I should say *how* we'd sleep, since the courthouse was closed. For answer Harlan turned me around and walked me back along the street we'd just driven, and all we did the whole rest of the evening was walk up and down looking in the windows until I was so worn out and so sick from hunger I couldn't go anymore. He set me down on a store step finally and went away, and when he came back he took me by the hand and guided me a few blocks to the front of a gray-looking house with a homemade sign tacked to a porch pillar, *ROOMS TO LET*.

I balked. "Harlan, we can't be spending money on a rented room. How much is it? I left my money home, you know I left my money. We can't cut into our money for our license!" I didn't know if he meant us to stay in a room together. I just wasn't about to do that, I couldn't, but I didn't know how to ask if that was what he meant. "Let's keep walking!" I turned and started back up the street, but he caught me.

"Here, now, sweetheart," he said soft against my hair. "I'm not having my bride sleep in a bar ditch the night before we marry." He bent to kiss me. Right then the door opened and a lady stood there, and Harlan took off his hat and said howdy to her instead. He fixed it up with the lady for me to spend the night and get breakfast in the morning for two bits, and another dime on top of that for something to eat now. Harlan led me by the hand up on the porch, he touched my throat and stepped down and limped away in the dark.

Hungry as I was, that Spam sandwich with mustard on light bread the woman gave me in her kitchen just stuck in my throat. Tired as I was, when I stretched out on the skinny bed in a wallpapered room with a wash basin and pitcher, I couldn't sleep. I lay in my slip on top of a starched and ironed sheet, staring up at a foreign ceiling, in a foreign room, in a foreign place, a foreign town, and I said to myself, It'll be all right . . . Mama'll get over her mad . . . we'll go back day after tomorrow . . . or the next day . . . or the next. I just wouldn't let myself think about where me and Harlan might be the next night, or what happens to a girl when she gets married, or trains. He'd talked about trains all evening. The Katy Flyer comes right through Muskogee, he'd said, and made a squealing train whistle sound. The Midland Valley. The Kansas, Oklahoma and Gulf. The Frisco. I didn't know what all that meant.

The rooming house lady fed me oatmeal and fried eggs the next morning. I don't know what Harlan ate, or if he did, but he came rolling up on the porch bright and early, he had his hat pushed to the back of his head and his face was shining. When we went down the steps in the hot sunlight my insides were rolling and tumbling, but I guess I was as glad as any girl on her way to get married might be. Harlan had fixed us up a piece of paper, signed in my daddy's name, saying Daddy was too sick to come to Muskogee but I had his permission to get married. Turns out we didn't even need it. A lady in red earbobs at a desk had me to sign a form saying I was of legal age, and Harlan gave her the two dollars, counted it out in silver, and the justice of the peace went ahead and performed the ceremony. It took about five minutes. I kept thinking I'd feel something but I didn't. The earbobbed lady stood at the back of the room, and she signed our certificate for a witness, and we walked back outside the courthouse, where it was hot.

We stood on the sidewalk a minute. "Hey, Mrs. Singer," Harlan whispered. He went to kiss me, but I pulled back. We were right out on the street.

"What are we going to do now?" I said.

"Well . . . now . . . *Miss*-us Singer . . . I'll tell you what." He reached in his shirt pocket for his harp. "Way I see it, a fella's first order of business on his wedding day oughta be to hunt him up a place where he can kiss his new bride without half the prying eyes of Muskogee, Oklahoma, looking to watch." He blew a line or two of a sweet country ballad. The sun was beating hard, I was sweating. "Let's go, Harlan," I said. And he stepped right out like he knew just where he meant to take me.

All we did, though, was walk around town again. I went along for a while, but we'd seen all the windows the night before, and there were lots of people on the streets now, and cars everywhere, and the women all looked like they'd had their hair done. It shamed me to stand outside and gawk at the store windows while people were going in and out. Finally I took the studs right in the middle of the sidewalk, I wouldn't budge, I said, "Harlan. Tell me what we're going to do now."

"Why, sugardoll, we're fixing to find us an empty boxcar with some nice fresh sweet-smelling hay on the floor."

"Find it where?"

"In the switchyard, darlin'."

"What if it leaves out while we're sleeping?" I said. My heart was beating so fast.

Harlan laughed. "What else would you want with a boxcar? Otherwise you might as well find you a toolshed."

I looked straight at him. "We're not going home to Cookson?"

He got real quiet. "No," he said, finally. And then: "Well, yes, one of these days, maybe." Then: "Aw, sure we will, honey, just . . . not for a while yet."

I felt his touch on my arm.

He said, "Sharon. Look at me. I'm going to take care of you. I am. And when it gets the right time, I'll carry you home to see your family. I promise you I will."

"What are we going to do? We can't stay here. I don't know anybody in Muskogee."

"Why, we'll just go around a while, see a bit of the country. Wouldn't you like that?"

"Go where?"

He sort of laughed. "Now that's the thing about *going*, babe. You don't got to think where, just hop on and ride."

I said to myself, I don't know this man.

"Sweetheart. Sharon. You're my wife now."

I am, I thought. That's what I did. I married him. That's me now, Sharon Singer. Sharon Singer. Of course, I didn't know then he'd made the name up. "All right," I said finally. "Let's find that boxcar."

He broke into a grin. "Oh, well, darlin', we got to wait till it gets dark."

We spent the rest of the day in the shade of a big elm across from the courthouse, and that's the first I remember Harlan talking about going to find Profit. I thought he was saying *profit*, little *p*, and I thought he meant a job of work, until I finally understood he was talking about a person. Then I thought he was saying *prophet*. "That's a sacrilege," I said, "to call somebody that."

"How so?"

"Well, what kind of prophet is he? Not the Old Testament kind, surely."

Harlan laughed. He reached over and touched my throat. "'What doth it profit a man,'" he quoted, "'if he gain the whole world and lose his own soul?'"

So then I knew what word he was saying after all, but I still didn't understand. Harlan said he'd been thinking for a while now that he ought to try to find Profit. The two of them used to travel together, he said, and he still owed the man. I didn't know Harlan owed money. I thought he'd ought to have told me. "How much?" I said.

He gazed at me, his eyes light under his hat brim. "Everything, I reckon."

Before I could ask where this man lived and how much was it really and how did Harlan aim to earn enough to pay it back and all the other questions swimming in my head, Harlan took out his harp and started to play. In a minute he lowered the harp and sang in his high, thin tenor, beautiful old ballads about girls getting drowned and snakebit, men getting hung for lost love. You'd think, from how smooth his face was and how delicate his mouth set, that Harlan's voice couldn't help but be pretty, but to be honest, it wasn't really. His voice had a kind of a whang to it, sort of gamey and nasal, but it was real well suited to those sad old country songs. People passing by would stand at a distance and listen. Harlan took his hat off and turned it upside down on the grass. A woman walked up with her two little kids, and she dropped a dime in. I frowned at her. I couldn't see what she meant by it. Then a man in a felt hat strolled by and tossed in a few pennies. Folks kept doing that, little by little. It made me feel strange. Up until then I'd thought they were stopping on the sidewalk to watch us just on account of how Harlan looked at me, how he sang to me, played his harp for me. I'd thought anybody could see it was our wedding day. When the sun started to lower, we got up and Harlan put the change in his pocket and we walked over to the switchyard.

That Muskogee yard wasn't much, compared to KC or Amarillo, but it was sure big enough to scare the daylights out of me. A railyard's always in the worst part of town anyway, so just the walk over there had me shaking, and then Harlan acted like it was a top secret activity, us poking around. There were three or four lines of cars and the switching rails and the through-lines, I couldn't begin to make any order of it, and then, when we got closer, a locomotive came barreling in like a big black belching barn roaring. I let out a yip and grabbed Harlan, he put his arm around me. But he was facing into the hot push of air the freight made, his eyes were shut, I could see he was smiling. I held onto his sleeve.

Harlan said we had to keep our backs down and our heads up, so we were sneaking low beside the cars on a side rail, kind of hunched over and gliding—*huntin' our honeymoon empty*, he kept saying, like those were words to a song—when, way down at the end of the line, a roundbellied man in overalls and a cloth cap came strolling around the front car. Harlan jerked me across the hitch to the other side so fast I didn't know *what* was happening. He whispered, "Lucky we seen him before he seen us!"

"Who is it?" I was terrified. I didn't know what kind of thief or murderer it might be.

"Shhhhh!" Harlan pressed two fingers against my mouth. They smelled like tin from his harmonica. *We got to be ve-ry quiet.* He shaped the words without making any sound. Then he had us creeping forward, the same direction the roly-poly man was coming from. Every time we'd get to a space where one car ended and there was a gap before the next one, Harlan would take his hat off and peek around. When he saw the coast was clear he'd glance back at me, put his finger to his lips, take my hand, and we'd dash across, light and quick.

I wanted him to explain to me what we were doing, but he wouldn't, he just pulled me along. We passed dozens of closed boxcars, but Harlan didn't try to slide the doors open, that would have made too much noise. We found an open door, finally, and he got me by the waist and jumped me up, I had to scramble, that ledge opening hit me at the top of my chest. I put my hand down, and he scrambled over the lip, took us inside to stand in the back.

Phew-ey. I'm telling you. I don't know what they'd been transporting in that freightcar, but it was something putrid that ought to have been buried six weeks ago. I never smelled anything so bad. We couldn't stay in that stinking dark, only just long enough to have a conversation.

"Harlan Singer, *what* on earth do you think you're doing?"

"Saving our hineys from that bull, sugarfoot."

"What bull?"

"That Muskogee bull."

"I ain't seen no bull."

"Oh yes you have"

"Well, who's that little man following us?"

"That's him, babydoll. That's what I'm saying, that fella is old Muskogee Fats himself."

I just looked at him. The word "bull" to me meant a male animal in a pasture—I'd sure never heard the word used for a railroad detective. Of course, at that time I didn't even know what a railroad dick was.

"What's he want with us?" I said.

"Shhh, sweetie, keep your voice down. He don't want nothing with us right now, he don't know we're here. If he *did* know, what he'd want would be to shake us down and take every nickel out of our pockets for riding the trains without a ticket, or that's what he'd tell us, but he'd put that money right in his overalls bib. Then he'd call the sheriff and have us arrested for trespassing. Or that's the general order of business, anyhow."

"But why would he *do* that?"

"It's his job, darlin'. That's what the railroad hired him for." Harlan sounded so nonchalant, so casual, like it was nothing special to worry about. "'Course, now," he said, "if that bull finds out we ain't *got* any money, then he's liable to knock my head around with his blackjack a while."

"Oh, my word, Harlan! We got to get out of here!"

"Well, that's what I'm saying, sugarfoot, what've I been saying?" Harlan went to the door and looked out. He turned and winked at me, wrinkled his nose to show we had to get out of that stinking car, and then he stretched out his hand.

So, that's how me and Harlan got to playing cat and mouse with Muskogee Fats. If that was even his name. With Harlan you couldn't always tell when he was pulling your leg about something, though the worst bulls did all have nicknames, I later found that out. Whatever the old guy's name was, he sure got after us. It wasn't long before he figured out there were trespassers in his yard, which we knew he knew because he'd take two steps, pause and listen, another step, pause, and like that. We stopped every time he stopped, we always kept a car or two between us, and he couldn't locate where we were at. You'd hear him slide a door open really quick, but we weren't in a boxcar on a side rail, because we weren't about to be sitting ducks, Harlan said. We'd skip off fast, go quiet, up and down, keeping the cars between us, and after a while it got to be fun, I got in the spirit of it, and I was laughing the same as Harlan. I caught a good glimpse of the bull one time, from a couple rails away. He had steely hair sticking out from his cap and a big belly, but he really was a short roly-poly fellow. I said to myself, well, he's too old and fat to run.

He was old and fat enough, maybe, but he sure wasn't dumb, because what he did was, he baited us. He went in a storage shed and got his supper and came back and climbed up in a car and sat in the door to eat it. Turned out to be a turnip-green sandwich on cornbread and a cold sweet potato, which might not sound too appetizing if you've got a full belly, but for people as hungry as we were and planning on traveling all night, it was a feast. Not that we knew just yet what it was, but we could smell the bacon grease the greens had been cooked in, and we could smell the ripe smell of the greens themselves all the way from the back side of the car where we were hiding. So when he dropped that paper sack on the ground and it thunked like there was a bate of food in it, Harlan shinnied under and grabbed it. That old bull jumped down and tried to stomp his hand. Harlan was too quick for him though, he snatched the sack and rolled back under the car, hollering at me to run, but I wasn't running without Harlan. He wriggled out from underneath, and I know his bad leg took a hair off how quick he could move, but even so, he was faster than Muskogee Fats. We took off laughing, and all at once there was a whistle scream and a rumble and a roar, and here came a hotshot highballer barreling into the yard. Harlan grabbed my hand and we danced right across in front of the engine, that whistle shrieked like a woman, oh, the engineer was mad. I saw his face yelling in the engine window, but we were on the far side of a moving train then, and there was no way that bull could get around it to catch us, and we had that bull's supper in Harlan's hand. The end result was, though, we couldn't wait for an empty like we wanted. We had to quick climb the ladder to the top of a car while the train slowed, we laid down flat, end to end, him behind me, on the catwalk in the middle. Harlan had hold of my ankles, not like a cuff or anything, just holding on to keep me safe, and we both had our faces down on the top of the boards, laughing, and in about ten minutes, that train started rolling.

When it began to gather speed at the edge of town, we sat up. Harlan put his arms around me, he had his legs straight out on either side, cradled around me. We were facing the same direction the train was headed. The sky was swept from one side to the other in lilac and dark purple, the wind was whipping my hair, there were cinders spitting back from the engine. Harlan had taken his hat off to keep it from blowing away, he scrunched it with the old bull's sack between his legs, I could feel them against my backside. It was just after twilight of a mild May evening. Straight ahead of us was one last lone streak of cloud lit up red-orange like a slash of fire. I thought it was an arrow marking the beginning of our lives. Harlan put his mouth to my ear, shouted, "I love you, Sharon Singer!" If I could've talked, I might would have said it back to him, but my heart was too full up in my throat, and we were going too fast, and the wind was beating too hard.

deepsong

in the silence, on the bed of white stones,
the singer remembers
    the whistle's hollow moan, the sound of wind, the slow
clacking rhythm the rhythm of breathing, wanting her, the quicker
clickclackingclickclacking west into dark, into night, into light again,
wanting her, the pale sweep of sky overhead, the earth flattening, west
toward elk city amarillo tucumcari, wanting her, but always there was
the hunt for food, an empty car, a place to lie down, always there was
the mumble of the bums' voices nearby in the dark.
he remembers
    standing in a boxcar door sounding out on his harp the hiss of
steam, the brakes' scream, down the long grade into albuquerque, the
shadows on the land purple, the light glowing, and in the distance a
lone mesa etched in violet, one side crimson, how she'd stood beside
him, holding tight to him, the top of her head at his shoulder, her light
voice crying out over the wind's thunder, oh, harlan, look!
    and later the smell of clay and cow dung, fresh hay, the earthen
floor warm beneath them, how soft it was, how soft she was, soft, how
he'd known then, believed then, he would never want anything more.
how he'd slept the sleep of the blameless, with sharon curled soft on
the barn floor beside him, until he jerked awake in the night, his heart
racing,
    listening.

remembers
    in california, the meat on meat sound,
    white men's curses, the crack of stone
    against bone, and in the san joaquin
    moonlight, the bright bloody
    cradle inside willie jay's skull.

Sharon

H*untin' our honeymoon empty.* You know how long that took? Four days. And then it wasn't even an empty boxcar at all but a clay barn near Albuquerque with cattle snuffling outside in the darkness and mice scritching all night in the straw. At first I was just glad to stretch out and not feel trembling steel underneath me, I was glad to be able to kiss my husband as much I wanted with nobody around to watch. But then . . . well. It wasn't anything like I expected. Harlan meant to go easy, he truly did, and I knew it wasn't sinful, we were married, that lady with the red earbobs signed our paper to prove it, but anyhow it still hurt. His chest was warm though, his arms tight around me, and the feel of his skin was smooth and soft. Harlan jumped up real fast before daylight next morning, started walking us back to the Albuquerque yards. I thought we were on our way to California, like he'd been singing, but when we caught out finally, along about noon, we were on a train headed back the direction we'd just come.

By noon the next day we were pulling into the switchyard in Fort Worth, Texas. I'd never seen anything like it, miles and miles of steel lines and freights and cattle cars. Harlan took my hand, and we dodged between the side rails till we got past the yards and found our way to a hobo jungle under a bridge. Harlan went around studying the bums' faces. I didn't get what he was doing. I didn't like the looks of the scrabby men either, how they stared at me, and the stink around there was strong. Harlan took out his harp and played train songs till everybody's eyes were on him, then he said, real casual, like he was talking about the weather, "We're hunting an old fella about yea-tall, got him a beard down to here, kind of gruesome and curly. A Scripture-spouting old man, pert as a garden rabbit, handy as a pocket on a shirt, he'll dance you a jig to no music, all you got to do is clap. Any of y'all seen him?" Nobody acted like they knew who Harlan was talking about, but they gave us some beans and a heel of light bread to eat, and for that I was grateful, and we walked back to the switchyard and caught out on a hotshot headed north.

A while later I saw a sign from the boxcar door that advertised a feedstore in Ardmore, Oklahoma. My heart squeezed up nervous, half happy, half scared. I thought we were going home now. I figured it must be time, like Harlan had said. I started rehearsing in my mind what it would be like to walk through the yard gate, I could see the kids tumbling out the door and Mama behind them,

Daddy coming from the field maybe, the dogs barking. A sinking feeling pulled through me. The picture seemed dull and awful. There wouldn't be anything to do after that, I thought, but housework and field chores and mending. No place to go until school started, except church. I felt guilty, dreading it so, but the hotshot we were riding whizzed right through Ardmore and on up to Oklahoma City. It stopped just a little while in the Oke City yards, but no bulls came around, and me and Harlan didn't get off.

We kept riding, on north across the flatlands all the way to Wichita, Kansas, and that evening we hopped an eastbound freight. Harlan started talking about carrying me to Chicago, where the buildings rise up as tall as a mountain and the great lake beside them is as wide as the sea. He played a song about it, and his voice when he spoke had the same dreamy sound it had when he talked about California. I didn't think I wanted to see any building as tall as a mountain, but anyway it didn't matter, because at Springfield we turned around and caught a freight heading west.

It's strange now to think how I hardly ever asked questions. Oh, well, I did sometimes—not that there was much point, Harlan seldom answered a question straight out—but most the time it never even crossed my mind to ask. I'd just start running whenever he did, jump up and grab for a handrail when he told me, bend my knees and hop down from the ladder with my legs scissoring, the same as him. I followed Harlan's lead in everything, and I wasn't scared. The earth was wide and flat and huge, which I never knew before, growing up in the hills, and the sky was a wonder, how it scooped from one side of the world to the other. I couldn't take my eyes off it.

We traded out my dress for a pair of boy's overalls Harlan swiped off a clothesline in Topeka. He said things'd go easier if I rode that way, and the overalls were patched and my dress wasn't, so it was a better-than-fair trade. I didn't care. I was just glad to not have men staring at me in the boxcars. I was also tired of having my knees cut and skint. Often we'd stay a day or two in a campyard. Harlan would play his harp in a downtown park and gather a few nickels, or he'd mow a lawn or chop wood for a widow lady in exchange for a meal. Sometimes he'd get to drinking with the old 'bos in the jungles, stay up all night playing music, playing cards, and naturally that bothered me, but then he'd come lay down beside me, wrap his arms around me, I'd tell myself never mind, when we go home to Cookson he'll quit doing that. He found a rucksack at a town dump and cleaned it up and folded our marriage license neat and slipped it in the bottom, and any bit of goods that came to us after that—a tin spoon or a soup can, a holey shirt, a pile of newspapers we could use for a blanket, anything—he'd stuff it in there, tuck that rucksack back under his arm.

And everywhere we went, Harlan asked about Profit. He'd quiz the bums sitting around the fire in any jungle, describe him to a lady in her backyard hanging out the wash. Now and then we'd meet somebody who acted like they knew him, but they never could tell us when they'd last seen him, or where, and we never could seem to run across the man ourselves. But we kept trying. You can cover a lot of territory if you keep traveling, and we did keep traveling, for days and weeks and months. In the nights, rocking in a railcar, Harlan still sang about a land where the weeds don't grow and the water tastes like cherry wine, but we never went there. That is one thing I asked him, one time, I said, "Aren't we never going to go to California and look at the ocean?" and he said, "Aw, sugarbear, you don't want to go to California. Things are bad in California," and I said, "What about the cottonbolls dancing in moonlight?" and he said, "Well, that's just a song."

Another time—it was in an empty cattle car where we'd got side-railed in Abilene, I remember—I woke in the night, and Harlan was completely stiff beside me. He was on his back, had his hands behind his head.

"What's wrong?" I said.

"Nothing, babe. I's just thinking."

"About what?"

"Blood poisoning."

"What?" I raised up on my elbow. I could see his outline in the strips of light shining through the slats.

"I had the blood poisoning real bad one time," he said. "Stubbed my toe on a river rock, the thing swelled up big as a pike's head. Not just my toe, my whole foot. He was walking out the other direction, coming from Tahlequah. Headed to Fayetteville he told me later."

"Who?"

Harlan stayed quiet. He wasn't asleep, I could see his eyes open, the faint glint of whites in the moonlight. I knew who he was talking about anyway. After a long time he said, his voice soft. "He seen me sitting at the side of the road, he crossed over and sat next to me. 'Let's have a look, son,' he said, and pulled my foot in his lap. My whole leg was white and tight as a drum, red streaks running all up it. He pushed on the tender parts, I let out a holler and a cussing. It burned like fire and throbbed like pure dread. 'You got the blood poisoning, kid,' he told me. 'If you don't get this looked after, you'll be dead by morning.' He set my foot back on the ground and stood up like he was fixing to walk off. I begged him to help me. I believe I was crying. Well, I know I was. It hurt like sin. He said, '*They that be whole need not a physician, but they that are sick,* Matthew nine twelve. Where's your people, son?' I told him I didn't have none, he said, 'You do now.' And he hoisted me on his back and carried me a mile into Tahlequah to the doctor."

"That was Profit?" I said. "That's when y'all first met?"

"That was him. We traveled together a lot of years, but that first mile was the hardest. I thought he'd collapse under me. I was a big grown fella by then. Well, not big, I hadn't never been big, but Profit wasn't much size either, and he was old as God already. He carried me piggyback, I hung my arms around his neck, my feet dragged the ground. I felt like my leg was about to come off, or I wished it would. He had to stop twice and set me down and give me a drink of whiskey to make me quit hollering."

"Is that how come you to . . . walk stiff?" I didn't like to say the word somehow. We'd never talked about Harlan's limp.

"Naw, babe, it was my right foot I'd messed up in the river." He was silent a minute, then he murmured, "Come to find out, me and him had a lot in common. Both of us without a home to speak of, we both liked to keep moving, travel around. He didn't have no people either, he said. For a time I guess we became each other's people, but then we had a falling out, and I quit him. Same as I quit the Letbetters when I was a youngster. I never could abide somebody trying to boss me."

"Ledbetters?" I said.

"Reverend Letbetter used to be the Methodist preacher in Sallisaw. Might still be, for all I know. His wife was a good lady. Stiff though. Awful proper." He drew quiet again. Then, like he was tasting the sound of it, he murmured, "Blood poison. Blood poison. That's strange, innit? I caught the blood poisoning in my right leg, and Profit come along and saved me. Then so many years later it's the other one. The other kind. And Profit was there then."

"Other kind of what?"

"And that's the last time I seen him."

"Other kind of what?"

Harlan didn't answer. I asked a few more times, but in a little while I quit, because that's how it was then. Whatever I found out, I learned in dribs and drabs when Harlan felt like talking, and if he didn't feel like talking it wasn't any good to keep on. I scooted next to him, put my arm across his chest. He pulled me close, cupped his palm to the back of my head, stroked my hair. After a long while he eased me over, very gentle. The floor stank of cow pies and urine, we hadn't had a wash in a long time, but the car was an empty, it wasn't moving, and for that I was glad.

And so we kept on, riding the rails, searching for Profit. I knew by then, of course, that he didn't live anywhere, that, like me and Harlan and a bunch of others, he just went traveling around. I can't say, though, when I first knew we were going in circles. After the weather turned, I guess. Or it wasn't even circles, exactly, but more like a giant figure eight, with Oklahoma in the middle, the squeezed-in hourglass place. We'd go in a sweep from the Texas panhandle, say, southeast toward Dallas, and there we'd catch out on the Katy Flyer, go barreling northeast through Oklahoma—McAlester, Muskogee, Pryor, Vinita—on up into Missouri and Kansas, then we'd turn and thread our way back down through Coffeyville, Tulsa, Henryetta, Okemah, west all the way to Amarillo or Albuquerque. Then we'd turn and start the same twisting loop all over again. Every time we crossed the state line, I'd think, All right, this time we'll go home, but we didn't. We just went passing through. Harlan changed directions sometimes—we got as far east as Georgia once, I remember—but eventually we'd circle back to Oklahoma, and very gradually, slow by slow, I came to understand that me and Harlan were tied to a tether. We could swing out only so far before the tie jerked us back.

By early winter there were starting to be so many men and boys traveling we hardly ever found an empty car to ourselves. The jungles were turning crowded, more dangerous, it was getting tougher to bum a meal. There were too many folks asking, I guess, too many wanderers—not just the regular old 'bos but young kids on their own, hungry, looking for work. That kind of thing really bothered Harlan. My husband was a tenderhearted man. Most folks don't realize that. You couldn't tell it from the outside, he had that drawly voice, sounded like he'd just woke up, and when he joked he kept his face serious, then he'd flick his grin sharp and quick. Some people took him for a smartaleck, but he wasn't. It hurt him to see folks living in misery, and misery was just plentiful then.

We were riding into Kansas City this one time, I remember. A cold front come through and the door to the car we were riding got jammed open, freezing rain was blowing in on us, but the car was an empty, and me and Harlan were glad for any kind of an empty boxcar, even one with an open door. We snugged up against the front wall as far out of the wet as we could get, the train clicking along making sixty or seventy miles an hour, and all of a sudden this skinny blond kid swings into the car with us. Well, it was nuts to scramble down from the top of a fast-moving freight but people did it sometimes, especially if the weather turned bad. This kid swung in so quick we didn't have the chance to help him, and then he crawled to a far corner and hunkered up against the wall, shaking with the cold. He looked to be eleven or twelve maybe, bone thin and pale as a duck. Harlan kept staring at him. The boy's hair was so short you could see his scalp through it, the crusty pink circles of ringworm spotted over his skull. He shook and shook, his arms wrapped around his knees, his head down.

After a while Harlan called out over the train noise, "Where you headed, son?" The boy didn't look up, he didn't answer. Possibly he didn't hear. Harlan took off his cap. He'd got himself a ratty-looking tweed cap to replace his lost snap-brim that got blown off in Arkansas. We'd traded a fellow some potatoes for it at the Joplin yards. Harlan started turning that cap in his hands. I knew what he was thinking. I whispered, "Harlan, that boy don't need your hat."

Harlan got up and made his way along the wall, he squatted down next to the kid and held the cap out. The boy jerked his head up, he looked scared a minute, and then he saw the cap in Harlan's hand. He bleated, "Oh, that's all right, mister." Harlan said, "I don't want it, son. The wool itches my scalp." So the boy took the cap and put it on his ringwormy head, it slipped down over his forehead, swallowed his ears. "Thanks," he said, and he laid down and turned to the wall. Harlan crawled back over by me, I said, "What'd you do that for? I don't know where you're going to get you another." He shrugged, gazing across the car at the boy.

That's all it was, no bigger an encounter than that. Me and Harlan hopped off when the freight started to slow coming into the KC yards, and the boy stayed where he was, curled up like a sowbug against the back boxcar wall. We never saw him again, so far as I know, but that blond kid stayed with Harlan, he troubled him for the longest, and I didn't know why. He wasn't the only youngster we ever saw in such a shape, believe me—we saw lots worse than that, later on—but for some reason that one ringwormy kid traveling alone really stuck in Harlan's mind.

We made our way to the nearest jungle that evening, found ourselves a place not too far from the fire. The men in the camp had their fire inside a steel drum next to a little running stream, the jungle looked pretty makeshift. Harlan asked around about Profit, naturally nobody knew him. We sat down and Harlan took a tin of sardines out of his jacket, opened it with his pocketknife. We'd carried those sardines from Saint Joe. I would have liked a cracker or a piece of bread to go with them, but from the sorry looks of the camp there wasn't going to be anything like that coming. Harlan pulled our clean can out of the rucksack and dipped us a drink of water from the stream, and that was supper, sardines and creekwater—a good one, actually, compared to sometimes.

I knew we were going to have to decide pretty quick if I was going to be a boy or a girl, because if I didn't have my mind made up firm to be a boy I'd always slip and show myself. If I was a girl, I could take my cap off and relax, and me and Harlan could sleep wrapped up together. But a girl asleep in a hobo jungle had her dangers, even in her husband's arms. We'd heard some awful stories. If I was a boy, it'd be safer, but we couldn't sleep together. Not how we liked. I said, "Honey, it's really cold." He nodded. I took off my cap, got our newspapers out of the sack—Hoover blankets, people called them—and I spread the papers open on the damp ground. We laid down, Harlan arranged his jacket across us for cover, pulled me in close. The rucksack was the pillow under our heads. I was about to drop off to sleep when I heard Harlan whisper, "We should have brought him with us. It's hard on a kid, traveling alone."

"He'll be all right," I said.

Harlan wrapped his arms tighter around me. After another minute he said, "I should've at least give him my jacket. He's liable to freeze to death before morning."

"We need this jacket, Harlan. I need it. We both do."

He got quiet again.

"You done what you could."

"No, darlin'," he said. "I didn't."

I popped off with something I'd heard people around home say: "Well, it's his misfortune and none of our own."

"Shush!"

Oh, it was like he'd slapped me, it was like a bolt smashed through him and cracked against me.

"I'm sorry," I said. "Honey. I'm sorry."

His chest was hard and stiff.

"I don't know why I said that. Harlan? I don't mean it. That's just an old saying."

He pulled me close, his arms taut like they had springs in them, holding me so hard I couldn't catch my breath. He didn't let go of me all night.

Then, for quite a while after that, if I'd see him staring at a campfire or a boxcar wall, I could just feel in my throat that he was thinking about that kid. Sometimes he'd mutter, "Wonder if he made it." Or he might say, "I had those sardines in my pocket, I could have give 'em to him. We could have got more."

I told him, "Honey, please, you can't do anything about it now. Quit bothering your head."

But Harlan couldn't quit. He was like my daddy in the kitchen, both of them troubled by something they couldn't help. Only difference, my daddy regretted doing something he felt like he shouldn't have—counting Oliver Teasley's dollars so slow—whereas Harlan kept going over in his mind what he should have done and didn't. I stopped trying to talk sense to him though, seemed like whatever I said only made matters worse.

And anyway after a week or two he was back to his same jokey self. He'd make up his funny songs and play them by the fire, he always visited around with people in the jungles and yards. Seemed like he was a little worse about staying up all night playing music, but it was better than him sitting and staring, and anyhow, every morning he'd jump up bright and early, grinning, ready to hit the stem.

deepsong

in the silence, on the bed of white stones
the singer remembers
  sitting up on a flatcar with his legs straight before him, sharon
in a double-curled heap on the floor, her head in his lap. how he'd
looked down and seen the bones sharp in her face, along her back and
shoulders, how he'd tried not to wake her, his leg hurting beneath her.
his left leg, numb as a sleeper. how he'd thought to himself then that
the jake must have known which side was stronger. not the jake, he
reminded himself. the poison it was laced with. a poison with a homing
instinct for what should have been the stronger side of a left-handed
man.

he remembers
  cold steel knifing his back, and the pale boy against the boxcar wall,
  shaking,
  the sound of ties clacking,
  how close to the surface the grief was,
  how he'd felt himself receding, descending,
  falling back,
  remembering
  the faint creak of new leather, the pinched sound, walking to the
front of the church to stare into the box, his chest shaking, his heart
cold. the woman's face bellywhite. the body swollen. the soft tump of
pine on pine, the lid closing, the slow rhythmic squeak of the screws
tightening, sealing in the fishrotting smell. the pump organ's nasal
hymn, the people staring, walking the aisle behind the men with the
pine box on their shoulders, walking behind the wagon, through the
dirt street in the summer sunlight, and in the graveyard, the broken
earth's smell.

Sharon

We were coming from the train yard in Oklahoma City, walking through the yellow weeds beyond the tracks at the edge of town, toward the river. Off to the west the sun was going down behind huge purple clouds. They looked like thunderheads but they didn't have any rain in them. All at once the sun broke through into open sky underneath the cloudbank. The light slanted sideways, lit fire to the red dirt and red water, outlined the shanties along the river in gold. Harlan said, "Look there, darlin'. That's godlight." He was holding my hand. I said yeah, even though I was tired, because I could see what he meant. When you see that slanting light shining on red earth and red water, even if all there is ahead of you is rows and rows of shabby tacked-together shacks, well, it makes you think of heaven.

The closer we walked, though, the more I realized the size of that encampment. We had stopped in Oklahoma City a few times, we'd always go down to the river to look for Profit, but the area had been nothing but a hobo jungle before. It was never so large, so full of women and little children. Seemed like a vast shantytown had popped up and spread along the riverbank overnight. We'd seen other Hoovervilles, of course, other families on the road traveling, but when I saw the size of that squatters camp on the banks of the North Canadian in Oklahoma City, I knew that the world was in a terrible mess.

We made our way to the water, walking past shanties built out of packing cases and old sheet iron, torn oilcloth, tarpaper, tin cans, used license plates, car fenders. You wouldn't believe what people will nail together to make a dwelling. At the same time that lovely slanting light turned every color so pure it nearly hurt to look. Harlan nodded at different ones as we passed, "Howdy, neighbor, nice evening," and so on, but nobody hardly answered. That was strange. Harlan had a way about him, he could very nearly get a bo'dark fencepost to speak, but not that evening. We kept walking. The godlight was pretty but it sure didn't do a thing to help the stench in that camp. Shew. It was worse than some of the hobo jungles we'd stayed in. You put a thousand families crowded together with no plumbing and no way to wash, well, it's bad. And the farther we walked seemed like the shelters got flimsier and poorer, and the smell of people living hard grew worse. The light began fading, it was coming on dark, turning cold, and that squatters camp didn't look like heaven to my eyes any longer. I was really hungry. I said, "Profit ain't here, Harlan. You know he ain't." Then I said the words I'd been thinking for quite a while, I said, "If you ask me, he ain't anywhere."

"Aw, sure he is, sweetheart," Harlan said, and he turned aside to talk to a big Negro man sitting on an upended apple crate.

I stood and shivered. The patches on my overalls were worn through at the knees, the chill was creeping in the holes right up my legs to my neck. I had a pretty good secondhand denim jacket that Harlan had dug ditches in Texas to get me and a cloth cap he'd traded his necktie for, but they didn't make up for holey britches. The water in the river was a low dark trickle. The shacks along the bank were just tattered tarps now, pasteboard boxes, and the people inside them and camped in front of them—whole families of people, some of them, camped out on the bare ground—they were all black. We'd walked right past the white section into the Negro part. Not that that bothered Harlan. I mean, to be the only white person in amongst all Negroes. Might have bothered *them,* but it didn't bother him. It did me, in the beginning. I just never did grow up around colored people, I was raised with a normal amount of prejudice, but Harlan wouldn't stand for it. The first time I bristled up about climbing onto a flatcar with some Negroes he lectured me like a schoolteacher. That was one of our first big fights. I can't honestly say I was totally over it by that evening in Oklahoma City, but I didn't buck up at him about it anymore. I heard him ask the man on the apple crate if he'd ever seen Profit, and the man said, "Naw, sir, not in a bunch of years."

Harlan laughed. He set our rucksack down and drew his harp out of his shirt pocket, and I groaned in my belly. I knew what that meant. Harlan ran a lick up and down. "Tell me something," he said. "How come white folks in these parts to be so unfriendly?"

The man was plaiting long strands of green vines together. I couldn't tell if he was making a basket or a lariat or if he was just keeping busy with his hands. He said, very even, like you'd talk to a stranger's dog you didn't want to get riled, "Can't say as I noticed 'em to be any more unfriendly here than most places."

"Oh, well, might just be me then," Harlan said. He played a slow, slidey lick. "Coming through yonder," he said, nodding behind us, "just seemed to me like folks showed a tad suspicious. Either that or they're just hungry."

I thought to myself, *I'm* hungry, Harlan. Me, here. Your wife.

The man on the crate watched Harlan, his fingers moving fast, over and under, over and under, pulling the vines through. "Maybe they thought you was from the government," he said.

Harlan whooped like that was the wildest idea he'd ever heard. "Why in the blue dickens would they think that?"

The man shrugged. "City officials come around with a move order this morning. Appears we're a health hazard, we don't meet the requirements. They're fixing to clear this place out."

"You think me and Short here look like we're from the government?"

"Wouldn't know about that, sir."

Harlan shook his head. He limped over to a big rock and sat down. The man's hands quit moving while he watched him. Harlan put his harp to his mouth, blew a long wailing note, let the sound fade. Then he commenced a slow in-and-out rhythm. He juiced it up, little by little, got the sound going fast, and then he proceeded to play what we used to call juke music or colored music, that dancing, lively, beer-joint kind of sound. A lot of people were watching, and listening, the big man on the crate and other Negroes right by us and the white people downriver too. Pretty soon the ones closest began to edge in. If I'd had the strength I'd have gone over and tugged Harlan's sleeve and told him to come on. Not that it would have done a bit of good. Once Harlan got started there wasn't any stopping him, not before daylight or somebody called the law.

So instead I picked up our rucksack and went over by a little campfire where a skinny colored woman in a sack dress and a raveled sweater was burning green willow sticks. It was making a terrible smoke but I guess that's all she could find for fuel. I said, "Can I stand here a minute?" She looked at me, suspicious enough, but after a bit she nodded, and I sat on the ground, wrapped my arms around my knees, put my head down. I could hear Harlan's music. Not his music, those people's music. After a while I heard a guitar and a second harmonica, a deep voice singing, not Harlan's tenor. All I could hear from Harlan was the quick ripply sounds from his harp. I guess I fell asleep, because when I roused later it seemed to me like only a few minutes had passed, but the night was full dark and there was a good-sized crowd of people gathered yonder. I wasn't cold anymore, somebody had put a piece of quilt across my shoulders. The hunger hole in my stomach burned though. I stood up and almost fell over into the fire, I was that faint. I held myself still a minute, trying to get steady, looking over at the bigger fire on the riverbank, where Harlan and a half dozen Negroes were playing in the middle of that crowd.

"You want something to eat?" a voice said. I turned, and it was the skinny woman in the sack dress. "We got soup is all," she said. "But it's hot." She dipped me up a can full of broth from a number two galvanized washtub, it was watery as anything, but it had a little piece of potato in it and a slick peel of onion, no salt. It tasted like heaven. I scalded my mouth right away, but I didn't care, I drank that soup down. I could feel it going through me, steadying me, helping to stop the hunger shakes.

The woman dipped me up a second can. "I didn't know you was a girl," she said.

I sipped this one slower. "My husband don't want people to know it when we're traveling," I said.

"Oh," the woman said. "He's the one told me."

I looked at her.

"When he come ask me for that cover to put on you."

I pulled the piece of quilt tighter around me. I heard Harlan's twangy voice in among the others. He'd sing a verse and then one of the Negroes would answer. It sounded like a piece of rusty bobwire strung across silk mudflats. I said thank you and set the can on the ground. I went over and pushed my way through, or I didn't push really, people stepped aside and made room, and when I got close I could see Harlan's features in the firelight, bright among the others, like a pink scald scar. If it had been a crowd of white people, Harlan would have been the darkest, but since it was black people, they made Harlan look white. He had his eyes closed. He'd do that a lot when he sang. He was playing somebody's guitar. You might not know it but my husband could play almost any instrument that had a string to it, guitar, mandolin, banjo, he just never could afford to own one. Anyway, we had enough trouble keeping up with a rucksack, I can't dream how we'd have traveled with something so clunky and hard to toss as a guitar. I didn't question how those people camped on the river came to have one, though, when they didn't even have a roof to go over their head. Folks who make music won't turn loose of their means to make it no matter how bad off things get. Not if they can help it they won't. I knew that from being married to Harlan.

The song ended, and Harlan opened his eyes. He grinned broad when he saw me. I smiled back. I was warm now, and not so hungry. The musicians didn't wait, they lit directly into another tune and Harlan went right along with them. I tried to be still and listen, but I'll tell you something, it's hard to go against your raising. If we'd been standing in a bootleg speakeasy with sawdust on the floor I don't think I could have felt worse. My own husband making that kind of music with Negroes, and a bunch of them were dancing, and the *way* they were dancing, well. I was just glad my daddy wasn't around to see. I felt like just me being there and watching was a sin. But then, here in a little bit, I found out I was moving to the music too. It went that way sometimes, me feeling like I was being torn in half.

Somebody started out a new tune on a mouth harp, and it wasn't Harlan. He was still strumming the guitar. I looked where he was looking and saw it was the big man he'd been talking to, that one on the apple crate, and I thought to myself, leave it to Harlan to take up with somebody crazy for a French harp. This man though, it's hard to admit this, but he was as good a harmonica player as my husband. Well, I don't know. Harlan likely would have had him beat on the natural sounds—my husband was like a mockingbird, he could imitate any natural sound he heard—but as far as making that type of juke music, well, this fellow was aiming to show Harlan the light. Harlan handed the guitar to somebody and pulled his own harp out of his pocket and proceeded to answer the big man, and right from there it was bye-bye-so-long. Three or four other harp players came in on it and a second guitar and a bull fiddle and over by the water a little bitty boy was drumming a washtub with two sticks, but it was Harlan and the big man leading, the others were just standing back and giving them their head. Then Harlan jumped out front, and, oh Lord, I'd never heard him play so good, I'd never heard him do half what he did that evening, he ripped up and down with those juiced-up rhythms, his palms flapping open, fisting closed, you'd have sworn he had a brass trumpet in there, a squeeze-box accordion, a church organ, and that big black man right with him, daring him, getting way out ahead of him, sassing him back. The crowd around was just going crazy, whooping and calling and dancing, I bet every live creature within a mile was moving, me included, and anytime Harlan pulled his harp away from his lips I could see him grinning so big.

And they just kept going, one song after another, a fast tune, and then maybe a slow sad one, and then a fast one again, and after a while the big man and Harlan got to taking turns singing. They'd each blow a lick and then sing a lick, then they'd trade off, Harlan's high tenor cut the night, followed by the black man's voice, sweet and deep, and they didn't have to tap a foot to keep the beat in between, because the others kept playing right through the voice parts.

But then, way up close to midnight, or even later maybe, the big man sawed into a slow thumping tune. *"Went to sleep this morn-ing,"* he sang, *"fell right out of bed / Went to sleep this morn-ing / fell right out of bed. Woke up in the eve-nin' / with the lim-ber leg."*

And Harlan didn't answer.

"Oh, jake leg, jake leg, jake leg," the man sang, *"tell me what you gon-na do / Been drinking that mean jake gin-ger / Got the jake lim-ber leg blues."*

Still Harlan didn't answer. So the man just took over and sang the song himself.

"When you see me com-in' / I'm a tell-ing you / When you see me com-in' / I'm a tell-ing you / if you got that mean jake gin-ger / betta give me crutch-es too."

Harlan just kept standing there gazing into the fire. I said, "Harlan?" He didn't look at me. All of a sudden I understood why he limped around with that slap-footed gait. Harlan had the jake leg. I was floored. I felt so stupid. I'd seen that high-stepping jake walk on hobo drunks, old souses in the yards with their bottles of rubbing alcohol and cans of sterno. They'd dip the sterno out with a soda cracker and eat it, when they stood up, they'd go limping across the yard with that limber-leg jake walk. I'd seen it so many times, I never made the connection. I stared at Harlan. If a person had jake leg that meant he was an old sot, didn't it? The same feeling came on me like in Muskogee the morning we got married, I thought: I don't know this man. Harlan raised his eyes to me, and I turned and walked away.

I went back over by the woman who gave me the soup. She was crouched on the ground next to her fire, it wasn't so smoky now or so small.

"They still going, huh," she said.

I didn't say anything.

"Selby won't quit before daylight." The woman reached behind her and snapped a slat off a half busted-up apple crate and fed it to the flame. I thought, She stole that big man's seat, didn't she? "Sit down if you want," she said.

So I did. They were playing a stomping rhythm now, somebody else was singing, not Harlan and not the big man. I got as close to the fire as I could.

"Watch out you don't burn that quilt," the woman said.

I pulled back a little. "Why don't you go over there and listen?" I said.

"My ears hear good enough from here," she said. "Anyhow, somebody got to mind the soup. Thiefs come sneaking around after dark."

I turned quick and looked behind me.

"Oh, they won't come with us sitting here. Sneak thiefs come around when nobody looking, snatch the food right out your baby's mouth. You want some more?" She didn't wait for me to answer, she dipped the can in the washtub and held it toward me. "Look like you fixing to blow away."

I thought, You are sure somebody to be talking, lady. Her face was as thin as a flint, her skin smooth in the firelight, stretched over the bones. I took the soup and drank it, and it made me warmer and it made me feel better, except this time I really noticed the dearth of salt. I said, "I just found out this minute my husband crippled himself from drinking." She didn't say anything so I said, "He's got the jake leg. He never told me. I thought he was born with that limp." The woman poked the fire, it flared up sparks. "He did it to him*self*," I said.

She said, "Sound like you bitter."

"It's a sin," I said. "Drinking's a sin regardless, but to cripple your own temple by taking spirits till you can't walk, that's really sinful. Don't you think it's a sin?"

"Tell you what's a sin," she said, and she drew herself a can of soup, wrapped both hands around it, put it to her mouth and held it there. "Putting poison in that jake ginger and selling it to poorfolks like it's medicine, crippling them for life, and doing it for no reason but for profit, *that's* a sin. I don't see no reason to blame the poor cripples that don't know any better than to drink it."

"Poison?" I said. I got a tight feeling then, remembering Harlan talking about blood poison in the dark boxcar outside Abilene that time.

"What is it you think?" the woman said. "A man don't get jake leg from too much drinking, he get it from one place only, and that's drinking poisoned jake. Don't take much of it either. My Uncle Porter shared a bottle of that Jamaican ginger with six other men, they all every one come down crippled, except Jim Saddle. He died. They didn't even get a chance to get drunk, just hand that bottle around the barber shop about twice, Clarence White go to stand up and fall flat on the floor, and then they all did. Couldn't none of them walk. Some got better after a while, but not Porter. They bought that bottle legal from a drugstore, too."

"But why would somebody do that?"

"Put poison in? Why else do you think? To cut it, to make it go futher so they can get themselves some more damn money. There's men all over this country been crippled by that stuff, and here Lottie Saddle is a widow with six kids to raise and my Uncle Porter can't walk and can't work, and what do you think happen to the ones that did it? Paid a money fine. That's it."

"You're the one sounds bitter to me."

"Naw, child. I ain't bitter. Ain't got time for bitter. I'm too busy trying to keep these children fed." She nodded toward the dark behind her, and for the first time I noticed the four little lumps lined up side by side on the ground just outside the circle of light from the fire. They were wrapped completely in blankets like little moth cocoons. "These my sister kids. They staying with me while she's in Wichita looking for work."

"Your sister left her kids to live out in the open like this?"

The woman gazed at the four lumps. "We was living on Second Street when Mona left," she said. "But Selby hadn't worked since they took his job at the packing plant. I been cleaning house for a lady on Fifteenth Street, but she don't want me but once a month now. We got behind." She snapped off another slat and fed the fire. "When they run us out of here," she said, "I guess we'll go on up to Wichita. I hate to leave though. I been living in Deep Deuce all my life."

"I don't think y'all are going to find any work in Wichita. Me and Harlan been to Wichita. It's no different."

"Well," the woman said. "We got people there." She hoisted herself with a grunt and went over to check on the lumps, tucking in the edges of the blankets. I pulled the piece of quilt around me and stretched out.

When Harlan quit finally the gray light was rising. I saw him limping across the cleared space. I kept my face to the fire, though it was nothing but orange embers now. My back side was cold. Harlan laid down behind me, wrapped himself around me, pulled me close. "Sugarbear," he mumbled. I could smell the liquor on him. The Negroes were still making music, not so many of them though, only a few voices, a couple of sad harps, maybe one guitar. Without turning over I said, "How come you never told me?"

"What?"

"The reason your leg's crippled."

He was quiet a long time. Then he said, "I had it in my mind to speak of it. Just . . . never got around to it, that's all. Maybe I thought you'd figured it out."

"Tell me now."

"Aw, honey, there's nothing to tell. I got hold of some bad juice one time, that's all. I'm luckier than most. Plenty other fellas can't walk."

I rolled over so I could look at him. He tried to snuggle me against his chest but I pushed myself back. I said, "It's a punishment, Harlan."

He looked at me, very still. His face was reddish colored from the embers. "God don't work like that," he said.

I said, "Why, He sure does. If God don't punish sin what's the point in having it? You wouldn't even have to have the word. Anybody could do whatever they felt like."

"Most folks do anyhow, don't they?"

I shut my mouth and turned over. He was making me mad. I laid still, and he wriggled in close, and I only let him because my back was cold. "What makes you think you know how God works?" I said. "You don't even believe in the Almighty."

He murmured, "Sure I do, sugar. Most days." He was breathing slow, about to go to sleep. Well, that made me madder. I poked my elbow against his chest, I said, "You can't half believe and half not, Harlan."

He didn't say anything for so long I thought he'd gone to sleep, but after a while he said, "How old were you when you got saved, Short?"

I was so surprised, it took me a minute to answer. "Six," I said. "Daddy baptized me in Rock Creek. That was before we moved to Cookson."

"I was twelve," Harlan said.

I didn't know whether to be doubtful or glad. He'd never once mentioned about being saved. I said, "Who saved you?"

"Jesus," he said against my hair.

I said, "No, I know. I don't mean that. I mean, who gave the invitation?"

"Jesus."

"Oh, quit. I mean where at? Who was preaching?"

"Jesus," he said again.

"It's a sin to joke about salvation."

"That's not what sin is," he said.

"You know so much, Smarty. What is it then?"

But Harlan didn't answer. I laid still a long while, staring at the red coals. This was one area that really troubled me in my marriage. Harlan talked Scripture more than a normal person, he could quote it chapter and verse near as good as my daddy, but then he'd twist things around to where they didn't sound anything like the way I was raised. After a long while Harlan blew out a soft whiskey snore against my hair. Lying there with the weight of his arm across me, his warm breath on the top of my head, I knew I ought to pray, but I just didn't feel like it. I couldn't actually think what to pray for. I watched the coals die and the dawn come. I heard the soup woman snoring soft beside the children. The folks by the river played slow and low, quiet, sad sounding. Then I heard something else, back behind us, toward town, distant yelling, dogs barking. I thought, It's late now, them people oughta hush.

Suddenly the woman sat straight up, I mean like a sprung trap, she hollered, "Selby!" and right at once the sorrowful music on the riverbank ceased. I heard the yelling voices plain now, and the dogs, and also children far away, crying. I sat up too. One of the near little kids in its quilt cocoon woke up wailing, and then the woman was on her feet, telling the others to get up, quick! Harlan was snoring with his mouth open, his curly hair spronging all over his head.

The light was good enough that I could see down the river. Men in hats with shotguns were breaking up people's lean-tos and shanties, or standing to one side with dogs on leashes, their guns cradled across their arms. The white families downriver were gathering their belongings, wrapping things in blankets, corralling their kids.

"Harlan!" I shoved him, and he roused a little, trying to sit up. "Wake up!" I yelled. He was looking around, his eyes bloodshot like Christmas. I felt like whacking him with my cap. "Get up, Harlan! Look what they're doing!"

"What? What?"

I didn't even try to answer, I scrambled to my feet and went over where the woman was wrapping her sister's kids, putting bindles on their shoulders, trying to tie them on with too-short pieces of twine, telling the kids hush, hush. Only two were crying, the two littlest ones, twins maybe, their bawling faces as alike as two crowder peas. The older two were girls, their hair in braids all over, they stood next to each other, trembling and silent. I said to the woman, "Can I help?" She acted like I wasn't there.

I saw the big man then, the harp player from last night, rushing toward us, he came and jerked the washtub off the embers and started tossing things in it, the tin can I'd drank soup from, a wooden spoon, an old blue graniteware coffee pot burnt black on the bottom. I was sort of surprised and not surprised at the same time, to realize he was her husband. He told her to grab the kettle. The man grabbed a pair of beat-up brogans from beside a bedroll and slung them right in on the dregs of broth. Behind me I heard Harlan's voice say, "I've seen some strange things throwed in a mulligan stew in my time, Sel, but that takes the cake."

I whirled around, he was standing there scratching his head, bleary-eyed, his hair like a bramblebush gone mad. The big man stopped what he was doing. "You," he said, very low and quiet, staring at Harlan. "You the one working for the Man." His voice was blaming, like he thought Harlan had brought the trouble, like Harlan played music with them all night just to trick them, just to set these people up for a raid.

Harlan stood blinking, his face baffled. "Whoa—" he started, but the big man looked straight at him and spat deliberately on the ground. Then he turned, and in one smooth swoop hoisted the tub to his shoulder, and him and the woman took the four children and walked to the water. They never gave us another glance. The two littlest ones were still bawling, the woman picked them up, one under each arm, and started wading across.

It was full daylight now, but the sky was overcast, the light couldn't seem to grow to anything more than gray. I saw other Negroes splashing through the water to the land on the other side. Downriver it was all white people, either the men in the hats and guns or the squatters they were rousting out, some of them walking with their families along the train tracks toward downtown. Upriver, it was all Negroes, and they were scattering a lot faster than the white people, slinging whatever they had into packs and blankets. Me and Harlan were standing in the middle, the sort of no-man's-land in between.

I said, "Harlan? Reckon we better go?"

He didn't answer, he was staring across the water. The whole side of his coat and britches were dusty red from where he'd been laying on the ground. I figured I was too, and I glanced down to check, and that's the first I realized I still had that woman's piece of quilt wrapped around me. I looked up to catch her, but she was already out on the open land, moving fast. Not far from us a man in a straw hat was using the butt of his shotgun to bust up a shelter hidden in the willow scrub. He had a dog on a leash with him, an old redbone coonhound, and the dog whined as it watched him. "Who are they, Harlan?" I said.

"I reckon they're from the government," he said. His face was so still.

"Where's their uniforms? Don't they need uniforms?"

"Appears not." Harlan limped over to the campfire and picked up our rucksack.

A little man in khakis and a snappy felt hat came through with a bullhorn, calling out, "This illegal squatters' camp is in violation of the health codes of Oklahoma City! We are hereby executing the move order you people received yesterday! Y'all get your stuff and get out of here! We're armed, folks, and we ain't afraid to use 'em!"

Behind him swarmed the army of men in denim work pants and straw cowboy hats, and if they were rough busting up the white camps, they were just awful with the Negroes, the ones that hadn't already run off. They'd jerk people away from their belongings and shove them toward the water, dump their packs upside down on the ground and toe through the contents to see if there was anything they wanted to keep for themselves. I saw one man smack a little colored boy in the head for no good reason that I could tell. I didn't see anybody shoot anybody, but it sure looked like they might if they were crossed.

Me and Harlan started walking back the way we'd come yesterday, toward the railroad tracks, but the fellow with the redbone hound stopped us. He didn't look like a man from the government, he looked more like a farmer. He had tobacco spittle in the ends of his mustache.

"Y'all can't go this way," he said. "You're going to have to go yonder." He gestured with his shotgun across the water to the open land.

"That so?" Harlan said.

"We got orders to clear this area. You squatters been spreading like the blame mange, we're not going to stand for this sort of squalor here." The man spat a stream of tobacco juice into the dust. "We don't need your kind in our town."

"What kind is that, mister? What kind are we?"

The man eyed Harlan from under his hat, and then he slipped me a glance. His face went still, I saw him registering I was a girl in overalls, or maybe it was the fact I was white. Anyhow he frowned and turned away, muttering, "Y'all keep moving now. Soo, Jerry." He clicked at the redbone, and the two of them wandered off.

"He don't have the right to talk to us like that. Does he?"

Harlan said, "Put your cap on, Short. Let's go."

I pulled my cap out of my bib and tugged it on, let the piece of quilt slide off my shoulders, rolled it up and put it under my arm. We started again toward the tracks. I smelled tarry smoke, not woodsmoke from the fires but something like rubber, and I turned to look back. We were on the grade leading toward the tracks, I could see a long ways, up and down the river. It looked like a war or something, people running every direction, shouting and yelling, the ground littered with busted crates and tents, scattered belongings. In the white section somebody had set a car afire. It was the tires smoking that made that smell. I said, "What is this, Harlan? I don't see why they're doing this."

Harlan didn't say anything.

"Looks like a twister, don't it?" I said. "Like a tornado come blowing through."

After a minute his voice came, very soft. "Well, but it's not weather, is it?"

We watched two men in light-colored cowboy hats shoving an Indian man toward a paddy wagon, taking turns pushing him in the back with the barrels of their guns. A woman was trailing behind them, she had a baby in her arms. I thought, I hope that baby's not dead. My stomach was burning. My chest hurt. I wanted to go home to Cookson, I wanted to see my daddy. I said, "Where's all these people going to go? It's whole families of people without any place to live." Harlan was still staring at the river. I said, "I don't see how them folks are going to get to Wichita. It's three hundred miles to Wichita. They can't put those bitty kids up to hopping freights."

Harlan raised his eyes over the flat yellow land. To me, there was nothing to see out yonder. I kept looking at what the men on the bank were doing. Afterwhile I started to understand what Harlan meant. It wasn't weather mowing the shacks down, it was the work of men, and that's what made it so awful. But, I thought, it could just as well be an act of God or a windstorm for all a solitary person could do to stop it. You couldn't stop it. I touched Harlan's sleeve. I was hungry. There was a little bakery on Robinson Avenue where we'd bummed some toppings the last time we were in Oklahoma City. I figured maybe we could try that place again. I said, "Harlan? Aren't we going to go?" But he had his harp out already, and he didn't look at me and he wouldn't answer me, he just cupped his hands to his mouth. The sound he made wasn't pretty though. It wasn't music. It was more like the rasping squeal of a red-tailed hawk.

deepsong

on his back, in the thicket, hard stones beneath him, starless night overhead, the singer remembers

how the silence came to him first on the banks of the flat winding river, the water russet, low, thick seeming, the water rust red and sandy, like the dirt.

how he'd tried to listen,
and could not hear over men's voices, the sound of wood cracking,
the odor of guns.

harlan? she said.
the silence like a spider's
web clogging his ears.
are you all right? she said.
listen, he said. listen.

hearing then, finally, not the sound he longed for, but the sound from his boyhood, the evangelist's voice at the front of the tabernacle, FOR ALL HAVE SINNED AND COME SHORT OF THE GLORY OF GOD! remembering how that voice had burned in him, throbbed in him, back then, in his boyhood, when his greatest sin was petty pilfering, when his sin was the sin of trying to feed himself. how the voice shook him through the night on the damp ground beside the brush arbor, how the gray gauze of guilt lay across his mouth and chest, long after the praising was finished, hours after the preaching had ceased and the people drove away in their wagons, how he'd felt the searing flame at the core of him, dreamed himself burning, how he'd cried out for mercy, cried out for his mama, so that when the sun rose he had been ready, or he'd believed himself ready, and in the evening he'd walked the sod aisle in the torchlight, he had fallen to his knees at the mercy seat to accept a perfect god's perfect forgiveness for his miserable worthless imperfect self, little sneaking thief that he was. useless one that he was. wretched urchin, unwanted wild boy from the timber. how he'd believed himself ready for salvation, when all he'd wanted was to be civilized, to fetch wood and wash in the cool waters of a clean basin, when all he'd wanted was to be fed.

how he'd committed the books to memory, genesis exodus leviticus numbers, studying in the yellow coal-oil light inside the dark toolshed behind the methodist minister's house. how he'd turned his harp to playing hymns only, *the old rugged cross, power in the blood, jesus paid it all*, and what a lie it had been, this salvation that lasted no longer than it took for him to run into that bootblack in muskogee, the negro boy as small as himself, traveling with a box guitar strung with catgut, who said he'd teach singer to play on the way to california if only he'd go with him and help keep him from getting his head battered in. how the singer's name was not singer then but willie. wee willie jonesy. but the bootblack boy from muskogee went by the name willie too.

Sharon

After we got run out of that squatters camp Harlan turned different—not completely, not like what happened later—but when I look back now I can trace the first changes I witnessed to then. His music was the main thing It got to where I didn't want to hear him play anymore. He'd cup his hands to his mouth, what came out was so raw and sour it hurt your ears. I thought his harp must have got damaged from all the travel, or else he'd just forgot how to make the thing work. He grew quieter, too, same as he did after we ran into that blond kid outside Kansas City, only now Harlan's silence was deeper, more settled. He'd sit in the corner of a clacking railcar and stare at the floor. He wasn't seeing the splinters or the rat droppings, he was seeing something inside his own mind. I'd say, "Honey? You all right?" Sometimes he'd shake his head and grin, crawl over beside me, if we were in a car alone he'd lay me down and love me. Other times, though, he'd just keep staring. Cock his head to one side, tell me to listen. Well you know you couldn't hear a thing but the roar of the rails. Plus, on top of that, seemed to me like his limp was getting worse.

It wasn't, actually. Jake leg don't work that way. You get the limber leg one time and then your walk stays the same right up till the day you die, I reckon, unless you'd be dumb enough to drink some more poisoned jake and make it worse. I couldn't realize that it wasn't Harlan's leg getting worse, it was me, it was inside my own eyes. Watching him go across the cinders in some switchyard, I couldn't seem to see anything but that slap-footed gait. When I had to reach a hand down to help him climb up in a car, I'd feel so ashamed, like that limber leg made him weak. Too weak to be my husband. Too weak to depend on. That bothered me a lot.

Another thing, after Oklahoma City, we never spent any time at all in one place. Used to be, we'd work a while somewhere, if we could find any work that paid, or Harlan would play his music on the street corners for change. Now, we'd stop just long enough to hustle a bite of food, maybe wash up in a creekbed, then we'd catch out right away. Seemed like Harlan had it in his mind that Profit was on the next train ahead of us and if we moved fast enough we could catch him. Well, and the more Harlan chased after Profit, the more I settled in my own mind that the old man wasn't real. I figured he was a daydream my husband had conjured to justify running. I told him so sometimes, I'd say, That old man don't exist, Harlan, he ain't going to be on the next train. Let's stop a while. Let's rest, honey. But seemed to me like Harlan couldn't hear.

And then, in the spring, I started being sick to my stomach. Whether I ate or whether I didn't, whether we were on a moving train or sitting still. It took me a while to know the reason. I was only fifteen. But I did figure it out, finally, one afternoon, sitting on a hill outside Henryetta, waiting for a westbound freight.

We had pretty much quit catching out on the fly if we could help it, that's absolutely the most dangerous way to hop a freight, but the long grade outside Henryetta made the engines go slow, and the Henryetta bulls were mean as devils, so sometimes we'd still try it there. We would wait till the front engine appeared around the curve, then we'd slide down the hill and run alongside the tracks till the train caught us, I'd grab the ladder and swing aboard and Harlan would keep running in his jagged lope, the rucksack under his arm. I'd reach my hand down to help him, he'd grab hold and pull himself up. We'd done that on that same hill three different times. Not today, I said to myself. I'm not doing it anymore.

The sun was hot on me, and I wanted to be sick, except I hadn't eaten since yesterday evening. I didn't have anything to throw up. I looked across the valley. In a little gully beyond the railbed some wildflowers were blooming. The pale little blossoms made me think of the dogwoods back home, how the blooms look like snow winking on the trees, deep in the woods, when you're passing by in the wagon. I said, "Harlan, what month is it? Is it May yet? We missed the dogwoods. I think we missed the dogwoods." And then all of a sudden, right from nowhere, I understood why I kept being sick.

Off in the distance a whistle was blowing. The freight was at the crossing a mile east. Harlan stood up, hoisted our rucksack. "Here she comes," he said. The train chugged up the slope toward us. I just kept sitting. Harlan said, "Shug, we better hurry." I could feel him watching, but I didn't lift my head. The freight drew near, coming slow, climbing, until it was right below us, rumbling past, picking up speed on the downslope, roaring away toward the west.

"What's the matter?" Harlan said.

I looked up at him. "You remember the morning we got married?"

"Sure do." He tipped his hat back, watched the train disappearing. He'd got himself a new brown fedora, well, it wasn't new really, but it was new to him. He'd won it in a card game in a campyard in Omaha. I don't approve of card playing, but I had to admit that hat looked nice.

"What did you tell me that morning?"

"I don't know, babe. Probably something like, 'I just married myself the prettiest little cotton-picker west of the Mississippi'?"

"I can tell you the very words. I can quote them exactly. You said, 'Sharon, I'm going to take care of you.' You said, 'When it gets time, I'll carry you home to see your family.'"

He was still peering along the line. "Is that right."

"You said, 'I promise you I will.'"

Now he turned his eyes to meet me.

"It's time, Harlan," I said.

He took me back the same way we left: we hopped an eastbound freight out of Muskogee, jumped off before it got to Vardis, started hitching rides from there. Every mile we drew closer, though, I got more scared. I scrunched down in the backseat of our last ride, a shoe salesman going home to Tahlequah. I put my face in my lap. I couldn't look up at the clotted hillsides. I didn't want to see any empty farmhouses or burnt cornfields or dry creeks. I heard Harlan say, "You can let us out here, mister. We're much obliged. My wife don't feel good." I climbed out of that drummer's coupe onto the dirt road. Harlan waved our thanks and the man drove off, raising a dust cloud, I had to put my hand over my mouth. I saw right where we were. We'd come up on the back side of Mr. Casper's place, it was a half mile walk to Cookson one direction, a half mile to our house the other. I was sweating. The hurting in my chest was so fierce. I don't know what my face looked like, but Harlan said, "You know we don't have to go, sweetheart."

I turned on him, for the first time in our lives I yelled at him. "Who's going to feed this baby? You don't even feed me, Harlan, you don't take care of me, not even enough to keep a cricket alive! We can't be traipsing all over the blessed country with a baby!"

It was so hot. Sickening hot. I went over to the shade at the side of the road and sat down. Then I leaned over and heaved several times, but I didn't have anything in my stomach. When the wave passed I looked up at him. What was in his face is hard to explain. I felt like he was *trying* to be scared for me. He kept his gaze steady on me, he met my eyes, like he knew he ought to give me that much, but he could just as well have been staring at a boxcar floor. Some part of him wasn't there. "Are you all right?" he said. I was too sick then to feel anything but misery. I nodded, wiped my mouth, stood up and dusted the seat of my britches. I took my cap off and stuck it in the bib, smoothed my hair down, dry, I didn't have any spit to use. Then I started walking. He came along beside me.

I could see the house from a distance, the yard gate and a corner of the smokehouse and the barn roof. The trees were leafed out, but the leaves were tiny and shriveled, dusty as August. I could see where the whitewash Harlan had put on the side of the house was fading, the gray shingles next to it, the uneven line where he'd quit work the day before we left. Nobody had finished his job. I didn't see any of the kids. No dogs slunk out from under the porch to bark at us. I didn't see any hens scratching in Mama's zinnia bed. I didn't see any zinnias coming up, either. We stood outside the gate and Harlan helloed the house. No answer.

"Something's the matter," I said. "Our house is never empty. Somebody's always here. Where's the dogs? Where's my family?" My voice started spiraling. "Harlan! What's happened to my family?"

"Look," he said. "The yard's swept. See it? Come on, doll, shhh, baby," and he touched my neck.

When I opened my eyes I could see the fresh raked strokes in the dirt, long perfect waves scratched with the brushbroom from the foot of the porch to the fence. Mama must have done it, none of the kids could have made it that perfect. Sweeping the yard used to be my job, every Saturday morning. To get ready for Sunday. I could see the kids' bare footprints going in crazy stitching, curlicuing and looping across the yard to the side gate. I started to breathe again.

Harlan opened the gate and walked me through. It felt so strange in the yard, on the porch, it felt like I'd been gone my whole life. Inside the house, though, the hurting in my chest swelled even worse. I didn't say anything. I just walked through the rooms. Mama's rocker and the four canebottom chairs were lined up against the wall in the front room. Four soft bundles sat in the chairs like people, each was a panel from the curtains wrapped around something lumpy, tied up with twine. Over the fireplace was a blank space where the picture of the beautiful tall angel helping the two orphan children across the bridge used to be. The kerosene lamps were missing from the mantel, the corner knickknack shelf was gone. In the dark dining room Daddy's homemade bench stood upside down on the bare table The wall was blank where the dish cabinet used to stand. In the kids' bedroom there weren't any iron bedsteads, the two mattresses were folded over, shoved against the wall. Mama and Daddy's room was completely empty. The floor was swept.

Old memories stirred in me, of what it was like when I was little, Daddy putting our things into the wagon, Mama taking them out and setting them around in a different house. Until I was nine we'd moved every year or two, from one landlord's place to the next, trying to find a better land to plant, a fairer landlord, someplace nearer where Daddy was preaching. After we got to Mr. Casper's we quit moving. The house was a good one, it was Mr. Casper's old grandma's place before she died, and Mr. Casper was a friend of Daddy's, and a Christian. I'd forgotten all about moving. I guess I thought my family would never have to move again.

In the kitchen I peeked in the keeper for leftover biscuits or cornbread, but the keeper was empty. The cookstove was cold. The dishpan was gone from its nail on the wall. I looked out the window. The truckpatch was a mess of pokeweed and dandelions. Harlan came in the kitchen behind me. I didn't turn around. "They're not gone yet, are they?" I said. "Do you think they're gone?"

"Don't look like it."

"They wouldn't leave Mama's rocker."

He put his hand on me but I shrugged him off. I stood at the counter. The door to the henhouse gapped open. The chickenwire fence had a tear in it. The gate was hanging off its hinges. Everything was quiet, completely silent, in a way no barnyard ever is.

"It's Sunday," I said.

I don't know how I all of a sudden knew that. I just did. I knew it was Sunday, and I knew where my family was.

I said, "We got to go on in to town."

We heard the singing as soon as we turned onto Main Street. That surprised me. I squinted up at the sun. It was almost noon. Through the church windows I could see the backs of people standing in the aisles. The front doors were open, and there were men and women on the porch, too, looking in. Cars and wagons lined the side of the road all the way to the schoolhouse. I hadn't ever seen that little Free Will Baptist Church so full, not even during revivals. And this was no revival. From the size of the crowd I thought it must be people from every one of Daddy's congregations. I thought maybe it was an all-day prayer service and camp meeting with dinner on the ground. Suddenly my heart stopped cold. *It's Daddy's funeral!* I thought. That had to be what it was. I broke free from Harlan's hand and started running.

When I squeezed through the crowd at the door and saw him standing in the pulpit, you know it was like the resurrection to me. His head was shining with light, it was bowed over, he was leading in prayer. Mama was sitting at the piano in her Sunday hat with her hands folded. Everybody's head was bowed. The prayer didn't last long, but it was long enough for me to look at my parents, and I saw in a long slow draining how much was changed. Even before Daddy raised his face I saw it. His hair wasn't shining with light, it was white, it had turned white on his head, almost completely. Mama's arms were slack-covered bones coming out of her scalloped sleeves. She had on her same Sunday dress, starched and ironed like always, but the navy was faded to gray, the white collar was missing. It must have been a bitter prayer my mama was praying, because her mouth was clamped so tight her lips practically disappeared. She got up quietly from the piano bench while Daddy was still praying. My eyes burned hard on her, I thought she'd feel me and look to the back of the church, but she just slipped into the fourth pew to wait for the sermon. I tried to see the backs of the kids' heads, but the sanctuary was too crowded.

"Forgive us wherein we have failed Thee," Daddy said, "and we'll be sure to give Thee the praise. These things we ask in Jesus' name, amen."

He looked up, stared out over the congregation, and I saw how badly his face was gaunted, how deep and baffled his eyes were. For me, it was like standing in the front room against the wall the night he came home from the bank in Vardis. Everything inside me wanted to sink to the floor. I felt Harlan slip in beside me, the people shifting to make room. I squeezed over behind a big woman in a print dress. I was afraid Daddy would feel the commotion, raise his glance and find me. I didn't want him to see me looking the way I did. He was reading from Psalms about the soul longing for God in a dry and thirsty land. My mouth was so parched I was spitting cotton, I thought, What my soul wants is a drink of water.

Then Daddy started in on the Rich Man and Lazarus. I'd heard him preach that sermon a few times, the rich man in torment and the beggar Lazarus being comforted in the bosom of Abraham. He'd paint the flames to make your soul tremble, make you certain sure you didn't want to end up like the rich man. This morning though, Daddy's voice sounded choked and quiet, too soft. I thought his throat must feel like my throat, raw and sore with thirst.

"Brethren," he said in a near whisper, "we know Lazarus was a poor man, a beggar, his body covered in sores. His people had to carry him to the gate so he could lay there and hope for a few crumbs from the rich man's table. Lazarus didn't beg for the crumbs, he just laid there and desired to be fed. That's what Jesus said, Lazarus *desired* to be fed. And the dogs licked his sores. That's hard to picture, isn't it? A beggar laying on the ground and all the old yella dogs in the neighborhood coming up to lick his sores. But that's how Lazarus lived. There wasn't any help for Lazarus on this earth. Isn't that like the times we're living in? No help for the poor and heartsick, the weary. No help."

I peeked around the side of the big woman to see the congregation, I expected some amens but everybody was silent, staring at the pulpit. My grammar school teacher Mrs. Lambert was sitting across the aisle. I recognized Marie Tingle's red hair down front, the Garrison family rowed up in a middle pew. I even saw our landlord Mr. Casper at the end of the aisle near the altar, I didn't know what he was doing in our church. Mr. Casper was a Methodist. A lot of the people though, I didn't recognize, they weren't from Cookson. How had all these people come to be here?

"'The poor ye always have with you,'" Daddy quoted. "No help for that.

No help. And poor old Lazarus died, and the Lord tells us the angels came and carried him to Abraham's bosom. What does that mean, Abraham's bosom? It's heaven. I guess it's just heaven, don't you expect? I think it is. I don't know. And the rich man died, and they buried him. We don't know what went with Lazarus' body. The Bible doesn't tell us. I hope they didn't leave it in the road for the dogs to eat. That would be terrible. That would be awful, but that's how some folks do. When a nation transgresses, the whole nation's got to repent. The Bible says that. Jeremiah tells us. Isaiah says it. The prophet Ezekiel told us there would be famine and pestilence and the sword. Famine and pestilence and the sword. Isn't that like the times we're living in? We are as dry bones scattered in a dry land. 'The pastors are become brutish. They shall not prosper. All their flocks shall be scattered.' Their flocks shall be scattered. They come got the cows. Killed the hogs. We ate the chickens, ate my wife's pea hen. My oldest boy shot the dogs. The flocks are scattered. The crops turned to dust."

Harlan tugged on the strap of my overalls, he was trying to get me to go outside, but I stood there, swaying. The church was going dark in front of me, I needed to sit down, to lay down. My belly hurt. I couldn't see Mama from where I was standing. I hadn't seen any one of the kids.

"We don't know where we shall be scattered," Daddy said, his voice cracking, "We don't know, do we? Only the Lord knows. This nation has sinned, like the children of Israel. A sinful nation has got to turn away from sin What is it, though? Our nation's sin. We've got to name it and repent it. When we do that, these hard times will pass. 'O ye dry bones.'" My daddy's voice quavered like an old man's voice. "'Hear the word of the Lord—'"

Harlan turned suddenly and pushed back through the crowd.

"'Return ye backsliding children,'" Daddy said, "'and I will heal your backslidings.'"

I wanted to stay, I meant to stay, for my daddy's sake, I desired to, but I couldn't help it. I turned and went back up the aisle, following Harlan. The people on the porch stared at me as I came out.

He was in the road, standing next to a blunt-nosed truck parked in the shade.

"What's the matter with you?" I said when I reached him.

"Matter with *me*?" Harlan's eyes were so washed in the bright sunshine, so pale. "Your daddy's cut to pieces, honey. He's broken apart."

"He's not either." I felt sucked out and hollow. I leaned against the truck. It was silent in the town, the air was heavy, too still. Houseflies darted and buzzed over a covered basket in the truck bed. I was so thirsty. I sat down on the running board. Daddy's croaking too-soft voice hummed through the open windows.

"Here," Harlan said, and he handed me a fried chicken leg.

"Where'd you get that?"

"Eat it, Sharon. You're fixing to faint."

Dry as I was, I gnawed that leg down. I cracked the bone in my teeth and sucked out the marrow. Then I watched Harlan reach in the truck bed. He handed me a chicken wing, he was stealing someone's food, somebody's picnic lunch, and I didn't care a whit. "Do they have any water?" I said. I watched his shoulders move as he felt around under the blanket covering the basket. He was frowning, trying to tell by the feel. He handed down a fruit jar full of buttermilk. Somebody had wrapped it in a wet rag to keep it cool, but it wasn't cool, it was warm as cow's milk direct from the bag. I drank it down. I was starting to feel better.

Harlan sat next to me on the running board. He pulled a chunk of meat off a breast and handed it over, started to eat around the wishbone. "The whited sepulcher," he said.

"What?"

"The nation's sin. Hypocrisy. That's what it is. They go around acting like they do, and then proclaim themselves in the name of the Lord. That's the whited sepulcher. That's sin."

"What are you talking about?" I said. I thought he meant my daddy, I was set to fly mad. If I'd had the strength I'd have been mad already.

"Sharon, don't you know what this is?"

I hesitated. I looked up and down the road, struck again by how many cars and wagons there were, and so many people in the church, and if it wasn't my daddy's funeral, what was it? I shook my head.

"It's farewell. Goodbye to your folks, so long to the Caspers, the Garrisons, the Seliys, they couldn't even list me all the names. A dozen families, they said."

"Who said?"

"Them on the porch. Turns out that fine upstanding Christian banker Oliver Teasley has foreclosed on half the county. Not all of them was poor farms either. I don't guess Casper's was. Teasley hit the Cherokees and the colored farmers awful hard, they said. I don't know how he managed to get Indians to take out a mortgage. But then again, I guess I do. Oliver Teasley is a mighty shrewd man." Harlan spat out a gristle.

"If Daddy had a place in mind for us to go, he wouldn't have said only the Lord knows. Would he?"

"A place for *us* to go." Harlan spoke the words flat, like a sentence, but his face wasn't declaring. He was asking.

"Well, we're going with them, aren't we?"

Harlan was quiet.

"I mean, we got to. I mean . . ."

The understandings all fell in place then, click click click click. Harlan didn't have to say anything. I knew my family didn't need any more mouths to feed. Not mine, and surely not Harlan's, and not our baby's either, when he came. It was no use me wanting to go home to my family, there wasn't any home here anymore. The house and the barn, the fields and the smokehouse, the truckpatch where Harlan first kissed me, the very bobwire around it, every bit of property belonged to Oliver Teasley. That made me furious mad. My strength was coming back, I could feel the blood rising. I took the quart jar of peaches from Harlan's hand, I drank the juice down, slithered a sweet half a peach into my mouth. I felt guilty, stealing some farmer's food, not guilty enough to stop though. I told myself we could watch and see whose truck it was, pay them back later. And then I thought, there won't be no later. Because I knew that if I saw my family up close, if I talked to Mama, if the kids swarmed around and hugged me, if Daddy looked at me with his sorrowed eyes, I might not be able to walk away again. Harlan would walk away, he would have to, but what if I couldn't?

And then, click, there was the last thing: when my family rode away in the morning with Mama's rocker and the chairs and the bundles rolled up in the wagon, I wouldn't have any way of knowing where they went.

Harlan was talking again, saying he didn't believe Jesus meant for poorfolks to pay the cost when it was rich thieves and hypocrites ruining the country, he couldn't figure how that idea had got so garbled in people's minds. I stood up and started to walk. We were thieves ourselves anyway. We'd robbed from the poor for our own sakes that morning, but the way I figured it, I had to feed myself, on account of my baby.

But then it turned out that even that wasn't true. Because we headed west across the Illinois River, walking the planks of the old Standing Rock bridge in the hot sunlight, carrying pieces of stolen chicken and a fried pie, and before we'd even reached halfway across the water, my womb had started to bleed.

deepsong

under the thicket, on the bed of stones, the singer remembers
how he'd tried to staunch the blood, on the road coming from
cookson, not knowing what it was, the dark stain spreading, until she
couldn't walk, couldn't sit, and he'd carried her into a hay field and laid
her down, the earth dry and hard and rough as cornstubble, he'd spread
open his coat, ripped the sleeves from his shirt and pressed the cotton
against the private place, and still the blood came. how he'd looked at
her and known she might die, and that if she died he'd die, or the rest of
him would, and still he couldn't make himself come forward. inside, far
back in the recesses, he was listening.

how he'd cut the small quilt into strips, pulled apart the cotton
batting to make it last, and when the quilt was gone he'd used his knife
to cut the sleeves from his coat, and still she lay bleeding. how he'd
looked at her face, pale in the sun, paler still in the evening, the life
draining, and said to himself, *if she dies.* the helplessness a cold weight
in his chest. how when the red clot came he'd laid it on the piece of
white batting and carried it to the edge of the field, knifed a hole in the
hard earth, buried the bloody cotton there, and still she bled,

even when he lifted her and carried her, too light, no more heft to
her than a child, over the stubbled field to the road, where he stood
with his wife in his arms until a man in a new car stopped, a new
chevrolet with chrome fenders, and helped him put her in the car, no
rug or quilt or jacket underneath to protect the scented leather from her
blood, how the man parked the car far back from the hospital door, the
indian hospital in tahlequah, telling singer to take the girl out, wheeling
away fast, tires crying, as singer laid her down on the grass.

how he'd used his chameleon tongue to tell them she was cherokee,
when they could see how pale she was, could see her skin stark beneath
the tiny freckles, her hair the color of cottonseed, seeing too, maybe,
that she was dying. how they'd taken her behind a drape, the white
doctor's hand against singer's chest, telling him he could not follow,

how when he heard her screams he'd shoved through the curtain,

seeing her legs strapped, the white doctor between them, the silver tool in
his hand red, and the indian nurse pushed him back, pushing him back,
yelling, the nurses yelling, singer yelling, and sharon, screaming, but
alive. how, even then, he was still trying to come forward, still trying

nights later, when he stole her out of the bed and carried her,
limping, to the dark highway, both of them limping, how he'd put his
fist out, thumb angled, not knowing, or thinking, then of where they
would go.

how she had fallen twice after they left the empty road, her head at
his shoulder dropping away in silence in the dark, and he'd picked her
up again, carried her into the brush, going by memory, going by feel,
through the tangle of vines and twisted undergrowth, until daylight,
when he could lay her down on the bed of white stones.

how in the end he'd carried her home, carried her to this place he'd
carved from the living thicket years ago, green brambles held back with
pilfered tin and sawed boards, a living cave beside the creek he'd named
in his boyhood

nokiller.

nokiller.

a trick name, a twist on the names of the other boys in the place
his mother took him in summer, the little town beside the chalky hills,
marble city, where he did not belong because he had no clan, because his
mother was white. where tommy fourkiller caught him behind the school
and bent his arm back and called him pretty-like-a-white-boy, called him
gehyooj. where jim mankiller laughed when he'd turned away, crying,
from the shot *tewa*, the young squirrel dead on the ground, eyes open,
its small hands fisted, its big tail flat to the earth. he'd run away then, far
into the brush, and found this springfed creek and believed in his boyish
mind that his eyes were the first eyes to see it. he'd claimed it for himself,
saying this place belongs to no man, and so it is mine. no man's creek. no
mankiller creek. no tenkiller, sixkiller, fourkiller.

and that had been in the time before they brought his mother back
to the white town, back to sallisaw, where he had no name, because he
had no father. because his father was dead. because his father was not
white. where they brought his mother from the river and laid her out
at the front of the church to let the people walk past with stone faces,
the ladies coming to him where he sat in the pew beside the minister's
wife, to pat his head or his cheek, to push the tangle of hair off his

forehead. and the minister's wife drew a handkerchief from her dress
sleeve, pressed it into his palm, as if he would weep, as if he were weak
like *agehyooj*, a girl. but the singer was dry-eyed, walking to the front of
the church to stare into the box, his chest shaking. his heart cold. he'd
watched them close the lid over the woman's face, swollen, bellywhite,
the smell horrific, watched them turn the screws to tighten it down,
seal it over the smell and the swollen woman, how he'd allowed the
minister's wife to put her hand on his shoulder to walk the aisle behind
the men holding the box, he'd walked with them to the graveyard, he'd
watched them lower the drowned woman in the box on three lengths
of strong rope into the earth, dry-eyed still, because it did not matter to
him what the minister said, what the town told him,

he knew that was not her,

not his mother, in the ground.

he'd only fled, he said, to get the feel of that white woman's hand
off his shoulder, had only run the many miles to nokiller because he'd
desired to feel the hard knots of the creekbed stones beneath him,
thinking of the names.

sixkiller. tenkiller. mankiller. no mankiller. no killer.

i will be brave, he'd said, but i won't be a killer.

but of course he had killed. he'd had to kill to live, he'd slit the
throats of a hundred *tewa*, a thousand rabbits, he'd learned to snare
them, skin them, roast them over the open flame. the silent boy in the
woods had taught him, calm bledsoe had taught him. the older boy
who, like him, was not white and not indian, who chose indian, who
chose cherokee, and would not speak english any more. but that was so
much later, long after the singer was starving, almost dead from hunger,
after he'd learned to steal, and then learned not to.

after he'd come to know that it was, truly, his mother inside that
swollen body, inside the pine box.

after he'd understood deep within himself that he had no mother
and no father, that, from now on, he was alone. and then he found jesus
and was not alone again. and then he lost jesus and went on the road
with the bootblack boy from muskogee, willie jay jefferson jones, guitar
and harp in perfect tuning across america, in peafields and migrant
camps, all the way to california, where white men bashed willie jay's
skull in, and the singer fled, hiding in the dark recesses of clattering
railcars, home to the secret timber, and that was where calm bledsoe
found him, half dead, and fed him, and taught him to hunt.

where are we going to go now, she said,

and he gave her no answer,

but gathered *chochani* at the mouth of the spring, dug wild onions when there were some, made snares from ivy and grapevines, and in the mornings left her on the dry creekbed, alone, while he walked north or east to check them. how he'd scraped the hides and staked them in the sun, swamp rabbit, possum, tick-ridden squirrel, knowing even then that calm couldn't sell them.

how he'd cooked the game for her, said, come and eat now, and in the evenings put the harp to his mouth, but the taste was ugly, the sound wrong.

and the silent web was still in his ears, down his throat.

the great clotted fullness.

he'd watched from deep inside himself, seeing how she grew thinner, didn't sleep, until he thought he would return one time and find her gone, her frail bones on the white stones, maybe, but her spirit vanished.

she didn't speak of her family, the doctor, the blood,

where are we going to go now, she said, the flat one-note sound,

how he became afraid to leave her.

he remembers

waking one dawn, seeing her curled round herself, curled away from him, sleeping, her narrow shoulder rising and falling with her breath, how he'd risen quietly, not to wake her, crawled out from the thicket and, turning to look back, saw her small face in the pinking light, her eyes closed, lips curled back from her teeth in agony.

so that then he'd gathered the stinking pelts, strung together with vine, put them on his shoulder, put his hand down for her, and they'd walked through the low sumac and scruboak, the grapevines and gnarled brambles. climbed out of the box canyon. walking toward the river, walking

all that one day, until the dogs barked below the rim of the hill, until they made the last turn and the cabin was there, and below it, the winding green snake of the river. and calm bledsoe on the porch, waiting.

how they'd stood on the path while calm called the two dogs off, motioned the singer to come down, and how her arm trembled as he guided her, the roots and ivy cunning, the path steep, calm's gaze gliding past the shedding pelts, past sharon stumbling along the path, her clothes stained thigh to belly with old blood. the dogs at the foot of the porch silent. their ears pricked, tails flat to the ground. come in then. calm's eyes showing nothing as he turned, went back in the house,

and singer nudged her forward, up the log steps, onto the porch, let the skins slide from his shoulder, a dull small sound on the wood, his hand on her trembling arm, frail as quail bone, how he'd made her go in.

remembers

the taste of the coffee strong and black, bitter, and the white gravy thick over the cold hominy, dotted with black pepper.

calm sitting on the lip of the cold stove, scratching the yellow dog's ears, picking ticks off and dropping them in the kerosene can on the floor, while the light outside turned lilac, the room growing dark, a lone locust whined in the twilight, calm saying what singer had already known: he couldn't sell summer pelts to the *yoneg* trader.

but it was already night then. and calm had said in cherokee, take the bed,

sharon was gripping his arm with her fingers, strong for such thinness, strong under the table, and he'd said no, they'd better be going. but calm tossed out the last of the coffee, rolled himself in a blanket and lay down on the floor between the two dogs.

how, deep in the night, he heard her, the gulping sound in her throat as she tried not to make any noise, the bed shaking. and then she was still, and he'd thought she slept, and so he slept, maybe, or went deep in himself, still trying to hear.

how when the first graying light came, calm's snores rising from the floor, and one of the dogs scratching, its leg thumping, he'd felt for the first time that the blanket beside him was empty and knew she'd gone down to the water.

he'd struggled fast down the path, the gravelbar barely visible below, the river lost entirely in white mist, knowing, before he heard the small splash, what she'd done,

running then, trying to run, limping across the gray expanse of river stones, calling her name, awake now, fully forward, and praying.

Sharon

Towards daylight I got up and went out to the porch. The treefrogs were hushed then, the whippoorwills silent. The sky was lifting, there was enough light to see where the path went around the side of the cabin. I followed it in my bare feet, a lighter streak through the thick tangles, going down, going down. At the bottom I could see white mist over the river. The bank was a gravel bar, long and wide, a sweep of rugged stones, gray-looking in the gray light. I stepped onto the rocks, knuckled hard under my feet as I walked toward the water. At the river's edge I loosened the clasps, shucked my overalls, pulled the filthy shirt over my head.

The water felt thick on my thighs, like coal oil. Everything above and all around me was white with river mist. I felt something, the touch of little fishes. I looked down to see the silver slivers, dozens of them, their tiny mouths nibbling at the hairs on my legs. On the far bank the undergrowth scrawled down to the water, a dark overhang, gnarled vines, deep cut-aways in the clay. I walked toward it. The river was cool on my private places, my belly. The current pulled strong out in the middle, it wanted to lift me off the rocky bottom. I resisted just a minute, and then I sank down with my arms spread and let my feet rise.

The river carried me downstream, my face to the mist, floating, turning a little, going down the Illinois. I thought, I'll just go. The river could carry me past Welling, past Barber and Pettit, on down to Cookson. But there wasn't any place for me in Cookson. There was nobody in Cookson. I'd have to go on. I'd drift past Vardis, past Blackgum, on down to where the Illinois joins the others, like Harlan once told me. Every drop of living water joins together in the end, he said. The Illinois and the Canadian, the Arkansas and the Verdigris, all the little Rock Creeks and Turkey Creeks, if you followed them, he said, if you could swim them, they'd every one carry you to the muddy Mississippi. Down the Mississippi, Harlan said, to the end of the land mass. Throw you in the wild sea. The mist was getting thinner, bleeding out, but still I could only see whiteness. I heard a faint splash up the river behind me, I thought, beaver. Or bass. I was on my back, floating.

His hands came around me and grabbed me, I struggled, my face going under, the burning Illinois water in my nose, down my throat. I flailed my arms,

I tried to stand up, but the water was too deep. The river had me, Harlan's hands had me, he hooked his arm around my neck and started pulling me toward the side. There was nothing I could do but let him take me, the water burning me, blinding me, until he turned me around and squeezed my chest to him, hard. My feet could reach the bottom, silky here, not gravel. The bank above us was steep. Harlan held me so tight it felt like he'd squeeze the breath out of me. I was embarrassed. I was naked. I was half out of the water.

"Don't you *ever*," he gritted, his chin like a stone against the top of my head.

I couldn't breathe, my face against his wet shirt. "Ever what?" I choked out.

He didn't answer. He just held me that hard.

It was a long time, I don't know how long, that we stood in the shallows, the river nudging, Harlan squeezing till I thought my ribs would crack. He let go finally, took my hand and clamped it to a knotted tree root sticking out, then he hoisted himself up the bank, kicking down dirt. I crouched in the water to hide myself. The current wasn't strong here, I felt it lapping around me. I held on to the root clot. "Sharon," he said, his tan hand reaching down. I shook my head.

"Come on."

"Go get my clothes."

"I'm not leaving you." His voice was low and quiet. I knew he wasn't about to give up so I reached for him. He lifted me like I weighed nothing, my legs kicking and turning, my own body naked as a possum's tail, white and hairless where my clothes ought to be, and it shamed me. I tried to cover myself. Harlan stood me among the vines, took his wet shirt off and wrapped it around me, hugged me a minute, not so fierce this time. Then he held me away from him by the shoulders.

"What in the world did you think you were doing?" he said.

The bank was a tangle of green ivy and brambles. Harlan's shirt was cool against me, dripping water down my legs.

"Answer me."

"I don't know," I said finally. I cut my eyes to the river. I couldn't look at him. He put a hand to my chin, raised my face, but I still wouldn't. "Where are we going to go, Harlan?" I said. "Head to Muskogee and catch out on a freight, ride whatever direction it's pointed? I can't keep traveling those same old loops and circles, I can't keep going nowhere, doing nothing. Serving no earthly purpose in this world."

"Where do you want to go?"

"I don't know," I said. And then I said it: "I don't know you." The words just came out, threaded out, following after.

He got really quiet. "That's not true," he said.

"It is," I whispered. "I don't know what kind of people you come from. I don't know how your folks died. I don't know their names even. All we do is wander place to place, chasing after some damn ghost from your mind. Oh," I said. "That's not it. That's not even it." I felt such a misery. Such a despair. I could see water drops on his naked shoulder, only a few left, his smooth skin drying fast in the heat.

"Sharon. Look at me. This is me here. I love you. When I woke up and you weren't in the bed, I thought . . . I found your clothes by the water . . ." His hands were trembling on my shoulders.

I said, "I killed my baby."

"No. That's not true."

"We did. Us together. By not doing right. It's a punishment, isn't it?"

"No, darlin'. Things happen. It's nobody's fault."

"Things happen for a reason. The reason is when people don't do right."

"Don't do right how? Traveling place to place hungry? Not having a job of work? That's half the folks in this country. The whole nation's a kicked-over anthill, Sharon. It's not just us."

"Who kicked it over? God. It has to be God. Look at the heat. Look at the drought. People haven't been doing right so they got to be punished."

"Aw, honey, that's your daddy talking."

I jerked away from him. "Don't you speak about my daddy. Don't you say one word."

He was quiet then. I kept my eyes to the river, I said, "Last night, laying in the bed, I tried to pray. I couldn't pray, Harlan. I haven't prayed in I don't know how long. The treefrogs were so loud. They were saying *give-it give-it give-it gimme-that!* I kept seeing my daddy in the pulpit, his fray-collared shirt, his hair white. His voice was so strangled, it was like he was choking. I'd see him sobbing at the kitchen table, Mama standing behind him, touching him, my mama yelling in the hot sunlight that last morning before I walked away from my family. Before you walked me away. You walked me away, Harlan. I could smell myself. I stank in the bed. The blanket under my arms was so scratchy, the treefrogs kept shrieking louder and louder, I saw Mama, she was shrieking louder and louder, like those frogs, only her voice said *hussy! shameless and immoral and hussy!* while I laid there stinking in those stinking boys overalls on a horse blanket in a half-breed Indian's bed, and whose fault is it? Whose fault?"

"Sharon."

"I let my baby die inside me and turn to blood. I let that doctor open my legs and scrape my dead baby out. No. Don't touch me. I can't pray anymore, I can't live anymore, I don't know what I'm doing. What are we doing? It don't make any sense."

"It does," he said. "It soon will." And then, so low I barely heard him: "Listen." And I did listen, but there was nothing to hear, only the hot whine of locusts. He was staring hard at me. "You're bone of my bone and flesh of my flesh, Sharon, I feel like I'd die without you. I really believe that I would. When you were so sick, coming from Tahlequah, I told myself, I've got to take her home. I've got to let her rest, I got to feed her. Get her well. Trouble is . . . this is all the home I know. Where we were camped on the creek, that's a place I used to stay when I was a boy. I made that place years ago. I cut it out of the thicket. I carried in that tin." His voice got really soft. "I never meant it to be but just a little while."

"Are you a heathen?" I said.

"What does that mean?"

"You sat there all night talking Cherokee with that Indian."

"How would that make me a heathen?"

"I don't know," I said, miserable.

"Sharon. Listen. I know I hadn't done a lot of things right. I know it's been hard on you. I'm trying to do better. I thought if I could get some money for them pelts, it'd go easier. We could feed you, we could maybe stay someplace besides hobo jungles and sheds."

"He can't sell them," I said.

"No. I know that. But when a fella can't see what to do, he'll just fall back on what he knows, even when it don't work anymore." He sighed, looking toward the river. "Profit used to say God enters us through sin, through the holes we cut in our souls by our own imperfection. I'd tell him, man, according to that notion I must be holy, holy, seeing how imperfect I am. You couldn't get him to laugh over it though. Some things he wouldn't kid about. I didn't see what he meant then, but I think I'm starting to." He reached for my hand. "We'll go again. We'll make it different this time. Sweetheart. Come here."

I didn't move toward him, but I did let him draw me, I let him kiss me. It felt like the first time, out in my daddy's truckpatch. It was that much a surprise on my mouth. That soft. He turned and cleared a space in the leaves with his foot, then he unwrapped his shirt from around me, spread it open on the ground. I didn't want to see my hipbones jutting out, my belly and thighs right outside naked in daylight, but Harlan laid down beside me, he covered me. And I'd been in the river a long time, I was clean anyway. Clean as the Illinois water could make me.

It took us an hour to get back to the gravel bar, pushing through the snarled timber. My clothes were a dark spot on the grayish rocks beside the water. We limped toward them. The stones were sharp under my feet, getting hot in the sun. I stared at the caked overalls wadded in a pile, the awful shirt. I shook my head.

"Harlan, I can't."

We were both quiet a minute.

"Well then," he said. "Appears like we got a problem."

Which I could see that we did. He didn't have any shirt on, and I didn't have any bottoms, standing out there on the open gravel bar. We surely could not get to wherever we were headed dressed like that. But I stared down at those stained overalls and they were everything bad to me. I stepped over and kicked them toward the water. It was too shallow, that close in, they just stayed on the stones, bobbing and swelling like a person was inside them trying to swim. I picked them up and waded out and threw them as far as I could. They floated a little in the current, turning in a slow circle, going down the river. I waded back and Harlan handed me the shirt. The shirt used to be yellow, now it was so filthy you couldn't tell what color it was. I balled it up and went out a few steps and threw it. The cotton bloated up with air, the shirt floated, following those overalls down the Illinois. They wouldn't float long, I figured, they'd snag on a branch somewhere or just soak full of water and sink to the bottom. I didn't care. I didn't even bother to watch where they went. I walked back and sat on a boulder away from the water's edge. I had to smooth Harlan's shirt under me, the rock was hot. He came in a minute and crouched beside me, his bare shoulder next to mine. He didn't say anything, just picked up pebbles and tossed them toward the river.

Naked, I thought to myself. I don't have any clothes. Not a stitch of my own to my name. I said, "Maybe I shouldn't have done that."

"I reckon you had to."

"That's right," I said. "I did."

"We'll figure something out."

"We got a lot of things to figure out, don't we?"

"We do."

I looked up at a hawk sailing the updraft over the water.

"I'm real sorry about your folks," Harlan said. I turned my eyes from the skies, watched the moving circles in the current where he was tossing in little rocks. "More than anything, I'm sorry about the other." It took me a second to realize he was talking about the baby. "I'd give anything in the world if that never happened," he said, very soft.

"I know."

Harlan stood up and threw a flat flint rock side-armed toward the water, but it only skipped a few times before it sank. "I've been watching how folks live," he said, his back to me. "How they get along, raise a little crop of corn or cotton, grow their kids up. Like your folks. Just like your daddy. Well, that's simple, or it would be if it wasn't for the likes of Oliver Teasley and his kind taking more than their share, but still, even so, that's a way to live, innit? It's a good way. It ought to be good enough. Except I never did live like that. I don't know how. I never had but one ability in my life, and that's making music." He got quiet again, staring at the water. "I lost it, Sharon. I can't hear the notes anymore. I try to listen, seems like all I hear is voices yelling, wood smashing, the popping of guns. I can't hear anything good or lively, only just what's wrong, what's rotten, you can't make music from that." He turned now and looked at me. "I been thinking maybe we could go back all the places we traveled, all the yards where I played music. I might hear it again in the crossties, a whistle blowing, the race of the wind. But then I think, no. That's crazy. I think, You just take care of your wife. Take care of Sharon, the rest will take care of itself. And then I think, how? How am I going to take care of you?" His face was so baffled.

I wasn't crying but my chest was shuddering under the damp shirt. It was a while before I could speak, finally I said, "Well. First thing you might try is getting me some dadgum clothes."

He blinked at me a second. Then he laughed out loud, came back and sat down.

"That's right," he said. "Get you some dadgum clothes. And a good meal to fatten you up a little." He held my wrist, circled it with his fingers. "Potatoes and gravy and lightbread. We got to put some meat on these bones."

"A dress, Harlan. I'm sick and tired of wearing britches."

"A dress, then."

"And some decent shoes besides those old brogans you traded that tramp for in Tulsa."

"We'll get you some shoes."

"How?" I said, but he didn't answer. "Harlan?" He still didn't say anything. "Reckon we'll have to steal them," I said.

"No, darlin'. I'm not too big on stealing."

"Stealing don't seem to bother Oliver Teasley," I said, "and he's a Christian. I'd think a heathen like you ought to be able to do whatever he wants."

Harlan laughed again. He leaned over and touched his two fingers to my throat, soft against the hollow part. He whispered, "I love you, Sharon Singer." Then he stood up and took my hand and we climbed the path to Calm's cabin.

Calm was standing on the step, drinking coffee. The dogs came down off the porch to meet us with their tails wagging. I didn't feel so scared of them as I did the night before.

"'*Siyo*," Calm said. He didn't bat an eye about how we were dressed, me in Harlan's shirt, and Harlan in nothing but britches. That was one of the strangest things about Calm Bledsoe. I'll bet a person could jump up and take off flying in front of him, he wouldn't even swallow hard. I figured that was where he got his name. I said so once to Harlan, but he said no, he said Calm's mama named him Irish. Well, I didn't get that, but *calm* is just exactly what the man was. He stepped down and went around to the firepit to get the coffee pot and some kind of little birds he had roasting back there on sticks.

We ate on the porch. Those birds were delicious, whatever they were, not quail, I don't think. Even the burnt black bitter coffee tasted good to me. Everything was good, even the sun high up over the tops of the trees now, burning murderous heat into the morning. Even the dogs watching every bite of bird as it went in your mouth. Even, or most especially, when Harlan got up to go in the house and came back out with his harmonica in his hand. He winked at me, whacked it against his palm a bunch of times before he sat down barechested on the steps. My heart lifted. But when he cupped his hands to his mouth, the sound that came out wasn't pretty. It wasn't the worst sound I'd ever heard him make, but it still wasn't Harlan's music. He palmed the harp into his pants pocket, very fast and quiet, went on talking Cherokee to Calm Bledsoe, and he didn't look at me any more, but I knew then, my heart sinking, that nothing had really changed.

Except, of course, everything had. Or soon would. We quit hunting for Profit, for one thing. Or at least, I should say, Harlan quit talking about him. I still didn't know where we were going to go or what we were going to do. We didn't own even a whole suit of clothes between us.

And yet. And yet. Things were more tender between us than they'd been since our first days in the truckpatch, out back of the smokehouse. We stayed at Calm's cabin another several days, and every single moment we were touching each other. Maybe not actually, maybe not with our hands, but our minds touched, or our hearts, or whatever you want to call it. I mean, I felt like I knew every tiniest thought he had, every sensation. I practically felt like I could taste the salty gravy as it went in his mouth. And I believe the same was so for him. It's strange to think it, but those few days we stayed in that cabin above the river were like the honeymoon we didn't ever get in the first place on account of how we were traveling so hard.

Calm helped us. He gave us clothes to wear, a shirt nine sizes too big for

Harlan and a pair of dungarees for me that I had to tie around my waist with a rope, and he fed us, of course, but I don't really mean that. It was just how he was. Quiet. His eyes never said nothing, never judged. Seemed like he always knew when me and Harlan were longing toward each other, because he'd call his dogs, they'd go off away from the house and stay gone a long time. Like that.

Something else that was different is how Harlan didn't have that faraway look anymore. He'd meet my eyes straight on, even when he was fooling with his harp, rubbing it against his pantslegs, spitting in the holes. He didn't play it at all now, but he kept that tin harmonica with him, touching it, touching me, like he had to have both of us right with him every minute. And it was one of those private times, when Calm was gone with the dogs and me and Harlan were alone inside the cabin, that we got our idea.

We were sitting at the table. I thought he'd nudge me to get up and come over to the bed, but he just kept sitting. After a long while he took his harp out and laid it on the table in front of him, cupped his left hand over it against the wood. I looked down at the soft brown skin on the back of his hand, I could almost feel the harp under my own palm, sweaty and warm. He said, "I been alone all my life, Short. Even when I had my mama I didn't have her. It wasn't her fault, she was just . . . crazy, they said. She told everybody that God was my daddy, so I reckon maybe she was. Even when I used to travel around with old Profit, it wasn't real in me. I didn't have any purpose. Just go around looking to see how the world works. Just make up a little tune. Take a drink of rye whiskey, share a bite of food maybe, a bit of talk, a train ride, a song. And then—"

He sat quiet a minute, gazing through the front window toward the river. "That morning I walked up the road and seen you standing in your daddy's yard . . . I recognized you." He turned to me, and at once the whole memory came to me: Harlan's light eyes in the shade of the bo'dark, Ellie bawling, the dogs barking. "Before I even got halfway close," he whispered, "I knew you. I'd been roaming the whole country trying to find you, I never understood that's what it was. I figured I could just fold you in my life, it wouldn't matter about your folks or anything. We'd go around a while, and then quit. Or not. I thought we could just keep going if we wanted, that'd be enough. Just to be together." He was rubbing the back of my hand, his other hand still cupped over his harp. "I never dreamed it could hurt you," he said.

"I know."

He sat watching me for the longest time. "I get this feeling in my chest here," he said. "My throat and ears, all in through here." He lifted his hand, made a slow sweeping gesture up and down his front. "I feel like I could bust open. Like any minute my chest is fixing to blow open, like there's a hot stick of dynamite in there. Other times I feel like I'm wadded up with something. I don't know what it is. Something white and thick, glommed inside me. Choking me. Wadded in my throat." He was watching me so hard, like he expected me to tell him what it was. "I can't hear the sound anymore," he whispered. "I can't speak right. I can't make the music. Something's the matter, Short, I—I got to *do* something."

"I know," I said.

And I did know, or I felt like I did. Right at that time I felt like I knew everything Harlan was feeling, what he was thinking, whether he spoke the words or not. For years I believed Harlan had it in his mind already, and that, sitting there with him at Calm's table in the twilight, my heart heard. Lately, though, I've been thinking maybe it was just my own mind talking. Maybe he wasn't ever planning it at all. Because Harlan wasn't the one who said the words out loud—about robbing Oliver Teasley's bank, I mean. That was me.

and it had not seemed a crime then, to clothe her, to feed her,

to stand on the vardis street, tossing greenback dollars out of a sack, waving calm's old broken colt pistol at the banker's nose, just for fun, thinking if only he could find the woman who'd stood with her dead baby in the bank lobby, if only he could roll up a dozen washington dollars and press them into the woman's hands, with sharon's eyes upon him, the eyes of the town upon him, then he would be glad.

it hadn't seemed criminal to walk off into the timber with the burlap sack bulging, had not seemed like sin to let sharon count the dollars, crouched in a clearing, her fine silvery head shining, her small quicksilver hands the hands of a young bandit coon, sorting bills, smiling as he watched her, his harp in his own hand, his belly still warm, still giddy, firing shots, firing thoughts, quick and joyful, like the hot rapidfire glow of whiskey, though he had not tasted whiskey in many months.

only later, when they'd returned to calm's cabin to give back the pistol and singer tried to pay him, the five sawbucks folded tight inside his palm, when calm stood in the porchshade meeting singer's eyes as if he did not know him, as if he'd never seen him before, then the quavering started

and later still, as they walked back to nokiller along the footpath, the top of sharon's head at his shoulder, her piping voice piping daydreams, when singer recalled with a sickening punch the great joyous burst in his chest at the feel of the town's eyes upon him, then he drew sick of himself.

in the silence the singer remembers

how he'd waked in the morning to a shaking sickness that was like vile moonshine sickness, that was like whitelightning sickness, bad oh-be-joyful sickness, waked in the morning hating himself, thinking, lord, what have i done?

how the notion began to open in him slowly, over the course of

days while he checked his traps or skinned game, nights as he lay
sleepless on the creekbank with sharon curled sleeping beside him:
    the knowledge that the wadding in his ears was the sound of sin,
    the silken webbing in his throat was the taste of sin,
    clotted, full, without flavor or taint,
    because he'd turned thief again, turned liar, turned fake and
    deceiver,
    because he had allowed himself to get caught in hopelessness:
    a prisoner, a spider's tumbled meal.
    how he knew he'd lost his song to sin
    but did not know how to be redeemed.

Part Two

folksay

1934

So we watched for Harlan Singer to rob us a big city bank, but "any day now" rolled on into months, and then years, and just naturally our attention began to wander. We were minding the elections, see, on account of everybody was ripe ready for Herbert Hoover to go. Plus, you had your labor riots and your sit-down strikes, your farmers rebellions, your kidnappings, your suicide pacts. We had a lot on our mind then. Truth is, most of us forgot to wonder too very much over Harlan Singer. Turns out he had us fooled anyhow, concerning his public career, or else we'd fooled ourselves, because time we heard his name again—that hard, hard summer of 1934—it was in no connection to banks at all but to an old broke-down white sharecropper's place some several miles below Sallisaw.

Nowadays folks tell all sorts of tales about what Singer did during those lost years. Some say he was in the panhandle bulldogging dust storms, and others say he's fled to California with his possum-haired girl, that they were out there with the rest of the Okies getting radicalized. A few swear Singer was wandering in the Sans Bois Mountains that whole time, while others say, oh, he was in the Sans Bois all right but not wandering: he was hiding out in a deep abandoned coal mine near McAlester. And so on. The only thing we know for sure is this: two years after the Vardis robbery, Harlan Singer showed up alone in the flat worn land south of Bokoshe at the Blessing family's sharecropper shack in the month the government began to kill the cattle.

The U.S. federal government had somehow figured out that the thing to do was to kill starving people's starving cows because that was bound to help, similar to the way dumping loads of milk by the side of the road and tons of wheat in the rivers was supposed to help when people were hungry in every corner of the nation. It might not have made right good sense to us, but we knew Mr. Roosevelt had our best interests at heart, and it was a voluntary program, they said—except that, for folks as desperate as we were, nothing much in those years felt very voluntary—but, so, in general we went along with the plan.

Now, the cowkillers didn't look like government men, they looked like your neighbor, and in fact, for the most part, they were going to *be* your neighbor, or somebody from the next county that looked just like him: a fella with a bunch of hungry mouths to feed who'd hired himself out at a dollar a day, glad to have a job of work and whatever meat he could drag home, and all he had to do was round up his neighbors' stock, stand off to one side and judge the weight of the animal, then shoot her.

Of course, there were two ways of looking at the whole proposition. One was, your cow was bound to starve to death anyhow, you'd just as well get your check from the government for letting them kill it. The other side was, that cow might have been in your family for years, you might have raised her from a calf, she might have kept your young ones alive with her milk when there wasn't anything else on your farm to feed them. So folks were of two minds on the issue. But at the Blessing family's place south of Bokoshe things took a little different turn, on account of the old man Tommy Blessing was an ex-an-archist Republican who'd lived at the Milton Socialism commune in an earlier time—which might be an impossible contradiction someplace else, but not in Oklahoma—and it was Tommy Blessing's oldest boy, Coy Ray, who'd hired on with the government to supervise the cowkillings. So these two minds, these two ways of looking at the notion of hungry folks killing their own cows and having the government pay them to do it turned out to be, in the Blessing fam-ily, sort of like one single mind divided against itself.

Other than their secret anarchist past, though, the Blessings were pretty well ordinary folks: a pa and a ma and thirteen redheaded kids, ranging in age from two to twenty. They had four cows, the people say, each one poorer than the last, but the cows had kept on giving milk through the lean years, even if it was tainted sour with the bitterweed, which was all those poor old bag-o-bones could find to graze off the wasted land. There were many times when the Blessing kids didn't have food to chew but they had buttermilk to drink and blinky sweetmilk to grow on and churned butter for their cornbread, when there was some.

The oldest boy, Coy Ray, had left home the year before, saying his hand wasn't fit to hold a hoe and he'd croak before he'd ever chop another row of cot-ton. He wandered around a few months, hungry all the time and hunting a job of work, until he managed to sign on with the LeFlore County cowkilling pro-gram. The main thing he liked about the job, he said, was that the government gave him plenty of .22 shells and left him on his own to figure the best way to conduct the killings. He'd headed to Wister first, tacked a notice on the post office wall for the people to bring their cattle to the stocksale lot on a certain Saturday. A dozen farmers came, driving before them their emaciated cows, and the whole town gathered to take home the meat. Even so, there was too much beef to eat before it spoiled in the heat, too much for all the women working in shifts to put in their pressure cookers and can, and the bawling cows and the bawling kids and the wasted carcasses all piled up to burn were too much for Coy Ray or anybody else to stomach.

So he made up his mind he'd go around from farm to farm; he'd ride a horse if he could get one, walk if he must, and that's how it come about that, just a year after he'd left, Coy Ray Blessing's ma stood on her porch watching her eldest son trudging home along the dusty track. When he got close she turned and went in the house to put another plate on the table. Old man Tommy Blessing stepped out from behind the barn, peered across the fields, and when he recognized his son he walked over and squatted in the shade of an old Studebaker truck. Coy Ray came into the yard. Mr. Blessing said, without looking up, "Son."

"Pa," Coy Ray said.

Tommy Blessing began to examine the right rear tire, which was flat as a flint, the silvered rubber shredded to the rim in a dozen places. He said, "What brings you back to these parts?"

"I come to shoot the cows," Coy Ray said.

"What?"

"Shoot the cows."

"What do you aim to do that for?"

"Six dollars apiece."

Mr. Blessing turned now and peered up at him.

"I can get you six dollars a head," Coy Ray told him.

Mr. Blessing took off his hat, smoothed his hair down with his palm on both sides of the part, put the hat back on. "I heard they was giving twelve," he said. "And three for the calves." He went back to skimming his hand along the flat.

"Out west maybe," Coy said. "They only authorized us in LeFlore County to offer six."

"Authorized," his pa said. "Authorized?"

"Six dollars a head, and a dollar for a calf. I don't reckon you got any calves though."

"Ain't got any use for a Roosevelt man neither."

"I'm not a Roosevelt man. I'm working for the county."

Mr. Blessing stood up, hitting the dust off his overalls with the flat of his hat. There were a bunch of little Blessings strung out on the porch and down into the yard. Mr. Blessing said, "Darinda, fetch me my makings." The littlest redheaded girl jumped up and ran in the house.

"You know what I think about a man taking handouts from the government," Tommy Blessing said.

"It's not a handout. They're paying you for your stock."

"Six *dollars* for a full matured milk cow? "

"How many dollars you got now, Pa? How many nickels tied up in a knot in the corner of Ma's apron? I'll tell you how many. None. Zero. Nothing. How do you aim to get these kids any shoes for school? They got the hookworm now, look at 'em."

"Them cows still give milk. That's something, till it rains."

"It ain't fixing to rain, Pa. How do you aim to make a crop? Hell's bells, Pa, how're you going to feed all these children?"

"I won't have that language in my yard," Tommy Blessing said.

The littlest girl skipped out of the house then with a greasy Bull Durham sack and a pack of papers. She sidled across the dirt yard, cutting a sharp blue-eyed look at her oldest brother as she handed the pouch and papers to her pa, and then she raced back up to the porch and hid behind the others.

Coy Ray watched his father roll a cigarette and light it with the kitchen match he pulled from his bib pocket. "I come to help you, Pa," he said. "I figured you could use some cash money."

"You ought to be moving along now, son," Mr. Blessing said. A tiny wind came up, danced a dust-imp across in front of him and over to Coy Ray, and then, whipping and skittering, out past the woodpile.

This is probably as good a place as any to make something clear. Those big black blowing dust storms people talk about? They were mostly just tales to us too. We weren't Dust Bowl Okies. Not that we didn't have our share of dust, we had some, but primarily what blew through here was a variety of low-to-the-earth brown tumbleweed storm: people's plowed and planted fields, dusted up and skimming along the horizon. The Joads wouldn't have left out from Sallisaw or anywhere else around here on account of tractors and dust. They might have left, but it wouldn't have been due to tractors and dust, no matter what some stranger might have wrote in a book. Truth is, some left, but most stayed, dumb as lambs to the slaughter maybe, but we were determined to live with the devil we knew. That devil wore a few different faces.

One face was faith. Not God-faith—we're all pretty much agreed over that—but politics-faith, money-faith, opportunity-and-greed-and-how-a-man-makes-a-living-faith, now, those have generally promoted some trouble in Oklahoma. Well, in the whole nation. Like, say, for instance, a fellow might start out believing it's a free country and all a man needs is opportunity and a little spit of land and the heart to work and everything will turn out right. But then, come hard times and corruption, why, that same fellow might turn into the type who'll tell himself, *The rest of them's doing it, why not me?* Now, apparently, according to what folks say, that's what happened to Coy Ray Blessing. He'd somehow gone from a decent young man trained up in the way he should go, to one who'd steal from poorfolks in his own native land, to one who'd steal from his own family. They say he'd come up with a mighty good scheme for getting those cowkilling checks put in fictitious names and mailed to the Poteau post office. Then he'd pay out six dollars to the poor farmer for his pitiful cow and put the whole twelve-dollar government check, signed over to him, in his own account at a Poteau bank. Naturally Coy Ray had a little banking help, he wasn't that smart of a young man, and there's rumors of every ilk and stripe about who else was in on it, though no names were named, and there was nobody ever indicted. But the upshot is this: on that murderous hot August afternoon in 1934, Coy Ray Blessing stood in his daddy's bitten, blowing rented yard, offering to kill his daddy's uncommon-ugly half-Longhorn, half-Jersey rib-slatted cows with a government-issued .22 and pay his daddy half of what wasn't half enough for the privilege, and he had himself convinced that what he aimed to do was right and moral and helpful.

"Pa," Coy Ray said, watching the little dust-devil disappear, "four times six is twenty-four. When's the last time you seen twenty-four dollars?"

"When'd you fix it in your head the government ought to hand a man a red cent?" Mr. Blessing pinched the fire off his half-smoked cigarette, put the snipe in his pocket to save for night.

Saying to himself, *I ain't a-going to argue,* Coy Ray stomped out across the land toward the cornfield. The stalks were stunted yellowed knee-high stubs, half of them lay twisted over on their sides, the flat parched leaves licking the dust. Coy Ray couldn't see an ear of corn in any direction. He raised his eyes to the cotton patch, rows and rows of shrunken plants darker than the dirt. No whitening bolls on any horizon. Coy Ray turned and peered back at the house, or, rather, shack—sharecropper's rented three-room shack of weathered puncheon, rusting roof, buckling porch sagging toward the earth with a dozen little Blessings crouched along its lip. He passed his gaze slowly over his pa kneeling beside the sinking truck, the rusted yard pump, the empty watering trough, where his pa's cows were gathered, tonguing the dampish splintered wood. Everywhere he looked it seemed like things were sagging: the shack, the barn, the cows' flattened bags, his father's freckled sunworn face. Coy Ray felt of the .22 pistol in his right coat pocket, his stash of bullets in his left, and began to walk back toward the yard. The old man stood waiting beside the truck, and the little Blessings watched in silence.

Nobody ever quite figured out why Coy Blessing did what he done, or at least not the way that he done it—though some said it was part of the mystery between a father and a son, and others declared it was no more complicated than the fact he'd walked from town with an unloaded gun and didn't want to take the time to load it—but anyhow, when Coy Ray got to the trough, he reached and pulled the chopping ax from out the stump and turned it over to the blunted edge and whacked the nearest cow in the head. Down she fell, dead as a door stop.

That particular cow was the oldest of the bunch, and an outstanding ugly one at that. The Longhorn really showed out in her. She was a kind of a pooty-looking tan, hips like fence slats, one horn twisted crazy out the side of her head and the other broken off sometime, somewhere. Even among the Blessings' ugly herd, that cow stood out for ugliness, but you'd have thought she was those children's favorite pet, the way they jumped off the porch and began to swarm and wail.

Well, old Tommy Blessing, of course, rushed over and tried to snatch the ax from out the crazy sucker's hand (is how he later put it) as the young ones fell on the dead cow and wept or grabbed Coy Ray's legs and clung on tight while he tried to swing that ax at the next old bellowing, backing-up, head-down cow. His pa kept hold of the ax, trying to wrestle it away and blistering him a torrent, but Coy Ray managed to wangle the ax far enough over to whack another bossy in the head, only this time he didn't get in such a good lick. The cow didn't die, she went to her knees, sprawled sideways, laid flat out on the ground bawling as loud and scared as only an old injured cow can, lending her distress to an already distressful situation. The blow had split the hide over her eye and so, on top of everything else, the blood was just a-pouring. Old Man Blessing and his son were still wrestling over the ax, the little Blessings were shrieking, the dust was flying, curses were thundering high and low and ugly enough to make a pulpwood hauler blush, and all at once here come this sound.

High, thin, and mournful.

Trailing out over the dry trough and the dry ground. Winging up to where the sky was white as a summer sail. They say it was like a sunset turned into sound, or like a meadowlark had lost its mate and turned its whole sorrowed self into song to go winging back and forth across the prairie. The little Blessings heard it first, and one by one, from the least little redheaded girl on up, the children stopped their yelling. Here came Ma Blessing from inside the house with her hands in her apron. Coy Ray and his pa both lowered the ax, though they each kept a tight grip on it. Apparently that mournful song, rising over the heat and the violence, was such a shock that in a bit even the bawling bossy shut up and lay still, watching her blood soak into the thirsty earth.

None of them seen where he came from. They claim it was like he'd pretty near materialized out of the dust of the road. Harlan Singer played for close on to two hours, and by the time he quit, they say, every living creature on that farm had tears in their eyes, including the rat snakes and the scorpions. The kids were sitting on the truck or on the lip of the trough. Their ma was in the yard, and their pa and oldest brother were still standing over the hurt cow, each with a fist yet on the ax handle, but slack now, their heads were bowed, outlined against the fading sky, like a father and son praying. The cow had made peace with her injury, it seems, or else she was just stunned, because she didn't try to get up but lay blinking one big brown tear-filled eye at heaven.

Harlan pulled out a blue bandanna, wiped his sweating face. "Yes sir," he said, "as near as I can make it out, the question is: Who made the cow? And who made the dollar?"

He knelt beside the injured cow, ran a hand along her bony spine, and the poor thing bleated like a sheep. He peered thoughtfully over at the dead one, who hadn't a mark on her. She was more beautiful in death than she'd ever been in life, though the flies were starting to gather at her eyes. Harlan said, "I'm trying to recollect what the Book says. Don't it say to render unto Caesar?"

The Blessings all looked at one another. They didn't know what the deuce he was talking about.

"Or is this a situation," Harlan went on, "where we're supposed to offer to cut the living cow in half, and that'll prove who owned it?"

Tommy Blessing, who considered himself something of a Bible scholar, knew the quote, but he couldn't see how it related. He was still trying to decipher the stranger's meaning when Harlan stood up with his old stiff-legged stance, murmuring to himself. "'Render unto Caesar the things that are Caesar's,'" he said. "'And unto God that which is God's.'" He looked up at the old man with a sort of wondering expression. "You reckon that applies here?"

Tommy took off his hat, scratched his part. "Well, sir," he said, "I don't see how."

Harlan nodded slowly, very thoughtful. He put his harp to his mouth again. This time he played a reel, the jiggedy highstepping kind that'll make even a deacon want to dance, and here in a bit the little Blessings were cavorting around in the yard. Coy Ray started to sneak off toward the barn, but somebody somehow or another tripped him, and when he got up his pa had ahold of his arm on one side and Harlan Singer had the other. The hurt cow was on her feet, though her head was hanging mighty low. She had Singer's blue bandanna tied over the gash above her eye, and the littlest girl, Darinda, was petting her neck.

"Ooo doggies," Harlan said, swiping his forehead with the back of his arm.

"It's hot for dark, innit?" He squinted at Ma, then at Pa, then at Coy Ray. The three standing cows were bawling, their bags were full. Old Man Blessing said, "Somebody better get to milking." Then he said, "Ma, go fetch the lamp. We got to get this beef cut up."

By midnight the grownups and the older Blessing kids were all sitting around the table, feasting on fried steak and drinking warm fresh-from-the-cow milk. The least ones were lined up around the wall, bouncing on their toes, and glad, because there was so much meat they knew it wouldn't run out before second table. Coy Ray sat between his ma and his pa with his hair slicked back and a shamed look on his face, but his countenance, nevertheless, for the first time in about ten years, was peaceful.

Why, it was a trick, don't you see? That Bible verse didn't have anything to do with the situation. Or not much. Not in a direct way, anyway. What happened was, the Blessings' mad and fear and thirst got bled away, same as the sun and the sky's colors and the cow's blood, drained off in a dark stain sinking into the earth, while Harlan Singer played his music. And then that awful old malingering human thing, blame, it got baffled and confused and couldn't find a place to land, because of Harlan bringing up that question. And so the Blessings slept peaceful through the night, believing to their souls that from this time forward their hearts would be gentle.

At daylight next morning, the old man and the old lady both agreed: they'd might as well adopt the young stranger. But when Ma Blessing went to the corncrib to wake him, Harlan Singer was gone On the pallet she'd placed on the crib floor the night before, in a wad, lay the blue bandanna, sweat-stained, smeared a little with the bossy's blood.

Sharon

It happened in Texas, or it started there, that awful night we got stopped by the bulls on the dark plain south of Pampa. This would have been the spring of '34—early April, I'm guessing. We'd been back on the road well over a year. I ask myself now why didn't I see trouble coming, maybe I could have stopped it, but I know that's just dreaming, because the fact is, when the engines started to slacken in the middle of the night in the middle of nowhere, I couldn't think anything, except I was glad. We'd been on top of that reefer seven hours, all night, all the way from El Reno, riding it into the teeth of a late cold front bearing down across the plains. Harlan had me strapped with his belt to a grip at the front of the catwalk. He kept his arms around me, but I was shaking all over. The freight ground down, shuddered, screeled to a stop, and Harlan fumbled with the buckle to unhook me. It took a while, his fingers were clumsy with the cold.

"Where are we?" I said. Harlan glanced over his shoulder. "Nowhere, shug. They just stopped to get water." Steam hissed up behind him, a boiling cloud rising over the tender, it showed the curly shape of his head. The brakey was yelling at the back of the train. "I'm freezing," I said. I couldn't get my teeth to stop chattering.

"I know, darlin'." He got me loose, straightened up to put his belt on. He leaned over and pushed his face against mine, his skin smooth and cold as stone. "You stay here," he whispered. "I'll go see about finding us a boxcar." He kissed me, crammed his hat on, disappeared over the side.

"Hurry!" I called after him, and laid back down. My face hurt from the wind, from all the little pecks of cinders. We'd climbed on too close to the tender, I'd been getting hit with flying sparks all night. Ordinarily we hunted for something better, but a bull in El Reno had been closing in on us, and that reefer was the easiest place to get on, but then we didn't have any protection when the weather turned. Some riders would climb down in the compartment where the ice goes, but we wouldn't. We'd heard a story from a fella one time, he said he'd walked past a reefer in Bakersfield and seen blood dripping onto the rails where a bum had climbed down in there and got crushed by a two-ton block of ice when it dropped in. There are lots of ways to die riding trains, but that always seemed to me one of the worst. Your blood dripping out the side of a refrigerator car onto the tracks.

The steel underneath me burned cold, I couldn't stop shaking. I sat up, but that didn't help anything. A sickle moon hung low in the sky. Off to one side I saw the dark shape of a water tank, the top of it yards taller than the train. Then I heard the bulls. Their voices had a sharp, vicious sound, you couldn't mistake it. They were coming from the front and the back of the train, moving toward the middle, rousting out the riders. Harlan! I thought. I grabbed my cap and scrambled down the ladder, fast.

I nearly ran right into one jabbing his shotgun underneath the car, checking to see if somebody was under there riding the rods. "Line up, punk!" he said when he saw me. He shoved me in line between a Mexican kid and an old man who stank to high heaven, and the bull kept moving, banging his gunbutt on the sides of the cars. A voice at the front shouted, "You bums think you can ride the Rock Island for free, y'all got another goddamn think coming! Turn 'em out, assholes! We're here to collect your fare!" Then there was a whap and a grunt where they hit somebody.

I looked around for Harlan, but I couldn't see him. I pulled my cap down over my forehead. My hair was getting too long, but there wasn't anything I could do about that. "Harlan?" I whispered—quiet enough, I hoped, that it wouldn't get a bull's attention, loud enough that maybe Harlan could hear.

"Careful now, son," the stinking old man said.

I turned to look behind me. The black sky scooped all the way to the horizon, I could see stars straight ahead, down low. The wind wasn't strong now. The cold had settled. I tasted dust grit between my teeth. When I turned back around, I counted five lanterns bobbing and swaying, and all along the line tramps stomped their feet on the crossties, hit their fists against their arms to keep warm. Everybody's breaths came out white, like the steam from the tender. Forward by the engines the water tower looked like a huge black bump on spindly legs in the starlight, rising over everything. I thought, This is a place to take on water maybe, but mostly it's a place for railroad dicks to bust heads.

Here came two shakedown bulls from the rear, one in front of the line, one behind. I could hear their blackjacks smacking people. Those hard little leather thumbs would leave a knot as bad as ball bat. One rider jumped back and took off running. The bulls shouted, I heard a gunshot and a bunch of curses. I couldn't tell if the guy got away or not. In a little bit another fella took off, and I guess this time the bull had his gun ready, because when the shot came we heard a yelp, and then a voice out in the dark, calling for help. Nobody went to him. Nobody jumped out of line again either.

The blows and curses were getting close now, my chest was thumping. I felt like I had a saw in my throat. I didn't have anything for them to take, that was part of what scared me. That could earn you a beating quicker than almost anything, except running or talking back. Or being a Negro. Me and Harlan had never got beat up, he would always ask a question, crack a joke, do something to get them distracted. But that was him. I couldn't do it by myself. I thought they must have found him already. I knew he wouldn't let me face the bulls alone.

"Harlan!" I whispered again, louder.

The stinky man said, "Easy kid, hold 'er steady."

I said, "Stop talking to me."

A voice cursed down the line just a little ways. "Take yer hat off. Shake 'em out, pussy, let's go. *Take your hat off!*"

I heard his harp then, one long soft note on the far side of the reefer, and my heart lifted. The sound was so faint, if you didn't know what it was you'd think it was a dry whispery wind. I watched for my chance to dart across the siding, jump over the coupling. We'd take off across the prairie on the back side of the cars, they'd never catch us. Then a bull was standing right there, telling the Mexican kid to take off his blanket. This bull didn't have a lantern, he just appeared out of the dark, and yet I could still see five yellow lights moving. I thought, No telling how many of them's out here. I thought, Maybe they don't even work for the railroad, maybe it's just a way to rob and murder people where nobody could find them.

The Mexican kid didn't move or say anything. He wasn't any taller than me. He must have been really young. The bull blackjacked him, it was an awful sound, that *thwap* on a bare face. The boy stayed silent. The stinking man said something in Spanish and the boy went to pull his serape off, but the bull smacked him to the ground. The kid tried to get up, the bull kicked him, yelling at him to take his goddamn shoes off, and even in the dark you could tell the boy didn't have any shoes on, you could see his pale feet scrambling in the cinders while he jerked around. That's when I heard Harlan's harp pierce a high thin note from the top of the reefer. I looked up. The bull saw me, or he heard Harlan, I don't know, anyhow he quit kicking the Mexican kid and turned to look where I was looking, and right away he hollered, "Brewer! Topside!"

A lantern broke off down the line, moved to the train and began to swing quick up a ladder. I tried to warn Harlan, I tried to cry his name, but the bull was shouting, "Over this way! He's on the goddamn reefer!" and the stinking man was saying, "Look out now, son, don't you mix in it," and lanterns were bobbing fast our direction from both ends of the freight. The yellow light moved fast across the tops of the cars. I expected Harlan to open the hatch and slide down where the ice goes, no matter if it was dangerous. It wasn't as dangerous as getting caught by railroad bulls. Or maybe I only thought that because hiding is what I would have done. What Harlan did though, before the man up top could reach him, he shinnied down the ladder and started sauntering toward us, completely casual, like he'd just been taking in the view a minute, he'd never intended anything but to get in line with the rest of the tramps. Two other bulls came trotting up, but Harlan was already standing in the line next to me. He tipped his hat. "Howdy, gentlemen," he said.

"Forget it, Brewer!" the first bull hollered. "We got him!" The yellow light on top swung back and forth to show he heard. The first bull waved the others off, told them to go about their business, he'd handle this, and the others went on.

"Turn your pockets out, shithead," the bull said.

Harlan tugged the linings out from his khakis. "Sorry I ain't got a little more to show for my travels," he said. "Maybe I will next go-round. I'll be sure and stop back this way to help you fellas out."

"Shut up," the bull said. "Take your hat off."

Harlan handed over his latest straw hat with its raggedy, windbroke brim. "Tell you what, mister," he said, "I been thinking here lately." He was watching the Mexican kid get up and slip back in line. The boy had his head down, he made himself small. "I believe I might like to try your line of business. Could you tell me how a fella gets hired to such a fine worthy job?"

The bull ignored him, ran a finger under the band, turned the hat over to check it inside. Harlan still hadn't made any sign he'd seen me, but I could feel him telling me to just go along.

"Shoes," the bull said, handing the hat back, and now it was almost like he was bored. He was probably ready to move on, except that when Harlan bent over to untie his brogans, for some reason he slipped his harp out from his ankle garter, palmed it under, trying to hide it. I don't know what Harlan was thinking, that the bull would make him roll his pantslegs up or something, I guess. I mean, it didn't make any sense. The bull saw him. "What's that?" he snapped.

Harlan raised up, his left hand was closed. "What's what?" The bull hit him. Harlan gave out a grunt, but he didn't go down. Maybe the bull caught the silver glint in the starlight, maybe he thought it was something more valuable than a two-bit tin harmonica, or maybe he was just the type bull that loved an excuse to beat up somebody, anyhow he hauled off and really smashed Harlan. By the thudding sound I could tell it wasn't a blackjack he hit him with, it was the butt of a gun. I cried out, and the stinking man said, "Easy, boy." The bull jerked Harlan around, I heard a thud and a crack, Harlan went, "Ah!" I started yelling, "Help him! Somebody! Help!" The riders stood motionless all along the line. "Stop it!" I tried to pull the bull off, but he knocked me back like you'd flick a fly off a biscuit, and then it was more thuds, loud and sickening, over and over. "*Help him!*" I screamed, though I knew it wasn't going to do any good. Nobody was going to help. We were so many, there were only a few of them, they couldn't kill us all, but nobody lifted a hand for Harlan. Nobody helped the shot runner out in the dark, nobody helped the Mexican kid. The bobbing lights came charging toward us.

"Ease off, Smythe," a voice said.

Another said, "Cut it out, hey, hey, goddamnit, Smythe, looka here. We got a situation!"

My cap had fallen off when the bull knocked me and anyhow I was shrieking, they could see what I was. The big one stepped back finally, breathing hard. He wiped his gun and flipped it around and stuck it in his belt. Then he bent over and picked up something. I caught a dull glint in the lamplight as he pocketed Harlan's harp. I struggled to get over there but somebody had me by the back of the neck. Harlan wasn't moving, his shirt was dark and shiny with blood, his face smeared. I had a sickening, sharp feeling between my legs, it twisted up in my guts, I felt like I was about to fold over. "Harlan!" He was too still. I could see his bloodied face in the lamplight, he didn't open his eyes. He was coughing a little.

"She's probably been pulling trains all the way from Memphis. Ask her."

"Smythe, shut the hell up. How old are you, kid?"

A lantern came up next to my face, it made me blink. I couldn't see Harlan then, and it scared me, I tried to go around it, I tried to go to him. The hand at the back of my neck twisted my face to the light. A voice said, "Hell, man, she ain't but twelve or thirteen."

"Harlan!" I cried.

"We can't leave her out here with all these spics and niggers."

"Sure as shit can."

"That's a white girl, y'all, it's thirty damn miles to a town."

"She got herself in it, she can get herself out."

"We'll turn her over to the sheriff in Amarillo."

"*Harlan!*" Why couldn't he answer me?

"Ain't nobody put a gun to her head to make her hop a damn freight."

"Look around, fellas. People are watching."

I felt my neck suddenly freed, and I rushed to where Harlan lay curled on the ground. I said his name again, but he didn't move. I was afraid to touch him.

The inside of my head was buzzing. Around me, the sky was spinning. I felt like somebody had shaken all the gravity out of the world.

"Aw, the hell with her," a voice said. "She's with that one, let 'er stay with him, we got work to do. Let's get this freight moving. You sonsabitches, turn 'em out! Shake 'em out! Better hurry it up, you bums got a mighty long walk to town!" There was laughter, and the yellow lights began to move away again.

I didn't hear when the train pulled out, barely noticed when the other riders started to walk away along the tracks into the darkness. The one thing I heard really loud was the calls from the hurt one out on the prairie, begging somebody to come help him. I felt like it was Harlan. I felt like he was calling me from somewhere behind his smashed face. I didn't know how to help him. I sat with his head in my lap, used my shirt as softly as I could, I finally got the blood oozing from his scalp to stop. Dawn came in a red line on the horizon. Harlan's face was nearly twice its size. His eyes were so swollen I didn't think he could open them even if he woke up. And he didn't wake up.

The tramps were mostly all gone by good daylight, walking the rails east or west. There were only a couple bums still stretched out on the siding, far down the line, and the old smelly man sitting yonder, at the foot of the water tower. The Mexican boy was asleep beside him on the ground. I wondered if the shot rider out on the prairie had died. He wasn't calling any more. When I looked that direction, though, I couldn't see him. I thought, Maybe somebody helped him. Maybe somebody carried him on their back along the rails. Or the coyotes dragged him off.

After a while I realized that the old man was watching us, or anyway he was watching Harlan. He peered at Harlan's face, studying his chest, I think to see if he was still breathing. I said, "Do you know how to help him?"

"I'm sure not no doctor, ma'am."

"He's in really bad shape," I said. The fellow got up and came over. His hair and beard were scud gray and matted, and when he got close the smell was awful, but he didn't move like an old man. He squatted down in the cinders, didn't say anything.

"Is he going to die?" I said.

"Reckon that's between him and the Almighty."

"I got to get him some help."

The old man was still peering hard at Harlan's face. He said, "Another freight oughta be along sometime. By how hurt your man is, maybe they'll let you ride. You got any money?" I shook my head. "Well, they might not then." He stood up, turned in a circle, looking off over the flat land. When he got halfway around, facing north, he stopped. He said, "Might just be my imagination, but

I think I see a windmill yonder. If it's a windmill, likely there's a house. Unless it's just to draw water for range cattle. Or unless it's not even a windmill." He shrugged. "Might be a piece of mesquite bumping the horizon."

I squinted but all I could see was craggy, flat emptiness wasting off into the distance.

"Be worth a try to find out," the man said.

"He can't walk," I said. "He can't wake up. Even if it is a house, I can't get him there. How could I get him there?"

The old man studied me, his eyes were the exact same gray as his beard. He turned and went back over and shook the Mexican kid awake, spoke to him in Spanish, and before I realized what they were doing, the two of them set off across the plains, walking north.

I thought, Oh no. Oh no. Don't leave. I turned to look down the line, but the last two riders were going too. I saw their figures getting smaller, disappearing east along the rails. Help me, I said. Please, God. Somebody.

That's the most alone I ever was in my life. To look out over the horizon, there was just nothing. Clumps of sage, sifting dirt, the two steel lines running east or west, straight as a straight-edge, out to a point where they came together and you couldn't see them anymore. No food, I thought. No water. "Harlan?" I whispered. I touched him as easy as I could. His hair was so bound with blood I couldn't smooth it. Seemed to me like the bruises on his face were swelling bigger, but it was hard to tell under the crusted blood. Help us, I said.

Harlan groaned. My breath caught. He was trying to open his eyes, but they were so matted, so puffed, I said, "No, don't, honey. It's okay. We're getting you some help. It's coming. Help's coming."

I wanted to believe that, you know, that they'd come back, the old man and the boy, but I knew it was just as likely they'd keep walking till they got to a town, they'd hop another freight, keep traveling. I knew I might be here holding my husband's head till he died, till another train came in the night and the bulls got out to beat people, till the sun claimed us. I thought, if he dies and I don't, what will I do then? Where will I go? I don't know where they are, how to trace them. Without family you're lost in the world. Lost. Harlan sank back under, his throat let out a rattle. I thought it was his death rattle, my heart nearly stopped, but when I touched his chest it was still moving. I started making promises then.

We just stayed. My legs fell asleep. For a while the air was still cool from the front passing through, but the higher the sun climbed the hotter the day got, and the sun began to burn down really fierce. I was thirsty. The water tower was right there, but I couldn't see how to get water from it. Besides, I wouldn't move

Harlan's head off my lap. It was way up in the afternoon when I saw the old man coming. At first I wasn't even sure it was him, he didn't have the kid with him, but then I recognized that gray scrawl on his head. He walked pretty fast but still it seemed like I watched him a long time before he got close enough for me to see his face. He was huffing and sweating, but either he'd washed or I was just really glad to see him, because when he drew near his smell didn't bother me half as bad.

"It's a house all right," he said, panting. "They're in a pitiful fix, but they got water." He handed me a water bag, and I turned it up and drank. The water tasted awful, it was iron water or something, but I had a hard time making myself stop soon enough to save some for Harlan. I tried to put the bag to his mouth, but his lips were too swollen and he didn't move. I was afraid I'd choke him. I poured some on my shirttail and used it to wipe his face. The old man said, "The wife said she'll send her husband when he gets back in the wagon. Their automobile's busted, that's unfortunate. But what's fortunate is, it's a houseplace, and the folks are decent. You can't always depend on that. But a lot of times you can."

"Can you?" Probably I sounded like I didn't believe it, because I didn't.

"Well," the old man said. "I'd call it sixty-forty. Sixty percent of the people might be willing to help you, the other forty's more likely to knock you in the head and take your shoes." He looked at the sky. "It's liable to be a while, ma'am. We better see if we can't get him out of the sun."

He helped me half-drag, half-carry Harlan to the shade under the water tank, and then he took a flat piece of hardtack out of his filthy pants pocket and handed it to me.

"Oh, thanks." I gnawed it down.

"Don't thank me," the old man said. "The missus there at the house sent it." He went and got the water bag, brought it over, but there wasn't much left. Neither of us could figure how to get water from the tower. Harlan's swelling had slowed some, or it didn't seem to be getting worse, and he wasn't bleeding. But he still wouldn't wake up. I held his head in my lap, that's all I knew to do, but we were out of the sun now, I wasn't so thirsty. I started to feel a little hopeful.

The old man talked a lot, I drifted in and out on what he was saying. The boy had stayed on to sleep in the barn, he said, the kid was pretty banged up too, from his run-in with the bull. He said that family out there was in as sorry a shape as he'd seen, trying to ranch this murderous country. But they were willing, the old man said, that was the strange thing about people. His voice was coarse and phlegmy, like he had little bits of wet gravel at the back of his throat. He said he knew better than to stay on the Rock Island past Elk City, but he'd just been too blame tired last night to jump. He'd figured he would take his chances, he said, but that was sure a mistake. I didn't say anything, I just fanned the flies off Harlan. I think the only thing I asked was if the Mexican kid was his traveling partner. A lot of bums would do that, hook up and travel in pairs for safety, but the old man said he'd never seen the boy before last night. Then, along towards sunset, we heard a train engine coming from the west.

"Here's your chance," the old man said. "They might take you on. Get your man to a doctor quicker."

"I thought you said somebody was coming."

"Well, probably. But that train would be a lot faster."

I looked at the glint on the train moving toward us, a spark of light hitting the steel from the lowering sun. Just the thought of riding a freight was like tasting something that made you sick enough to vomit one time, you never wanted to touch it again. But I looked at Harlan's face, and I said to myself, Well, if they'll take us, we'll go. The train roared in, steaming, to take on water. The old man went to talk to the brakeman. Way off towards the end of the line I saw a bunch of riders on the tops of the boxcars, rowed up on the edge like starlings on a telegraph wire. The old man came back, shaking his head.

"They won't take us?" I said.

"They're from the lower forty, I reckon."

"What about you? Are you going with them?" I stared at the rows of tramps perched on the rear cars. "Don't look like they're carrying any bulls."

"Oh, I expect that rancher will be along directly. Besides!" the old man called out over the noise of the freight starting to move again, "I might need to see how the thing turns out!"

The rancher did come, finally, at almost dark, in a farm wagon with one horse. Him and the old man loaded Harlan into the bed, we drove overland what seemed to me like four or five miles, and when we got closer I saw the shape of a windmill outlined against the evening sky. It was right there in the yard. I couldn't imagine how that old man could have seen it that far. A woman came out on the porch, there was just enough light left in the sky to see her. They didn't have any light on in the house at all. I heard a little child inside crying. The rancher drove us on to the barn, and in a minute the woman came with a kerosene lamp and held it up while the old man and her husband unloaded Harlan and carried him into a stall. The stall smelled like it had clean hay on the floor. They laid Harlan down and then the husband went to unhitch, and the old man disappeared.

The woman said, "I only got the one blanket. You want it under him or over him? We could roll him onto it, maybe."

I didn't know. It wasn't cold now, but it wasn't hot either. It might get cold later. "Over him, I guess." The woman gave me another piece of hardtack from her apron and a Mason jar full of water. "Get yourself settled," she said. "I'll be back for the lamp." She set the lamp on a shelf outside in the aisle and left. I could hear the old man talking overhead in the hayloft, the kid's soft, high, fast answers, that rippling-water sound. Spanish. I smoothed the blanket over Harlan, drank some of the iron water. There wasn't anything else to do to get settled. I didn't need to go outside to pee because I hadn't had enough water to drink to make any. I laid down next to him, put my hand on his chest. His breathing was steady, but so slow. It was a terrible long wait between each rising. I'd get scared every time, waiting. I sat up and moved over to where I could lean against the stall wall, and very carefully I eased Harlan's head into my lap. After a while the woman came back and picked up the lamp, she said, "Sorry I can't leave the light for you, but you'll be all right. Drought's about got all the rats." She stared down at Harlan. Her face in the lamplight was so gaunted, it looked like a skeleton staring down. She said, "If he's still alive in the morning, maybe Sam can carry him in to Pampa. Provided we don't get hit with another duster." She left again.

I guess I slept, because I remember being surprised to see red strips of sunlight slanting across the barn floor, but it seemed to me like I stayed awake all night, listening to the barn rats that the woman thought were all dead from the drought, listening to the horse stamp or snort in the next stall. Listening for Harlan to breathe. I was relieved to see it was morning, and that Harlan was still living. He's going to make it, I thought. We'll carry him to a doctor now.

I heard the old man climbing down from the loft, he came around the corner and stopped a ways inside the stall. "How's he doing?" he said.

"I think maybe he's a little better. Does he look better to you?"

He squinted at Harlan. "Hard to say."

The Mexican kid slipped in behind him. The boy had a bad bruise on his cheek, otherwise he didn't look too very hurt. His striped blanket had little pieces of straw stuck all over it. He stared at Harlan with somber eyes.

"He needs to see a doctor real bad," I said.

"Well," the old man said. He left the barn, the boy trailing him like a blue heeler.

I eased Harlan over as gently as I could, stood up and stretched. I felt like I'd been wadded in a knot all night. Then I went outside. The old man and the boy were nowhere in sight, nobody was. The people's house was practically a shack, the wooden sides wind-scoured to silver. The roof really sagged. It was large enough, though, had a long porch across the front. I went around behind the barn to pee, and when I came back the old man and the rancher and the Mexican boy were standing in the yard, looking up. The woman came out on the porch, and three little kids followed her. Did you ever see those pictures of the Okies in the camps in California? Well, these people looked like that, only they weren't Okies—they were Texans, I guess, or they were just people who looked like that in those years. Worn-out, lank-haired, bony, their skin the color of dipping snuff, their teeth bad. They every one looked too tired to move hardly. That's one thing hunger does. Makes you so tired. Sometimes you're too tired to look for food, and then you know it's bad. I couldn't tell if being hungry was what was wrong with these people, but I understood better what the old man meant when he said they were in sorry shape.

The old fella was coming toward me across the barnyard, the Mexican boy behind. "When can we go?" I said.

"He's not sure he's able to do it today," the old man said.

"But—we got to!" I stared over his shoulder at the family. The rancher was still looking up at the sky, frowning. The woman took the kids and went back in the house.

"Go talk to him," I said.

"I don't think it'll do any good. Man says he's afraid another duster's fixing to blow in. He can't leave the wife and kids alone to face a dust storm. Anyhow he says you can't see to drive in one, he'd get lost going to town."

I looked up where the rancher was looking, to the north and east, but the sky there was clear blue. It was clear everywhere, a little dun colored toward the horizon is all. There wasn't any wind, not even a small breeze. The morning was turning hot already. "How can he tell?" I said. "He can't tell."

The old man shrugged. "He's says we'll go in the morning. Lord willing and a duster don't blow in."

"That'll be too late!"

"No it won't," the old man said, and he sounded so sure that I turned and went back inside the barn to see about Harlan. I sat down and took his head in my lap. Oh, you wouldn't dream that anything could change a face so much. If I didn't know it was him, I'd never believe that was my husband. It wasn't just the swelling and the dried blood and the bruises. His features were all changed. They weren't slim like Harlan's face, they were wide and bulky, like a fat man's. Like a stranger's. The old man came in, with the kid shadowing him. "I'll bring you something to eat if I can," he said, scratching his armpit. "I believe that woman'll try to fix you something afterwhile, if she's able." Then him and the boy left.

I drank the rest of last night's water. After that, everything was the same. The exact same as yesterday, except we were inside a barn where it was shady, which helped, but the hay dust and the plains dust sifted the air, clogged my nose, made me cough. Harlan wasn't coughing. I didn't know if that was good or that was bad. The rancher came and got his horse and led him out, he didn't look in to see how Harlan was doing. I expect he was probably too ashamed. He knew my husband needed to see a doctor.

The old man came back later and brought a piece of rabbit jerky and a plate of beans, oh my Lord, it tasted good, and he had another jar of that awful water. He left, and came back and took the plate away. After that, he came in every little while to see how we were doing, and each time, the Mexican kid would be right behind him. The old man squatted on his heels like a farmer. The boy stayed standing at the stall door. He had that somber stare, you'd think he'd never laughed one time in his life. Sometimes it was Harlan he stared at, but mostly it was me and the old man talking. The boy watched our lips, like maybe he could understand what we were saying if he studied us close enough. I remember thinking, That old man might not believe that kid is his traveling partner, but the kid sure thinks it. He couldn't shake him loose now with a stick.

Harlan didn't seem to change at all, one direction or the other. Sometimes he'd come awake enough to groan, but he'd always sink back. I didn't try to wake him up anyway. We weren't going anywhere, he'd just hurt if he woke up. The rancher came again in the late afternoon and mucked out the other stall, he brought the horse in, fed and watered him, combed him down, but he still never once poked his head in to see about Harlan.

When the old man brought me a piece of hardtack at sunset, I took it, but I wasn't too glad to see it. Not nearly as glad as the day before. I said, "They ain't got any more rabbit?" The old man cut me a look. "Oh," I said, "they got some, they're just not giving it away."

The old man sort of grunted. I took that for yes, and I ate the hardtack. The old man watched me, and the Mexican kid did too, standing at the stall door with his big eyes. They watched me so close I thought maybe they didn't get even that much, they were hankering after mine, but in a minute the old man said, "I was trying to remember what-all you had to eat yesterday. Before that woman sent you the biscuit and water."

I knew he knew I hadn't had anything before that, I was parched and starving before that. I knew he meant me to be grateful. I didn't feel grateful, though. I felt hungry. The piece of hardtack was already gone. I looked down at Harlan. "He needs to eat too," I said. "But he can't wake up enough." I touched him. "I can't believe what they've done to him." I brushed my hand over the top of Harlan's caked head.

The old man was quiet. I thought he'd left again, but when I looked up he was sitting crosslegged on the floor at the front of the stall. The boy was still standing.

I said, "That was sure some duster today, wasn't it?"

The old man didn't say anything.

"He just wanted to stay home. He'd went to town yesterday, he didn't care to turn around and go back."

The old man shrugged. His eyes were smoky, like greenwood smoke, the kid's eyes were the color of tar. I wished they'd quit staring. The old man said, "They've had a lot to deal with, these people."

"Well so have we."

"Yes ma'am. I can see that." He picked up a piece of straw and chewed on it. "You ever witness one of these dusters?"

I didn't answer. Me and Harlan had ridden out a few dust storms, twice inside a boxcar with Harlan's shirt wrapped over my mouth, once in an empty silo with the dust blowing through the cracks, making squiggly gray patterns on the floor. I figured that wasn't any of the old man's business.

"I been through nineteen of 'em," the old man said. He took the straw out of his mouth. "Wouldn't care to go through another." He turned to look outside at the pink swath of sky showing through the open barn door. "It's strange how you can see the thing coming miles off. Boils up like water, don't it? Turns the sunlight that beautiful lilac green. You'll stand and watch it rolling in, high in the sky as a thunderhead, looks like a firestorm coming, only it's all them colors, purple and blue and dark green. You can't help thinking, what an awesome thing. What a beautiful, awful, awesome thing. Crows flapping and squawking, jackrabbits scrambling, trying to outrun it, and the one thing you know is, you can't outrun it. Same as a twister. You can't outrun a twister, neither." He turned and looked at me. "A twister's a hopper though. It's a hit-or-miss type of destruction. Somebody might very well have the luck to dodge a twister. A dust storm, though, it covers the whole world." Now he looked down at Harlan, narrowing his eyes a little. It was getting dark inside the barn. "Takes feed and water for that horse to go to town. Costs more to draw a wagon twenty miles than it does to go out and round up a few longhorns, I imagine."

"That rancher just don't want to be bothered," I said. "No misfortune of *his* if my husband's hurt."

"Maybe," the old man said. He looked back to the sunset. "I reckon that explains him driving out to get us yonder at the train tracks."

I didn't have an answer for that. The old man yawned. He said something in Spanish, and the boy sat down behind him, pulled his serape over his knees.

I said, "Looks like it wouldn't have killed them to share one more little piece of jerky anyway."

"If they had it to spare," the old man said, "I believe they would. Didn't see any jerky when I was in there. Nor any beans left over neither. All I seen was an empty cupboard and a lot of grit on the floor." He stared at the barn wall, in the direction of the house. "Their littlest one's got the dust pneumonia," he said, very low and quiet. "I didn't want to tell 'em. I reckon they'll all have it before this is over. I don't believe these ones are going to make it."

"They can always go to California," I said. "Like everybody else."

He shook his head. "Maybe."

I'd been glad for his company before, but now I wished he'd go away. He kept sitting there, chewing on his straw. "How long have y'all been on the road?" he said.

I started not to answer, but then I said, "Longer than I ever wanted. Three years."

"I guess y'all've run into a bunch of sixty-fortys."

It took me a second to realize what he was talking about.

"Funny," he said. "Seems like you can always recollect the ones from the forty percent way more than the sixty. Probably because they're generally so damn mean." He pondered Harlan's face in the dusk. "Reckon how many strangers y'all've run into that went out of their way to lend you a hand. As opposed to how many beat the hell out of you. You got any opinion as to what y'all's percentage might be?"

I touched Harlan's cheek. I wouldn't answer. What I really felt like telling him was to please shut up.

"I like to check my figures with other folks," he said, "every now and again." His gravelly voice meandered on, but I quit listening. I was thinking about the skinny colored woman at the squatters camp in Oklahoma City. I didn't know how much out of her way she'd went, but she fed me when I was about to drop. I remembered this one church lady in Durant who cut my hair to a boy's cut when we asked her, out on her front porch with a dishtowel tied around my neck. She cried the whole time and fed us a piece of pie after. I thought of a family in Kansas, the lady gave us soap and water to wash up and then let us sleep on her screened-in back porch, in a bed with quilts on it. That seemed like such a long time ago. I cradled Harlan's head, lifted it, shifted my legs.

"Probably y'all've helped a lot of folks, too," the old man was saying. "Like these people here have helped you."

"If my husband dies," I said, "I'm not going to be thinking they're such a big help. We should have went today. They should have carried us to the doctor *today.*"

"That woulda been good," he said. "But here we are."

"We didn't have to be! They just don't *care!*" The old man didn't say anything and by his silence he made me feel what a lie that was. "Not enough," I said. I put my hand on Harlan's chest. "If he dies," I whispered, "I'll hate them forever. I'll blame them with my last living breath."

"Blame them," the old man said, his voice flat.

"Yes, blame them! Blame that damn bull, blame the railroad owners! We weren't doing nothing! What did it hurt? What did any of us hurt, riding their damn freight? It's going where it's going anyway, none of us stopped it or slowed it down or caused one iota of damage. They got to send those bulls to beat people, they got to hire the most vicious men on earth to do their damn dirty work. Just for nothing. Just for the love of hurting somebody, is all I can see."

"Yup," the old man said. "Plenty blame to go around."

I didn't like how he said it. "Look what they done to him!" I said. "Look!"

"Yes, ma'am," he said. "That's bad."

"It's bad all right, and it's wrong, and I hate their damn guts!"

I picked up the Mason jar and drank from it, my chest was on fire. I wet my shirttail and tried to wipe Harlan's face. Oh, his poor face. His lips were so huge and cracked and black with blood. I couldn't tell if he'd lost any teeth. I was afraid to try to pull them apart to look. The old man spoke to the Mexican boy, and the kid jumped up, came got the nearly empty Mason jar and took it outside. The old man just kept sitting.

"Hard to figure why somebody would do something like that," he said, gazing at Harlan. "You just can't figure why there's so much meanness in the world, can you?"

"Sin," I said without thinking.

"Is that it," the old man said.

"I don't know. That's what my husband says." I touched Harlan's swollen cheekbone. I was afraid it might be broken. "Why there's so much meanness, so much sorrow. Harlan says it's on account of the whited sepulcher, people acting clean on the outside when they're full of rotted flesh and stinking bones in their hearts. Harlan says that explains the bread lines and folks losing their farms and a few other things, but it don't explain all of it."

"Don't explain the snakes and scorpions, does it?"

I looked up at him.

"You wonder how come there's sidewinders and stinging scorpions and black widows, why the world's made so all God's creatures got to kill each other to live. Why a mama sheep will butt away her own baby sometimes, or why the panther that comes along and finds it has got to tear that lamb's throat open and leave it lay there uneaten in the field. How come there's cyclones and earthquakes and dusters, so many people living their whole lives in the most miserable hard luck."

"Well," I said. "I don't wonder it. Harlan does."

"Does he," the old man said.

"I think so."

"What'd that bull take off you people? I seen him put something in his pocket."

"Oh. My husband's harmonica," I said, remembering that too, suddenly, with an even worse pain in my chest. I got so mad then, it just swelled up in me, it made my whole face hurt. "That was absolutely one of the cruelest things they could've done. That is sure enough sin. My husband's music is like the breath of him. I don't know what he's going to do when he finds out it's gone." The thought of Harlan not being able to make his music just smacked me.

"Plays a French harp, does he?"

"Ah, you wouldn't believe, mister. He's the best harmonica player in the whole world. Or he used to be. He got a little out of practice for a while, but here lately he's been sounding really good. I can't think how we're going to get him another, but we will." I touched Harlan's forehead. "When he wakes up we will. We got to."

The boy eased into the stall then and set the jar of water on the floor. He stood nearby, a little shadow in the dim barn, and then he leaned down and patted Harlan, three soft pats on Harlan's shoulder. He slipped back to his place by the door.

"Matthew," the old man said. I thought he was naming the boy, but he went on: "I believe that's where that verse is."

"What verse?"

"'Woe unto you, scribes and Pharisees,'" he said, "'hypocrites. For ye are like whited sepulchers, which appear beautiful outward, but within are full of dead men's bones.' That's Matthew twenty-three twenty-seven, if I'm not mistaken."

I stared at him. It was getting too dark to see. "Yeah," I whispered. "That's the one."

"Your husband coulda fell between the couplings and done worse than that to himself, he coulda cut his durn head off, but seems like it's only when people hurt each other we shake our heads and say, I can't understand it."

"Well why do they?"

"I reckon you said it already, ma'am. Sin."

"*Sin's* not the reason that bull half killed my husband! That was just plain meanness, that's just being a, a, an out-and-out bully, it's . . . "

"Takes a bunch of avenues, don't it? Sin. Probably that's whycome the Book's got so many different names for it. According to all I've seen there's a whole lot of meanness-sin in the world, plenty of greed-sin, selfishness-sin, lust-sin. Pride-sin. Laziness-sin. Stupidity. I reckon that's a sin, although I expect some folks can't help it. To me, it depends on how much a person can help it, their worst sinning. A fella can't help being afflicted with the lust-sin maybe, but he could help being afflicted with the greed. Or that's my opinion. But it's not just mine. The Book says it right out, says it don't profit a man anything to gain the whole world if he loses his soul."

What doth it profit a man.

I stared along the dark length of the stall, trying to see him.

"To me," the gravelly voice said, "everybody's got their choice. A fella can join the sixty or he can join the forty. Or a girl can, just anybody. But even there, you get to decide how far along the scale you want to go. Seems to me like a person sitting at the bottom of the sixty, somebody who sees what's right to do and don't do it, even if he don't do anybody any harm, well, I don't expect he's a whole lot better than a fella sitting at the top of the forty, who maybe sees what's wrong to do and how it'll advantage him, but is just too blame lazy to do it. Either way—"

"What's your name?" I blurted. My heart was thudding so hard. I'd never asked because I'd never wondered. His presence was just there, he was just the smelly old man to me.

"Oh," he said, scratching his leg, "some folks calls me one thing, some another. I been traveling around so long I'll answer to whatever folks feel like they want to call me."

"Do you know my husband?"

"That's him there?"

I nodded.

"Ma'am, I never seen the likes of that face before in my life."

"Well, you couldn't tell, he don't look like this. His name is Harlan Singer. Do you know him?" But the old man was back to staring out through the barn door at the last of the light. The sky was faded pale turquoise, the sun was gone now. He didn't answer. I whispered, "My husband's always hunting for an old man called Profit."

"Is that right," he said.

"Is that what they call you?"

"Ma'am, I don't take a name for myself. Names get you in trouble. They'll let somebody keep a tab on you."

"You don't know Harlan Singer?"

He turned his head now, turned to look at us. "I've run into a whole mess of folks traveling," he said. "Hundreds of 'em. Thousands. I couldn't say if I know your husband or not. I'm sorry for your troubles, ma'am. Real sorry. But I believe y'all are going to make out all right." Then he got up, stretched, said good night and went up to the loft to sleep. The Mexican kid followed him.

In the morning, as soon as I came awake, my legs numb under Harlan's head, I listened for them overhead, but I didn't hear them. The rancher came and got his horse and led it out to hitch it to the wagon to carry us to Pampa. He said the old man and the kid had left before daylight, walking back across the plains to the train tracks.

I told the doctor in Pampa that Harlan would pay him when he woke up. "My husband makes money playing music, he can when he wants to," I said, talking fast, "people drop coins in his hat we could start doing that again and I know how to sew I could take in piece work we'll get you your money I promise we will." I was afraid he'd send us away, even though he was the one went outside to help the rancher carry Harlan in. But that doctor was already working on him, touching the swelled places above Harlan's eyes, feeling all over his head with both hands. The rancher left, and I never even thanked him. I feel bad about that to this day. I never told him to tell his wife thank you for the hardtack and the water. I didn't even notice when he walked out.

The doctor had to shave Harlan's skull to put in the stitches. He stitched him in nine different places, that's where all Harlan's scars ended up being, under his hair—except for a small white ridge at the corner of one lip, and underneath it one of his teeth was chipped. That's all that showed later on the outside. It took him two more days to wake up. The doctor wouldn't let me hold his head in my lap anymore, but he set a chair for me to sit next to him. At first, when Harlan roused enough to say something, he still couldn't open his eyes. The swelling in his eyelids had gone down, the doctor had cleaned off the dried blood where the lashes were stuck together, so that wasn't why. Just seemed like he couldn't open them. But he was awake. He said, "Sharon?"

"I'm here," I said.

"They came to meet me," he said. He sounded groggy, half dopey. "All them people."

"Shh, baby."

"They had their hats on." He tried to turn toward me, his shaved head, the ugly black stitches. "Working hats," he said. "Overalls."

"Oh, darlin', it's all right. Everything's all right now."

He settled back down.

I didn't know if those blows had knocked him crazy, but I told myself I didn't care if they did. Harlan was alive, he was breathing, coming awake. A day or so later he got to where he could sit up, drink a little broth, but by then he didn't talk at all. He was silent in a way I'd never seen him. The bruised color around his eyes was still bad, but it wasn't how they looked outside but inside that scared me. I wouldn't look at them. I told him the story how we got there, about the rancher and his wife and the old man and the Mexican kid, but he didn't seem interested. I didn't tell him what I suspected about the old man. I was afraid he'd be too heartsick if he found out he missed him, he might take a backset. I told about the bulls, though. Harlan didn't remember them. There was a lot he didn't remember, but other stuff he did. Things I couldn't. Like, he said he'd heard people talking, a man and woman saying that he—meaning him, meaning Harlan—wasn't going to make it, he'd die and they'd have to bury him, and what were they going to do about the girl? He said he'd heard a little kid crying, coughing and coughing, other stuff I couldn't imagine, but it scared me. I changed the subject when he talked like that. And it was almost a month—we were standing on the highway outside Pampa, trying to hitch a ride back home to Oklahoma—before he came right out and asked me what had become of his harp.

I said, "Honey, I told you."

"You did?"

He looked so completely baffled I just didn't feel up to repeating the story. He never could seem to understand it. Maybe I didn't tell it right. A fellow with a load of chickens stopped to get us then, and I said, "Come on, babe, let's hurry," and I ran and scrambled onto the back of the truck, reached a hand down to help him climb up.

deepsong

in the silence, on the bed of white stones,
the singer remembers
 waking up from the dream/notdream,
 bearing witness to an imperfect god's perfect
 creation. made in the image.
 believing he had seen not just what men were
 but what they wanted to be, believing
 it was not hell's road but the road to an imperfect
 god's perfect heaven that was paved with good intentions,
 because he had seen the tenderness in men's souls,
 the caverns of sorrow, believing
 he knew sin for what it was,
 now.
 paltry.

Sharon

The man with the chickens leaned out his cab window, said he was on his way to Kansas, I said which way's that and he said north. I told him we wanted to go to Oklahoma, and he said he'd pass right through Oklahoma when he cut through the panhandle, and I said, well, all right, because Harlan had the headache really fierce. Those headaches he took after that beating could make him blind nearly with how bad they hurt. We rode in the back with the stinking chicken crates for a lot of hours, which, I didn't mind the smell so much, but I felt like it might be bothering Harlan, and I didn't want us to accidentally cut straight through the panhandle and end up in Kansas, so when I saw a sign for the Farmers Cooperative of Goodwell, Oklahoma, I pounded on the glass. The man stopped. He seemed surprised we wanted to get out there, but he waved his hat as he drove off, and me and Harlan went over to the side of the road and sat down. There wasn't any shade to sit under.

The land didn't look any different from Texas, just flat and raw, the dirt piled in drifts against fenceposts. I could see a grain elevator in the distance but it was too far to walk. The wind was steady, not too strong, flicking dirt around everywhere, grit in our eyes. Harlan took off his cap. He looked terrible, his hair sticking up like little black straws around the scabs, his whole skull red. I said, "Babe, you better keep that on, otherwise I don't think anybody'll ever stop."

That wool cap had to be hot, it was May already, at least a hundred degrees, but Harlan did what I told him. We'd got the cap the same place we got the skirt and blouse I was wearing—the Salvation Army at Pampa. I believe the old man would have said those people were from the sixty percent. They fed us for a month and clothed us. The doctor too, he let us sleep in his back storage room until Harlan could walk without stumbling and it was time to take the stitches out. He said Harlan ought to go easy a while yet, but I wouldn't listen. We walked out to the highway the next morning. I was just real anxious to get home. Well, it's hard to explain that. We didn't have any *home* to get to, of course, I still didn't know where my family went, but the whole time I'd sat beside Harlan, praying for him to wake up, I promised we were going to start living right. We'd settle down, I said, quit hopping freights. I promised to get right with the Lord, get right with my family. But first I had to find them. There was only one place on earth I could think of to start.

"You hungry?" I said. Harlan shook his head. I was famished, but there wasn't any point in saying it. "How you feeling?"

"Not too good," he said.

I knew that already. He'd get this cloudy look when the headache came on, it made his eyes daze even worse. I squinted, looking around, shading my eyes with the flat of my hand. I didn't have a hat to wear, they never gave me one, and my face was sunburnt already from riding in the back of the truck. "Looks to me like that's a crossroads yonder," I said, pointing. "Maybe we'll have a better chance to catch a ride there. Can you walk?"

He nodded, and before I could say anything else, he started out. From behind he looked like a lame scarecrow walking. My husband was always slight, but right at that time he was so skinny I didn't trust but what the wind might pick him up and blow him away like so much high-plains dirt. I caught up to him and held on to his arm. He felt like a stranger. Denim overalls and a tweed cap weren't any kind of clothes that suited Harlan, but it's all the Salvation Army people had and that's what they gave him, and it felt like I was walking along with a farm boy. The wind whipped my skirt too, but I was more bothered by the specks of dirt in my eyes. I didn't know if it might blow up a duster, but I figured as long as Harlan could walk we'd keep moving. Maybe we'd find a ride or someplace to get out of the sun.

He had to stop and sit down every little while. I couldn't see anything like a crossroad now. Maybe I'd dreamed it or it was a heat vision, or else it was hidden in a fold of land—except the land didn't appear to have any fold *to* it. All you could see was bare-naked ground sweeping off in every direction, empty, but then keep walking and you'd come up on those arroyos cut deep. They were dry though, sagebrush clinging to the sides where the dirt showed white or tan or dark red. I couldn't see any cars coming, either. The road was covered in that white powdery caliche, I should have been able to see car dust from miles away. The grain elevator was still yonder, off to the north, but it didn't appear a bit closer than when we started. I thought to myself, Sharon, that was sure some stunt. Take a ride headed to where you never wanted to go in the first place, and then quit it before it gets you anywhere at all. Well, I said to myself, setting out walking again, it's still better than riding the rails.

I don't know how long we walked but I know I was boiled as a beet by the time that lady stopped in her Pontiac car. She was coming from behind us, I didn't even hear the motor till she was nearly on top of us, I think because of the wind. She pulled alongside, the white dust roiled up like a kettle, but the wind blew it away quick, and I could see her reach over to shove the passenger door open. She said, "*What* in the world are you children doing out here? Get in. Get *in*. My word."

I was shocked it was a woman driving, we hardly ever ran into women drivers, or not ones that would stop to pick us up anyway. I couldn't get in that car fast enough. She carried us into Goodwell, which turned out to be quite a few miles, right where the grain elevator was. By the time she drove up to a house at the end of a nice street with a brick church and trees all along it, she'd got me to tell her how old I was, how long we'd been married, where we were from, where we were headed—which, to that I just said, "Home"—what had happened to Harlan. I don't know how she got me to blab so much, just from asking questions. Turns out she was the newspaper editor's wife and she was coming from Texhoma with next month's advertisement orders, that's the only thing she told us about her. Harlan didn't talk at all. The whole drive he'd sat beside me with his eyes closed, and when we got to the house he climbed out of the car and sat down on the lady's back steps.

The lady fed us, gave us cold milk from the icebox, she told us we could sleep in her front bedroom—her *front* bedroom, on a bed with a white bedspread, she opened the door and showed us—and all we had to do was put up with her questions. Well, it's not like she said we had to put up with them, but she sure never hushed. The lady's hair was too black to be right, it didn't have any tones to it, just one same color all over, blacker even than Harlan's. I couldn't remember ever actually meeting somebody that actually dyed their hair. I wondered if she was a loose woman, but she didn't seem like that type at all. Her dress was too shirtwaisty and flowery, the way she talked was too, I don't know, smart. But she sure asked a lot of questions. I couldn't see what she was getting at though, there didn't seem to be any rhyme or reason. She wanted to know what kind of hair my mama had and did Harlan contract the polio one time and where did our people come from before they got to Oklahoma, how many stitches did the doctor have to give Harlan, what type of work were we looking to do. I felt like saying, What business is it of yours? I wasn't brave enough, though. I'd just mealymouth some answer or say I didn't know.

Her house was closed up against the heat, there were rolled rags on all the windowsills to keep the dust back, but you could still hear it grit under your feet when you walked across the floor. Her kitchen was real sweltery, so we went out to the front porch to wait for her husband to get home. I hadn't sat on a porch in I don't know when, and it was a nice shady porch, a nice house. Even with all the lady's questions, I was glad to be there, except for how sick Harlan felt.

I looked at him sitting in the porch swing with the little pained stitch between his eyes and that hot wool cap on, I told myself, Sharon, you're going to have to do better. Because I thought then that the main difference between before Harlan got beat up and after was that I was going to have to start deciding things. The only big decision I'd ever made for us was to try to get our clothes money from Oliver Teasley, and that didn't work out, so after that I'd just went back to depending on Harlan. But he was in no shape now to guide us, and I didn't know when he would be, so when the lady paused a breath between her questions, I told her we'd be leaving for Cookson in the morning. She didn't know where that was, and I said near Tahlequah, and she didn't know where that was, so I said not far from Muskogee, and she said, "Well, my stars."

Then the lady looked over at Harlan. She could tell he was really sick. She said, "Son, why don't you go in the bedroom and lie down? Come on, I'll put the fan on." And she got up and went and unplugged the black electric fan from the living room and put it in the bedroom for Harlan. The furniture was all covered with bedsheets, on account of the dust, she said, but she went right over and swept the sheets off the dresser and the chest of drawers and rolled them in a ball and stuck them in the closet. It was a real closet, too, with a door on it. Harlan pulled off his shoes and the knit cap and laid down on top of her chenille bedspread, dirty as his clothes were, and his scalped knob shining against that white spread. The lady never said a word, she just plugged in the fan and aimed it on him. To me, that was such a kindness, I'd have probably answered any question she asked then, but when we went back out to the porch, she was quiet. She sat in the rocker, and I got on the swing again and we just sat and rocked. She was fanning herself with a cardboard fan that had a picture of Jesus in the Garden on one side. I thought it was church fan, but later when she turned it over I saw it had an advertisement for a funeral home. In a little while she said, "You youngsters have really been through it, haven't you?"

"Through what?" I said.

She shook her head, and leaned back in the rocker, fanning herself, her eyes on the tall bank of pillowy clouds over downtown. The red lipstick she'd had on when she picked us up was eaten off now, and her face powder was sweated into the creases on her neck. She had a nice permanent wave though. Her face looked tired, a little old. She must've felt me watching because she sat up, frowned over at me.

"That's a bad sunburn you've got there," she said. "There's some Cloverine Salve in the kitchen window. You can put some on it if you want. Oh, dear, what is it? What's the matter?"

"Nothing, ma'am."

"Why, there sure is," she said.

"Only just—my mama used to use Cloverine." I wiped my face. I wasn't sobbing out loud or anything, I just had that clamp on my throat and the tears squeezing down.

"Well," she said. "I guess it's good you're going home, isn't it?"

"They're not there." And then I just told her everything, I don't know why, seemed like the words poured out of my mouth, I said, "Mama used to get her Cloverine from a neighbor girl. Marie Tingle? She delivered our GRIT too, but I don't know if she still does because my family left Cookson, I think the same day me and Harlan left, or the day after. We haven't ever went back. They couldn't keep us, they couldn't even keep themselves. My brother Talmadge shot the dogs. Daddy told that from the pulpit. He went sort of crazy, well, not crazy but he broke apart. That's what Harlan called it. My daddy couldn't preach right. That's what come of him taking an outside job, he'd went to work for Oliver Teasley, that's the banker in Vardis? He made my daddy give the people back their money too slow, and it really bothered Daddy, he went downhill from that. For a long time I blamed Mr. Teasley, but just here lately I've been thinking maybe it was Daddy's own fault. Maybe he shouldn't have taken a job in a bank. But then you'd have to say it was Mama's fault, really, because she made him. I was thinking that one way we could look for them is to go to all the Baptist churches, but I don't know how you'd ever get to all of them. How would you?"

"It'd be hard."

"It would," I said. "And I wouldn't know what state to look in, either. They might've went someplace else. Me and Harlan have been to a lot of states, I can tell you. Thirteen, I think, all told. We don't stay long though, we just go passing through. We're fixing to head for Cookson now, though, that's what I decided. I been thinking somebody there might know where my family went."

The lady had quit fanning herself, she was frowning at the brown grass under the cottonwood tree in front of her house.

I said, "I was going to have a baby one time, but it died. Like that woman's in the bank. Only hers was borned already and mine wasn't. I don't know whose fault was that. I used to blame Mr. Teasley, I guess. I blamed him for pretty much everything, except I didn't know I was doing it. Harlan pointed that out. He said not to feel too bad though, he said people are just made to where they like to have somebody to blame when sorrow hits. I tried to argue with him, I said, Oliver Teasley's got all the money and we haven't got a stitch that fits us to our name, I said, Half the poorfolks in two counties lost their farms to that man, and you know it yourself for a plain fact. Plus, I told him, if it wasn't for Oliver

Teasley I'd know where my family is this minute. That is not *blame*, I said, it's the gospel truth, and Harlan said, Well, what do you want to do about it? and I said, Go get some of the people's money back."

"My," the lady said. "That's a thought."

"Oh, we tried, but it didn't work really. On account of Harlan. Something about touching that money perturbed him. He said folks had put it in the bank for safekeeping, what sense did it make to rob the dollars and sprinkle them in the streets or go around putting them inside people's milkboxes and barns. How were we going to know if the right people got the right money. I said, Well, but what about all the money Mr. Teasley got from foreclosing on people's mortgages? and Harlan said, How are we ever going to sort that out either? So we gave it back. He paid a little boy from Webbers Falls six bits and a new pair of overalls to carry that box to Mr. Teasley. I wanted to buy us some clothes out of it first, but Harlan said that would be just plain stealing. We finally swapped our too big clothes for some that fit though. At a campyard in Dallas. Calm Bledsoe had given them to us straight out, they weren't a loan, so Harlan felt like we had the right to trade them. I guess everything worked out, like Harlan said it would, or seemed like things were working out, until we run into those Texas bulls."

I shut up then, for a minute. I really was trying to make myself keep quiet, but somehow the way the lady didn't look at me or ask any more questions but just sat and rocked and stared out at her burnt yard, I couldn't help myself. I said, "My husband always acts like he knows what he's doing, but lately I've been thinking that, really and truly, he don't. Like, for instance, all he wants to do is play his music and cheer up the people. We've been going around for ages doing that. Just here lately though I been asking myself what good is it."

"I don't know," the lady said. "Might be some good." Her cardboard fan was in her lap. She had little sweat beads on her lip, above the worn-off lipstick.

"Well, it don't feed anybody. That's partly my own fault though. I knew from the beginning he wasn't too work brittle. He showed that out the first week in my daddy's cotton patch. Boy. I hate cotton. I mean I hate messing with it. Chopping it. I really hate picking it. I guess anybody does. We picked cotton at Tipton one time, before the drought got so bad. I always could out-pick Harlan. Even a five-year-old kid could do that. He'd start off with the rest of us, but if nobody was keeping tabs, before you knew it he'd be standing in the field between the rows, playing his harp. Or he'd go over with the colored pickers and get to singing, embarrass me half to death. All they pay you for is just however many pounds you've got in your sack, and all we had mostly was what was in mine and that wouldn't even feed us, much less clothe us, so I figured we'd might as well be on the road bumming handouts at some lady's back door. Oh. Excuse me. I meant to thank you for lunch, ma'am. That ham was so good. I really liked it."

"You're welcome," she said. She picked up her fan and went back to fanning her neck.

"And thanks for stopping to get us. I had no idea it was this far to town. I can't ever tell anything about distance out in this flat country. I grew up in the hills. Harlan did too, but he traveled around when he was young, I guess he got used to it, but I never have. Back home, you always know how far away things are."

"Do you."

"Uh-huh, and most generally, if you can see it, it's not too very far. I been thinking how lucky it is we run into you. But we've always been lucky that way, me and Harlan. Considering. I thought our luck had all run out down there in Texas, but maybe it didn't. Because, look. Here we are." I gazed at the other nice houses on the street, the gray square of the grain elevator downtown. "This is a nice porch."

"Your husband's a musician?"

I thought about it a minute. "I guess you could call him that. Musician don't sound just exactly right, he's a . . . I don't know what you'd call him, ma'am, he's just Harlan. He plays the harmonica really well. He can play any instrument, actually, just about. He makes up songs and keeps time with his foot. Songs that tell people how the hard times are fixing to get better, or maybe songs that sound religious but aren't really, he's pretty bad to do that. He'll turn his hat up and collect a few pennies, or I will, I should say. He don't much like to do it. Harlan's got peculiar notions about money. Robbing Mr. Teasley's bank turned him like that. I can't say why. He couldn't abide the feel of that money, couldn't stand the touch of it in his hands. I told him *I* could abide it, but he said, Not for long you couldn't, shug. He said, We'd better just keep on how we are. And I guess it was the right thing, because our luck held all that time, till they stopped us in Texas. They beat him to a pulp in Texas, or that one bull did, he liked to killed him, and on top of that, he stole Harlan's harp. I don't know what Harlan's going to want to do when he gets back to himself."

The lady wasn't staring at her yard or the sky now, she was looking right at me.

"He nearly died, ma'am," I said.

"Yes," she said. "I can see that." She was quiet a minute, and then she said, "Dear, would you like to take a bath?"

"Oh, could I?"

See, that lady was in the sixty percent. High up in the sixty, if you ask me, even if she did dye her hair. At first I wasn't sure, but it's one of the things I got to thinking in her bathtub. I figured her and her husband both were. Of course, I hadn't met her husband yet. They must be rich people, I thought, because they have a bathroom with plumbing and an indoor toilet. Plumbing and a Pontiac car and a yellow table with shiny metal legs in the kitchen. She'd only let me run an inch of water—because of the drought she said—but it wasn't even iron water like in Texas, it was clear. I felt like I could sit there for a month. Here's something I don't like to tell, but it's the truth and I might as well say it: I didn't even think once about how Harlan was doing alone in the front bedroom while I was sitting in that tub.

What I thought about mostly was the old man. What he'd said about there's plenty blame to go around. I knew he wasn't saying to blame the ones worth blaming, he meant there's so much of it, why bother blaming anybody at all. That didn't seem right to me—I couldn't make it go with how I felt. But I kept studying on it. I thought that must be how the old man did, went around saying things to make you keep thinking about them. Like that sixty-forty business. I couldn't get that out of my head. I said to myself, If these are rich folks here in this nice house, and they're in the sixty, how does that square with the camel through the eye of the needle and all that? It goes against God's Word. And then I thought, Probably it's just by what you do, how you act, it don't matter if you own a Pontiac or not. And then I thought, But how do nice people get money? If it's not somebody like Oliver Teasley taking it off poor people, how do they get it? We can't rob any more banks, Harlan won't go for it, and anyhow we might get caught and sent to prison, or shot all to pieces like Pretty Boy Floyd.

All of a sudden I remembered Harlan's face after the robbery, how sick he'd looked crouched on the creekbank, turning his harp over and over in his palm. He said the old man had told him God enters us through sin, and that was the thing he couldn't quit thinking. He said those words just kept going round and round in his head. At the time I jumped up and went to see about the fire or something, I didn't want to hear such talk, it made me nervous, and besides, I didn't believe in Profit then. But sitting in the Goodwell lady's bathtub that evening I affirmed in my heart that the stinking man was Profit, he had to be, because it was the same with me as with Harlan. That old man's words were completely stuck in my head.

The lady knocked on the door. She didn't come in, she just hooked a clean housedress and underpants on the towel rack, said, "Here, dear, see if these'll fit." In a minute she knocked again, and set a jar of Cloverine on the floor. Well, I can't explain how I felt about that, because just her mentioning the name on the porch had set me crying, but now, seeing that old label, it didn't make me feel any particular way at all. Later, though, the smell did, when I put it on my face, so I smeared it on real fast and wiped my hands on the washrag before I reached for the clothes. They were her own clothes, I could tell, the underpants wouldn't stay up, I had to tie a knot in the waistband, and the dress swallowed me, but still. They smelled so clean. I was real careful not to get salve on anything. I wadded up my dirty Salvation Army clothes under my arm, opened the bathroom door and listened, but I didn't hear her, so I went up the hall to the front bedroom.

Harlan looked awful. He was asleep on his back with his mouth open. I could see his chipped tooth and the swelled purple ridge in his lip right above it. His poor scalp was so burned. You wouldn't think somebody as brown as Harlan could get so red, but I guess if part of you comes uncovered that's been covered all its life, it's bound to get pretty burnt in the sun. I laid down beside him on the bedspread. I kept as still as I could. I knew he needed to rest. The doctor had told me that, but I wouldn't listen, I'd just longheaded on. I stared at the ceiling and promised to do better. We'll go slower, I said to myself. We been gone this long, what difference does it make how quick we get back? "I'll go easy, babe," I whispered, and touched my hand to him, but I didn't look at him anymore. For a while I stayed there, but that shut room was suffocating, even with the fan on. I'd never laid under an electric fan in my life, the buzzing sound felt like it was sawing right through my brain. Plus, the little white bumps on the bedspread prickled my sunburn. So I got up and went out to the porch. There sat the lady, waiting on her husband. Her lipstick was back bright on her lips.

When I spied a man in a tan suit coming up the street I knew it must be him by how he slid his eyes at me. He didn't care to see a stranger sitting in his porch swing, I could tell. The lady stood up and told him my name, told him I was from Muskogee and that me and my husband were spending the night but we'd be leaving in the morning. The man didn't say anything—he didn't even glance at me—and then we all went in the house. He took off his hat and coat, washed his hands at the kitchen sink, and sat down at the table in his suspenders. He had a bit of soft-looking baby hair fringing the back of his head, otherwise he was pretty much bald. The lady motioned me to have a seat while she uncovered the leftovers. I bowed my head for the blessing, but the man started eating, so I raised my head and did too. Harlan was still asleep in the bedroom. The lady said to let him sleep, she said it was a cold supper anyway, it wouldn't be any colder an hour from now. The man said, "Maybe Mr. *Roosevelt* will cook him a hot plate. I'm getting partial to these cold suppers myself."

The lady just looked at him. They looked steadily at each other, and that's the first I understood they weren't so much alike. I helped the lady clear the table, and we all went out on the porch again—to wait for things to cool off a little, the lady said, so she could open up the house.

"Things aren't going to cool off, Ila," the man said. "Haven't you heard?" He grunted as he bent over to untie shoes. "Ask Reverend Bascomb over there at First Church. He'll tell you very well things are only going to get hotter, since it's the end of the world."

"Oh, John," the lady said.

"Did you know it's the end of the world, missy?" The man tossed one shoe toward the front door, and then the other. They hit with two soft thuds against the house. He started undoing his bow tie. "All the preachers around here have it that these black blizzards are the end of the world coming," he said. "And the *New York Times* has it that it's our own fault. Can you bear that?"

I studied the porch floor. It hadn't been painted in a while.

"Can you?" the man said.

I said, "I guess not."

"John. You're scaring her."

The man let out a long breath. He got up and went in the house and came back out with a red tin of Prince Albert and a packet of papers. That surprised me. I would have figured rich people only smoked store-bought. But then I asked myself, how many rich people have you ever actually met? and the answer was zero, unless you counted Mr. Teasley, which I did not. So, well then, I thought, how would you know? The man talked the whole time he was rolling, even while he was licking the paper to seal it, and just like his wife, he asked a lot of questions. There was a big difference though. The lady asked because she wanted to hear your answers, which you could tell by how she listened, whereas the man asked so he could tell you his own answer. He'd put his opinion inside a question and then ask what you thought about it, or he'd tell you some long involved information and start the whole thing with *Did you know* . . . The lady watched him with her mouth crimped, like she expected him to do something embarrassing, but all he did was fish a match out of his vest pocket and strike it on the porch rail.

"Let me ask you this, little lady," he said, drawing on the cigarette, his voice mashed. "By just what percentage would you suppose that the population of this county has decreased since the drought began?"

He was staring at me so hard I thought he wanted an answer. I shrugged.

"Hardly three percent!" He shook the match out, pinched the head off, threw it over the rail. "That's all we've lost from our farming population! People back east think we're dusted out. We are not dusted out. Not by a long shot." He smoked a while, frowning. The tobacco smelled good in the evening air. I turned to watch the huge white boiling clouds. They stood so high I had to tip my head back to see them. The tops disappeared above the porch roof.

"Sandstorms are nothing new in this country," the man said. "Didn't you know that? Our people know how to adjust to the vagaries of weather, but just try explaining that to the people back east. If that half-socialist *new deal* federal government would leave things alone, we could get some capital moving. What business in its right mind is going to expand with the people in Washington all wringing their hands and bawling woe is me?"

The lady leaned forward, touched my arm. "Dear," she said, "do you think your husband could eat a bite now?"

I started to get up and go see, but the man said, "Too many people asking for a handout in this country. Sit around and expect the government to feed them if the church won't. Know what's the matter with them, missy? They don't have any faith! They don't believe wheat prices are bound to rise if people will just cinch in their belts and wait it out. Quit crying the sky is falling."

The lady snapped, "Faith doesn't keep hungry children alive!"

"Neither does hysteria," the man said.

Oh, that made the lady mad. She didn't like that word one bit.

"We've got to get this economy turned around, Ila," the man said. "That's what's going to feed people! And just as quick as it rains, we will!"

"Feed the people," Harlan said. I jerked my head to look, and there he stood, behind the screen door. I was so glad to see him on his feet and not squinting with the headache and actually talking, I didn't know what to do. He pushed on the screen and stepped out. He'd forgot to put his cap on, but even so, he looked better. His eyes were bright anyway. Probably by how scarlet his skull was, it helped them look brighter.

The man stared at him. "What the hell happened to you?"

"Nothing too much," Harlan said. "Run into a few folks who don't cotton to the ones looking for a handout."

"How's your headache?" I said.

"Gone." Harlan limped to the porch rail and looked up at the clouds, turning pinkish now with the lowering sun.

The lady said, "Are you hungry?"

He cocked his head, like it was a hard question to answer. I said, "Harlan, you better eat a bite."

"I'll fix a plate," the lady said. She stood up, threw her husband a look, and went in the house. I wanted to go in and help her but I had a bad feeling about leaving Harlan alone with that man. Harlan stood with his scalped head tipped back, staring up at the sky. You can't help it, out in that country. Sky's such a force there, like wind, like the weather. Plus, you never knew when a dust storm might blow in. Harlan kept moving his hands around, patting his empty pockets. He glanced back at the man. "I could sure go for one of them smokes, mister," he said. "If it wouldn't trouble you too bad."

Oh Lord, Harlan, I thought. The lady's husband had done nothing all evening but gripe about folks asking for things, here was Harlan bumming him straight out for a cigarette, and Harlan didn't even smoke. Or, not yet he didn't. I guess that evening right there in Goodwell is when he got started—or unless he used to smoke before he met me and had quit and after that beating he decided to take up the habit again. Or, more likely, without his harmonica to hold, he was just looking for something to do with his hands. Anyway, I was shocked to hear him ask for one, and even more shocked to see the man make it. The man frowned a lot, but he tapped tobacco into a paper and rolled Harlan a thin little cigarette.

The lady brought a plate of food and set it on the porch rail. Harlan was standing by the banister, smoking and looking up. He said, "I don't smell any dusters. Do you?"

The lady said, "Not this evening."

"That's good, innit?"

"Yes," the lady said.

All at once Harlan turned around with his arms spread and announced, "All men are created equal!" The man and the lady stared at him. Harlan went on in an amazed voice. "Created equal. Why, that's a promise, innit? But, now, here's your question: Is this the promise that says folks were created equal to start with, but after that it's every man for himself? Or does it go the other way around?"

I whispered to the lady, "Them bulls pistol-whipped him, ma'am." I wanted her to know Harlan's brains were just temporarily addled, I didn't want her to hold it against him.

"It's not just rightly true what you said, ma'am," Harlan told her. "About faith don't feed the kids. It don't mostly, but it can. Feed the kids. Move the mountain. Looka there," he said, motioning down the street. "I don't see mountain one. Do you?"

I got up and went over there. "Honey," I whispered, "don't aggravate them."

The man was hunched forward, his bald dome near as red as Harlan's scalded knob, and the lady too. She wasn't red in the face but she was sure frowning. Harlan gazed at her. "What makes you think, ma'am, that there's a government answer for a human nature question? Or," he said, peering now at the man, "that there's a human answer for government questions? Looks to me like y'all could just throw 'em both out, both them notions, and ask yourself an old question that's been rolling down since the beginning of time—like about sin. But then where would you be? Back at the beginning. That's not progress. Oh well," he said, patting his pockets, and the look on his face was so sad, so . . . despairing. "What's the use in trying to fix it?" he murmured. "You never can." He turned to face the sky again.

I said, "Harlan, I think we better go."

The man said, "I think you'd better." The lady didn't say anything. Her lipsticked mouth was pulled tight. She didn't look at me. So I went in the house to the front bedroom and turned off the fan. I picked up my skirt and blouse from where I'd left them on the floor, took her clothes off me, put mine back on. They felt like my clothes now, that was a difference. They hadn't before, from the time the people at the Salvation Army gave them to me, but now they did. I smoothed up the bedspread, folded the lady's dress as nice as I could and laid it out on the foot of the bed. I heard her in the doorway behind me, or I felt her, I guess, because she didn't say anything. I said, "I'm real sorry, ma'am. That bull hit him hard."

She said, "No, dear. I'm the one who's sorry. It's getting late anyway, it'll be dark in a little while. You kids better stay here."

"It'd just be a fight if we did, ma'am."

"That would scarcely be a first in this house." The room was reddish orange with the sun going down, but the light was behind her, I couldn't tell anything about her expression. I could tell she was looking at me though.

"How can you live with somebody like that?" I blurted. Oh, I knew that sounded awful, even though how it sounded was about what I meant. I just didn't like the man. I tried to say it better. "What I mean, somebody so. . . different than you."

She sighed. "I married him, dear." She came on in the room, went to the dresser and started fiddling with the brush and comb set. "People change, don't they?" she said, catching my eyes in the mirror. "Over time. But it's not *real* change, I find, it's not fundamental. Not transformation. They just become more of themselves. If you've loved the essential self, the surface change is immaterial. It only makes life . . . interesting."

"Do you think somebody could change if something bad happened to them? Change inside, I mean."

"I don't know," she said. "Possibly."

"Do you think they'd have to change for the worse if it was really bad, the thing that happened?"

"Not necessarily." She picked up the hairbrush. "Come here, dear." I hesitated. But the lady motioned me and I went over and stood in front of her, and she brushed my hair. I didn't look for a long time, I just didn't want to, but finally the room was getting dark enough and it felt so good, her running that soft brush along my scalp. I turned my eyes to the mirror. I guessed it was me, I mean, I knew it was, but it felt no more like looking at myself than it would to look at a picture postcard on a rack. That girl's hair was too light colored, she had too many freckles, her skin was too red. And she was older. Older than I'd ever been or was yet. She looked female at least anyway, in a smudgy light blouse, with her hair growing out. I said to the lady, "Did you ever have any kids?"

"Yes," she said.

"Where are they?"

"My son teaches in Guymon," she said, and then she was quiet. Her hands were so steady, brushing my hair. Brushing and brushing. After a long time she said, "Our daughter died a long time ago. Before we came out here. Sarah had just started walking. She'd be about your age now, I guess." The lady twisted my hair up in a knot, held it there with one hand while she felt around in the top drawer for some hairpins. "It's not good to judge a man unless you've lived his sorrow. Is it?" she said. She pinned the knot down.

I didn't say anything. I was thinking how that sounded a little like the old man.

"If you want to get out of these dusty clothes," she said, patting my shoulder, "I'll wash them and have them ready for you in the morning."

"They won't get dry in time, will they?"

The lady sort of laughed. "You don't know this western wind." She turned to go.

"Did she starve to death?" I said.

"Who?"

"Your little girl."

"Oh. No. No, dear. She died of diphtheria."

"Mine did. Starved to death. We just couldn't feed me, so I couldn't feed him. We think that's what happened."

The lady looked at me a long time. Then she went to the bed and picked up her dress and brought it over and held it out to me. She turned around so I could shuck out of my skirt and blouse and put her dress back on, and then she took my clothes, touched the top of my head, very light, I barely felt it, and she went on out of the room.

"Thank you, ma'am!" I called after her. I hope she heard me. What I was thinking was, really, it would be good to start for home in the morning in clean clothes. I never dreamed we'd get up and leave in the middle of the night.

A little while after the lady left, Harlan came in the bedroom. He switched on the fan and laid down on the bed in the twilight, staring up at the ceiling. "What's wrong?" I said. I was worried he'd got the man madder—maybe even mad enough to call the law. "Oh, honey," I said, "what'd you have to provoke him for?"

"Sometimes when you're trying to make the peace," he said softly, "you got to draw their fire to yourself."

"What's that supposed to mean?"

He didn't answer.

"Harlan Singer," I said, "that is the peculiarest reasoning I ever heard in my life." I took the lady's hairpins out of my hair and laid down beside him. After a few minutes his breathing deepened, became slow, and I knew he was sleeping. But I couldn't sleep. I kept listening for a town cop or a sheriff to come stomping up the porch steps. Oh, not on account of the Vardis robbery, no. We'd sent that money back. I didn't think you could be a criminal if you gave back what you stole, and anyhow, we'd been on the road ever since, I couldn't keep up with what month it was hardly, much less an unfathomable notion such as that. The idea of Harlan being wanted was about the fartherest thing from my mind. But we'd been arrested plenty for vagrancy, in Nebraska and Illinois, once in Mississippi. Usually they'd let us go when they saw I was a girl, they'd drive us to the edge of town and tell us to get going and never come back, but a few times I'd had to spend the night in a hard chair in the sheriff's office while Harlan sat in a cell in the back, and once they threw me in the clink right along with him, and *that* was what had me worried, and why I stayed quiet on the top of the bedspread, listening, though all I heard was the restless whine of the high-plains wind.

Well, and now I had the Goodwell lady's words stuck in my mind right alongside the old man's: what she'd said about people seeming to change over time but not really, how really they were just becoming more of themselves. But if that was true, what did it say about my daddy breaking apart in the pulpit? It would have to mean he'd always been crazy a little, and I just didn't believe that. I thought too about all the times Harlan seemed like he was changing but then didn't. Like how he'd turned so quiet after we met that ringwormy blond kid, but later he got back to himself. Well, but then he turned even *more* quiet the time they ran us out of that Hooverville, and that was also when he'd quit playing his music, and what would you call that but a real change? Except, after we gave back Teasley's money, he started playing again.

Lying in the gathering dark on that soft bed my mind swept through all our time on the road since, nights in the hobo jungles, days spent scavenging food, hunting work, Harlan joking in the camps and railcars, playing music for the people, and the sound from his harp wasn't harsh or sour anymore. It wasn't perfect either—not even as good, really, as when I first met him—but every day he played a little sweeter, a little stronger, like a toddler child learning to walk. Now, though, he didn't have his harp to play and I couldn't see how we were going to get him another, and nearly two years had passed since we'd went home and seen my daddy preaching strange in the pulpit. I was worried there wouldn't be anybody left in Cookson who'd know where my family went, and that thought made the urgency choke up inside me even worse. I laid there sweating on the bedspread with the electric fan buzzing and my mind rolling and tumbling, and I don't believe I slept, I truly don't, but next thing I remember Harlan was leaning over and nudging me, whispering for me to get up.

"What happened!" I said, my heart pounding.

"Shhhh." He put his finger in front of my lips, acting so secretive I thought for sure the man had called the law. I sat up fast and put my shoes on and followed Harlan through the dark house. We eased out the front door, and he let the screen to very quietly. Dawn was still hours off but there was a good moon. I could see his pale shirt under the overalls going before me along the walk. After we got down the street a ways I asked him again what had happened.

"Nothin', shug," he said. "It's just time to go."

"In the middle of the night?"

"Aw, it'll be light soon." He took my hand, and we walked through the silent town. I sure hoped there weren't any constables around hunting vagrants, but the truth is, I was relieved to be back on the road. Harlan seemed rested, he walked pretty fast, heading toward the black bulk of the grain elevator. When we got there it was right by the railroad tracks, naturally, and I realized what he was doing. I stopped still. "No, honey," I said. "No more trains. I told you that."

He frowned like he didn't remember, but then he shrugged and we kept walking, on out past the edge of town. The wind had settled, the moon was a million miles high, and so white, almost full. It was a beautiful night. We left the town lights far behind. Harlan was quiet, ambling the road in his slow rolling gait.

"I'm glad the wind laid," I said, "aren't you? What a pretty night. Look how bright the road is. Oh, honey, you never did get any supper, did you?"

"Yes I did."

Then I remembered the lady bringing the plate to the porch. Then I remembered I had on her dress. I looked down. "Oh shoot. I'm fixing to walk off in that lady's clothes."

He squeezed my hand. "It's all right," he said.

"Are you sure?"

"Yes."

"Well, I wisht you'd told me we'd be leaving before daylight, I'd have kept my Salvation Army clothes. This thing swallows me."

"Salvation don't come from no army," he said. His voice sounded strange, it made my throat catch. I started walking fast. Harlan came along beside me. I kept my eyes on the road. The caliche shined pure white in the moonlight. That was good, I thought. I didn't want to be stepping on any nightcrawling sidewinders. I knew there wouldn't be any rides for hours, but Harlan was stronger than yesterday, and the sky was bright, and we were walking east across the top of the world. Have you ever been out there? Out on the high plains? Feels like you're passing over the rim of the earth. It seems nearly impossible, the way you can feel so high up when everything around is so flat. The moon showed the black line of the horizon before us, a few pale washed-out stars down low, and it wasn't hot and it wasn't windy, only a little warm, with a soft breeze blowing. For a while there, walking that night road, I felt glad.

"Two years isn't so long, is it?" I said. "Somebody's bound to still be there that knows them. Don't you think? I'll bet Marie Tingle's still there. I was just thinking, the baby's nearly five now. Ellie Renee. I can hardly imagine. She won't even know me, will she? When she sees me? She won't remember."

Harlan murmured, "'Lovest thou me?'"

My heart nearly stopped. I knew he wasn't talking to me. He wasn't asking if I loved him, he was saying what Jesus said to his disciple. I thought to myself, Oh, Harlan, no.

"'Lovest thou me?'" he said again in that low, flat voice, and then he answered in the same voice, "'Feed my sheep.'"

He let go my hand, started feeling all around his empty pockets. "Harlan," I said. "Honey, what's the matter?"

"Where's my harp?"

"I've told you and told you, the railroad bulls took it! Oh, foot, Harlan, that harp don't matter. We'll get you another. It's just an old piece of tin." We'd stopped walking, we were standing in the center of the white road. I could see our shadow on the caliche. Harlan's hands were wandering all around himself. I couldn't help it then, I burst out, "Listen! That old man? That was *him*! I know it was. They beat the living breath out of you! They took your harp and left you for dead, but he saved your life. He saved mine. He was *there,* Harlan."

"What old man?"

I felt like I could nearly shake him. "That old *man* you been *hunting* ever since I dadgum *met* you. That Profit! Good Lord, Harlan, what is the matter with you?"

"I've been longheaded, Sis. Did you know it? Longheaded and wrongheaded both."

"What?" I stood in the road, hardly breathing. Sis was my nickname at home, that's what my whole family called me. Sis or Sissy. Of all the pet names Harlan used for me, in all our lives together, he'd never once called me that.

"You can't depend on a man, Sissy," he said. "No man. Not your good ones or your bad ones, your powerful ones or your weak. Not your daddy you never knew, nor the one that you did. Not even that old fella I took up with, good as he was. He don't know. He don't know. It's not one human you can depend on, and it's not a thousand. It ain't human work, see. That's what I was looking at all wrong."

"I should have stayed on that reefer," I said. "I should have stayed right where you put me."

"No. No, baby. It's how it was supposed to go." His hands began roaming around himself again. "I thought it was going to be easy. All them folks come to meet me, I thought . . . " His voice trailed off. "We're made in the image," he said, shaking his head. "That's the mystery. That's the one thing I can't figure." He got quiet again. After a long while he said, "It's *real,* Sharon. It is."

"What's real?"

"Ah," he said, "I can't explain. It don't go into words."

I stared at our shadow in the moonlight, mine shorter than his, and stiller. No space in between. I thought, There's a gulf fixed all right, like my daddy used to preach it. One that nobody can cross over. But it ain't between rich and poor, nor saved and sinner. It's between somebody who's come that close to dying, and somebody who has not.

The sky was beginning to lift a little, graying out straight ahead in front of us. I took Harlan's arm and we started walking east again.

We were still walking an hour later when the sun broke over the rim. It hurt to keep my eyes open. I was really wishing I had a hat. We heard a car engine behind us, and I turned to see an old black jalopy, coming fast. Harlan stuck his thumb out, and I suddenly realized he didn't have on a hat either, he'd left that wool cap behind, and I said to myself, Reckon how long it'll take his hair to grow out. We might have to keep walking till it will.

But the man in the car stopped for us.

"Looks like you people can ambulate anyway," he said. "Can you bang a pan?"

"I believe so," Harlan said.

"You'll do then, get in."

And we did, Harlan in the front and me in the cramped little seat in the back. The man said, "We'll be late if we're not careful," and he gunned that old lizzie, the dust flew in the windows, and I hunkered down. The man talked at Harlan, his voice loud over the wind and the motor, but I couldn't really make out what he was saying. We drove a good while. By the time we stopped it was full morning, and we were way out on the bare prairie. I didn't see a sign of a town. There were lots of people though, men and women, and plenty of children, and cars and trucks everywhere, lined up as far as I could see, all facing the same direction.

"Harlan," I whispered, "what are we doing?"

"Looks like we're fixing to earn our ride."

Nobody explained to me anything. To this day I don't think that was fair. They just stuck a saucepan and a lid in my hands, gave Harlan a tin dishpan and a big cedar-knot stick and told us to start thirty feet apart, and we went over and got in the row of people, and before I could think or ask anything, everybody started moving, all the same direction, walking north, yelling and banging their pans. Some of the women and the littlest kids jumped in the cars and trucks and came driving along slowly behind us, blaring their horns. Now what are you going to do in a situation like that? You do what everybody else is doing. You think it must be the right thing. They all looked like normal white farming people to me, I figured there was bound to be a reason. I started clanging my pan and lid together and yelling, the same as everybody else. I'd lost sight of the man who brought us by then.

And here go the rabbits, jumping out in front. Blacktailed jackrabbits is what they were, with those long jackrabbit ears and powerful legs and graybrown fur. At first it was just a few, zigzagging like crazy, but soon we were herding dozens of them, and then hundreds, along through the clumps of buffalo grass before us. I glanced over at Harlan. He was limping along, pounding the bottom of that dishpan like a drum, smiling, he had a peaceful smile on his face. We were raising such a racket I couldn't have asked questions right then if I'd wanted, but I didn't need to anyhow. I could see what it was. The ground was just alive with rabbits, thousands of them, leaping and darting ahead of us in panic. A few tried to come back on us, but we were moving closer together as we walked, and if one zigged back, some of the men or boys would jump over and knock it in the head.

After a long time, almost an hour maybe, I saw another line of people way off to the east, and then one coming from the west, squaring up with us. I knew there was a line opposite us too, coming down, though I couldn't see them yet, but I could see very well what we were doing: we were driving those jacks toward the huge pen in the middle, standing out on the empty land, tall and closed and wooden, with openings at the sides for the rabbits to go in. A bunch of men and boys started rushing forward, pouring in through the openings, and by the time me and Harlan got there, the killing had begun.

Have you ever heard a rabbit scream? It's a terrible sound, I think it's worse than any cry a noisy animal makes, like, say, a hurt dog. Their nature is silent, rabbits have a completely silent nature, so when they scream it's the most wrenching sound in the world. And of course the people couldn't shoot them to kill them quick because they might accidentally shoot each other, they had to kill them with their sticks. The thudding sound was everywhere, it gave me the sick pitless feeling like I'd had when the bull was pistol-whipping Harlan. I wanted to stop and walk away, but here went Harlan, in through the opening with the rest of them.

I got such a panic, losing sight of him, I rushed forward. Inside, the grass was worn away and the dust was roiling. I got jammed up behind the people crowding in. I couldn't see him. All I could see was rabbits, thousands and thousands of rabbits, kicking and leaping and trying not to die, and some of them screamed, yes, but many were silent, scrambling to hide where there was nothing to hide under but some other jack's dead body, or they'd freeze, trying to blend in, and that just got them clubbed quicker. To this day I can't get the pictures out of my mind, their mashed heads, furred legs, blunted feet, jerking and twisting, I can still see people's fists raising sticks and ax handles and homemade clubs, crashing down again and again. Bits of fur flew up in the air with the dust, and also there was the smell of blood.

I saw him finally, Harlan, yonder by the fence with his cedar-knot stick and his dishpan. He was breathing hard, his chest heaving up and down, fast, under the overalls, fast like the rabbits' chests, their small hearts thumping, and I thought, He's scared, and my heart wrenched too. I shouted his name, pushed toward him, but before I could get there, he suddenly threw his head back and let out a long, high, wobbling throat-cry, a gobbling sound, like a wild turkey gobbling, only terrifying. I'd never heard any sound like that from a human throat. Then he waded in with his cedar stick and began to kill.

Oh, I wish I'd never seen it. I'd give anything not to have that picture inside my mind, Harlan's face twisted, his arm swinging the knotted stick. I screamed his name, I shoved through the people to reach him, I jerked hard on his sleeve, calling him, but he couldn't hear me, he couldn't feel me, he just kept bringing the stick down, over and over. The blood and fur flicked up, specking the washed-out denim covering his legs.

deepsong

thud and smack stone on bone,
the sound of weeping,
teeth gnashing, the earth cracking.
run and hide, boy!
hide and run!

silence.

the old man's voice in the tulsa campyard:
god enters through the wounds of imperfection

harlan? she said.
hush now. listen.

deep in the bottoms.
no wind.

Sharon

Maybe it didn't last nearly as long as it seemed to me then. I waited outside the pen for what felt like hours, but the sun wasn't even quite overhead yet, I remember, when the men began to drift out, one by one. I was standing next to a farm truck. A new mother sat on the running board, nursing her baby. Cars and trucks were lined out all around us, most with women and kids on the turtlehulls and sloped hoods. I watched for Harlan. Some of the men coming out were holding dead rabbits. I asked the mother feeding her baby, I said, "Who cooks all them rabbits? It'd take a long time, I guess. But they sure won't keep in this heat."

She said, "Oh we don't eat them. Too much rabbit fever around."

"Well, but does somebody buy the skins?" I said.

"You can't get anything for them. There's millions and millions of jacks in this country. We've been holding drives once a week since February, except when the dusters keep us from it. Arliss was hoping we'd be finished by now so we could try another planting, but . . . " She shrugged. "Seems like there's always more."

"What do y'all do with them then?"

"Burn them, if the wind's not too bad."

I watched her shift her baby to her other side. He was bald as a little scalded pig. I could see tiny blue veins running under his scalp. "Don't it make you sick, though?" I said. "To see it, I mean. To smell it."

She glanced at me. "Where I get sick," she said, "is watching a scourge of jacks swarm on our place eating every nub of wheat and alfalfa my husband plants. Every sprig in the garden. They gnaw it to the bare dirt and then dig up the roots and eat them." She gazed down, smoothed her baby's naked head. "As if things weren't bad enough."

"Looks to me like there'd be some other way to do it, though."

Her head shot up and she stared at me dead on. She had thick eyebrows, auburn hair, like my mama's, only hers was straight. "Another thing makes me sick," she said, "is hearing all the time how people everyplace else think we do this for sport." She eased her baby away from the breast, put him to her shoulder, buttoned her top button. Then she got up and walked off.

I didn't know what to think, except that I wasn't going to talk to any more of these people. Something the lady at Goodwell said was trying to nudge me, about how it don't do to judge somebody unless you've lived what they've lived. I thought, Well, maybe so. But they don't have to be rude.

Then I saw Harlan coming. His limp seemed really bad. His hands were empty, he didn't have that pan and stick anymore, or any dead rabbits either. The whole lower half of his legs was streaked red. I started to rush at him, but his face stopped me. There was something awful in the way it was set. His eyes had that cloudy look too, the deep stitch between them. I thought to myself, Lord, how long is it going to be like this? I went to him very slow, took his arm and led him to a different car so he could rest a minute in its slip of shade. I didn't want to be by that same truck if the woman with the baby came back. Harlan sat on the ground, he put his scalped-looking head down on his arms, cradled across his filthy knees.

I laid my palm on his neck and stood there, hunting all over for the fellow who brought us, or at least his old car, but I didn't see him. Men and boys were toting carcasses out from the pen now, five or six in each hand, holding them away from themselves by the ears or legs. They carried them off a ways and threw them in a pile, then they'd go back in and get some more. You'd think the men would be tired—we'd walked for miles, plus all that hitting they'd done—but they acted cheerful, or het up, anyway, like some mighty foe had been licked. I rubbed Harlan's neck, watched some boys pouring kerosene on the pile of rabbits. That grayish-brown heap was taller than most of them's heads, covering a piece of ground near as large as a barn—it took a lot of kerosene. Before long the coal oil smell was stronger than the dust smell or the blood smell either one. Then they lit the fire, and here came the odor of hair burning, and then the air started to smell delicious, like roasting meat. A stab of hunger nearly cut me in two. I thought, What a waste. This is such a waste. Somebody ought to do something. After a while, though, the roasted meat scent turned to a nasty burnt-black smell, and that wasn't so good. People began to load up in their vehicles. I didn't want to talk to any of them, but I didn't want us left out there in the empty prairie either.

"Get up, Harlan," I said. "Honey. Come on now."

He took a while but he stood on his feet, finally. His face had the old dazed look. I grabbed his hand and we started walking, Harlan's foot was dragging. In a minute I saw our chance, a flatbed hay truck headed east with forty or fifty people clinging on the back. I said, "Hurry!" and started running to catch up. The people saw us, they saw Harlan struggling, and they called to the driver to stop, which, he didn't come to a complete stop, but he slowed down enough that we got there and climbed on.

We started out riding at the back, our legs dangling, jouncing along on that bucking truck straight out across the open land, but it wasn't long before I made Harlan crawl through the crowd of people to sit in the middle up next to the cab. He was limp as a ragdoll. I was afraid he'd fall off. He sat swaying with the bumps then, gazing down at the splintery truck bed, and the people all stared at him. After a while I announced, very loud, "My husband fell off a hay truck last week and scalped himself!" I just got tired of them gawking at him. After that, they quit.

I couldn't tell you the name of the town they carried us to, I forgot to look. I wasn't paying attention to anything except Harlan, if he was going to be all right, but I do know it was a really little town, even if it did have two grain elevators by the tracks. I also know it took us the whole rest of the day to get there. We kept stopping to let off different ones at farms and ranches along the way. Whole families of people, a man and woman and maybe five or six kids, would all scramble down at once. I figured as long as we had a ride going generally our direction, me and Harlan had better stay put. When we reached that little town, finally, the last five men jumped off, and me and Harlan went to climb down. The men were already scattering to their automobiles parked along the street. Nobody said a word to us. The hay truck drove away, left us standing in front of a furniture store, which was closed. All the stores were closed. Across the road and down a ways were the twin elevators, five stories tall and metal gray. I could see blue sky between them, all the way to the ground.

"How's your head?" I asked him.

"Not too bad," he said, but I could tell that was a lie.

I glanced up and down the street. A few cars were angled to the curb, but there wasn't a living soul in sight, not even a town dog. I thought, Maybe it's Sunday. And then I thought, No, probably not. I doubt there's a hundred people in this whole state who'd miss church to kill rabbits, much less the bunch we saw out there. More likely it's Saturday, I thought. After five. Naturally the stores would be closed. Everybody's gone home to supper. Well, we hadn't had a bite since the lady fed us in Goodwell, so getting something to eat is just what I had on my mind. I didn't know what I was going to do with Harlan though. If we knocked at a back door to ask for something he might scare the people. Not just by his scabs and spattered legs but because of the look in his eyes. I said, "Come on, babe," and took him across the street, and we walked down to the elevators. The office was shut, the doors locked, and I couldn't see any place at the foot of the bins to put him, but there were a couple of rusty grain cars on the sidetrack. I led him over to the coupling. "Sit here," I said. "I'll be back in two shakes." I walked away fast, I didn't want to leave him by himself for too long.

It only took a couple of minutes to find the kind of house I wanted. When you've been on the road as long as me and Harlan, you sort of get a hunch which house is likely. I saw one a few blocks away, it hadn't been painted in a while, but it didn't have rotted porch boards either, or a bunch of junk in the yard, and when I went to the back door I could smell bacon frying. I guess I looked hungry enough in that swallowing dress, because the woman that answered the door said to come in, she said they were just sitting down to supper she'd fix me a plate, but I said, "No ma'am, my little brother's waiting on me to bring him something," and she said, "Well, he can come in too," and I said, "Oh, no, ma'am. He's down at the train station. He's a cripple, he can't walk. I'd have to carry him and I'm too tired." She still wanted me to come in, but I said, "Ma'am, I really 'preciate it, but I'll just wait here." I sat on the steps and in not too long she brought out a big paper sack. It was heavy when she put it in my arms, and I thought, Boy, what a good hunch I had.

When I got back to Harlan and climbed up next to him to open the sack, though, I found out that what made it so heavy was two big ugly rutabaga turnips the size of a cat's head. I could have laughed. Us without a knife to cut them and no pan to cook them in nor any way to make a fire if we did have. But she'd also put in a pint jar of sweetmilk and a cold Irish potato, and laid in on top of that four slices of lightbread with crisped-up bacon between them and some soda crackers smeared with butter and pressed face-to-face, all wrapped inside a clean blue bandanna-type handkerchief. That was worth everything right there. Harlan started looking better as he ate, and that made me feel hopeful. I thought to myself, We'll keep the turnips, even if they are heavy to carry. We might can trade them for something better.

The high clouds were starting to tinge a little towards the tops. I told Harlan we'd better get on out to the highway if we hoped to reach anywhere before dark. He started to climb down, and I told him, "No, here, wait a minute. Bend your neck." I shook the crumbs out of the blue bandanna and wrapped it around his head and tied it. It made him look foreign, like a gypsy or something, but it was still better than his scraggly scalp and the scabs. We set out walking, but we hadn't even reached the edge of town before he faltered. I said to myself, Sharon, hadn't you learned nothing? He's *got* to rest.

So I took him back to the siding by the two grain elevators and found us an empty. Yes, I'd said no more trains, and I meant it, but that's where we'd been living for so long, railyards and hobo jungles. A storage rail or a train yard was the only kind of place I felt like I knew. The car I found was riddled with holes, the floor rotted through in places, both doors standing wide open, but it was the only boxcar there. The others were all grain cars or gondolas. I jumped high, locked my elbows, scrambled over the lip, turned to help Harlan climb in. I was praying it was a discard, that there wouldn't be somebody come along before daylight and make it up into a train. "If this thing starts moving in the night," I said, "we're jumping off."

It took every bit of strength I had to drag the rear sliding door closed, Harlan was in no shape to help me. A crossbreeze would have been cooler, but I only wanted to have to keep an eye on one door. We sat against the back wall and watched the light fade, and then we laid down. I started to drift off. All at once Harlan let out a yell. I jerked alert. I was scared it was tarantulas or something. He rolled away from me and sat up against the back of the car. He was shaking. I mean, just quaking and trembling all over, like the blond kid who swung in the car with us at Kansas City that time, the way that kid curled up against the wall and shook and shook.

"Babe, what is it?"

He wouldn't tell me, but in a little bit he quit shaking, and we laid back down and I put my arm across him His breath started to come slow. Okay, I thought, he's going to sleep now. Then he cried out, sat up shaking, just the same as before. The whole night it kept happening, over and over, and he still wouldn't talk to me, or he couldn't. I gave up trying to sleep, and we both sat in the dark, leaning against the car wall. The wind rose. I heard it crying through the little holes, skittering grit through, but it was blowing from the north and couldn't come in the open door. I dozed some, I think, off and on, I was just so tired, but way deep in the night Harlan stirred, and I bolted awake. The moon made a square of light on the floor. The clouds were moving quick over it, light, and dark, and light, really fast.

"The earth can't hold all the dead," Harlan said.

I reached to touch him. His heart beat fast under my hand.

"I fell asleep on the creekbank," he whispered. "I was real young then. It was after my mama. I seen them, Sharon. They were so many. The earth couldn't hold them. They came pouring out, millions and millions. The ground had to spew them. The dirt and mud spewed them." He turned toward me. I could see his shape in the shifting moonlight, the kerchief binding his head. "That was the war dead," he said. "But they're only part of it. Just a little part."

"Shhhh," I said, touching him.

"There's something terrible inside us, Sharon."

"Hush!" I said. "Don't say that."

"The lion can't lay down with the lamb, it can't. We got to answer what's in us. And it's bad, what's inside us, it's dark there. But it's frozen, too. Like the sea."

I kept my hand on his chest. There was nothing for me to say. I couldn't think of anything. I just prayed to God it would turn light soon.

And when morning came he did seem better. He was weak, he was tired, we both were—I went to swing down, my bones felt like they could crack open—but at least Harlan wasn't saying such things anymore. We left that town, I couldn't shake its dust off my heels fast enough. We caught a ride on the highway, and from that ride we caught another, and another. He still looked bad, but I'd rubbed dirt on his overalls to cover the blood stains, and the bandanna helped.

Every mile farther east we got, the steadier he got. If he was hurting you couldn't tell it, he never breathed a word of complaint. In no time he got to where he'd visit with whoever stopped to pick us up, farmer or drummer or delivery man, he sounded almost like his old self, friendly, sort of jokey, except for he'd started asking those peculiar questions. Well, sometimes Harlan's questions made sense, but a lot of times they didn't. Oh, like, for instance, he'd be as apt to ask a rancher if the wheat was divided from the chaff as what direction the fellow was headed. But Harlan was getting his strength back, whether we walked or whether we didn't, whether we ate good or not, and that was the main thing I cared about.

By the time we got to Blackwell, he was downright cheerful, strolling along the main street, making up songs and singing them under his breath. The bandanna was tied around his neck now. His hair was grown out enough he didn't have to keep it covered, but it was still so short and tight to his scalp, it made him look different. Made him look older somehow. The words he sang were all about pumpjacks and blackjacks and scores of bloody blacktailed jackrabbits, but he didn't sing them sad, he sang them to old square-dance tunes.

We'd been seeing those rocking-horse type oilfield pumpjacks as we rode along, and the giant grain elevators, of course, you can see those for miles, so we knew they worked oil and wheat both around Blackwell. I don't guess they were working either one too good though, because most of the pumpjacks were stilled, and the town, when we got there, had a bunch of boarded-up stores, FOR SALE signs propped in the windows. It looked like they were having a hard time in Blackwell, same as everywhere else. We knew the town's name because the water tower carried it in huge black letters, BLACKWELL, and that word must have got stuck in Harlan's head, because he kept repeating it, limping along. Then he went to singing it, way too loud. *"O Black-well, poor Black-well! Ah, Blackwell, my soul! Hie thee to Good-well, where the sweet waters flow! Good-wa-ter, Sweet-wa-ter, Still-water too! Black-well, ah Black-well! Where the dark waters go!"*

I said, "Honey, don't you think you might make somebody mad? Singing words like that?" But he just winked at me, patted his bib, singing, *"Well, well, well, oi-ll wells and wa-ter wells, I've roamed the world o-o-o'er! From Still-well to Black-well, Where the black waters flo-o-ow!"*

There was no point in talking to him when he got like that, so I let it go. What I had on my mind anyway was hunting a hobo jungle where we could trade our turnips for something decent, or maybe even a cafe where we could beg a bite to eat. Harlan stopped in front of a drugstore, staring in at the window.

"What?" I said.

He pushed through the door, a little bell jangled, and I followed him, of course. I didn't know what he was up to. We hardly ever went in stores. Merchants don't care for our kind—I mean us with no money and always on the road—so most generally me and Harlan didn't trouble them, only bakeries and cafes, or every once in a while a grocery store. There was a man at the very back, behind a counter, and Harlan moseyed toward him. It had been so long since I'd seen the inside of a Rexall, though, I have to admit I got stuck at the front, gaping around at all the nice things. They had one whole glass shelf of lipsticks, just twisted up and sitting right out there, you could see all the different reds. They had Coty face powder in gold boxes, and light-brown and dark-brown hairnets draped over cardboard cutouts shaped like a woman's head, and all kind of bobby pins, brown and black and silver, rowed up in stacks on pieces of paper. I heard the man ask Harlan if he could help us—his voice sounded like he really doubted it, and I thought, oh, honey, let's just go. But I heard Harlan say, "Yes sir, I just believe you can." So I hurried back there.

"Well?" the drugstore man said. He was standing behind the counter where they give out the medicines, he had a big head of white hair, a white coat buttoned up at the throat.

"Have y'all got any pantydine tablets?" Harlan said.

The drugstore man frowned, not so much like he was suspicious as like he was studying the question. He reached up and pushed a hand through his snowy hair. I'd never seen so much white hair on a person, it bushed high at the crown. He reminded me of a leghorn rooster or something. "What do you need them for?" he said.

"Truth is, mister," Harlan said, "I got the miseries mighty bad."

The man pondered a minute. "What kind of symptoms?"

"Ohhhh," Harlan said, "some nights it's the headache, and some days it's the leg. Some mornings my heart aches so till I can't crawl out of bed." Well, you could take one look at Harlan and know he didn't have any kind of a bed to crawl out of, but the man came from behind the medicine counter and went towards the front. And then, all in one slick second, I saw what Harlan was after:

inside a glass case on top of the glass counter, there amongst rows of pocket knives and scissors and fountain pens, sat a blue-and-white rectangle box with the word HOHNER on it. I was still wondering how he'd seen that from all the way out on the sidewalk when Harlan reached over the counter. The drugstore man came back holding a little two-cent envelope of BC Headache Powder, but all I could really see was the blank spot in the case where the harmonica box had been, shining bare as a scab. I stared up at Harlan's face. I couldn't believe it. He asked the man, real casual in his friendly twang, if there was any sweeping-up work we could do to pay for the powder, but the snowy man shook his head. He looked uncomfortable. "Here," he said, and pushed the BC packet at Harlan. "Y'all better head on now." Then he turned to step back behind the counter. We got out of there fast.

"That's stealing!" I said on the sidewalk. But Harlan was already walking away. I hurried to catch up, I grabbed his overall straps from behind in both fists, jerked back on them like reins, he was laughing, I started laughing too. I couldn't help it. I knew it was bad, but he was just so slick. I turned him around. "Harlan Singer," I said, "I'd be ashamed!"

"Would you," he said. His left hand was deep in his pocket.

"I would," I said, "and so should you." I glanced over my shoulder. There were people on the street, cars passing, a man in a straw hat coming out of the feedstore across the way. I lowered my voice. "You're liable to get us arrested," I whispered. To my own mind now, what I think I'd meant to do was make him give it back, like he made me give back Oliver Teasley's bank money. I believe that's why I stopped him. But all I said was, "I wisht you'd let me know we were fixing to take up thieving again. I'd have gone for something besides a two-dollar harp. Like some dadgum food."

"Aw, Sis," he said.

"Quit calling me that."

He tilted his head, blinked at me a minute, like he was puzzled. Then he said, "Them folks in Goodwell? They're good people. Decent people. But look how they boss and contempt around at each other."

"Somebody's got to do some bossing," I said.

"You think so?" His hand was fumbling in his pocket, I could see the bump moving, like a mole under the earth. "You know, shug," he went on in that dreamy voice, like when he first woke up, "I have believed some, and I've doubted more, but . . . I'm starting to see things clear now."

"What things?"

"You can't think your way to God, Short."

"What's that supposed to mean?"

He frowned then, started singing under this breath, testing the words, backing up to try them different ways. *"Farewell to Blackwell, where the tar waters, black waters, night waters flow . . ."*

"Let's go." I tried to walk off. But Harlan had fumbled the harp out of the box inside his pocket, and when he pulled his hand up into the sunlight, I about fainted. That Hohner harmonica gleamed like a brick from the streets of heaven. It looked like pure gold. I grabbed his arm. "Put that away!" I whispered, but I was too late. He already had it to his mouth. He blew the most glorious, wrenching, wonderful sound, one long crying note, and when the sound died, the street was still. Then everything happened at once.

The druggist man was coming fast out the Rexall door, calling, "Hey! Hey!" and the farmer across the road stopped with his feedsack on his back to gape at us, and then there were people everywhere, turning their faces to gawk, or coming toward us, and I only had an instant to meet the eyes of the snowy-headed drugstore man before Harlan grabbed my hand and we ducked down a side street.

We ran into an alley, in through the back door of a store that smelled of grain and sawdust and raw meat, and then back out when we heard somebody coming from the front, we darted between trucks and wagons, down another side street, into another alley, in and out, laughing, keeping our heads low, making for the highway, and it felt the same as a thousand times we'd run from any railyard bull, it felt like that first time playing hide'n'seek with Muskogee Fats, only this was different, because I'd seen the snowy man's eyes. He wasn't one of them. He might have been a merchant, but he was trying to behave decent. He'd thought we were like him. Filthy as we were, bedraggled and bloodspattered and useless-looking and homely, the man believed we were worth helping. He'd given Harlan that headache powder straight out for free, and we stole from him. I mean, that was what was in his eyes. His surprise.

It's one thing to steal from the likes of Oliver Teasley, or to take somebody's chicken lunch when you're hungry, but to filch that snowy man's harmonica and run away like Jack and the Beanstalk, laughing, when the man hadn't done a thing but try to help us, well, it was wrong. It was bad. I got scared, running, thinking for the first time that Harlan was different to what I'd ever believed. I kept seeing him in the pen with the rabbits, how he threw his head back and gobbled in his throat, and here I was joining in with him, running away from the snowy man, laughing, a laughing pair of thieves. I felt sick. Sick about Harlan. Sick of myself. But we had to keep running.

We ran along a street of houses, kept running until we reached the outskirts, and then we slowed down and walked fast. Harlan was limping pretty bad. The road played out at a fenceline a mile or so out of town. We sank down in the tall grasses at the side of the track, breathing hard. "When I told you we'd get you another," I said, panting, "I wasn't talking about that."

Harlan didn't say anything. He had the harp in his hand, turning it over and over. The gold on the sides bounced sunlight, I could hardly keep my eyes on it, the glint and shine was so bright.

"We oughta take it back, honey," I said. I stretched tall, trying to see if any cars had followed us, but I couldn't see anything, the weeds were too high. I didn't hear any motors though. "We'll wait till it gets dark," I whispered. "Then we'll walk back. You can put it in his mailbox or something."

Harlan was watching a grasshopper climb a spear of Indian grass, slowly, awkward with its crooked legs. There were hundreds of hoppers all over, eating the edges of the bluestem, flipping from the tips of the switchgrass like peas off a peashooter.

"We can get out to the highway before anybody sees us," I said. That one hopper reached the tip of the Indian grass, clung on a moment, took off buzzing, yellow-and-black wings spread. It flew a dozen yards and dropped, disappeared. "All right? Harlan?"

For answer he put the harp to his mouth and blew a sound that was a little like that grasshopper's wings. Then, in a moment, seemed like the sound wasn't just one hopper but a whole chorus, a prairieful, and then it was a million black-

and-yellow-winged grasshoppers, flying every direction. Harlan blew bird sound then. *Bob whi-ite. Bob whi-ite. Bob whi-ite.* A lone mama quail calling her lost chicks. He blew a high-sailing hawk crying its hunt cry, the quick scuttle of a field mouse, the barest whine of a dragonfly standing in the air. He blew a faint creaking thump, like a faraway pumpjack rocking its nose up and down. Harlan was making natural sound, the living world's actual sound, and then in just a minute, he turned that sound into music, but it wasn't a tune or a melody, it was a song, it told a story, about a hot, dry, windless afternoon, a summer prairie afternoon. That song seemed to say sitting in dry grass beside a fencepost in burning sunlight was the most precious thing on earth, too precious and sorrowful, hardly, for a human soul to bear. A feeling started to rise in me, lifting from my privates through my chest through the roof of my mouth. I felt like I could go winging across the prairie with those grasshoppers in joy and destruction. I felt I could call my lost babies forever, knowing every moment they would never come. I sat in the weeds with the tears running down, running down, until Harlan quit. Then it was just quiet, except for insects whining, a crow cawing somewhere.

After a time he leaned to one hip and pulled the Hohner box from his pocket, opened it, nested the harp on the red velvet. He sat with the lid open, gazing down.

"Reckon what something like that costs?" I said finally, because I knew already we weren't going to take it back.

He shook his head. "More than you and me's ever seen, I imagine."

"I 'magine," I said, but I was thinking about Oliver Teasley's bank money. We'd had our hands on that much one time, I couldn't think even a gold harmonica would be worth more than that. I looked up at the sky. Dark was still a ways off, but there were violet thunderheads boiling high in the west. I thought of something. "Harlan?" I said. "Can you blow that yonder? Those purple clouds up there?"

He raised his face that direction, was silent a moment, then he shook his head. "No, ma'am." He smiled, the new little chipped place in his tooth showed. "I could blow you a duster if you wanted."

"No thanks," I said. But I wasn't scared then. I didn't feel sick anymore. Harlan kept staring at the harmonica. The look on his face was so peaceful and still. I said, "How did you see that from all the way out on the sidewalk?"

"I didn't see it, shug. I felt it."

"How?"

"You just got to listen."

I pondered a minute. "I could listen till the end of Glory," I said, "if I didn't see it with my two eyes I'd never dream it was there."

He laughed, touched a fingertip to the gold side, left a little smudged place that faded in a bit after he lifted his finger away. "You know who taught me how to play one of these?"

"I reckon I thought you taught yourself."

"Oh, I did, mostly. Taught myself to make a tune. But it was a colored boy from Muskogee taught me how to *play*. A bootblack at the depot. He kept his shine box at the depot. Or he did till we went on the road. His name was Willie Jones. That's funny, innit?"

"Why?"

"Aw," he said. "It just is. He was a few years older than me and way littler than me. Willie Jay Jefferson Jones. Man alive, that boy could play. Taught me guitar, too. He carried an old six-string, we slung that guitar from car to car all the way to California." Harlan sat looking straight ahead, but there wasn't anything to look at, only the tall grasses. "They killed him in California," he said. "Right outside Modesto. Killed him for that guitar and a good pair of shoes. Or maybe that's why they killed him. They took them anyway, his guitar and shoes. Took his harmonica, too. Left him with his eyes open, flies on him, his face smashed to pulp."

"The bulls killed him?"

"Naw, shug," he said, and drew quiet again.

"Who then?"

"I don't know," he said, sort of absentminded. I waited. After a while he said, "I'd gone to town to scrounge food. When I come back and found him, I didn't know what to do. I just walked off and left him in the weeds at the side of the track." A shudder passed through him, like in the boxcar that awful night. I was afraid he might have another spell, but he just went on talking. "I was twelve or thirteen then. Thereabouts. I used to wonder if they would've killed me too. If I'd been there. But then, I couldn't have been there, could I? Because it's all a pattern, innit? Like fence shadows across a field at sunset, or like blackjacks scrawled across a hill. Cobwebs in dew at daylight. Like frost. One huge ordered pattern, beautiful. Absolute." He looked at me. "See? Can you see what I mean?"

"I don't know."

"Or it's not exactly a pattern," he said, "because there's sound in it too. It's more like . . . an orchestra painting. How it all goes together so perfect. It couldn't be an accident that I'd went into Modesto that morning. I used to think it was. I thought you could make a choice and do something, by accident or on purpose, and change how the story goes. Now, though, I don't think so. Or maybe you can, but then you're going to change everything, not just the little part you wanted but the whole story, the whole . . . everything. But then," he said softly, "when you look backward, seems like it all had to go the way it went. Don't it? Don't it seem like I had to be in Modesto that morning? So I could come walking out the road from Cookson years later and see you standing in your daddy's yard?"

"I don't know, honey," I said. "Seems to me like life just is what it is."

"I was supposed to pay him. We had a deal between us. He wanted to see California. He felt like traveling with a white boy would protect him. I told him according to the folks in Sallisaw I wasn't all that white myself, but he said I was white enough to suit him. He kept his part. He gave me the music. But I was gone to Modesto when they killed him. I came back empty-handed. Not that Willie Jay could have eaten anyway. He'd been dead so long the blood on his face was starting to set."

"You couldn't help that, Harlan. How were you going to keep something like that from happening?"

"Maybe so. But I still owe." He was quiet a minute, looking straight on at me. "I never paid your family for taking you away either," he said.

I didn't know what to say to that. A low grumble of thunder rolled in the distance, and I turned my eyes west. The bank of clouds was rolling higher, towering toward heaven, I could see the heat lightning flickering inside them. I didn't have much hope for rain from them though. If there was any, it'd likely be those few scattered plops racing through, puffing up dust like a bunch of doodlebugs doodling, just enough to make the earth smell good, make you long for a downpour, and then the clouds would pass on.

"Calm had him a dog once named Heat Lightning," Harlan said, looking up. He started to untie the bandanna from his throat. "That was a long time ago, back when he used to talk English." He leaned toward me with the bandanna, wiped the sweat off my face.

"Calm Bledsoe speaks English?"

"Not any more." Harlan wiped his own face. "Ol' Heat Lightning and Blue Streak. They were good tree dogs. Bad to run deer, though." He squinted west, where the clouds now were blocking the sun. "After Willie got killed," he said, "I run back to Oklahoma. I rode by myself. I wouldn't hook up with anybody. Went back to the hills, back to Nokiller. I don't know what would've happened if Calm hadn't found me. Oh, I do too know. I'd have died if he hadn't come along. I *was* dying. I didn't care anymore." Harlan sat quiet a long time then. "I tried to pay him," he murmured, "but that wasn't no way to do it." He raised his eyes to meet me, they were the same color as the sage grasses dying in the summer heat all around. "I don't want to lose it again."

"You won't lose this one," I said and touched his shoulder. "I told you. We're through hopping freights."

"Not this," he said, lifting the Hohner box. "That...sound. When I was a boy I could hear it any time I wanted. But it quit me. You remember? On the banks of the river. I thought I lost it on account of sin, but that wasn't it. Or not the kind I thought."

"Reckon we ought to head out now?" I said. I didn't want him getting off on that kind of talk.

"I run off from the Letbetters, I quit Profit. Walked away without a word of thanks, nothing. But when you been given a gift you got to return it. The old ones will tell you. If you don't pay it back you're bound to lose it again." He sat staring down. "Things go how they're supposed to go, Sharon. There's a reason why we suffer."

I got to my feet in a hurry. "C'mon, babe, let's go."

Harlan kept gazing at the harp in its nest of red velvet. All at once he snapped the lid closed, stood and crammed the box in his pocket, and we started walking back along the dirt track.

I'd thought we would head to the highway, but Harlan insisted on toting that packet of BC powder back to town. We watched from an alley while the snowy man closed up his store for the evening, and then Harlan went and slid the packet under the door. He stood a minute, looking around. I tried to get him to come on, he had that filched harp right in his pocket, I was scared we'd get arrested. "It's all right, babe," he said, his hand cupped over his pocket. "We'll be back to Blackwell one of these days. We'll come pay the man."

"Will we?"

"We will."

Harlan eased the sack of turnips out of my hand then and set it on the sidewalk in front of door. After that we got us a long drink at the town spigot and walked on out to the highway. Before we'd cleared the edge of town Harlan had the harp out, making music. People were driving by, I wanted to tell him to put it away, but the sound was so pretty I couldn't get myself to say it. That stolen harp just had the sweetest, purest sound.

We walked south, the blacktop was tacky as chewing gum, but the sun was low then, slanting sideways from underneath the western clouds, and the prairie light was shining on everything. That beautiful godlight. Meadowlarks called across the fields, there were scissortails perched on the wire fence along the side of the road. Harlan's song sounded like that, like the meadowlarks and the godlight and the flycatchers on the wire with their pale heads and pinkish bellies and perfect long black-and-white tails scissored down. They'd flutter up and soar away when we got close. The shadows stretched long across the blacktop, the rolling sweep of land. The fenceposts made a perfect straight pattern in front of us all the way to the horizon. We walked until a farmer with a load of hay stopped for us right at first dark.

deepsong

the singer remembers
 sin.
 the sins he'd never paid for
 not theft only, but deceit. how he'd lied to her. both in the telling
and in the not-telling, because he'd said he was gone to modesto to
hunt food when they killed willie, when in truth what he'd done was
run.
 run and hide, boy, hide and run
 and yes, he'd come back hours later and found willie dead with his
eyes open, head smashed, the purplish blood turned to jelly, and yes,
he'd left willie jones by the side of the tracks and come home, riding
alone, curled in a boxcar, but the lie was about why.
 because he had watched when the other bums turned on willie, for
the sake of a lie, for the sake of someone else's transgression. watched
as they snatched him from the ground and began to beat him, saying
nigger, saying *thief*, saying *sonuvabitching coon*. watched, moving
backwards away from them, to the edge of the camp, watched the many
fisted hands, the glazed eyes, not willie's eyes, but the eyes of the men
raining their rage on him, their darkness, their sin.
 watched in silence from the protection of his mother's skin,
 walking backwards,
 till he could reach the water ditch
 and run.

 run.
 the old man's voice, years later, yelling
 run, boy!
 and that had been on a morning in fayetteville, the two of them on
a street corner, the singer playing harp to draw the crowd, and profit
balanced on a milk crate preaching his whited-sepulcher sermon, his
don't-store-up-treasures-on-earth sermon, his love-of-money-is-the-
root-of-all-evil sermon, saying they were all the same thing, greed and

pride, hypocrisy and fear, all cut from the same sin. the sin of no faith. the sin of nonbelief. thus preached the old man who called himself profit, and singer next to him, making up hymns on his tin harmonica, his soft cap turned upside down on the sidewalk before him, to receive coins.

hide!

when the crowd of men came, and the sheriff and the deputy with them, saying we'll not have this blasphemous goddamn socialist wobbly talk in our town, and profit said, *lay not up for yourself treasures on earth where moth and rust doth corrupt,* and the men at the front hollered, *bring up the tar bucket!* and brandished a fat feather-stuffed feedsack and an iron rail, and the sheriff moved to wrestle profit from the crate, then the old man cried out, *run and hide, boy, hide and run!*

and the singer did run, darting into an alley, quick as heat lightning, running fast, both legs good then. and he did hide, secreting himself in an abandoned outhouse behind a brick school until he could steal enough clothes from a clothesline to change.

remembers how long it took to find profit, down along the river among the reeds, stumbling upon him finally, moaning, half out of his head, and the old man yelped when singer tried to pluck off the feathers, how it took two days to steal enough gasoline to take the tar off, three days more to clean it, the old man spouting scripture the whole time, preaching to singer alone on the riverbank, *it's all in matthew, son! every blessed thing he come to tell us! check my figures if you don't believe me, the master said to consider the lilies of the field!* ranting, still out of his head, until singer yelled in his ear, *shut up, shut up, for godsakes, old man, can't you never shut up!*

but that wasn't when they'd parted,

that came a year later, in the campyard in tulsa,

that was another lie,

another lie he'd told sharon,

because it was not singer who'd quit profit, but profit who'd quit him.

Sharon

I felt like we were taking *such* a long time to get to Cookson, and the longer it took the bigger rush I was in. Rides were getting harder and harder to come by. Some days we'd stand at the side of the road all afternoon. Harlan's hair was grown out good, but that didn't hide the fact we hadn't had a bath in a long time, or washed our clothes, and see, that's a big difference between hitching and riding the rails. Hitchhiking, you've got to depend on what people think of you, or else on the decency of their hearts, whereas, hopping freights, you just need to be good enough at it that you're not going to fall under the wheels and get run over. Well, and know how to stay out of the way of the bulls.

We got stuck outside Sapulpa for eight hours one day, right out in the hot sun on the Will Rogers Highway, trying to go east on Route 66. Harlan played his harp, and the sound made the time pass, but it still couldn't calm the hurry I felt. I waggled my thumb at every car passing, nobody would stop. I was about ready to give up and say let's walk to the freight yard. I was feeling that desperate. Then along towards evening a Negro preacher in a Ford car stopped for us. He carried us into town and up to the top of a hill and let us out in front of his church. If I didn't see the painted sign out front that said SHINING LIGHT TABERNACLE HOUSE OF THE LORD, I wouldn't have known it was a church. There wasn't any steeple, just a bell hanging between two posts beside the sign. The outside walls needed painting, the porch roof sagged. The man said, "Y'all go on in and get cool, I'll be back in a minute." And he drove over to the house next door and parked in the yard and went in.

So me and Harlan sat inside the church on one of the hard benches, but it wasn't a bit cooler in there, so we went back outside and sat on the edge of the porch till the preacher came walking across the yard with some slabs of saltpork between cold larded biscuits. I had to stop myself from snatching one out of the man's hand. I wolfed it down, oh my word, it tasted like a feast.

"This is mighty kind of you, mister," Harlan said.

"My wife'll send supper when it gets ready," the preacher said. He looked uncomfortable, standing back from the porch in his dark suit, his forehead shining in the heat. Harlan took another bite of biscuit, set it down next to his other one on the bare porch boards, and picked up his harp. My two biscuits were gone already. Harlan began to play a hymn, "The Old Rugged Cross," and it wasn't long till the preacher quit looking uncomfortable, standing there quiet with his lips pursed, nodding, though he still didn't come up on the porch with us to get out of the sun. Two little black kids came out of a house across the street. They ran to a tire swing in the yard and one boy scrambled bellydown through the opening, the other climbed on top and stood with his hand on the rope while the tire went round in a slow circle, and the boys kept turning their heads as the tire turned, watching Harlan. I could just make out a woman standing inside the screen door. Then I spied another Negro woman looking at us, holding her clothesbasket real still in the backyard one house over. The preacher had his eyes closed, listening like he was praying, and it reminded me of my daddy, how he'd sit at the table when Harlan played his hymns back in Cookson, and I felt like I wanted to jump up and go right then, but I just kept sitting. Pretty soon the preacher's wife came out of their house and stood on their porch, listening. Everybody within earshot was listening, I guess. That sweltery evening in Sapulpa was the first time Harlan played his gold harp for anybody, or it's the first I remember, but you know something? That harp wasn't even gold really. Or not true gold. Gold don't tarnish, does it? Already the side-plates were dull as pewter from Harlan's fingers, and in another week's time they were smudged down even duller than that. But I tell you the truth: no matter how tarnished that harp got, it never lost its pure sound.

Harlan finished then, and the preacher murmured, still nodding, "Yes sir, that is sure right." Then he said, "Y'all are welcome to stay the night in the sanctuary here."

"Sanctuary," Harlan repeated, like that was the sweetest word in the world.

And we did stay the night in that church, on the wood floor with the windows open, and it was hot, and there were mosquitoes because the windows didn't have any screens on them, but it was still better than laying by the side of the road like we'd been doing, and anyhow, I was glad to be clean. The preacher's wife, when she brought us beans and cornbread and green onions for supper, I guess she got a good whiff of us, because she went back to their house and got a basin and a bucket of water, a bar of soap and a hairbrush and a washrag, and some clean clothes. We cleaned up right there in the sanctuary, which, that was a fairly strange sensation, taking a basin bath inside a dark empty church. The dungarees she'd brought for Harlan had patches all over them, and the cotton dress she brought me was so worn from laundering it was soft as mullein, but they were clean, and we were clean, and my belly was full. That felt like a miracle. The woman had put a hamhock in the portion of beans she brought for us. We'd even had sorghum to go with the cornbread for dessert.

Me and Harlan loved together that night for the first time in a long time—since from way before he got hurt. I had a self-conscious feeling about that too, but I told myself that since it was a Negro church maybe it wouldn't count the same way. I just didn't want to think loving with my husband could be wrong, even in the House of the Lord. I curled over on my side afterwards. My hip and shoulder ached from the wood floor. I kept seeing my daddy in the pulpit—not how he was the last time I'd seen him, how he was when I was a little girl. Thundery. Full of the passion of the spirit, the fear of the Lord. I kept thinking if he saw how me and Harlan were living he'd say I'd forgotten to live in fear and admonition of the Lord. I did fear Him though, when I thought about Him, which I tried not to do too much. But there inside that church I couldn't help it. I whispered to Harlan, "My daddy preached security of the believer. No matter how a person's been living. I don't know if all Free Wills believe in it, but Daddy did. Do you think it's true?"

"There's no security, darlin'. No place on earth."

"Well, but it's not for here, it's for the Hereafter. Once saved always saved. Don't you know what it means?"

He was quiet a long time, his breathing slow and regular. I thought he'd fallen asleep, but after a really long time I heard his voice in the dark. "'For I was an hungered,'" he quoted softly, "'and ye gave me meat. I was thirsty, and ye gave me drink. A stranger and ye took me in. Naked and ye clothed me.' That's what salvation is."

"Salvation's by faith not by works, Harlan. The Bible says so. I could show you if—"

I stopped, my heart beating fast. I'd just suddenly remembered my Bible inside the traveling bindle under my bed at home, the small white Holy Bible Mama and Daddy gave me for my twelfth birthday. I hadn't thought of it since the morning me and Harlan left, not even when we went back and walked through the empty house. In my mind I could see Mama turning the mattress for spring cleaning and finding that dusty floursack on the floor. I could see her opening it, pulling out my skirt and blouse wrapped around the square shape, opening that and finding the twenty-eight cents I'd made from swiping her eggs and selling them in town. Oh, it made me feel sick with guilt. I squeezed tight against Harlan, his voice went on quiet, murmuring, his lips pressed against the top of my head. "'. . . I was sick and ye visited me . . . in prison and ye came unto me . . .'" I wanted him to hush, but I was too trembling inside my heart to speak, too scared.

Harlan was outside talking to the preacher when I woke up. It was just barely daylight. I heard their voices through the open window, I scrambled to my feet and went out there. Harlan turned to me. "Morning, babydoll!" He looked more like himself in patched dungarees and a white shirt than he ever did in those ugly overalls. His eyes were fresh. He had the blue bandanna tied at his throat. "Me and Reverend Perry was just fixing to engage in a word of prayer before breakfast," he said. "You hungry?"

I gave him a careful look. I didn't want him mocking prayer in front of a preacher, but then I could see he wasn't doing that. He had a light look to him, but he wasn't making fun. The preacher carried a basket up to the porch and unpacked it. He didn't have on a suit like yesterday but khaki workclothes. He prayed over the biscuits and gravy, prayed the Lord to guide us and keep us, prayed the Lord's blessings upon our journey, and Harlan said amen. The preacher left then, he said he had to get to work. The red-eye gravy in the bowl was starting to set already, but the coffee was still warm.

When we got ready to go, Harlan folded our filthy clothes and laid them on a bench in front of the pulpit. He stood a minute, gazing down, then he raised his head and looked all around the church, frowning, his palm over the Hohner box sticking out of his shirt pocket. "Reckon that'll have to do," he said.

"Do for what?"

Harlan didn't answer, but I knew anyhow. He meant it for the same reason he'd set the sack of turnips in front of the Blackwell Drugstore, same way he'd always leave his old hat behind whenever he filched himself a new one. I thought to myself, Who's going to want such a nasty pile of washing? That's no pay if you ask me. I didn't say anything though.

I guess the preacher's prayer worked pretty good anyway, because our rides sure got easier to come by, and in another two days' time me and Harlan were walking east over the Illinois River across the Standing Rock bridge.

The first thing I thought was how strange it was that Cookson looked so much the same, like nothing had changed, when so much had, really. Daddy's church didn't appear changed on the outside, except it wasn't Free Will anymore. The sign in front said Cookson Missionary Baptist. There was nobody inside, of course, the day was a weekday. Nobody on the street either, but I could see Stratton's store was open. "I guess I'll start at the store," I said.

"Whatever you want, sweetheart."

I made to cross the street, but he didn't come with me. I turned and looked at him. There was something, I don't know, hesitant or unwilling in his face, but I couldn't read it, and anyhow I had my mind on my purpose. "You coming?" I said. He stuck his hands in his pockets and came on. The little bell jangling over the door was so familiar I got a real hopeful feeling, but behind the counter stood a big blond girl I'd never laid eyes on before. I looked at Harlan, but he had his head tilted back, he was squinting at the tins of deviled ham on the shelf by the door. "Where's Mr. Stratton?" I asked her.

"Oh, him and Aunt Vera went to Broken Bow yesterday," the girl said. "Their daughter's real sick down there."

"Who are you?"

"Edie Squires."

Squires, I thought. I don't know any people named Squires. "When are they coming back?"

The girl shrugged. "I'm just supposed to take care of things till I hear." She nodded at the telephone on the wall. "Either close the store and come on, or they'll be back in a few days. But I hadn't heard anything."

"Do you know Marie Tingle?" I said.

"No, ma'am."

"She's redheaded, lives down by Snake Creek. Rides an old white dray mare."

"No, ma'am," the girl repeated. "I'm sorry."

"Well, do you know the Caspers?" I said.

She shook her head. I could tell I was scaring her.

Harlan came up behind me, I heard the little whisper of the harp being slid out of his front pocket. "Fixing to be another hot one, innit?" he said, very casual. "*Whoo*-ee. Folks need some relief." The girl didn't say anything. Her eyes were real big. Harlan started to play a light airy tune then, feathery, joyful, and at first the girl bit her lip, frowning, and glanced at the door. But here in minute I watched her face smooth out, getting easy, and then she was smiling. "That's 'Gather Up the Money'!" she said when Harlan finished. "My grampa used to play that tune on his fiddle! We used to jig-dance to that tune right here in this store."

"Is that right," Harlan said.

The girl nodded. "When I was a real little girl. We used to drive the wagon over from Barber of a Saturday evening. Aunt Vera's my ma's sister. But they turned Baptist, Ma and Aunt Vera both, and they wouldn't let him play for dances anymore. But I sure remember that song. Grampa played it fast as anything. Folks couldn't even move their feet as fast as he jumped that bow!" She was smiling broad now. In my mind I could hear my daddy preaching against the sinful Saturday night dances going on right in our own community, right in Stratton's store. Oh, that seemed like such a long time ago.

Harlan said, "Tell me something, how come it's so ghostlike in town here? There's not even any dogs laying around in the shade."

"I can't really say, mister. Maybe it's the heat? My brother just drove me over from Barber yesterday morning."

"Well," Harlan said, and he ran a little trill up and down the harmonica. Its sides were dull as pudding in the grayish store light.

"Might be on account of all the talk," the girl said. "They say they're fixing to flood the river." She leaned on the counter. "Supposedly they want to build a dam down at Gore or Blackgum or someplace and stop the river, back it up all the way to Pettit, and if they do that, well, Cookson'll be under the water."

"Who wants to do that?" I said.

"I don't know. The government? Uncle Bud says maybe they're going to do it, and maybe it's just talk. He says even so it'll take years and years, he's not worried. But there hadn't been a single customer in here all morning, so I don't know."

"Well now," Harlan said. "Much obliged for the information." He turned to leave, but to my mind we didn't *have* any information, nothing to go on, and I said—I know I sounded mad but I couldn't help it—I said, "Don't tell me you don't remember the Thompsons. Brother Earl Thompson, lived out east of town on the old Casper place?"

The girl said, "Ma'am, I'm from Barber."

"Daddy preached at Barber! He preached all over these hills!"

The girl looked to Harlan for help, and he said, "C'mon, Sis, let's go. I expect somebody at the school will know something." I let him take my arm and lead me to the door, and just as he reached over me to open the screen, the girl said, very soft, like she was half scared to mention it, "Y'all know the school's closed."

I whirled around, I felt so mad, like she was doing it on purpose. "For good? When did that happen?"

"No, ma'am. Just, you know, till the end of the month."

"What month?"

She shut her lips tight, glanced at Harlan. "This month," she said. "August." She gestured at a feedstore calendar tacked on the wall.

August, I thought. It's August already. I couldn't imagine how so much time had got past. I remembered shivering with cold on top of that reefer in Texas, but seemed like that was just a few weeks ago. I mean, I knew the weather was hot, but it was hot so much of the time, that didn't seem to say anything. I just couldn't fathom that summer was almost gone. We went on out and I stared at the empty street. Where was I going I find somebody to ask? The Garrisons and Seliys weren't here, I knew that from two years ago. I tried to remember names of people. Mrs. Lambert! I thought suddenly. The grammar school teacher.

"Come on, Harlan," I said, and started walking. She lived in a rock house at the south end of town, I knew right where it was. I went straight up on the porch and knocked, Mrs. Lambert came to the door with flour on her hands. She was wearing a house dress and a full apron. Her hair looked combed and perfect, all silver white under a light hairnet.

"Why, Sharon Thompson!" she cried. "What in the world are you doing? Come in, come in here, my goodness gracious." She pushed the screen open with her elbow, her floured fists in the air. "How are your folks, dear? Oh, we miss your daddy's preaching, we surely do. Let me go wash my hands." And she went back to the kitchen, and me and Harlan stood just inside the door.

"She knew me right off," I whispered.

"Well, why wouldn't she?" he said.

I couldn't explain why it didn't seem like anybody would know me, or why I felt so grateful to Mrs. Lambert because she did. She came back drying her hands on a tea towel. "Have a seat, dear. I'll put the coffee on." She looked at Harlan.

"We can't stay, ma'am," I said. "We just . . . " Mrs. Lambert was glancing back and forth between me and Harlan. "Oh, this is my husband, ma'am. Harlan. We're on our way . . . " And I stopped again. On our way where? We'd been on our way to Cookson for ages, since Pampa anyway. Now we were here. I couldn't think how to say what I wanted to say next, so when Harlan stepped on in the room and took a seat on the sofa, I followed and sat next to him, and when he started to visit with Mrs. Lambert sitting across from us in a big chair that had crocheted doilies pinned to the arms, I just let him, because my words were clogged in my throat.

The two of them talked about the weather, the news about the dam, a farm program or a relief program, something. Harlan was trying to make her feel easy, I think now, only I couldn't imagine Mrs. Lambert feeling uncomfortable around anybody ever in her life. I'd gone to school to her from the fourth grade through the eighth grade. I always liked her, Mrs. Lambert, she was good to me. She was good to all of us. I just suddenly thought about the time she let me and Clara Fay Jordan out of class to help the town ladies trim the tree for the Christmas party. We held the ladder while one of the ladies draped strung popcorn and berries around the top.

"Do you ever hear from Clara Fay Jordan?" I said.

"Why—no." Mrs. Lambert seemed surprised. "I haven't heard from any of the Jordans," she said.

"How about Lydia Seliy?"

Mrs. Lambert shook her head. "Most of the ones that left when that awful thing happened, well, we haven't heard any news."

"What awful thing?" I said.

"Oh, you remember, when the bank had to foreclose on so many. That was a terrible time. Just sliced the heart out of this community. To my mind that's what set the stage for this notion about flooding the river."

I said, "He didn't *have* to."

"What's that?"

"Oliver Teasley didn't *have* to do that. He just wanted to."

"Well," Mrs. Lambert said. "But what about your folks, dear? Where's your daddy pastoring now?"

I cut my eyes at Harlan. He said, "To tell you the truth, ma'am, we were hoping you might could tell us."

Mrs. Lambert frowned. She gazed at me a minute, and then she said softly, "Oh, well, no. I'm afraid not."

"What about Mr. Casper?" I said. "Do you know where the Caspers went?"

"Seems like I heard they're in Alabama. I believe Evelyn's family came from down in there."

"Who would know where my mama and daddy moved to? We tried the store already but that girl don't know when Mr. Stratton'll be back."

"No. Their daughter's really ill, isn't she? Bright's disease I heard. But I don't know that Mr. Stratton would have any idea about your folks, Sharon. I believe he'd have mentioned it to me if he did. He knew how much I thought of your father."

"Who would then? Somebody's got to know where they went!"

Mrs. Lambert was watching me so steady. I couldn't meet her eyes but I felt them, blue and quiet, I was afraid I'd start crying. I jumped up and went to the door.

"Thanks a lot, ma'am. Nice to see you. It was really nice seeing you again. Come on, Harlan." But he didn't stand to follow me, and when I looked across the room, he had his harp out. "Come *on,* Harlan. Let's *go.*" I felt such a panic, I don't know why, I just—I felt I was losing control, that I was going to do like I did with the lady in Goodwell, confess everything me and Harlan had been doing for three years, and I knew it wasn't *bad,* except for robbing the Vardis bank, but it wasn't right either. It wasn't how normal people are supposed to live. Harlan put his harp to his mouth. I shouted, "Stop!" He held it there, looking at me. "That don't work on me," I said, staring straight at him. "You can't joke me or music me or sing me to quit caring. There's not a thing in the world you can do to help it. So just stop."

Very slowly Harlan lowered his hands. He reached in his shirt pocket for the Hohner box and snapped it open, laid the harp inside. The parlor got so awkward and silent. Mrs. Lambert cleared her throat, she was standing next to her chair then, she said, "Sharon, you all stay to supper, dear. There's plenty. I'll think on it some more, see if I can't come up with somebody who might—" She paused, shook her head. She wasn't going to think of anybody who knew where my family went, and she knew it, and I knew it. Harlan sat gazing up at me, his eyes telling me he was sorry but he knew it too. He'd known it all along. He stood up, said, "Thanks anyway, ma'am, but we'd best be going. We got a long ways to travel before dark."

"Oh? Where are you headed?" she said, and Harlan said, "Sallisaw," and Mrs. Lambert said, "My word. You won't get *there* before dark." Harlan said, "No, but we'll get as far as we can."

I shoved open the screen and walked out on the porch. I'm not making excuses for myself, I know it was rude as anything, but in my wrought-up feelings I just let that screen door slam. I stood on the porch and stared at Cookson. In a minute I heard the screen open, I felt Harlan's hand on my shoulder, but I shook him off. I stared at the school, far down the street, thinking about those big community Christmas parties we used to have there, how folks would come from miles up and down the river, and each of us kids would get a paper sack with an apple and an orange and some nuts and a handful of hard Christmas candy. I stared at Stratton's store, seemed like I could almost smell the rubbery red sawdust Mr. Stratton sprinkled on the floor beneath the butcher block to soak up the blood. I hadn't smelled that smell in such a long time, not even just now when we went in there. What I'd smelled then was tin and kerosene and humid heat. I turned my eyes to Daddy's church. That memory was smell too. Mama's laundry soap and the starch in her dress, the twins' sweaty outdoor smell where they squirmed next to me, all of us trying to sit still through one of Daddy's long hellfire sermons, trying to stay out of the way of Mama's pinch. I didn't get saved at the church in Cookson, I didn't get baptized there, but I'd rededicated my life at that altar three times. I felt a grief welling up in me so terrible it was almost like I knew the town was going to one day vanish forever, be drowned under the river. But of course that wasn't what it was. I didn't have any inkling. I can't say how it would have been if I could have known, but I don't believe the hurt could have sunk in me any worse. Harlan was beside me, I could hear him breathing, feel the heat of him.

"Reckon we ought to go then?" he said.

"Go where?" I said, my voice dead. I'd already forgot what he'd told Mrs. Lambert.

"Well," he said softly, "it's no point in staying here."

I stepped off the porch, and he came down and touched my arm, and we started walking, but before we reached the gravel road I stopped.

"This road goes to Vardis."

"It goes through there," he said.

"I'm not going to Vardis."

"All right," he said, and we turned and walked back to town. But when we reached the school, Harlan tried to turn east on the dirt lane past our house. I stopped again. "No. I'm not going by there."

"The only other road out of town is north, shug, that's way out of our way."

"Out of our way to where?"

"Sallisaw."

"What are we going to Sallisaw for?"

"Just . . . I don't know, darlin'. Seems like that's right."

"Oh, I don't care," I said, and I didn't. I felt like it didn't matter anymore where we went or what we did, because everything was gone past, my family gone and no hope to find them, no hope now, because the world was too damn big. Too big.

deepsong

the town lies beneath the waters now, catfish and crappie swim through
the rock-framed door, the empty churchhouse windows. the town is
drowned with the canyons, the rotted oak and soft blackgum beneath
tenkiller's waters. but in the silence on the bed of stones beside the creek he
calls nokiller, the singer remembers

the river flowing thick and slow around the bend below cookson,
how they'd stood on the rock porch as he watched the long truth settle
in her. how he'd reached to touch her and she would not receive it but
stepped off the porch and walked away.

how his chest tightened, the fear cold, and he'd hurried to catch up
to her, touching her again, turning her south toward sallisaw, because
the pull was strong in him to return the gift if he could find his way to
it, so they could go on.

no. not true. another lie he'd told himself.

so *he* could go on.

to be free to hear the sound again, to play the sound again, to
surrender.

how she'd balked, would not walk south on the gravel road, and so
they had left cookson traveling north, the wrong direction,

how, when the first ride stopped, sharon climbed wordless into the
cramped car and turned to look back, her eyes on the church.

Sharon

We ended up traveling nearly twenty miles north to Tahlequah and all the way around by Stillwell to get to Sallisaw, it took us three or four days, but Harlan was just cheerful the whole time. He played for every ride that stopped, and sometimes folks would carry us miles out of their way just to hear him play a little longer. He had a new kind of look to him ever since we'd stayed at that church in Sapulpa, and the sound from his harp was faster and wilder and sweeter than anything I'd ever heard. After we left Cookson seemed to me like Harlan's face grew even lighter, or his eyes did, his spirit, and the lighter Harlan got, the duller I felt. I had this notion my insides were the same as the plate outsides of that brass harp, getting duller each day from all his handling.

In Sallisaw Harlan walked directly to a yellow house beside a church, a nice house with a porch and flowers, but he didn't go up to the front. He strolled around back and I followed. He stood a minute, looking from the house to a toolshed or smokehouse or whatever it was, a little scrappy building back there, and in a minute he took the Hohner box out of his shirt pocket and set it on the back steps of the house.

"What are you doing?"

"Shhh," he said, and turned, and we went out front and walked along the side of the road away from town.

"What was that for?" I said.

"For a lot of things," he said. "Mostly learning me to read."

So then I knew whose house it was. "What do you aim to do," I said, "steal you another?" Because naturally I thought he'd left the harp, but when we got to the outskirts of town he pulled it from his pants pocket and started playing, and I thought to myself, Well, that's about like him, leave somebody an empty box. What good does he think that's going to do? Then I thought, Maybe he's trying to send them a message, those Letbetter people, though I couldn't see what it might be.

Something else came to me then, walking along the road south of Sallisaw, a thought so ugly I don't like to remember, but I do remember. My mind said: He might think he's paying things back, but he hasn't paid me for taking away my family, and he could never pay for it, there's not enough empty harp boxes and dirty clothes, not enough songs or sounds or loving in this world.

Oh, it scared me, thinking that, and I hurried to catch up to him where he was strolling ahead of me, blowing his harp in the dry August heat. I hooked a finger through his empty belt-loop, walking beside him, holding on.

But once you think a thing, sometimes, it's hard to un-think it. And so the idea stayed with me, not the words exactly, but the feeling that Harlan owed me, that he ought to be trying to make up for it—not just that he should have given my mama and daddy something for taking me, but that he had never yet given me anything in place of them.

Maybe that's why I started feeling mean toward the people Harlan took up with. Well, not mean, exactly, or I hope not, but just, I don't know . . . jealous, I guess. We'd catch a ride in a car or a wagon, in no time he'd have the people clapping and singing. I'd sit in silence with my arms closed over my chest. We'd be at a house or a campyard and he'd go to making up words, patting his foot to keep the rhythm, his harp in his hand and the words ringing, the people laughing, I'd walk off and stay gone as long as I could. Half the time when I came back he didn't act like he'd even noticed I was missing. I felt like he cared more about strangers than he did me, and on top of that, seemed to me like he always hunted up the most hangdog-looking people in the world to play for. I asked him one time, I said, "How come every sorry old wino and blabbermouth shoe salesman we run into means more to you than I do?"

"Oh, darlin'," he said. "You know that's not true."

We were standing at the side of the road under a bo'dark tree east of Stigler, waiting for a ride. This would have been late August, I guess, or early September, because there were dozens of yellow-green horseapples tumbled around on the ground. Harlan leaned down and picked one up. Osage oranges, some people call them, but they're bigger than any orange you ever saw. Their skin is all mottled and squiggly, they're that bright lime green color, and hard as a club. I guess maybe horses will eat them but otherwise they're pretty much useless.

"You act like the very scum of the earth's your best friend," I said.

"Aw, sweetheart."

"You do."

"Most folks are doing the best they can. Before I had that accident in Texas—"

"It wasn't no *accident*, Harlan. That bull half killed you and he did it on *purpose*, and you haven't never been the same since."

"I'm just saying . . . " He stared at the horseapple like there was secret writing all over its wormy skin. "I come away from that beating, I'd had this dream. But I don't think it was a dream really. I think it was real. I seen all these people, hundreds of 'em, thousands, gathered in bunches as far as I could see.

It was folks like your folks. Common everyday people. They were waiting for something." His voice dropped. "I believe they were waiting for me. But I wasn't finished yet. Listen. Sharon. I've got a job to do."

"I wish that was true," I said. "I wisht you had a real job, earning some real money, we could get ourselves something decent to eat."

"I went down there," he said, his voice soft, "I was so full of rage. Rage and hate, that's a terrible thing. You don't want to live in 'em and you sure don't want to die in 'em. But what I seen . . . what I know now . . . people can't help how they are. They can't help what happens."

"That bull couldn't help beating the living tar out of you? Oliver Teasley couldn't *help* stealing people's homes?"

"Oh, babe. Most folks spend their whole lives on their knees, they don't even know it. They're just lost, they're feeble. We all are. Like that kid riding alone."

"What kid?"

And Harlan didn't say, but anyhow I remembered the blond kid in the railcar thundering towards Kansas City all those years ago.

"That's just exactly what I mean," I said, my teeth gritted. "You get yourself worked up about some strange kid in a boxcar, meanwhile you drag your wife around all over the blame country, you, you—oh, never mind. Forget it." Because it just felt to me useless. If Harlan couldn't see the difference, there wasn't any point in me trying to say it again. "Look yonder," I said. "I think I see a car coming." I started to walk toward it, but I could feel he wasn't coming behind me. I turned around. Harlan's face was sallow in the shade of the bo'dark.

"Things go how they're supposed to go, Sharon."

"Quit saying that."

"I had to take that beating."

"Hush!" I said. "Don't talk crazy."

"Not crazy," he whispered. We stood looking at each other. The locusts whined in the oak trees. I heard the car's motor coming nearer. Harlan held the horseapple out to me like a present.

"What do you expect me to do with that?" I said.

"Nothing," he said, and let it fall to the ground.

A drummer in an old Chevy stopped to pick us up then, and Harlan played him tune after tune for hours until the man pulled to the side of the road in a burnt-looking valley at almost sunset and let us out beside a bunch of dried-up cottonfields. Way off in the distance I could see a tiny gray sharecropper's shack, and beyond that a low ridge of blue mountains just barely showing in the south. Otherwise there was just nothing. I was furious. We'd passed right through the town of Bokoshe, where we could have got out and walked around and found a bite to eat, except Harlan was playing "Turkey in the Straw" for that salesman, and he'd let him drive straight through town and miles past it, and then leave us off in that empty cotton land when he turned onto a dirt lane heading north. I was tired, I was hungry and thirsty, most of all I was fed up. Just sick to death of *going*. I wanted to be still somewhere for a while and just sit. And that's what I did. I sat down in the road. I told him I didn't aim to get up before morning or a car came through and ran me over.

"Come on now, babe," he said. "There's a houseplace yonder. See it? They'll feed us. They'll let us stay the night."

"You go any damn where you want to," I said. "I'm not walking another step."

He tried and tried to coax me, but I sat with my legs crossed under me and my mouth clamped tight as a latch. Harlan's face had a look, well, it was just sort of desperate really, but I wasn't budging. I don't know what I expected him to do, but what he did, finally, was walk off. He left me sitting by myself in the dusty road while he walked away towards that shack in the distance, and I didn't try to call him back.

After a long time I heard him though, or I heard his harpsong. He was playing a powerful lowdown mournful sound, floating high over the shriveled cotton plants and the loose fences. Oh, it made my chest hurt. At first I thought it was the song he'd played in the weeds outside Blackwell, it seemed so familiar. I felt like I must have heard it before. But it wasn't the same song. This sound was more aching, more full of hurt. I drew my knees up, touched my forehead to them. The sun was starting to go down, and the sky was so beautiful I didn't want to look. I thought then that the song was the one he'd played outside my daddy's truckpatch, telling me what would happen to him if he never met me, but it wasn't that song either. This sound was higher, and deeper, full of remembering, full of longing, like if you heard the voice of a dead loved one from long ago, or like seeing them in a dream, knowing they're there but you can't touch them. A sound like the whole lost sorrow of the world. I didn't cry, I didn't weep, but when Harlan stopped finally—after a really long time, the twilight was already coming—when the sound ceased, I got to my feet and began walking toward the tin-roofed sharecropper's shack I could see way off on the horizon in the middle of those dark wasted fields.

When I drew near the shack finally, the sky's light was gone. All I could see was shadows of people butchering a hog or a steer in the yard. I smelled the blood and the raw meat, heard the crack of an ax hacking through bone. In the lantern light I saw Harlan leaning against a truck fender, his hat cocked at an angle, his harp cupped to his mouth. He was playing a lilty tune now while the grown-ups worked and the little kids jig-danced, same as my brothers and sisters used to dance around the table to Harlan's music while me and Mama cleared the dishes back at home. I waited for him to notice me, to feel me standing in the dark lane, but he didn't. He never even glanced at the horizon where he'd left me alone hours ago.

I stood in the road between two rows of plantings, dried cornstalks rustling on one side, burnt cotton plants on the other. I watched Harlan, listened to him playing a high-stepping song like he hadn't a concern in this world, and I thought about everything, our whole lives together, from the hot May morning he walked into my daddy's yard right up to now. I asked myself, Sharon, what on this earth have you ever wanted? I could only think of two answers, and one was Harlan, and the other was my home and my family. I couldn't have them both together, not ever, and that's what made me feel torn in half most of my life. I thought, Your family's gone, they're dead maybe for all you know, and look there. See for yourself. Your husband left you sitting in the dirt road to go play music for strangers, that's what he chose and that's what he will always choose, because he can't help it. Never in his life could he help being how he is—any more than you could ever help going with him.

I thought, *You could help it now*. You could walk away and leave him.

And in that moment I suddenly knew that I could. I could get a job some-where, quit traveling, live quiet and sane and normal in one place. I could walk away from Harlan Singer and keep on living in the world, and not be afraid. I pondered the words in the justice of the peace's office in Muskogee. Till death do us part. Fourteen years old and ignorant as pudding, but that promise made up the truth of my life—not because I'd said it. Because it was what I wanted. What I always wanted. I took a step toward him.

The screen door slammed, and Harlan's harp went silent.

A woman's voice began calling her kids to come on in the house now, come in and wash up for supper. I listened to that mother calling to her children, like the mama quail in the switchgrass calling her lost chicks. And I knew then that even death would not part us. Because I remembered then the third desire of my heart.

I stayed in the lane, listening to the children's laughter, their voices skipping across the yard, the men's voices behind them, the screen door opening and slamming, opening and slamming, until there were none left, only silence. Then I turned and went to sit in the dark cornfield. So many of the stalks were snapped over, broken, dying from drought. I sat down to wait. My stomach cramped with the smell of meat frying inside the house, my mouth watered, but I kept on sitting in the dirt, listening.

The sound came finally, Harlan's harp sound, long late in the night, the house was quiet, the fields dark, and I got up from the ground and walked to where the sound was. I could see a line of light leaking around a shed door. The notes were trilling up and down, glad-sounding, like a flute or a songbird, but when I opened the crib door I found Harlan sitting on a blanket on the floor, and when he raised his face to me, his hands cupped, I saw the trembling. I saw how miserable his eyes were. The air inside that log crib was close and hot, it smelled of dust and kerosene, old rat droppings. The bandanna in Harlan's lap was covered in blood.

I went to him and put my hand on the back of his neck. With my other hand I reached down and took the harp from his fingers. The plate was smooth and cool, wet with Harlan's spit. I put it to my mouth. It tasted of brass and saliva. I blew air out, made a sound, not one note but several notes together, not pleasant, not ugly, just plain harmonica sound. I sucked air in, blew out again, many times, and the sound was like a pump organ wheezing, but it wasn't hymnlike. It wasn't pretty. Harlan put his hands over my hand, held the harp to my lips like a mama holds a cup for her child. But I couldn't make music, nothing that sounded like music, and I didn't really like how the harp tasted, how it smelled. I pulled it away from my mouth, handed it back to him. He sat there holding it.

"Are you hurt?" I pointed at the bloody bandanna in his lap.

He glanced down. "That's just cow's blood."

"Might as well leave it then," I said.

deepsong

on his back, at the edge of the thicket, staring up at a pale washed sky overhead, he remembers

    her eyes furious in the shade of the bois d'arc,
    the earth littered with hard yellowgreen fruit.
    how he'd picked one up and handed it to her.
    what do you expect me to do with this?
    it's like you, bois d'arc is.

    overhead the tree arched and cascaded, gnarled branches bending earthward with their burden of fruit. from the lower trunk the young branches sprang skyward like willow twigs, covered with thorns. but it was the wood of the bois d'arc that was like her, like sharon: tougher than hickory, small veined, knotty, and it would not rot. all over the hills the people cut bois d'arc for fenceposts because of how it lasted, resisted fire, insects, the soft rot of rain, but the old ones used to steal the heart of the bois d'arc to make bows for their arrows because of its springlike character, its bending nature, because no matter how tough and rot-resistant it might be, it could still bend.

    he'd tried to tell her.

    well I guess you mean useless then, she'd said and dropped the fruit on the ground.

    no, his mind whispers. *i don't mean that.*

Part Three

folksay

1935

After the Blessing event, the cowkilling in '34, we began to hear stories. He'd been spied at a farm auction near Heavener, somebody said, handing out dough from a sack—except the folks around Heavener didn't look a bit better off than before, so nobody much believed that story. He was roaming the Ozarks playing harp for funerals and revivals and meatpackers' strikes. Somebody said they'd seen him in Joplin playing hymn songs for strangers, though others swore it wasn't hymns but union songs, and it wasn't in Missouri but atop a poisonous pile of hard-rock mining chat outside Picher. By the time Harlan Singer showed up in McAlester that cold bright afternoon in March 1935, at the commencement of the coal miners' hunger siege, his name was just common in people's mouths again, though none of the stories seemed to match each other, and we'd all forgot what he looked like, or anyhow, the fact is, nobody recognized him.

Well, we weren't expecting him, see. We had our heads down, about like those bawling cows marked for slaughter. The mines were shutting down then, cutting shifts, cutting pay, folks couldn't feed their families. Everybody was suffering, of course, but mining people had it worst, because if you were trying to make a living off the land, it was hard but your young'uns didn't starve, but if you were trying to make a living *under* the land, there wasn't any hope for you. Naturally it was mining folk who'd come up with this plan to seize the county courthouse and hold on till somebody did something to help the situation, and the ones that did it, they say, were the ones in so much despair they didn't care, plus the handful with enough hope left to believe they could actually change something. Folks say it was the plain amount of hope and hopelessness on the courthouse steps that caused Harlan Singer to show up that day. He stood off to one side, a slight, wiry figure with snuff-colored skin and green eyes and a familiar look about him. He had his possum-haired gal with him, and that French harp, of course, and his hat, but he just seemed like one of us. He could have been any one of that disgruntled crowd milling around in front of the courthouse, restless, disorganized, hungry.

"Line up, people!" somebody called. "We're going in!"

And the people began to move. It was laid-off miners and union men, women in cloth coats and worn hats, youngsters with their shoes tied on with string, mothers carrying their fevery children, and so on, all mounting the courthouse steps, and Harlan Singer and his girl mixed in among them. The siegers marched in through the front doors and up the inside stairs, spread out over the courtroom on the second floor, and somebody sent the county workers home, and somebody told somebody to go notify the sheriff. Several women had brought along scraps of blankets or old quilts, intending to stay all night or just however long it took, and they began to claim their little territories between the benches and along the walls.

One of the leaders, Mrs. Violetta Stapleton MacIntosh, hoisted herself onto the dais and began shuffling papers on the judge's desk, calling out to the women spreading their blankets around, "I hope y'all brought everything you need, ladies, because we are not leaving this building until we get some help for our children!" Mrs. Mac was the widow of a deputy union chief, she'd taught school at Wilburton once upon a time—till they fired her for radicalism and promoting books—so folks figured she knew how to conduct this hunger siege operation. "This is going to be a long campaign, people!" she called. "It's going to take a lot of organization and a lot of cooperation! Y'all settle yourselves so we can get down to business!"

But the people kept milling. Some of the union men, familiar with just how long-drawn-out a strike night can get, had brought along music instruments and decks of cards for playing pitch, plus a few samples of liquid entertainment tucked into boot tops and hind pockets, which they were trying to sneak past the siege committee. Plenty others were yet arguing or roaming the big room, trying to find their best position, and then Harlan Singer limped forward, and folks quit their bucking and bossing. They turned to watch the slim stranger push his way through the low gate, ease past the lawyers' tables and on up to the witness stand, where he took a seat and began to play a quickhearted little marching tune, boom-taboom-taboom. The possum-haired gal slipped through the crowd and sat down crosslegged on the floor in front of him.

Mrs. MacIntosh squinted at the pair a minute. "All right, listen up, people!" she said, turning back to her work. "Our first order of business this afternoon, we got to lay out our list of rules and regs!" She brandished a long sheet of paper. "I'm not going to read the whole list now, we'll post it on the door, but I think you'll find everything reasonable and fair! Our siege committee drew it up! Just one rule I want to declare outloud right now, and that's Rule Number One: No liquor! Y'all hear that?"

A honkytonk sound sawed into the bright air from between Harlan Singer's cupped fingers. Mrs. MacIntosh cut him a surprised, disapproving look. Singer lowered the harp and winked at her. "Just so everybody knows," she said, "any man found drinking or importing liquor will be out the door on his ear!" Mrs. Mac was the veteran of seven mining strikes. She felt she had a pretty good sense of the dangers. "No liquor," she repeated, "and no night fraternizing! I don't care if you're married! We don't intend to give reporters any wedge for criticism or scandal. Oh, that reminds me," she said. "Rule Number Six: When photographers or outsiders come in, nobody speaks to them but a committee member! Now, these here . . . " She fluttered a handful of blank pages. "These are the sign-up sheets for the sanitation committee, the patrol committee, and so on. I want to see every adult person's name down here somewhere. Now, as most of you know   Hey! Hey! Y'all can't play tag in here! Mothers! Mind your children! All right. So you all know, I think, that we sent a delegation of our hungry and unemployed to Oklahoma City last night? Well, we just got a wire. Our people are camped out on the governor's lawn right now!" Grunts of approval sounded around the room. "Folks!" Mrs. MacIntosh declared. "We are determined to make the powers-that-be answer for something! And we mean to start directly at the governor's mansion!"

A few of the siegers called out, "Yes, ma'am!" and "That's right!" Others bent down to wipe their children's runny noses.

"Because we all know perfectly well," Mrs. MacIntosh declared, "that we're not getting our share of relief here in Little Dixie! We aim to find out why that is! And we intend to fix it!"

"You said it, lady!" a lone voice hollered, but the rest of the miners were quiet. Yul Tannehill stepped forward. He'd been the pit boss at Carbon Number Five before the coal company shut it down. A good man. An honest man. Everybody there knew him. "No disrespect meant, ma'am," he said, "but we don't want charity. We want jobs to work."

"It's not charity if you're paying taxes!"

A kind of shuffling, throat-clearing air of discomfort choked the room. Some of the men looked at the floor.

"What's the matter?" Mrs. MacIntosh said.

A smattering of men's voices mumbled: "When's the mines going to open again? That's what we want to know." "I thought we come here to strike till they put back on some shifts." "They got to open the pits, ma'am. They got to give us some work."

"Well, yes," Mrs. Mac said. "But in the meantime you intend to let your children starve? We need relief, people! It's due us! We're suffering in mining country!"

Some of the women began to say, "The children are hungry," and others said, "Well, but our menfolks need work," and there was a general contrary muttering in the aisles and along the courthouse walls. *What we need is food for our children's bellies. We aim to see the mines open again. Milk for our babies' bones. Money for the rent. Earn a living wage. Milk. Work. Cheese. Jobs. Corn, our children are hungry, bless 'em! our men need a job of work,* until a voice bellowed out from the back of the room, "Y'all are all full of baloney!"

Everybody turned to look. A hulky fellow in overalls and a mashed cap stepped away from the wall.

"Ain't nobody gives a good goddamn about us," he said. "Don't you know that?"

"Rule Number Four," Mrs. MacIntosh said. "No profanity."

The young man began to make his way to the front. He was a large-headed, soft-jawed, handsome kid, with wavy hair and bad skin and a tattoo on his arm that spelled out *Cheryl Ann*. Nothing too remarkable about him, just your ordinary overgrown fatherless boy, homeless and jobless, without a pot or a pillow or a place to call his own. His name was DeWayne Tallent. He had happened along the street that afternoon and seen the people waiting to climb the steps and thought to himself, Well, whatever it is, I see girls, and he'd got in line and marched in with the rest. He'd been wandering between the benches in the back, tugging up his shirtsleeves and flexing his arms in the vicinity of any legal female who had most her teeth, which was few enough in that humble gathering, but some of the words being muttered near the front had caught his ear, especially *hungry* and *relief* and *charity* and *children need it*. Hearing them, he'd stopped his strut, and listened, until he couldn't stand it anymore.

"No. Damn. Body," he repeated now, the bitterness flowing from him as he continued his slow swagger down the aisle. He stepped around toddling youngsters, over pallets of sleeping babies. From the witness stand now came the lonesome strains of "Wayfaring Stranger."

"Watch your mouth, young man," Mrs. MacIntosh said. "We're not riffraff and rabblerousers here!"

The boy shrugged, turned the court clerk's chair around and sat spraddlelegged on it backwards. He scanned a curled-lip sneer around the room. Mrs. MacIntosh frowned, but the boy was quiet now, so she went back to her lists. "Can I get some volunteers for the chiseling committee? Hazel? All right, good. Lois Childers. That's good," she said, writing the names. "Now, the committee's job—"

"There's no damn jobs, lady."

"I warned you about that language."

"No *durn* jobs. Ain't that why we're all here? Ain't that why all these old men, and young ladies . . . " He doffed his cap to the possum-haired girl. "Come down to the courthouse? Ain't it all a man wants in this world, if folks would just let him have it, a blame job?"

Now, the truth is, DeWayne Tallent was the type of fellow who likely never would have worked a day in his life if there'd been any jobs to be had, but since there weren't any, he figured he had a right to bellyache about it. "Ain't that right?" he said, cocking his head to catch the miners' eyes, and a few of the men nodded.

"Jobs, yes," Mrs. MacIntosh said, "we'll put that in our demands, naturally. But we've got to get relief for our children right now!" Several women seconded her. "This is a *hunger* siege, son. I promise you, not one bit of government will be conducted in this county till we get what we came for. "

"Gov-erment, *hah!*" DeWayne Tallent said. "What's the gov-erment ever done for us?" Men's voices rumbled along the walls, a groundswell of agreement. Never had DeWayne Tallent been inside the right opinion of any gathering of men in his life, and his chest swelled with the rising voices behind him. But the old lady butted in:

"That's what this strike is all about, son! We intend to make them! Who can I get to head up the chiseling committee? That committee's job," she said pointedly in the direction of DeWayne Tallent, "is to go to the downtown merchants and dun them for coffee and sandwiches, lamps, kerosene—"

DeWayne jumped up from the chair and shoved it aside. "Y'all are wasting your blame time! This ain't no way to make a change. Organize, my foot. Strike, my hind end. What good does it do? Ain't my daddy tried that?"

The harp music stopped as Singer tumped the witness chair down on four legs—gently, but every eye in the room swung to him.

"My daddy joined the dang union," DeWayne said right at him. "My daddy went out on strike with the rest. And he's just as dead as any other poor coaldigging fool. Hunger siege! Pah!" DeWayne spat on the floor, stared around at the mining men. All at once he turned and climbed onto the defense table, stood tall, crowed over the crowd: "We ain't got to sit here like a bunch of dumb ducks in a courthouse!"

"No standing on the tables!" Mrs. MacIntosh called.

"What we got to do is convince those sonsabitches with a shotgun!"

"Which sonsabitches is that, son?" Singer asked, very mild.

DeWayne swung around to glare at him. "Any son of a bitch tries to tell me what to do, runt. You fixing to try to be one of 'em?"

Harlan Singer stood up then, and the girl scrambled to her feet.

Plenty witnesses swear it was from this minute everybody knew him. They say Singer's name passed through the room like a sigh of wind, but of course these are folks looking backwards, they know the whole story, how everything went, and so naturally they like to claim a little knowledge. Like as not, though, the majority of the people in that courtroom were still peering at him, thinking to themselves: *stranger*. But as he stepped down from the witness box and proceeded to saunter toward the defense table, a little murmur went up from every corner, because he did, you know, Harlan Singer had that air about him made you feel like you knew him somehow, from somewhere deep in your past, only you couldn't quite place him.

"You sure think you're something, don'cha?" DeWayne sneered, though he took a step back from the edge of the table. "You look like a midget from up here, did you know it? What are you, some kind of a pinko? Pinko gimpo pretty boy runt."

Harlan paused a few feet away, tipped back his hat so that his curly hair showed. When he reached for his shirt pocket several men at the front of the room flinched, but all he drew out was a white cigarette pack with a red bullseye on the side. At once every-man-jack's lungs went tight, every mouth watered, every chest burned with the nicotine hunger. Some hadn't tasted even so much as a roll-your-own in months. Harlan thumbed a Lucky Strike into his mouth, lit it, and the perfume wafted through the courtroom. You could hear sighs in every corner.

"So, your daddy's dead," Harlan said. He smoked his Lucky a while. "Mine too." He squinted up at Tallent. "Reckon that gives us something in common."

"My daddy got killed in the Sanboy blast," DeWayne said. His soft handsome face went even softer with the recollection of how he'd been made an orphan before he was born, due to the greed and avarice of the Sans Bois Coal Company and the ungodly worlds of explodable gas laced through the bowels of southeastern Oklahoma. "My mama died from TB. In the sanatorium at Talihina."

"I'm real sorry to hear that," Harlan said, and he did look sorry, like he could understand the insides of that sad story. He shook out another smoke, lit it, handed it up to DeWayne, who took the cigarette, but he had to stoop and stretch over to get it. When he straightened up, puffing, he cocked his cloth cap over one eye to regain his dignity. He stood with arms folded across his overalls bib, the Lucky smoldering from his bottom lip. "Hunger siege," he muttered again. "Baloney."

Harlan leaned down to pick up a banjo from the floor under the defense table, he slid the banjo strap around his neck, and strummed the strings, a disharmonious sound. "Whyn't you tell us about the time your daddy died," he said. He passed the crumpled Lucky Strike pack to a fellow standing nearby, and that fellow took a smoke, relayed the pack to the next man, and there was grateful murmuring along the walls as Harlan tuned the banjo. "I'd be interested to hear," he said.

"Ain't nothing to tell," DeWayne mumbled.

"Plenty folks in this room would be proud to hear about that Sans Bois collapse. Any mine collapse." Harlan turned a key, chorded the neck, smoke from his cigarette trailing up in his eyes. "They all got the same story."

"Let them tell it then," DeWayne said.

"What's the matter, son?" Harlan's fingers paused. "Didn't nobody ever tell you your daddy's story?"

"Hell yes," DeWayne said, but you could see by how he said it that what he really meant was hell no. Harlan began to play then, he didn't pick the banjo, only strummed, a sort of plinky sound, and after a while he began to hum, and then to sing "Don't Go Down in the Mine, Dad." It was a mournful-sounding tune, a familiar, sad old mining song—maybe there's no other kind—and some of the women wept silently, the courtroom grew melancholy and quiet.

Then Harlan began to make up new words to go with that old tune. Folks knew they were new words because nobody'd ever sung about Oklahoma's mining disasters, though we'd had plenty, Oklahoma's coal fields being some of the deadliest in the world, and for a while the people were glad to hear Harlan sing about the hundred men that died at Krebs (*"I-talians and Ger-r-rmans,"* he sang, *"the Scots and the Wel-l-lsh"*); he sang of the huge Sans Bois blast near McCurtain (*"and the number that di-i-ied there,"* he sang, looking quizzically at DeWayne Tallent, *"was seventy-threeee"*); he sang of the 1926 gas-and-dust explosion at Wilburton (*"and the number that di-i-ied there / was over four score and tennn"*), the dozens of miners killed at Samples and at Old Town (*"the Ne-groes and Mex-i-cans / the Slo-vaks and Poles"*); he sang of the oil fire at Haileyville, the cave-in at Adamson, the windy shots and the dynamite blasts, the fallen timbers and the cages crashed, and while he sang the people all stared at the floor, remembering, because it was their own story, or their daddy's story, or their granddaddy's: they heard the whistles blow and smelled the belching smoke, they saw the living miners scramble free of the pit, watched them turn and go back down to the dying screams, the voices begging underneath, the killing silence that was worse; they saw mangled bodies red with blood, black with soot, burned beyond telling, laid out side by side, end to end, over acres and acres in their towns, in Hartshorne and McCurtain, in Carbon and Lutie, in Alderson and Tahoma and LeHigh and Dow, and beside the bodies, weeping, were the widows and orphans, widows and orphans, and orphans, and orphans.

DeWayne was striding back and forth on the defense table, clenching and unclenching his fists.

"Them that mourn shall be comfort-ed," Harlan sang, *"Them that's last shall be first."*

"Shut up!" DeWayne cried at last. "Shut up, you son of a gun, I'll break your face!"

And Harlan Singer did hush, right in that moment, he opened his two hands and dropped them away from the banjo, they hung loose and open-palmed at his sides. The girl moved up to stand beside him. The room drew quiet again, except for a hungry baby mewling in the jury box. After a moment the people began to murmur and stir. One of the mothers snapped at her child, "Get over here before I smack you!" Men ground out their Luckies on the floor. One or two wondered outloud if maybe it was time to collect the wife and kids and go home. Others muttered, "We ain't looking to bring up all that old stuff."

What it was, you see, Harlan Singer had turned into a lightning rod for our buried sorrows—or not a lightning rod, more like a dowsing rod, a slender, forked peachwillow stick bending to the earth, pointing the way to things we'd shoved under, our secret flowing fountain.

"We're not talking about the past here today," Mrs. MacIntosh said. "We've got needs right now." All around the courtroom folks nodded in silent, tight-lipped agreement.

Harlan took off his hat, held it in both hands before him, in front of the banjo. His eyes were green as two bottleflies' bellies gliding over us. "Well," he said after a bit. He turned his hat over a few times, sort of casually examining it. "I met an old man once," he said, "told me something strange." He looked up. "Man said there's an unforgivable sin. I told him, Fella, you're going to have to show me where that's at in the Book."

We glanced around at each other. We couldn't see how this followed from that.

"I told him, Mister, from what I remember, the Word promises if you're washed in the Blood you'll be white as snow," Harlan said. "It don't say you'll be mostly white with one dirty spot yonder at the tail. Well, we were traveling at the time, we didn't have a Book to look at to check our figures, and I'll admit it took him seven days and nights to do it, but that old man finally convinced me there truly is one sin a merciful God won't forgive. Or can't." He peered out at us with his head cocked to the side, looking a lot like a banty rooster eyeing a sowbug. "Y'all know which sin it is?"

Well, that was a terrible question. That was a question nobody wanted to answer.

Harlan put his hat on, pushed it to the back of his head. "I used to know a young fella suffered this sin something awful." Harlan began to feel his pockets, searching, finally his hands came to rest on the banjo neck, but he didn't play anything. "He was only a youngster, but he got to roaming around in the timber just a-sinning and a-sinning, I reckon he didn't even know it was a sin. He was hungry all the time, he couldn't never get filled. He'd go off and sit on a creekbank, pretend to himself he was fishing, but he didn't put any bait on the line. Half the time he'd wouldn't even put a line in the water, he'd just sit there and watch the ripples and say to himself, It's no point. No point in nothing. I'm hungry, ain't nobody to feed me. I'm weary, I got no place to rest. I'm sick, there's no one to heal me. I'd as soon go on and die this minute, if only I knew how. Reckon I'll be dead soon enough anyway, and there won't be nobody give a good. God. Damn."

DeWayne was wagging his handsome head side to side, he had his cap crushed in his hands, wadding it, wadding it.

"This kid," Harlan went on, "he'd lay down to sleep on the creekbank, when he woke up he'd be covered in seedticks, poison ivy, a thousand chigger bites welting his skin. He'd be hungrier than when he laid down, but there he'd still be. Still living. Still sinning. He'd have to get up and go try to find himself something to eat." Harlan's voice dropped so low we had to strain to hear him. "What it was . . . " he said, gazing steady at DeWayne Tallent, "this fatherless boy . . . this motherless son. This hungry orphan wandering the Oklahoma hills what he done was . . . he quit hoping."

"That ain't how it was."

"Oh," Harlan said, "Are you trying to tell me you've got some hope then?"

DeWayne was caught off guard, he didn't know how to answer.

"Hoping or hopeless, it's only one of two answers." Harlan tilted his head back, like he'd just noticed something strange on the ceiling. *"Abandon hope, all ye who enter,"* he said, like he was reading the words off the scrolled tin. "They tell me that's what's wrote at the gates of Hell." He paused a beat, squinting upward. "'Course, on the other hand, it might read the other way around. *All ye who enter, you abandoned hope.* Who's to say?" He returned his gaze to DeWayne Tallent. "I been studying on that. Why hopelessness, or despair, or giving up, whatever you want to call it, why that's the one sin the Almighty won't forgive. I think I come up with the answer. It's not Him. It's us. A hopeless man don't ask for forgiveness, on account of a hopeless man don't believe in it. He don't care. About that or anything else. He don't see the point in living. That's a kick in God's teeth, innit?"

"I told you, that's not how it was!" DeWayne was in a terrible distress, his voice wobbled. "I never give up nothing! I never quit! I'll tear this place up, I'll bust your dang face if you say it again! I got plenty hope, mister, let me tell you what my hope is! It's to get what's due me!"

"Oh? And what's that's, son?"

"What's due any redblooded American! A place to live and a job of work! A drink of whiskey and a lady friend! A suit of clothes that ain't ragged and filthy, a little piece of bread and a plate of beans!" Some of the men began to murmur agreement. "It ain't right how my daddy slaved in the mines for slave wages and died on account of it! It ain't right how the whole world turned its back on me when I didn't have my mama to help me no more!"

"I see." Harlan nodded. "So this hope of yours, it's causing you to want to try and change these things that ain't right?"

DeWayne glared at him. He knew it was a trick question.

"Because I'd got to wondering," Harlan said, "if you'd showed up here to-day because you were looking to make a change—or if you were just looking to make trouble."

"I'll make you some damn trouble!" DeWayne shouted, and he leaped from the defense table. Harlan made a little sidestep, and the orphan boy landed on his feet with a thump; he scrambled for his balance, whirled around with his fists raised. A couple of the miners moved in to stop him, but Harlan held up a hand.

"Wait," he said. "Let's hear him."

DeWayne's throat worked, his face got very red. He longed for a shot of rye whiskey, to throw a punch, to yell something at the world. Harlan Singer just stood there, too damn little and too mild, too crippled, it wasn't fair. That's what DeWayne wanted to say, he wanted to yell it right out, *No fair! No fair!*

"So you were saying?" Harlan said. "About this hope of yours?"

"I got nothing to say."

Harlan waited.

"We're not getting our rights here," DeWayne said after a while.

Still Harlan waited.

"Things are all wrong."

Harlan nodded, he turned his eyes from DeWayne, gazed around the court-room at each hungry individual slumped in a pew or leaning against a wall. The people, in turn, began to look around. One factor stood out: there were too many bones in that courtroom. Too many sunken jaws and narrowed faces. Too many stunted feet and darkened teeth. Too many mining widows made pale and drawn by their children's bowed legs, and too many men beat down by no work and no way to feed their families. You said to yourself, This ain't America, or you said, This ain't how America's supposed to go.

After a while Yul Tannehill said softly, almost like he was talking to himself, "I hope Carbon Five opens up before long, that's my hope. I got to find me some work." Several voices agreed with him. A woman's voice came from the back of the room: "I hope Jimmy Don's shoes don't wear out before Rollie gets big enough to wear 'em." Another voice called out, very simply, "Rain." An old man near the front said, "I'm hoping somebody knows how to get this country out of the fix it's in," and somebody said, "Roosevelt's trying, ain't he?" and somebody else answered, "Not hard enough."

"What I'm hoping for," Mrs. MacIntosh said, "is for working folks to wake up in this country. We got to *fight* for what's due us. Capital's not about to just hand it to us. And we got to stick together!"

"That's right!" a bunch of voices said.

"I hope . . ." DeWayne said. He cut a glance at the girl. "I just wisht . . ." Then he squinted at Harlan. "Is hoping and wishing the same thing?"

"Depends," Harlan said. "If you're wishing something was different that's already over and done with, that's a useless proposition, innit? That hopeless, I guess. But wishing for something to be different that ain't happened yet but still could, why, sure, that's hope. Or close enough."

"Well, then," DeWayne Tallent said, "I wish things would come out fair in this world."

"We all wish that, son!" Mrs. MacIntosh said. "But we're going to have to get ourselves a new system to see it!"

Harlan pinned his bright green gaze on her. "You believe changing the system will fix things," he said, more comment than question.

"By golly it's a start!"

A commotion sounded near the door then, and everybody turned to look. Coke Jessup was crouched to one side of the big double doors, hissing and making faces, his hands flapping like pigeons as the county sheriff strolled in. Poor old Coke kept hissing and flapping while Sheriff Bob Doolittle made his way through the crowd toward the little gate, so folks understood that Coke Jessup, at least, had managed to sneak in a bottle.

"Hello, Vi," the sheriff said when he reached the judge's bench. He lifted his handsome gray Stetson. The swell of khaki over his gunbelt gave you to know he hadn't missed quite so many meals as the folks lining the walls.

"Sheriff," Mrs. MacIntosh said.

"Afternoon, Yul," the sheriff said.

"Afternoon," Yul answered.

The sheriff looked at Harlan Singer, nodded to him, too, though he didn't say anything. Then the sheriff's gaze skimmed over DeWayne Tallent with hardly a pause. He peered around the courtroom, very slowly, shaking his head, like it grieved him to see us all in such a situation. You had to wonder, though, by how long he paused at different ones, if he wasn't maybe also trying to commit some faces to memory. "Folks," he said at last, "we're all friends and neighbors here. I'd really hate to see y'all get yourselves into trouble."

"We're *in* trouble, Bobby Lee," Mrs. MacIntosh said. "Hunger's trouble, if you ask me."

"What I'm saying," the sheriff said, "I'd hate to have to arrest somebody for criminal trespass, unlawful assembly . . ."

"Unlawful! What's unlawful is our children going to bed without enough to eat! No jobs and no money, *that's* criminal!"

"I got all the sympathy in the world for these people, Vi," the sheriff said. "I really do. But you know I been elected to keep the peace in this county."

"We're the people of this county, aren't we? By gosh, we're peaceful!" Mrs. MacIntosh declared. "We'd be a little *more* peaceful with a little dadgum food in our bellies! We got a message for you to take to the governor, Sheriff, and to the chief of police and the press and whoever else you want to take it to, including that fat Congress and the very President himself: This courthouse is hereby under siege. The hungry citizens of Pittsburg County own it, our taxes paid for it—same as we pay your salary, Bobby Lee—and we're not budging from these premises till we get the relief we been promised!"

"Folks," Doolittle said, "now, y'all need to just go on—"

"*You* go on, Sheriff," Mrs. MacIntosh said. "Go right ahead and do your *job*! Arrest these hungry women and children! Take us right out to the state penitentiary and lock us up, same way the governor done our husbands during the last labor strike. That'll play mighty fine in the papers! That's guaranteed to win you the next election. Well, you'd have to feed us anyhow. I guess we wouldn't mind that, would we, ladies?"

There was a rippling murmur of agreement and hope. Harlan Singer eased forward, touched the brim of his hat. "Tell you what, Sheriff," he said, very friendly. "You provide these fine folks with something for their kids to eat, maybe a job of work and a bit of hope for their future, why, I bet you'll see this courthouse cleared in a jiffy. But then again, that's not your line of work, is it? Your job's to keep the peace. That'd make you a peacemaker, wouldn't it? I always admired to be one of them."

The sheriff studied him. "You ain't from around here, are you?" he said

"Sure not," Harlan answered.

"You look kindly familiar." The sheriff pulled at his clean-shaved upper lip. "What's your name, fella?"

"No man," Harlan said, and he picked a few banjo notes.

"Norman what?" the sheriff said.

"I's just wondering, though," Harlan said, like he was answering the question, "where *is* this peace you're intending to keep?"

"You're a smart aleck, ain't you?"

"Don't mean to be, Sheriff. I just wonder about things from time to time."

"Where you from, buddy?"

But Harlan only looked down at his fingers as he plucked a soft banjo tune.

"Yul," the sheriff said, but he wasn't looking at Yul Tannehill. His eyes were hard upon Singer. "Clyde. Leon. Elvin. Y'all've made your point. Whyn't you quit this sorry business and go home."

"Don't reckon we can do that, Sheriff," Yul Tannehill said.

The plinking banjo stopped. The room went still. Doolittle turned and gazed around at the people. The men all stood taller. The women glared at him with their fists on their hips. The children stared, unblinking, unsmiling. Nobody made a sound. The sheriff's sideburns began to quiver, his complexion bloodied a shade or two darker, you could see it going all over him: he didn't like folks challenging his authority. He placed his hand on the butt of his pistol. "Well," he said. "Looks like I'm going to have to arrest the instigators of this mess." He turned his narrowed gaze back to Singer in a manner that gave you to know he believed the cause of all the trouble, all this discombobulation and hungryfolks' rebellion, was purely the green-eyed stranger standing before him. He reached toward his back pocket for the handcuffs, but just then the orphan boy stepped forward. DeWayne Tallent folded his arms, barreled out his chest, spoke to the lawman, though his eyes, too, were on Singer, and it was tough to tell which one of them he was challenging when he said, "*I'm* an instigator, Sheriff. Arrest me."

In a beat, Yul Tannehill said, "Better arrest me, too, Bob."

Mrs. MacIntosh puffed as she climbed down from the judge's bench, "Arrest me while you're at it, Bobby Lee."

Lois Childers walked up with her youngest in her arms. "Arrest me, Sheriff."

From the back of the room: "Over here, Doolittle, arrest me!"

The people began to crowd forward, some of them holding their wrists out for the cuffs. "Here you go, Bob, arrest me."

"Arrest me, Sheriff."

"Arrest me."

Sheriff Doolittle, seeing he'd lost the skirmish, took one last careful look at Harlan's face, turned and strolled back through the low gate and on out the courtroom doors.

Oh, folks got as giddy as horseflies on gelding day. Somebody fetched up a couple of guitars and a mandolin and a fiddle, and all of a sudden there was a powerful rising of music in that courthouse, and singing and handclapping and what might have been construed in a less Baptist-like country as dancing. Men slapped DeWayne Tallent on the back, set him up on the defense table with his legs dangling, somebody put a pair of spoons in his hands, and after a minute he began to knock them together on his dirty denimed knee. Harlan lit into a quick little jig-dance tune, nodding at the children scattered around the room. The little ones started edging forward, giggling, then they went to prancing, making circles, holding hands, singing, "ARREST ME! ARREST ME!" Somebody produced a jug of rye whiskey and passed it in secret along the walls. Mrs. MacIntosh drew the district attorney's chair to one side and sat in it, clapping and singing along, and Coke Jessup jigged in the aisleway on his limber legs as Harlan plinked the banjo and the other players strummed and young Perry Eagleton sawed his fiddle to a flat fare-thee-well. The people all reckoned the sheriff was vanquished. We reckoned the courthouse was ours and we had the rest of a Friday night to do whatever we wanted, we might as well celebrate.

Harlan Singer climbed back up to the witness box, and from there he proceeded to give us hoedowns and breakdowns and goosedowns and every kind of frolicsome music you can think of. He had the gift, you know, he could just call up words at the drop of a biscuit and sing them to any tune you wanted, and he started making up funny words about roosters and red-eye gravy and carbide lights, singing them to old foggy mountain reels, and folks laughed and nodded at each other in recognition. Seemed like everything he sang was funny, because it was true. He sang a made-up song about train bulls and railroad justice and lawyers and thieves, and DeWayne Tallent bellowed from the defense table, "That's right! Every blankety one of the blankety lawyers is thieves!" Singer nodded, like he approved the boy's approval, and we all laughed and clapped. We recognized the tunes mostly, the other players all kept up, but couldn't none of us sing along now, on account of we didn't know the words. They were new ones every minute. He sang a song about burnt crops and boll weevils, jackrabbits and dust. This one wasn't so very funny, but he sang it lively, to the tune of "Sally Gooden."

After a time, though, Singer's words began to twist and change. The meaning inside them turned strange, turned sadder, turned peculiar, and a little while longer after that, they quit making good sense. Oh, for instance, to that old tune "Clementine," he sang, *"O my bald knob, o my bald knob, o my bald knob, turpen-ti-i-i-ine,"* looking out at us and grinning like that was a mighty good lyric, but if it was, we couldn't see how. The sun was slanting through the tall windows near the back now, flooding the room red, and Harlan Singer stood in the witness box in just such a position that the whole room could see him. His face was tipped up to catch the light, his hat was pushed back. Every so often he closed his eyes, like he was full of some kind of emotion, like he was singing alone to himself, even though you knew that he knew every eye in the room was on him. You started to want to look some other direction. You started to wish he'd lay down that banjo and quit making up words. He sang a song about a new white tombstone being laid on a rotted grave. He sang about a baby dead in its mama's arms. That's when Perry Eagleton put his fiddle away, and soon the other players did the same, but Singer kept on plinking the banjo and singing, and the girl stood beside the witness stand, watching his face.

One by one, folks got up and stepped out to the front hall for a sip of water. They would wander back in and sit down, but here in a minute they'd get up and walk out again. Restless. Elvin White and Yul Tannehill stood near the door with their heads together, muttering. Mrs. MacIntosh made her way to the dais, started sorting her papers. DeWayne Tallent sat on the defense table with a confused look on his face, the spoons in his fists forgotten.

"Up-on the bannks of the blood red ri-ver," Singer sang, *"we took their gooods, we smashed their homes."*

"Now wait just a minute!" Mrs. MacIntosh slapped some papers on the desk.

"We stole their sonng, and gave no mer-cy / We drove them ouuut, heartbroke to roam."

"What kind of music is that for a hunger siege?"

"We broke their heaads," Singer sang, *"We smashed their fa-ces / We dragged them throough the tar and loam."*

"Hush that up now!"

"We stole their shoooes, and beat them senseless / Be-side the traacks, they died a-lone."

"Honey," the girl said, "don't."

Singer drew quiet then, he stood with his hands on the banjo neck. "Just singing about some things I seen, is all." His gaze settled on DeWayne Tallent. "Folks don't want to hear it though." He shrugged. "Can't say as I blame 'em."

"What we need is songs to lift us up!" Mrs. MacIntosh said. "Songs to help us remember what we came here to do!"

"Well." Harlan patted around his pockets, feeling for something. "And what is that?"

Mrs. Mac narrowed her eyes. "Who you working for, fella? Are you on the side of capital? Because if you are, you are sure in the wrong place."

"Ma'am, I'm not on no side, that I know of."

"Then what'd you come here for?" DeWayne Tallent's face wasn't confused now, it was twisted up tight and furious. "You got to be on some side! You got to stand somewhere!"

"You do," Harlan said in a tone that was so completely a cross between a question and a confirmation you couldn't tell which he meant.

"You do!" the orphan boy said, and there was no doubt how he meant it. "You got to stand for something!"

"And stand together!" Mrs. MacIntosh declared.

"Stand up to them that's got their greedy paws on everything and won't turn a-loose of it!" DeWayne shouted.

"Stand united!" a miner bellowed.

"Stand strong!" another called.

A croaky voice in the back began to sing "Union Miners Stand Together," and soon the whole courtroom was singing in chorus, except for Harlan, who was removing the banjo strap from his neck, and the girl, who stood nearby and watched him. DeWayne Tallent wasn't singing either, he watched Singer and the girl, his chest rising and falling with deep feeling as the people sang about union, and when the chorus came around a second time, he hopped off the table and joined in. Slowly the red sunset light bled away, the room darkened to lilac. The song finished. The courtroom fell silent. Yul Tannehill stepped to the door and put his hand on the lightswitch, but he didn't flick it on. Seemed like we were all waiting for something. Seemed like we knew something was supposed to happen next, we just couldn't recollect what.

Along the aisleways and walls then, in the twilight, you could hear husband-and-wife disagreements starting up, old-friend arguments grumbling along, little kids whining and crabbing or fighting with their brothers. Coke Jessup meandered toward the far pews where a bottle was being passed. DeWayne Tallent stood glaring straight on at the witness box. From the bench Mrs. MacIntosh called out instructions, but nobody was listening. All around the courtroom folks were arguing and griping and complaining as the little gal stepped up and took Singer's hand and led him down from the stand and out the rear private door, through the judge's chambers.

Sharon

That stairwell was dark. I could just barely see him. They only had one tiny window up high, it didn't let in enough light for anything. I don't know how a judge could even find his way up and down those hind stairs. We went down slow, a step at a time, feeling our way, and when we got to the bottom we went out the back door, climbed the hill behind the courthouse, turned east.

Harlan was quiet, he had his head down and his hands in his pockets. We walked past all the nice houses we'd walked by that morning. They were two and three stories tall, some of them, with white columns in the front and porches and big windows. It wasn't full dark yet, but the houses had their lights on. I stared through the windows at the beautiful furniture, the baubly lights hanging down, thinking to myself it sure wasn't none of those folks in the courthouse that lived on this hill. Next thing I knew Harlan was walking far ahead of me, and I had to hurry to catch up. At the edge of town we came to a cemetery. I could see the pale square stones lined up in rows. Harlan walked straight through the gate, flopped down on the ground next to a tall white headstone. I went in and sat next to him.

"All right," I said after a bit. "You want to tell me what that was about?"

He looked down at his harp, turning it in his hand.

I said, "Harlan, I'm going to tell you something. You strum a banjo just fair, and I'll admit you're quick with words but if I never hear you sing another note it won't bother me." I waited for him to answer. "You're not fixing to have another spell are you?"

He shook his head.

"How come you didn't play your harp for the people?"

"I don't know."

"Well, you shouldn't have picked up that banjo."

He turned and looked at me.

"That just tempted you into showing off," I said.

"You think that's what it was?" His voice was really quiet.

"I know so," I said. "Let's go, honey."

"Reckon how many kinds of gluttony there are?"

"I never heard of but one." I laid my hand on my belly, trying to think how far it might be to the next town. I didn't want to go back through McAlester to hunt dinner. The thick, full feeling was in me already, all through my chest and belly. I tell myself sometimes that's the reason I didn't see how bad it was getting. I wouldn't see. I wouldn't listen. I had only one thing on my mind then. The third desire of my heart. "I need to eat, Harlan. I really do."

"Gluttony for drink," he said. "That'd be one kind, wouldn't it? Gluttony for music."

"It's getting dark, honey."

"Gluttony for somebody's eyes on you."

I stood up. "Come on."

But Harlan kept sitting. "Profit used to claim he could count six kinds of gluttony," he said. "And nine kinds of greed. I tried to get him to name 'em, but he said he was still counting. Told me if I wasn't careful I'd be one of the ones liable to suffer gluttony."

I couldn't help it, I burst out in a laugh. "You could stand to suffer a little more of that, if you ask me. I never saw a man cared less about food."

"It's not that kind of food he meant."

"Well *that* kind of food is important. Why else would half the county storm a courthouse like that? Anyhow, it's right to feed people, you said so yourself."

He raised his eyes then, but they were just shadows in the blue darkness.

"You did," I said. "Don't you remember? Last summer. In that colored preacher's church? You were quoting Scripture and everything. Let's go, Harlan, I'm starving. And we still got to find someplace to sleep."

He got up then, really fast, started walking. I caught up to him, touched his back, asked him to slow down, but Harlan didn't slow down, he kept walking quick, his limp bad, away from the town lights, deep into the country along a dark rutted road. And I went with him. Of course I went with him. Because after we left that sharecropper's shack near Bokoshe I never turned aside anymore. We'd gone from Heavener to Poteau to Spiro, east to Fort Smith, north to Fayetteville, Springdale, Joplin. In the Joplin campyard, Harlan said he wanted to go to McAlester, and I said, All right, honey. Whatever you want to do. I knew what he wanted to do, because every time we heard about a labor strike or a farm auction, a brush arbor revival meeting, anyplace a crowd of people would be gathered, he'd always want to go. He bought potted meat and a loaf of bread with the two dollars the picture lady gave us, he got himself a pack of Luckies, I remember, and we left for Oklahoma the next morning. I'd made my mind up in Bokoshe, and I'd told him. I promised. I said, Harlan, I'm not going to buck you anymore. When he set out on that night country road, I went with him. I stumbled a time or two, but the moon came up afterwhile, and then I could see how to follow him very well.

He stopped at a house finally, a little shotgun shack with a light on inside and a cinderblock step. I watched him go up on the porch and knock at the door. Somebody came in a minute. I could see the crack of light and Harlan standing in it, his profile lit perfect under his hat. Harlan said something I couldn't hear. A man's deep voice answered, Harlan said something again, but I couldn't hear that either, I was too far out in the road. Harlan turned, just as the door was shutting, and walked back to where I stood. I asked him who the man was, but all Harlan answered was: "I believe you said it right, Short. I believe folks have got to be called to the table." He turned and kept walking.

I saw the next house then, or I could see the black outline of it, this one didn't have on any lights, but Harlan went right up to the door. I could make out a row of shacks behind it, their tumbledown shapes, and I knew then it was a little mining town, a coal community, and I knew, too, that the people were suffering, because I could see the boarded-up company store across the road. Harlan knocked at this second door. I waited till somebody inside turned a light on before I went up and stood next to him on the porch.

folksay

All through the evening and into the night the people in the McAlester courthouse argued and grumbled. The youngsters fretted, pinched and kicked one another on their pallets. The women tried to sooth their bawling babies. Some of the miners fell asleep, others sprawled on the benches or against the walls with shoulders sunk down. Mrs. MacIntosh sat slumped in the district attorney's chair with her eyes closed, fanning herself with one of her papers. DeWayne Tallent snored softly on the floor with his mouth open, like a child. Gradually, bit by bit, we saw the life seeping out of the project. We were too hungry, some said, we couldn't keep our strength up. But most of us knew it wasn't strength we lacked. What it was, our hope was flagging. One or two thought to ask what had become of that singer fellow, but others just shrugged. By the time grayish light began to seep in through the floor-to-ceiling windows, you couldn't help but notice the dirt and smell and hunger. You knew that the whining of the little ones wasn't just worn-out kids acting cranky from sleeping on a too-thin blanket on a hardwood floor, but that little by little, degree by degree, tissue by tissue, our children were dying. You could still detect a bit of that old ear-back doggedness in a few of the men and women—mining folk aren't a breed to give up easy—but you could see others losing faith by the second, and others so tired and hungry and sick and heartsore they were just waiting for the end to catch them.

So when Coke Jessup came to around nine and wandered downstairs and out into the street, and then ran back in flapping his hands, crying out, "Holy Moly!" nobody paid him any attention. "Look out the window!" he kept yelling. Finally some of us slouched to the back and looked through the tall windows, down into the street, and it was a powerful sad sight that greeted our eyes.

Across the boulevard, in front of the new Aldridge Hotel, a closed-in army transport truck stood parked at the curb, and in front of the truck, lined up on the paved street in the morning sunlight, were dozens of National Guardsmen. Their rifles were shouldered, their round, flat-brimmed steel hats were perched perfect, they looked like a bunch of doughboys just home from the Great War.

Why, sure that was sad. You don't think it's sad and worrisome and downright *wrong* to look out your county courthouse window and see Americans lined up to shoot Americans? It is. Especially if you're among the Americans liable to get shot. Naturally we thought they were there for a fight, what else would they be armed for?

The adjutant general broke away from the bunch and marched across the street, up the courthouse steps, and in a bit we heard his boots clunking on the inside stairs. His graying handsome head poked through the courtroom doors. "Citizens of Pittsburg County!" he declared, "I'm here as a direct representative of the governor's office!" He stepped on in the room, stood very stiff, facing the far wall. "Governor Marland wants you to know he has taken you people's plight to heart! He has personally bought and paid for a thousand emergency food rations to be delivered to McAlester. Y'all come outside now and line up. We'll get these hungry kids fed!"

"Don't fall for it, people!" Mrs. MacIntosh cried. She was plenty awake now, and fighting mad. "They're just trying to get us outside! They'll wait till we go out on the street and then they'll bar the courthouse doors." She stood with her arms folded, glaring at the general. "Bring those rations inside the courthouse to feed us," she said, "or take 'em back to Oklahoma City!"

The adjutant general went on staring stiff-chinned straight ahead. "The governor has sent enough rations of corned beef and crackers to feed a thousand."

"Corned beef!" Mrs. MacIntosh snorted. "We can guess where that beef came from! Wouldn't be that old rank canning factory at the edge of town, would it? The state's been shipping dead cow carcasses to this county for months. Our people have been canning that government-slaughtered cattle for nothing wages, it's mighty white of the governor to send the same old stringy beef back here to feed us."

"We don't want table scraps, mister!" a miner called out from the crowd. "We want jobs to work!"

"And clothes!" Mrs. MacIntosh said. "And decent food to feed our children! Go back and tell that oil-rich governor we're not budging from this courthouse till we get what we came for!"

"Amen, lady!"

"You tell 'em!"

"That's right!"

"Y'all can holler all you want." DeWayne Tallent's voice came from near a back window, where he'd been looking down on the street. He turned toward us with a strange look to his face, a kind of mixed-up mess of fear and anger and longing. "Ain't nobody going nowhere," he said. "Nobody's eatin' nothin', either." His gritty eyes turned to the adjutant general. "Irregardless." The courtroom grew very quiet. You could hear the boy's denim overalls swishing as he made his way toward the front—and something else, too, a kind of whine or a low moan in the distance. DeWayne Tallent stepped up into the jury box, turned and gazed out over the people. "Ol' Coke's falling down on his job, folks, did you know it?"

We couldn't figure his meaning. Coke Jessup was slumped against the east wall with his eyes closed, head lolling. We noticed then how the room was turning peculiar, too dark-seeming and airless for a sunny March morning.

"That old sot's supposed to be our canary, idn't he?" DeWayne said. "I believe he appointed himself to the job. Or maybe some of you elected him?" The cloth cap came off, DeWayne reached up and rubbed the back of his dirty neck. He jerked his head toward the rear of the courtroom. "That sorry old drunk just missed the biggest sight of all."

The ones in back turned to look out the windows, there were gasps and similar noises, and then in the next heartbeat, silence, and we all heard it for certain: a low, deep, terrible-sounding groan, and behind it or under it or weaving through it, another sound, thin, high-pitched, lonesome. Those of us that could get there all crowded to the windows, others went out into the hall and across to the offices on the other side to look down.

The entire boulevard, as far as your eye could see, was thronged with poor people, desperate people, in overalls and straw hats, shabby dresses and mining caps, milling around like they didn't know what they were supposed to do now. They were shivering, had their collars pulled up. Their raggedy shirtsleeves and holey coats flapped in the wind. Even the Guardsmen across the way were huddled down in their uniforms, you could see that the temperature was dropping, and you knew just what was bringing it down: the same force making that terrible groaning sound. That wind. That cold blowing moaning northwesterly wind.

You knew what was making the other sound too, the high thin lonesome one, but you couldn't see him yet. You didn't know where he was. That harp sound—you wouldn't call it music—that thin crying sound seemed to be coming from the lobby downstairs. Or that's what you first thought. But then, turn around, seemed like it was filtering from above, like he'd drifted to the rooms on the top floor, or even farther away, up in the attic, or on the rooftop. Here in the next instant, though, seemed like it came from a baby bawling outside on the sidewalk, crying for its mama, now the sound was a dog howling on the high hill in back of the courthouse, now a rain crow calling behind the little door where the judge has his chambers.

The throng outside tried to get in out of the wind. Look down, you could see them crowding into the sheltered courtyard, pressing against the front doors, but the weight of them kept the doors closed against them. Maybe you recognized a few faces, some I-talian folks from over around Krebs and several black miners and their families, a teacher from the L'Ouverture Negro School, a couple of hungry-looking Indian kids escaped from Jones Academy. But there were hundreds of others that you couldn't fathom where they'd come from, all these hungry hordes, except you knew they belonged to you, they were folks just like you who couldn't make it anymore in an America gone wrong, gone sour, gone dark from its dream, and right then is when the dust began to blow in.

It came in a giant red cloud, rising up over the tallest buildings, filling the sky above the grand Masonic Temple on our highest hill above town, moving fast. The cloud billowed up, swarmed over the city, fell in a red choking blanket. You heard the people outside coughing, the children crying. They were pushing, shoving, desperate to get in, they couldn't breathe, they couldn't see how to get the doors open. The soldiers across the road had disappeared in the dust. All you could see now were the beams of a few caught-out automobiles crawling along Choctaw Avenue with headlamps lit, tiny and dim, like they were miles away.

And still the sound wailed. You began to think you were dreaming. Except you could see the red dirt, so vivid, you could smell it, feel its grit between your teeth, iron taste on your tongue, and you could hear the music then, not the high thin cry, but voices, not voices, a rhythm chant you seemed to remember, *your tired your poor your huddled masses yearning*, you needed to breathe free, you wanted to breathe, wanted to breathe, you tugged your shirt over your nose and mouth, you tried to make a mask for your children, the dust was silting in, silting in, and the sound changed, dropped low, went sorrowful and deep, singing about freedom, being carried to freedom, the sound turned high and keening then, wailing, coming from somewhere down below, deep-bellied, dark in a ship's hold, and then it fell into a low steady thumping, a drumming, fierce and slow, BOOM boom boom boom BOOM boom boom boom, hard on the downbeat, BOOM boom boom boom, the drumbeat, the heartbeat, the voices, not voices, *wey-yah-hey*, far away, you couldn't hear the words, *wey-yah-hey-yah-wey-yah-hey-yah-wey-yah-hey until it came to an abrupt*

stop.

Outside, the sky opened. Rain fell through the dust, it fell in thick red mudballs. Everything was splattered with freezing mud, the courtyard and the slick steps, the cars and the transport truck, the flag in front of the courthouse, the street lamps and telegraph poles, all the people. The world was lost in a rusty blizzard, a ruby fog, a bloody red mudfall.

Inside, there was silence.

We didn't know how to act. It looked like the end of the world. We were saved Christian people caught in destruction, this wasn't how it was supposed to go. We'd been reading about it, hearing about it, we'd never expected to see it for ourselves.

The adjutant general wheeled around and left the courtroom, taking the stairs two at a time. He shoved hard against the courthouse door, pushing the people back until he could muscle the door open, and at once, all along the steps and the courtyard, there went up a cheer. As the adjutant general shouldered his way through the mob to go see about his men, in through the courthouse doors poured the people. They swelled into the downstairs lobby, swarmed the offices, flowed up the stairs. Soon the entire building was filled, all three floors plus the basement, and in with the people blew more dust. You couldn't keep it out, it silted red on the windowsills, our eyes, the damp corners of our children's mouths like smeared blood.

That was the worst dust storm to ever hit this part of Oklahoma, did you know it? And you know what else is strange? It was our own dust. They said you could always tell where a storm started by its color, black from Kansas, brown from Texas, dun from Colorado, red from Oklahoma. That's how we knew it was our own rust-red topsoil, lifted off the heart of the state, blowing south and east across our mountains.

Mrs. MacIntosh and some of the women went to work, bossing and relieving, telling folks where to sit or stand, monitoring the lines at the drinking fountain. But quiet. Everybody talked in somber tones, low, like at a funeral, or maybe it was the dust itself that muted everything. And of course then's when Harlan Singer walked in.

He was limping bad now, worse than ever, his used-to-be-white shirt was the color of bricks, his tie was muddy, his straw hat splattered with red blotches. Behind him came more people, crowding into the room till you couldn't turn around, couldn't move hardly. You wanted to tell these newcomers to get out, go home, this was *our* hunger siege, we'd been here from the beginning. Well, and what made it worse, Harlan Singer was grinning. Here we'd been thinking it was the end of the world, and he comes sauntering in like it's a Democrat barbecue at the town park, and just naturally that went all over some people. You didn't know but what some of the rougher men might be getting ready to jump him. But then again, some of us found ourselves grinning right along with him, on account of the jokey way he doffed his hat to the ladies, shook hands, kissed the babies, like a congressman running for re-election. He limped through the crowd, climbed up to the judge's bench and stood beside the padded chair, looking out. The dust hadn't cleared yet, but it was clearing. Outside the wind was still moaning, but soft, like a girl.

"Folks," Harlan said, like he was just continuing an old conversation, "y'all are the salt of the earth, did you know it?" He pulled up a corner of his shirttail and proceeded to polish his harp. "Plenty of times," he said, "out west travel-ing or just anywhere on the road, different ones'll ask me where I'm from, I'm always proud to tell them I was raised up around Sall-i-saw, Oklahoma. Y'all know what *sallisaw* means? *Saltworks*. That's French. I tell 'em *sallisaw* means salt, and that's what my people are, mostly. I tell 'em, Go look that up in the Good Book, if you want to know what the Lord thinks about it."

A few people laughed.

Mrs. MacIntosh said, "What in the world do you mean, dragging this mess of people in here in the middle of a disaster."

"Disaster?"

Mrs. MacIntosh sputtered. "This—! This—! Good Lord, man, this *dust!*"

Harlan took off his mud-battered hat, ran a hand through his curly hair. "Well, ma'am. We didn't know about the dust, we can't take credit for that. We had another notion in mind." He gazed at the back windows. "We aimed to feed the people, like the Book says. I guess it was the right thing, because time we got back to town here, the Almighty'd already parked a whole truckload of supper across the street yonder in front of the hotel." Harlan put his hat back on, lifted the harp toward his mouth. "Don't seem like anybody knows who's to blame for the dust, though. Some folks say tractors. Some say plow-ing. Some say it's the judgment of the Lord. I knew an old man one time told me it wasn't a thing in the world but the American plains getting back at us for stabbing its heart. Said it was the steel-stabbed prairies, plus all the buffaloes shot and skinned and left to rot, thousands of 'em, millions, that used to make dust and thunder on the prairie, all turned to dust now and mounted up to heaven. Blowing back over their home prairie earth." He blew the distant whine of wind. Then he blew drumbeat, blew hoofbeats, blew the wind's roar, distant rolling thunder. He paused, then he blew a long high note, like a bone whistle.

"Of course, that's just one old Cheyenne man's opinion," he said. "I seen some of these Cheyennes in heaven. Least I think they might've been Cheyenne. Could've been Arapaho." He stared at us a minute, then he went on talking slow and dreamy. "Folks, when them on the other side come to meet you, you're go-ing to find they look just like you. They'll have on their straw farming hats, some of them, or their carbide lights clipped to their caps. Sun bonnets shading their faces. Cotton rags tied to their foreheads. Workboots. Cowboy hats. A bunch of them will be in dirty overalls. Lined up in the thousands, the millions, every color, shade, and variety, to the very ends of the earth . . . Or not the earth," he said, seeming to come to himself. "Heaven."

"If we don't get some relief soon," Mrs. MacIntosh said, "a bunch of us are liable to get there ahead of schedule!"

Harlan grinned a lopey grin, reached up and scratched the back of his head under his hat. "Tell you one thing I sure noticed. There's no rich folks in heaven. Did you know that? Of course, the Lord said it's easier for a camel to get through the eye of a needle than a rich man to get into heaven, but most people don't believe it. I didn't. But from what I seen, it's a true fact. No rich folks and no hypocrites either. Won't be any whited sepulchers there. I don't guess we'll have to put up with too many congressmen."

Some of the miners laughed.

"Mighty few senators and governors." Harlan straightened his muddy snap-brim. "No bankers or revenuers or wealthy oil men."

"I ain't worried about heaven!" one of the miners called. "I want to know how to feed my family this morning!"

"We're all believers here, son," Mrs. MacIntosh said. "That ain't the question."

"What is the question then?"

"Why, where's the next paycheck coming from!"

"The next pair of shoes!"

"The next jug of milk for my children."

For answer Singer climbed onto the judge's black chair, he stood in the seat, raised his harp, and blew a loaded coal car rumbling toward the tipple. He blew a train whistle coming, got the train clacking on the crossties, nearer and nearer, close by on top of us, *whahh-a-whah-a-whah-whahhhhh*, he disappeared that roaring freight train away down the tracks. He blew a rooster crowing, a calf lowing, the spitty pitpat of rain on a tin roof. We could hear it then, our hearts lifting: work and good times, ordinary times, we heard wood being chopped and postholes being dug, a cotton gin humming, locusts whining, a fiddle playing, water running, a little child's laugh. Hope was flooding back into the room with that music, or not music—sound. The sound of our living.

"It ain't practical!" a voice cried from the jury box. Harlan paused, looked to the box, where DeWayne Tallent stood with his cap pushed back, his fists clenched, his throat working. "It don't help nothing! That noise ain't going to save us!"

"Save us," Harlan said, his voice mild.

"We don't need music, mister! We need a durn job!" The orphan boy's voice was choked, his face red, and some of the people began to grumble agreement, but others said, "Hsssht, listen. That's us he's playing. The very likeness." One of the newcomers, a farmer in a mud-beaten straw hat, called out over the people's heads, "Son! If you'll remember, you invited us to supper!"

"Oh." Harlan glanced toward the back windows. "I believe that's being took care of," he said.

"When?" the people wanted to know. "How?"

"There's all kinds of food," Harlan murmured. He stared out over the courtroom, pausing at each of the upturned faces, and when he spoke his voice had that dreamy sound. "It don't go into words, folks. That's the trouble. Y'all have seen it though. You know the very truth. You can remember who's the poor in spirit, if you'll just think it over."

His gaze passed to the orphan boy. He put the harp to his lips again, blew a slow, aching trill up and down, and then from between his cupped hands came a sound so familiar, so tender and hurtful and strong, you felt like you'd heard it from the cradle—or before that even, like it was borned out of creation itself. Inside that sound you heard the mercy in your mama's touch, you smelled the scabs in your baby's throat, felt the burn of rage behind your eyes, the taste of sin upon your tongue, and in your chest, the slow heave of pity. The sound began to rise, began to lift toward something—joy maybe, or helplessness, or sorrow—but the double doors slammed open, and Sheriff Doolittle shoved in.

The song stopped.

"You! Harland Singer!" the sheriff called out.

Harlan held his cupped hands away from his mouth. "Howdy, friend," he said.

It took us a minute. It took us a little while, we were lost in that place of remembering, the unfathomable mystery, but in another instant a different sound soughed through the room: *Harlan Singer Harlan Singer Harlan Singer*, the whisper passed from lip to lip. Well, if there'd been anybody present who didn't know the name before, we surely knew it now, and we repeated the whisper as we watched the sheriff shoulder his way to the foot of the bench.

Doolittle stood peering up at Singer with his hand cocked on in his gun-belt, thumb twitching. "I thought I'd seen your mug somewhere before," he said. "Took me a little research." The sheriff's smile came so broad and quick it made his sideburns pop. "But I got my answer." He plucked the handcuffs from his back pocket, hoisted himself onto the dais. "W. William Jones," he announced, keying open one side of the cuffs, "alias Wee Willie Jonesy, alias Harland Singer, you're under arrest." The sheriff snapped the circle closed, yanked him off the chair. Harlan landed hard on his feet, his weak leg buckled, he nearly fell, but he caught himself and stood still. Doolittle intoned very loud, so that the entire room heard: "You are hereby charged with robbing the Farmers and Merchants Bank of Vardis, Oklahoma, on the ninth day of July, Nineteen Hundred and Thirty-two! I'm adding in a charge of inciting to riot. Plus unlawful assembly, trespassing on government property, and if you don't come along peaceable enough, resisting arrest!"

"Leave him alone!" voices cried. "Let him finish his song! He ain't done nothing!"

But one of the newcomers complained, "That fella brung us here under false pretenses! He promised to feed us! You oughta slap a charge on him for that!"

"Aw, shut up and go home!"

"*You* go home!"

"Y'all are *all* fixing to go home," the sheriff said "I've about had it with you people."

"Threats don't scare us, Bobby Lee."

"Vi, you stay out of this. Now I'm taking this fella in, and when I come back—hey! Watch it! Look out, somebody hold that door!"

It was too late. The ones who'd been stuck outside the courtroom were pushing hard to come in, hungry to see what the stir was about. All at once you had bodies ramming you from every direction, elbows in your belly, shoulders against your ribs, boot heels on your toes. Now, nobody likes that, but we're a real open-country type of people, we need room to breathe, we expect it, and we don't care a whole lot for being touched by our own kin, much less being rubbed up against by rank strangers. "Move over, buster!" people said. "This is *my* place!" "We were here first!" But the outsiders kept shoving, crowding into a space too small to hold the ones already in there.

Doolittle unsnapped his holster. "I'm giving you folks one hour to clear this courthouse! Anybody still here in an hour I'll march 'em straight out to the state pen!"

"The hell you will." DeWayne Tallent swung a leg over the ledge of the jury box, but Harlan Singer raised his free hand toward the boy, palm out, like a witness being sworn in. DeWayne stopped astraddle the ledge.

"This here ain't the one," Harlan said.

DeWayne stared at him.

"No sense in blaming the blind if they can't see. Or the deaf for not hearing." He held the boy's eyes. DeWayne's face had a struggling look, like he was trying to remember something he'd known once—or like he was trying hard not to. "You seen it, same as me," Harlan said. "It ain't about the dark place. That's just sin. That's misery. It's something else, innit? Look around." The orphan boy sat astride the jury box, his jaw working as he stared out over the courtroom, gazing face to face to face.

Now this here, this is a hard part to explain. It went by so fast and it felt so strong, and it was a little like hope and a little like wonder, but it wasn't neither one of them. It was just a feeling somehow, almost like a scent, a faint odor sweeping the air. The peacefullest look settled over the orphan boy. For one flickering instant you felt like you knew what this was all about. You understood what you were here for. What you were capable of. What you'd been given.

"Quiet!" The sheriff yelled. He jerked Singer's free hand behind his back to lock it with the other, snapped the steel ring closed with a final-sounding click.

There was a beat of silence. Then folks began to holler, to clamor and shout. "Let the man play!" "Shove over!" "Give us room!" The crowd jamming the door tried to squeeze in. There were feet being stepped on and ribs being jabbed, little children crying, babies wailing. Different ones began to climb up to stand on the pews to see, blocking the views of the ones too slow to think to do that, and them on the floor started hollering, "Down in front!"

The sheriff pulled his sidearm. "You people clear this courthouse! I mean it now!"

"Aw, shaddup, Bob."

"Go home."

"Go back to Texas!"

"Move aside!" the sheriff called. "Clear these aisles! I'll arrest the whole lot of you!"

"*Let him go!*" a voice called, a shrill, piping voice, like the cry of a killdeer a hundred times loud. We all turned and looked, and there in the doorway stood the possum-haired girl—and that's the first most of us even remembered we'd forgot her, she was such a little mouse. Folks were backing up to give her room, on account of she was holding a 30.06 with a bayonet strapped to the end. She was covered in red mud, too, just caked in it, cheek to foot. Her hair wasn't possumlike anymore, or, that is to say, what little we could see was plastered down and matted the color of the redbrick stores all over town. A flat mud-spattered steel helmet perched on her crown, sort of loose and perilous, with the leather strap doubled under her chin. She looked like a little red clay doll wearing an upside- down pie plate on her head.

The sheriff tried to ease the safety off his pistol, but the girl raised the rifle to her shoulder, and the people held their breath, squeezed back.

"Unlock my husband," she said.

What else was he going to do? Doolittle pulled his keys out, opened the cuffs. But there were going to be consequences, wasn't anybody present who didn't believe that.

"Come on, Harlan," the girl said, but he just kept standing with his hands behind him, like they were still cuffed. She came on in the room, moving toward the bench. We could just barely see the top of the muddy helmet gliding through the crowd, but you could see that bayonet real well, swaying and dancing, pointed straight up. People were stepping all over each other, backing up to give her room. The sheriff waved his pistol, called out, "You're under arrest, missy!" But the tip of that bayonet just kept gliding toward the bench. Then you heard the girl's voice let out a sound, there was a flurry of movement at the front and—

Ker-BLAM!

Everybody jumped, some hit the floor, others stampeded. As terrible as the rush to get in had been, it was a hundred times more terrible getting out. The weak and the elderly got crushed to the side, little children were trampled, the glass in the double doors shattered. The panic lasted about a minute. When it was over, we counted three broken arms and a broken leg, a half dozen busted ribs, too many knots on foreheads to count, and the orphan boy dead on the floor.

Nobody seen how it happened. Oh, later on, lots of folks claimed to. Some said the girl fired the rifle by accident or on purpose, and others claimed Harlan had hopped down to take it away from her and somehow caused the gun to go off. There were plenty who swore it was Bob Doolittle's pistol that done the damage, and some who swore it wasn't even a gunshot at all but a stick of dynamite stolen from the mines, smuggled in and exploded by secret anarchists, and it was just the misfortune of the Tallent boy to be standing in the wrong place, that was all. In the long run, though, it didn't matter how many stories went out on the subject, because the official story that came down—and the one that put a price on his head—was the one that declared Harlan Singer shot that kid in cold blood.

You didn't want to believe it, of course, but then, the guilty run, don't they? And when we looked around in the chaos and the dust, there were only two things we knew for sure. One was that help was on the way, for we all recognized the wail of mingled hope and terror in the sirens. The other was the fact that Harlan Singer and the girl were gone.

Sharon

I stood in the doorway. I didn't want to go in. I hated so many eyes on me. Harlan might have liked it, but I didn't. And I was tired, I felt thick and faint and quivery. We'd walked the whole night. Plus it made me just sick to see my husband with his hands locked behind him, a prisoner, his hat knocked cockeyed, and he couldn't even get his harp to his mouth. I waved that tall gun, motioning for the sheriff to unlock him, which really made that lawman furious, but I didn't care. Harlan kept standing there. He was free, his wrists were free, he could have walked off. I couldn't tell what was wrong. I thought maybe he was upset with me because I'd quit trying to feed the people, that's what he'd asked me to stay outside and do.

"Let's go, babe," I said, but he didn't move. I got a sinking feeling then, like he was ashamed of me. All those people staring at me, filthy in the doorway, covered in mud. Then I thought—this happened so fast, how I was thinking, just in an instant while I stood at the door—I thought maybe Harlan didn't like it that I'd stolen that guardsman's rifle and hat. "It's a borrow, not a theft!" I told him. And it *was* a borrow, even if that soldier asleep in the hotel lobby didn't know it. I had every intention of giving them back. The steel hat I only took on account of the muddy rain falling. What I'd snuck in there to get was a gun. Alls the gun I'd ever fired was my daddy's shotgun at a bobcat on top of the henhouse one night, and it knocked me on my tail, too, but I felt like I had to do something. I'd seen the sheriff coming out of the post office with Harlan's picture on a piece of paper. It was just a pencil drawing, it wasn't even a good likeness, but I knew what it was. Harlan was taking too long. I was scared the sheriff was going to snap the cuffs back on him. "Harlan, come *on!*"

But he wasn't listening. Not to me he wasn't. He turned his eyes to the big loud kid in the dirty cap sitting on the ledge in front of the jury box. I saw it then, the look on Harlan's face the same now as all those years ago, the way he used to stare at a campfire or a boxcar floor, and all of a sudden I understood. I knew why he picked him, why he played for him. To Harlan this kid in McAlester was the same as the other one, the skinny blond boy in the freezing boxcar on the way to Kansas City. I don't mean he thought they were the same person, I mean he thought they were equal. Like whatever Harlan had failed to do for the ringwormy blond kid, he could do for this one. He could make up for it now. I half expected him to take off his hat and try to hand it over, but the big kid already had a filthy cloth cap cocked on his forehead, and anyway that's not what it was. It wasn't the tin of sardines or the jacket Harlan never gave him.

We should have brought him with us. It's hard on a kid traveling alone.

No! I thought, or I said it out loud, I don't remember, but I know that right in that moment I knew I was done. My mind said, No sir. No sir. He is not coming with us. I've went the second mile, Harlan, and the third mile, and the seventy times seven, and this is it, Harlan Singer. It's finished. I'm not doing this any more.

I started to push past the people, but the crowd was too jammed around me, I couldn't see anything until I got right to the platform, and then I saw his left hand rising. Everything just went really fast: Harlan raising his harp and the sheriff swooping his pistol and that boy in the dirty cap leaping from the jury box, all at once. And the sound was so loud. It knocked me on my hind end, same as Daddy's shotgun back in Cookson, and in the next second everybody was yelling and running and Harlan was beside me. He must have practically flew from the back side of that desk.

He picked me up and set me on my feet, we went out the same way as before, ducked through the judge's door as if we'd planned it, down the stairs and out the back, running north, away from the sirens, both of us coughing in the dust. We'd had a lot of practice running from bulls but we hadn't done it in a long while, and I got a stitch in my side before we were halfway up the hill. We paused for me to catch my breath, I couldn't breathe that dusty air, and when I looked behind I could just barely see the back of the courthouse below in the red haze. Harlan undid the strap under my chin, fumbling a little, in a hurry, and he laid that helmet on the sidewalk in plain sight where the owner could find it. After that we walked fast.

Harlan was limping awful bad, but we kept angling north and west till we got to the rail line. We walked alongside, and here in a little bit I heard the train whistle. I turned and looked, and I'll tell you something, I was never so glad to see a freight train bearing down on me in my life. I saw right off it was the good old Katy Flyer, coming from Texas, and I turned and started running the same direction the freight was headed, north towards Muskogee. Harlan was panting behind me. He had good wind, my husband, even in a dust storm. His lungs were strong from so many years blowing harp. The engine was barreling at us, I could hear it, I knew it was going too fast, but I just busted out running faster, the cars flying by, and I kept running, I grabbed a handhold and it jerked me off my feet, but I held on like anything. The freight speeded up faster and faster, the whistle blaring, and I hooked my arm through the ladder, turned and reached a hand down to Harlan, but he was falling behind, limping, half loping, he was trying to run, but that leg wouldn't let him. That damned jake leg.

I yelled for him to *run!* though I could see already he wasn't going to make it, I'd have to jump off. I looked at the ground flying past, faster and faster, and I knew it was too late. If I jumped it would kill me—and not just me but also my baby, the one I was carrying. My Ronnie. I didn't know I was carrying him when that lady took our picture outside Joplin, but by the time we got to McAlester I knew. I hadn't yet told Harlan. I aimed to. I just hadn't. I screamed for him to meet me in the yards in Muskogee. He kept running, trying to run, limping hard, yelling something back at me, but I couldn't hear what it was.

Singer

Nokiller! he shouted, still running, Sharon calling back to him, her hand cupped, the wind snatching it, the train barreling fast away from him. *Nokiller!* he kept shouting, praying she heard. Long after the freight disappeared he was still running, shouting the word.

He walked back toward the railyard then, slow between the houses, the hurting in his leg fierce, watching all the time east toward the town, toward the courthouse, through the dust. A siren cut the near air once, and he jumped into a backyard, cried out when the pain shot to his groin. He hid behind a line of washing hanging straight down, rust red, mud-caked, but the siren wailed off in the other direction, and Singer limped on toward the switchyard, the pain like a knife's edge at the front of his leg. An engine was coming toward him, not a freight but a passenger train, pulling slow enough he thought, and he turned and loped north with it, north toward Muskogee, the pain cutting his breath as he grabbed on, still running, swung himself up to stand between the cars. He pressed himself against the Pullman, riding the blinds, the earth racing fast beneath him, the hurting in his leg growing worse; he'd felt the shinbone jar when he leaped off the platform, but it wasn't broken, he could walk, he could run if he had to, it wasn't broken, and Muskogee wasn't so far.

In the blur of earth beneath his feet he saw the orphan boy's face, blue eyes open, bib overalls bloody, the dirty soft cap still on his head. Singer closed his eyes against the image, but he opened them again, quick, the earth racing, his leg pulsing, a swimming black dizziness trying to make him let go. He forced his eyes open, pushed his cheek against the shuddering Pullman. If his grip loosened even a little he would fall beneath the wheels, be crushed in red tumbling pieces, he'd seen it happen one time, long years ago, to a tired rider who'd nodded off just that once. *Sharon.* She would know to jump off at Muskogee, wouldn't she? She'd know to go through the brush to the creekbank. Even if she hadn't heard him, she would know. He longed to pat his pockets, feel for the harp, make sure it was still there, but he needed both hands to hold on. A tune came to him then, humming inside him, and for a moment the gladness returned, as it had in his boyhood, walking the dirt track between the trees, the old wagon road from Sallisaw through the hills to Marble City, walking along playing the tin harmonica the man had given him.

Here boy, the barber said, grinning in front of the Rexall, *see if you can't make a tune out of this.* And standing on the Sallisaw sidewalk Singer had opened his hand for the first time to receive it, a mouth harp, a cheap tin harmonica, but it lay smooth and cool in his palm, familiar already, and he'd closed his fingers, picked up his cap, shaking the pennies into his fist. He'd slipped the coins into his pocket along with the comb and the packet of cigarette papers, started walking toward the hills. It was summer then, and his mother had been gone a year. He'd walked along the dirt track, trying to make that sound, the sound of his mother gone, thinking maybe it would ease the hard burn in his chest, but when he put the harp to his lips only glad sound came out. He'd tried many times, but all he could hear was a sound like skipping stones across water or like the calliope at the Sequoyah County fair. A bird trilled in the top of a hickory, and he'd stopped in the road. He couldn't see the bird, the leaves were too lush, but the sound broke beautiful and clear, and he'd put his lips to one end of the harp, his tongue to the holes, tried to make the same sound. The bird answered. He'd called the bird again, and the bird answered—or the bird went on bragging to its rivals, or calling its mate, or singing just because it wanted to sing, no matter. He'd started walking again, and inside the harp the bird sound turned to song, a skipping, gliding flutelike sound, a little glad song, and that glad song turned into another, and if he paused to think, if he tried to practice or make a tune he'd heard somewhere, the sound turned flat and wheezing, sour, but if he walked along in the speckled shade forgetful, playing how he felt, the sound came out glad, and he felt glad.

The whistle screamed from the tender, the engine was slowing on the downgrade into Eufaula, and he knew then he would have to jump off before the train reached the station, else they'd find and arrest him. He felt again the cold clasp of steel at his wrists, his arms locked behind him, his harp imprisoned useless in his fist—and Sharon waiting for him, alone on the creekbank. But in his leg the pain throbbed, pulsing from thigh to ankle, he didn't know if he could swing down running, as the old man had taught him, running before his feet hit the ground so as not to roll wildly, break his neck, slip under the wheels. He crouched slightly, the pain stabbing upward, both hands ready on the grip, waiting for the moment to jump, waiting as long as he dared, because a train moving slowly was still moving too fast, but the engine only slackened a little near the station, whistle blaring, before it began to speed up again, and Singer understood it was a passenger express. He'd breathed relief then, because he didn't have to jump yet.

The countryside was passing slow enough he could see dust layered on the rooftops, car fenders—but no rain here, he thought, no sign of the red mud. The air was tinged pink, like sunset, though he could see the soft coin of sun burning high overhead through the haze. How quiet the fields, quiet the towns, all work stopped because of the duststorm. In a field near the tracks a yellow-haired boy walked across a pasture, a spotted dog leaping behind him. The boy raised a hand in greeting, but Singer dared not loosen his grip to wave back. The train gained speed again through the low blackjack hills, crossing the North Canadian, the water here the same dun color as the wide winding bed, paler than out west, where the water ran russet, the color of the red dirt it cut through, the color of the riverbank in Oklahoma City where the silence had first glommed itself inside him. No, he told himself. Not that now either. He wouldn't think that either, he'd think nothing, he would sing maybe.

But the thundering rails kept the sound inside his mouth. He ached to know if he still had his harp. His hat had blown off in the wind, but his harp—surely he'd slipped it into his pocket when he leapt down to go to Sharon, jumped and landed hard, trying to reach her because he believed they had shot her, she fell so fast, dropped straight away in the roaring blast. But it wasn't that. Not Sharon who'd been shot. *the orphan boy dead on the floor. eyes open. chest apart.* Not now. Not now, notnow notnow notnow notnow. *I am a poor wayfaring stran-ger,* the song came to him, *traveling through this world of woe,* the words sang inside him, the old words, the first words, as he'd learned them from a white picker in the cottonfields outside Muldrow: *But there's no sick-ness, toil, or dan-ger / in that great world to which I go.* His arms were tired, his palms burned, the pain in his leg throbbing, swelling, like the white taut pain of the blood poison all that long time time ago, when Profit carried him, yelping with every step, into Tahlequah to the hospital, and Singer thought, his hands tight on the grip, he thought, It'd be mighty good to have a drink of rye whiskey this minute, to kill the pain. Then he thought: *Sharon.*

Surely she would know not to go into town? They'd be looking for her in the towns, in Muskogee or Tahlequah, in Sallisaw, Cookson, any of the towns. If they caught her they would put the steel cuffs on her wrists, as they'd clamped them on him. Surely she would know to go east through the timber, into the hills, where the creekbed was hidden, the springfed creek with its bed of white stones. *I'm only go-ing over Jordan, I'm only go-ing over home.*

Going home. Going home. As he'd gone home after they killed Willie Jones, riding alone curled against a boxcar wall hearing the thud and smack of men's fists on Willie's face, their curses as they beat Willie for stealing the tin of deviled ham and the cube of salt meat and the flat little flask of sweet wine, because Willie did have them in his rucksack, because Singer gave them to him, because it was Singer who'd sneaked into someone's bedroll in the night and taken them, traded them to Willie Jay to barter more time practicing on the catgut-strung guitar. He'd longed to make it stop, but his feet carried him backwards because he was afraid, because he was a boy then, because he hadn't known men held that darkness, that meanness in them, he hadn't understood inside himself yet what men were capable of.

No. Not to think of that now either. The train was nearing Muskogee, he could see the first crossing just ahead, he had to get ready to jump.

But the train screamed through Muskogee, slowing only as it passed the station, where Singer's eyes met the rail agent's eyes, staring hard an instant before the man ducked inside the depot to telephone ahead. No matter, Singer told himself. He wouldn't be on this train when it stopped in Tulsa, because he would jump now, he would jump, the engines churning toward the outskirts, gaining speed, the whistle screaming, and he couldn't wait to look for a good place, a safe place, couldn't let himself think, he had only to grasp tight with both hands and kick his legs out into the speeding air, running—

He awakened in the dark to pain, and it was nothing like waking in Texas with Sharon asleep in the chair beside him, swimming up from the darkness, from the dream that was not a dream, groping, Sharon's voice to guide him. In Muskogee he awakened only to pain. He had no memory of the jump, the roll and tumble, no memory of anything but the hard pain boring through every part of him, flowing from his leg upward in hot burning circles, and he wondered if he'd broken some bones when he fell. But he could still move his arms, lying on his side in the darkness, he could move both legs, though he wouldn't, because it hurt. He felt for his harp, the small hard shape of it in his trouser pocket, yes, it was there, and he thought to take it out and play, but the pain was cutting him too bad, cutting his breath. He lay still, waiting for day.

When first light came he saw he was in weeds many yards from the track. The dust had blown here too, coating the dry grasses. He raised up a little and saw the backs of houses not far away, small and gray and set wide apart. He would have to go there, to those houses yonder, he would have to knock at their doors, not to invite the people to supper but to ask for help, to beg a ride—

No. He couldn't get someone to carry him to the creekbank, or even near it, because then he would not be the only one in danger, because then they would arrest Sharon. He would have to walk. No matter the pain, he would have to. But he couldn't go in daylight. No good to go in daylight limping along the side of the road where they would see him, he'd have to wait again for dark.

He lay very still, gazing down the length of himself, seeing for the first time the dark circle on his caked trousers, darker red than the mud, there on the side of his thigh where the pain was most fierce; he stared at it a long time, a mystery, until he realized it was bloodstain. He must have injured himself when he jumped from the train, he thought, and then he thought, no, because the blood was dried already, and it was some of where the pain was coming from, but not all. He reached his hand down to touch the leg beneath the stiff khaki. His left leg. The bad leg. He could feel the fire in it. He thought to look at the wound, but he had nothing to cut the cloth with and he was too tired to take the trousers down. He put his hand on his pocket where the harp hid, shut his eyes a moment to rest.

All through that day and into the evening he awakened and slept, waked and slept, and each time he woke he tried to curl tighter against the earth because he was trembling with cold, or with fever, but when evening came, he made himself stand up and put weight on the leg, and the pain was so bad he felt like it wanted to kill him, but he made himself walk. The moon was full, the night cold, and he walked without stopping but even so, when grayish light began to lift in the sky some, he saw he still had not yet reached Pettit. So he hid himself in the timber again, to wait for night.

There in the brush he lowered the trousers and discovered the small
place on the side of his thigh, low, near the knee almost, oozing blood a
little where the khaki had been pulled away. In his mind he heard again
the gun sound, saw Sharon and the orphan boy dropping to the floor
at almost the same instant, but he didn't want to, and he took out his
harp and put it to his lips, blowing very soft, almost only breathing. A
flesh wound, he told himself. From the sheriff's pistol. That must have
been what happened. It would be all right, when he reached Nokiller
he'd send Sharon to Calm's cabin. Calm Bledsoe knew plenty enough
medicine to heal a flesh wound.

In the day, inside the filtered shade, he lay listening to the
earthsounds: a robin's laugh from a far clearing, the brown oak leaves
above him, whispering, stubborn, clinging to the branches against the
tiny buds pushing up from underneath. Seemed like he could hear
the scrape of steel on rock, rhythmic, the way it repeated in him, the
sound of his own feet in cramped leather shoes, squeaking, walking
to the front of the church, the swish of Mrs. Letbetter's skirt, the soft
tump of pine against pine, squeak of metal screws tightening, the dry
scraping sound in the graveyard, rope against earth. *I'm go-ing there to
see my mo-ther.* She'd been good to him, Mrs. Letbetter, taught him his
letters *She said she'd meet me when I come.* But Brother Letbetter had
treated him like a halfwild creature, dangerous, strange, and would not
allow him inside the house, though the minister had fed him, hadn't he?
Taught him to haul water, read the Bible, cut wood. *I'm go-ing there to
see my fa-ther.* But Profit had carried him on his back to the doctor, to
save his leg, save his life. Profit had taught him how to scrounge food,
scavenge clothes, ways to find drink and good will and music in the
most barren places. *I'm go-ing there no more to roam.* Taught him verses
to spout from a side rail or a soapbox, and Singer had learned religion
the same as he'd learned to play harp and jig-dance, the same as he'd
learned to place hickory nuts in empty windows when he'd snatched
the cooling pies for himself, *I'm only go-ing over Jordan,* because it was
easy to act agreeable, to pretend pleasant, play joyful, *I'm only go-ing
over home,* because the harp hummed in him that glad sound, and he
had always known how to hold grief in a hidden place, keep despair in a
deep place, though the old man had always seen.

Listen, boy. God enters through the wounds of imperfection. The old
man's voice in the Tulsa campyard. *You got to look inside yourself.*

Shut up, old man. Let me sleep now. Because Singer's head

hurt, his mouth hurt, he'd been playing all night, drinking all night, dancing, while Profit watched from across the Tulsa yard, measuring him, judging him, he thought, and Singer had only danced harder, played louder, campsongs and reels and ragtimes, with the rest of the bums cheering him on, whooping and clapping, until he'd forgotten the old man, forgotten pain and hunger, forgotten everything but the blaze in his chest and the pure clear sound in him and the noise of men clapping, until it was daylight and the sun's rays had blinded him, and all he'd wanted was to roll up in his blanket and sleep. But there sat the old man combing nits from his beard, preaching at him: It's a good thing or a bad thing, sin is. Just depends on if you're willing to use it. That's the wound the Lord enters, son, but it ain't magic, it ain't pixie dust. You got to look inside yourself.

Aw go to hell.

Sin of gluttony comes in a bunch of flavors, son. Sin of greed does too.

You're full of shit, did you know it?

And Profit had stood up then, grunting, using both hands, he'd bent to roll his blanket, saying over his shoulder: Worst is a greedy spirit, son. But I reckon you can't know that yet. He'd touched two fingers to his forehead, turned and walked east with the bedroll under his arm, and Singer had yelled after him, The hell with you, old man! Who set you up to be my judge! And the old man, still walking away, waved a hand over his head in farewell. Singer had thought he'd gone off to scrounge food and would be back by evening, and he'd curled up in his blanket and slept. But when he woke near sunset to the bloody winter sun shooting fierce rays between the buildings downtown, he'd found that the old man had not come back. And the next morning he still hadn't, and he didn't come, and didn't come, and Singer left the Tulsa campyard finally, went back on the road alone. Just for that. Just for nothing.

That just tempted you into showing off, Sharon said.

Sharon.

He had to stand up, he had to get to Nokiller, no matter that it was daylight, he had to go.

Sharon

I stayed in the Muskogee yard a long time, waiting for Harlan, trying to keep out of the way of the bulls. There were two of them now, not the little roly-poly man but two burly fellows who patrolled the tracks with their blackjacks out. I watched every train that pulled in, and Harlan didn't get off. I considered hopping another freight back to McAlester, but I knew he wouldn't stay there after all that had happened, he'd just take the next freight after me, running north. Harlan knew the trains, he knew the Katy Flyer went through Muskogee. Then I thought maybe he didn't want to take a chance on another run-in with a bull, he'd jump off early, so I walked to the edge of town where the trains start to slow coming into the first crossing. I saw a couple of tramps make the jump, but not Harlan, and I was afraid I'd miss him in the switchyard, and so I went back.

For a day and a night I waited. I thought a lot of things. I thought maybe he fell asleep and ended up in Pryor, or maybe he'd accidentally got on the line that branches off to Tulsa. I wanted to go look for him, but I was afraid I might miss him, he might be on his way back to Muskogee while I was traveling to Tulsa. Then I thought, Well, what would Harlan think? He'd know I'd want to go home to Cookson. Harlan would know that, I just felt it in my heart that he would. So I came on back here, walked up to Mrs. Lambert's porch and knocked on the door.

When the law showed up the next morning, I knew it was something bad. They weren't sheriffs or town cops, I think they were G-men, or at least they weren't wearing khakis but dark suits and blue ties. I don't know who told them I was here. For a long time I believed it was Oliver Teasley, or I blamed him with it, but I don't know how he'd have known either. Anyway, when those lawmen showed up, that's the first I learned the kid in the overalls was dead. It was also the first I learned they wanted Harlan for murder on top of bank robbery, which, that was just stupid. I tried to tell the lawmen that. They said yes, ma'am, and went on asking questions: when was the last time I'd seen my husband, had I had any contact with him, and so on. I told them the truth, nearly—I only left out the train part, I didn't want them hunting Harlan on freight trains—but I could see they didn't believe me. They left afterwhile, but the next morning one of them moved into the big room above Stratton's store. To my mind, that's part of where so many tales about Harlan got started, from that lawman moving to Cookson to watch Mrs. Lambert's house.

To be honest, though, I felt relieved. I understood then why Harlan hadn't come for me. It was four or five days already since that accident in McAlester, and I'd thought so many times about going to look for him, but to think it made me just sick, worse even than thinking about trying to find my family. It'd be like us hunting Profit all those years, chasing him, chasing him, and who knew if he was ahead of us or behind us or on a freight passing us, going the other way. I had such a terrible feeling again, about how the world is too big when people are trying to find each other. So when I heard that the governor had put a reward on Harlan, I thought, Well, that's why. He's too smart to walk into the middle of that, he'll hide out and wait till the trouble's settled, and then he'll come scratching at the screen before daylight to get me to come go with him. And I thought to myself, Be patient, Sharon. Just be still and wait.

But it was too hard to wait, because I knew where he was now. That creekbank. That place way out in the bo-jacks with its little cave inside the brambles where he'd hacked away the blackberry bushes and wild roses and propped them back with old sheets of roofing tin. I knew absolutely that's where Harlan would hide out, and I felt like I just had to go to him—except I couldn't do that either. I didn't know how to get there. It's way deep in the hills, there's no road to it, no path, and if I did know how to get there, the law might follow me, they'd arrest Harlan, they might kill him, and even if they didn't, just the fact he had a price on him would make it nearly impossible to clear his name. So I pondered what to do for another several days—that one lawman didn't try to keep himself a secret, he'd sit right in the store and swap lies with the old hunters—and finally that's when I thought of Calm Bledsoe.

I wasn't sure if I remembered how to get to Calm's cabin either, but I thought maybe I could. He lived right on the river, and there was a footpath, I'd been back with Harlan to visit three or four times. I worried that the law might follow me there too, but I thought, well, if anybody could give them the slip it'd be Calm Bledsoe, and I decided to take the chance. Mrs. Lambert borrowed a pair of britches and a cap from one of her nephews, and I put them on and left before daylight, walking fast.

Singer

Why wouldn't she come? She must know he'd be here. Even if she
hadn't heard him, she had to know this is where he would be. A day
and a night he'd limped through the brush, supporting his leg with
the crutch of tree limb until he could walk no longer, and then he had
crawled, pulling himself along the forest floor until he'd reached the
creek at daylight, and with clawing hands and useless leg he'd dragged
himself onto the tumbled bed of white stones. He dreamed himself
standing up from the creekbed, walking fast through the timber,
walking fast and strong, going to find her. Or he could send Calm. He
dreamed Calm Bledsoe stepping off the porch of the cabin, climbing
the rise above the river, going to fetch Sharon, to guide her to him
through the gnarled and clotted woods. But the pain was fierce, and
Singer could only dream it. He rolled a little to one side, drew the harp
from his pocket. His lips were dry and cracked, he had no spit, it was
hard to make his tongue work against the holes. But the sound was in
him, he could hear it so clearly. The sound was more ready in his ears
than it had been since he was a boy. He played it, and for a short while
the pain disappeared.

On his back, at the edge of the thicket, staring up at a pale washed sky
overhead, he remembers her eyes inside the bare corncrib, long months
ago, when she'd followed him across the burnt fields and waited,
hidden, while he played for the sharecropping family, the Blessings,
hungry, angry, divided against themselves. Sharon's eyes in the coal-oil
light black and fierce, her voice asking: Howcome every sorry old sot
and loudmouth drummer and lonesome kid traveling means more to
you than me? And he'd said, Baby, that's not true.

But he had left her sitting in the dirt road, hadn't he? Walked away
trusting her to follow, and she did follow, slipped in the corncrib door,
her eyes changed. She said, Tell me, and when he put the harp to his
lips she held up her hand. No. *Tell* me.

He'd gone deep then, remembering, straining to shape words for that which could not be worded, he said, That beating belonged to me, Sharon. When them bulls beat me in Texas.

No, she said.

Everything had to go the way it went.

No it didn't.

They beat a kid to death on account of me, on account of my thieving. Kicked his head in, I saw his teeth scatter. I saw white bone shining inside the bloody cradle in Willie Jay's skull. It could have been me, Sharon. It should have been. I walked away. I kept walking, stepping backward, but it isn't just that. Listen. There's a reason why we suffer. I couldn't see when they beat Willie, I had to see when they beat me.

Hush, she said. That's crazy.

Do you want me to tell you or don't you?

And she'd stood over him in yellow lamplight, listening, her hands folded across her belly while he tried to tell her how he had feared that living was only emptiness, how from his boyhood this had been his vast and aching fear: that the earth was just men walking in darkness, the worst icebound darkness, that there was no point in living because there was no reason because there was only emptiness, only nothing, coming from nothing into nothing, no hope. How when he'd seen her in her daddy's yard he'd believed that loving her was the force to give meaning where there was no meaning, and how that hope was filched from him, lost to him on the banks of the sandy river when they'd stood on the slope together and he'd seen again what men are, what they can be, when he'd lost the sound inside himself and could not make music because he had quit believing because he'd quit hoping because it had all seemed to him futility and darkness, not his only but everyone's, all mankind's darkness, how he'd wanted redemption, longed for it, but did not know how to find it, until he'd awakened in Texas and knew the reason: knew he'd had to die a little to live again, to hear again, to see. Because he had witnessed men's souls fixed equal between the dark and the light, but the hope was in the light, how he'd come awake knowing sin for what it was then, an imagination, a paltry daydream, and that was what he had to sing.

She'd said nothing. After a time she put her hand out for his harp, and he laid it in her palm. I'm going to go with you, she said. I'm not going to buck you. But I want you to know something, Harlan. You're just as wrong as you can be. She took the harp to her mouth then and blew a loud, pure note. And anyhow, she'd said, lowering the harp, staring straight at him, that don't answer my question.

Howcome every sorry old sot and lonesome kid traveling means more to you than me?

It's not true, his mind whispers. Nothing on this earth means more to me than you. O my love my darlin my heart's life *Sharon.* Why wouldn't she come?

Sharon

Calm's dogs set in to barking before I even reached the footpath, I could hear them far below. I started down the path, winding toward the river. The roof of the cabin came in sight, slab-shingled, a deerskin spread open on it. I could see the green glint of water. Then I took the little turn, and there was the whole cabin snugged against the slope, and behind it the outhouse and the smokehouse, and on the firepit a thin trail of smoke rising. The log walls were almost all covered in staked pelts. Before I got close I could smell them. I'd never seen so many together in one place, possum and rabbit, fox and raccoon, beaver, skunk, coyote, a couple of solid black ones that looked like they could be mink. It had to be a whole winter's worth of trappings. I waited on the path until Calm called the dogs off, *Wa'hyah! Gehyooj!* He didn't seem surprised to see me, but then his wasn't a face that showed surprise anyway.

"*Osiyo,*" I said.

"*'Siyo.*" Calm motioned with his chin for me to come down. I stopped in the yard, or what you might call a yard, it was really just a clearing. Close in like that, the odor was fierce. On the side of the cabin I could see that some of the foxes and possums still had their heads on. Their eyes were dull, their mouths sewed shut. The dogs sat on their haunches at Calm's feet in the shade under the porch roof with their tongues out, panting, their ears pricked. Curs of some kind, or not hounds anyway, one black and one yellow. They weren't wagging their tails.

I didn't know how to start. Harlan had told me that Calm could speak English but I'd never heard him talk anything but Cherokee. Alls the Cherokee I knew then, or to this day even, is just what most white folks around here know, o-si-yo for hello, chooch is boy, gay-hooch for girl, yoneg means white man, and like that. I sure didn't know enough to say something so complicated as everything had turned out to be. I stood a minute, trying to think how to say it, and Calm waited, leaning forward a little to scratch the yellow dog's ears. Finally I blurted, "The law's after my husband, they want him for killing somebody, which he absolutely didn't do, you know Harlan, you know he didn't do that. They want him for other stuff too, but murder's the worst thing, and he can't come get me. I wanted to know if you could go find him, take him a message."

Calm's eyes passed over me in that seeing-not-looking way he had. He turned his gaze along the path, up the slope, said, "You got any good idea where he is?"

It took me a second to answer, I didn't expect it. I mean, I knew he wasn't a fullblood—Bledsoe's a white name, and anyhow his hair was too brown—but Calm Bledsoe talking English just really threw me, no matter what Harlan had said. Then I was glad, of course, and I rushed on: "They put a price on him, five-thousand dollars, and I don't think they mean to quit till they find him. It wasn't Harlan's fault. I shouldn't have never taken that gun in there. I didn't know what else to do. They were fixing to arrest him, well, they *did* arrest him, he was standing there in handcuffs when I walked in the door. But it wasn't even Harlan's idea to rob Teasley's bank in the first place, I was the one wanted to do that, and now they're hunting him all over, and I can't go to him because they'll follow me. He's out there on that creekbank, I know he is, because that is absolutely where he would go. That little stream where we camped when he trapped all them worthless pelts, you know where that's at?"

Calm nodded, looking toward the river.

"Tell him I'm fine, I'm staying at Mrs. Lambert's, but tell him don't try to come get me. The law's watching for him in Cookson. Be sure and tell him that. They aim to use me to bait him, but we're too smart for them. We're not going to fall for it. Tell him when it looks like it's safe, I'll send word by you, we can meet close to the rail line, past Vardis, we'll catch out on a night freight. Tell him . . . " I was thinking about the baby, but I was too embarrassed to say it, and anyhow I wanted to be the one to tell Harlan myself. "Tell him to be careful."

The black dog was whining. She didn't know why we were just standing there, Calm on the porch and me out in the yard, but Calm put a hand on her and she hushed.

"He's a good trapper," I said, "but maybe you could take him something nice to eat?"

Calm nodded.

"It was a pure accident," I said. "That kid dying. I don't know how it happened. Harlan raised his harp and the sheriff swung his pistol and that kid went to jump down. The rifle just went off. It just went off. I fell backwards, and then Harlan picked me up and we had to run, we had to get out of there."

I quit talking. My throat was too tight. I knew in my heart I was lying. I stared down at my feet in old brogans, my belly not even rounded in borrowed britches. I felt like I did in my daddy's yard—*my fault, my fault*. I never meant to hurt him. I didn't. Only scare him. Only wave him off. I couldn't let Harlan bring him with us. We had our own child to feed now. Not some stranger. Not some orphan.

From across a great distance I heard Calm talking, he had a kind of thick deep-throated English like the words were rocks in his mouth. "I got some squirrel gravy left."

He brought me a plate, and I ate outside on the porch. The food made me feel better and in a while I was able to finish telling the things I wanted him to tell Harlan, including the fact there was a G-man living over Stratton's store. Calm listened in silence, every now and then he'd nod. By the time I left an hour or so later, filled up on stewed squirrel and gravy and black coffee, I felt sure everything was going to be all right.

But walking back on the gravel road to Cookson, I started to be scared again. The brush scrubbed in close on both sides, all tangled together, it wouldn't let through a breeze. I had a choking feeling in my chest, like I couldn't breathe. I tried to tell myself it was just me carrying my baby, but the feeling was too powerful, and anyway I wasn't sick with this baby like I was with the first one, I felt strong, I felt normal, at Mrs. Lambert's I ate like a horse. The only difference was, in the beginning, I had the dull, clotted feeling in my chest and belly, and there on the road to Cookson that feeling got to swelling in me thick and warm, like dough rising, stronger and stronger, till I felt like my chest could explode outward, or my throat could.

I remembered it then, that time we stayed in Calm's cabin, when I knew everything, every little thought Harlan had, what he was feeling inside himself. I could hear his voice, soft in the twilight, miserable, aching: *Feels like I'm wadded up with something. I don't know what it is. Something white and thick, glommed inside me. Choking me. Wadded in my throat.* And I felt it inside me, there in the road, that full-up glommed feeling. I was scared Harlan was feeling it too, right in that moment, where he was hiding in the brush by the little trickling creek, which I couldn't find my way to alone and wouldn't dare to go to even if I could, because the law might follow and hurt him, and, oh, I wanted more than anything in the world to go to him. I felt like I was going to die if I couldn't go to him. I turned and started walking back to Calm's cabin, I didn't care, I didn't care, I just wanted him to take me to Harlan. But I went only a little ways and stopped. I stood a minute, listening. I thought I heard a footstep crunch the gravel behind me. The sun was down behind the hills, night was coming. I stood so very still, listening. I couldn't hear anything then, but I was scared. I turned around and started toward Cookson. But I only got a little ways, and that feeling was huge and full and swollen inside me, and I swung around in the road and walked toward Calm's cabin again. Four times I did that, back and forth on the gravel road, while it kept getting dark.

deepsong

On his back at the edge of the thicket, the hard creekbed stones beneath him, the singer stares at the blue twilight, the sky deepening royal, the shadows on the far side of the creek turning dark. How silent she'd been, walking the night roads with him, through the mining towns, and past them, out into the country, how close she'd kept beside him when he stood at the doors and knocked. He had sent her off alone. To feed the people he'd said, while he walked the other direction, gathering sheep, never faltering, until he saw her in the courthouse door, her clothes muddy, her hand on the long gun. *maybe they caught her.* Maybe that was why she did not come, they'd put the steel cuffs on her wrists, as they'd clamped them on him, he can feel the cold rings snapping shut, his arms locked behind him, the harp imprisoned in his hands, that had been the worst part. Nearly the worst part. *the orphan boy dead on the floor eyes open.*

No.

He closes his fingers, places the harp to his mouth, he's got no spit to play it, no wind. He is thirsty. His leg is throbbing. If he could crawl to the water he'd be all right. He can see it there, a dozen yards away, not far, not so very far is it. When morning comes, he tells himself, I'll stand up and walk to the water.

In the silence, on the bed of white stones, he can hear the soldiers laughing, cursing, the old man's cracked and graveled voice saying, *you might not know it, son, but there's such a thing as a gluttonous soul.*

and that had been in the soldier town, yes, in Lawton, in a dark side-railed boxcar with a half-dozen soldiers ringed around him and the jug being passed. He remembers the bedroll tossed through the boxcar door, and then the grey scrawl of hair and the stink of Profit scrambling over the lip, how the old man hadn't seemed surprised to see him, only nodded like he'd known singer would be there, shuffled over to the corner to sit. How the singer folded his cards at once, though he was holding three sevens, went and squatted on the railcar floor: Where the hell you been? I waited a week in that tulsa campyard.

grey eyes squinting in the darkness. I been traveling, son.

Why didn't you come back?

No sense in going back, Profit said. Only forward.

Forward in blame circles you mean. That's all I ever seen.

well, but life don't go straight, does it? Time don't. It spirals, turns in circles.

the soldiers laughing in the middle of the boxcar, cursing, making bets. Hey, harp man! one yelled, Play us a tune, willya?

his hand in his pocket, rubbing the tin. Pass that jug over here! and when it came he took a long pull, but the taste was bad.

That ain't going to satisfy you, the old man said.

he drew it out then, his tin harp, the old one, the first one, played a juiced-up ragtime, but the soldiers went on bidding and cursing and laughing, they didn't seem to hear him, and the singer stopped, whacked the harp against his palm to knock out the spit.

you sure got a gift, profit said. Where'd you get it from you reckon? Didn't give it to yourself. No more than you give yourself breath.

howcome you left?

I been studying the difference between sins, son. Between greed and gluttony. there's gluttony of the flesh and a gluttonous spirit. A greedy body or a greedy soul.

aw hell, the singer said.

sin of pride and sin of glory, them two's a whole lot alike. sin of doubt and black despair.

you ain't changed a bit.

well sir, probably not. profit squinted across the darkness. *You* have though, I'd say. Sin of pride can sure kill a man. sin of doubt can too.

Hey fellas! Singer sang out, Send that jug back thisaway!

It's empty, man. Play us another tune.

Wait, hold it hold it, a young soldier said, I got a bottle a jake in my kit.

Ah, that's a bad business, profit said. I wouldn't take a drink of jake ginger these days on a bet, boys, hadn't you heard?

But the soldier was already stumbling across the car, fumbling in his pack, and the singer raised his harp and ripped out *sally gooden* as fast as he could play it, and when the medicine bottle came around— though the old man gripped his arm, the old voice in his ear rasping, *don't, son!*—the singer drank long and deep.

god enters through wounds of imperfection.

he'd crippled himself, hadn't he? out of willfulness. out of pride and anger. hunger to feel the soldiers' eyes in the dark boxcar, admiring him, and the old man defeated. the old man shown up. It had been the same on the night roads, inside the courthouse, the same sin, the singer's pride, his vanity, the old endless hunger for glory in men's eyes. *that just tempted you into showing off.* no, darlin. No, Sharon. *the orphan boy on the floor.* No.

The night is cold. He slides a hand along his hot thigh, unable to see in the darkness. The leg doesn't seem to belong to him, the swelling so tight it feels like his skin will split open. ah, it'd be good if it could split, spill the poison onto the creekbank. he stares at the winks of stars between the leaves, shivering. *wounds of imperfection.* if he weren't so weak he could nearly laugh. he'd had two good legs like a normal man, two good legs three times wounded, blood poison in his boyhood, jake poison in his young manhood, and now this.

bullet poison, he thinks. *lead poison.*

when Calm comes he'll take a knife and open it, make clean the wound, heal the wound, he can do that. he knows cherokee medicine, if calm comes to save him that will make the third time. Once when he found the singer starving and fed him, twice when he stared at him from his porch like a stranger, so that singer had had to look inside himself. this time makes three.

three's a good number. three for the trinity and the three wise men. his throat aches, his tongue is swollen his lips cracked with thirst. *four for the four directions four's a good number too.*

he can't seem to breathe. he isn't hungry though, he is too sick for hunger. and there's a kind of lightness too, like he could float if he had a mind to, he could just rise up and go.

on his back, in the darkness,
trying to know the difference between sins.
between greed and gluttony.

he remembers her standing in her daddy's yard,
her hand on the brush broom, her eyes big.
the scared tender way she'd looked at him.
remembers
the great blast, the blinding dust,

how in the chaos and screaming he lifted her and they'd run through the judge's chambers, down the back stairs, quick and low through the town, running, leaving behind on the courthouse floor the orphan boy dead eyes open chest apart. the white bone inside the dark cradle in willie jay's skull. how he'd used his knife to cut the sleeves from his coat, and still she lay bleeding, how he'd looked at her face, the life draining, and knew she might die, how when the red clot came he'd laid it on the piece of white batting and carried it to the edge of the field, knifed a hole in the hard earth.

he presses the cold harp to his lips not to breath in it, not to play, but only to taste the brass plate, to feel the smoothness in its touch.

shut up old man! singer shouts aloud, struggling up from the creekbank. *shut up to me. please.*

no salvation without redemption, profit says, no redemption without repentance.

no repentance without confession of sin.

what sin? his mind demands.

no confession without acknowledgment.

no acknowledgment without pain.

in the silence on the bed of white stones the singer asks, what sin?

if it was sin then what sin was it that caused him to steal her away from her family drag her around the country starve her half to death lose the child. what sin caused him to send her off alone while he walked the other direction, gathering sheep, calling the people—

he can feel it now, remembering, how the gluttony for men's eyes rose from a place deep inside him, from his gut into his chest into his throat, the thundering thrill the great excitement, the endless hunger that could not be sated. the thirst that could not be slaked.

the other was centered in his mind, locked in the high loose dreamy part of him that would have called the whole lost wandering world to himself, because he too was once lost and now was found, because he'd been faithless, and now believed. sin eater. greedy spirit. spiritual greed.

in the darkness he sees the orphan boy,

eyes open,

chest apart,

the dirty soft cap still on his head, and on his forearm the eternal pledge spelled out in blue cursive, *cheryl ann.*

I did this, the singer whispers.
no, his mind tells him.
Yes.

in the chill before dawn he fumbles the harp to him. the sound is clear,
ringing inside him, but he can't play it. he has too little breath. the
sound is in him, inside the stolen harp, tarnished to dullness. he'd never
gone back to blackwell to pay the man, and he won't go now because
it is too late now, because he is dying. the singer is dying, but he can
still hear the song, echoing through the timber, the clotted canyons,
against the far bluffs. it wasn't pride. not vanity, not greed or glory that
had called him to sing the people into the courthouse, drawing them
along with his harp's song. because he had always known that the sound
did not belong to him, he didn't create it, he could only translate it
sometimes from the hills' haunted cry.

the world's echoes deep in the canyons.
worst is a greedy spirit, the old man tells him.
you're wrong, the singer whispers. *there's forgiveness for everything.*

the light is coming, he sees its glint upon the water. no struggle now.
the willing surrender. peace like a river. on the far side the people are
gathering.

Sharon

I try to tell myself everything had to go the way it went, because that's what Harlan would say, but it's hard not to think it could have made a difference if I'd went back to Calm's cabin that night when I kept walking back and forth in the road, because Harlan was still alive then, I know that he was. But the last time I turned I was facing toward Cookson, and I kept walking. I was afraid for Harlan. I was afraid for myself, for my baby. I came on back here to Cookson to wait. All night I lay in Mrs. Lambert's back bedroom, staring into the dark with my palm open on my belly, my heart swollen huge in my chest, beating fast, beating hard. The full thick feeling kept in me all night and into the next morning, and then one minute, standing at the kitchen sink helping Mrs. Lambert peel potatoes, all of a sudden it was gone.

I thought then that it meant I was going to lose this baby too, and I went back to the bedroom and laid down. But I got up in a little while and ate supper, I helped clear the table, went to the front room and sat on the divan with a breathless feeling in me, a waiting feeling, because I was still hoping even when in my deepest heart I knew.

You remember how during the war you'd hear those stories about mothers or whole families beginning to weep when they saw an army officer getting out of a vehicle in front of their house? That's how it was for me. I looked up at Calm Bledsoe standing with the morning sun behind him and Harlan's harp in his hand, and I knew the truth in that moment, but I got up and went to the screen and let him in anyway, I stood and waited for him to say the words in English, Mrs. Lambert coming from the kitchen drying her hands on a tea towel, I waited until Calm said those two words: He's dead. And then I dropped straight down on the floor, every strength I had sucked out of me in an instant. Mrs. Lambert put her arms under me to try to lift me, she tried to help me get up, but I couldn't. I stayed there saying I can't, I can't, and sometimes just No.

So, well, after that, it didn't matter anymore. The law could follow me any damn where they wanted, they couldn't hurt Harlan, they couldn't arrest him, so when Mrs. Lambert said, "What do you want to do, dear?" I said, "Go to him."

Next morning, Calm took me out there. It was a beautiful day. The elms had their little reddish buds out, and the cardinals were just going crazy, darting low from brush to brush like flashes of fire in the woods. I was really glad Calm Bledsoe was with me. I never in this world could have found it by myself. Harlan told me once that when he was a kid he used to go a different way every time he went there so as not to carve a path anybody could follow, and there sure wasn't one. We had to practically claw our way through the scrawl of timber, the tangled underbrush, it took almost the whole day. I was worried Harlan would be already starting to smell a little, or that he'd look awful, like he died in agony, but when we stepped out of the brush onto the creekbed of white stones, I saw right at once how peaceful he was.

He was curled on his side like he was sleeping, half in and half out of the thicket. His hands were cupped toward his mouth, like he was pulling his harp toward him. I hadn't thought about his harp since I'd seen it in Calm's hand through the screen door, I couldn't even think then what we'd done with it, but there in the clearing I was wishing I had it with me so I could put it back in Harlan's hands. They just looked so empty. Later though, when I went home and found where Calm had set it on Mrs. Lambert's mantel, I was glad. I was grateful to have that much of Harlan left.

I stood a ways back, looking. His hair sponged every whichway against the stones, black and curly. I wondered how come he didn't lay inside the thicket where the piled leaves were nice and soft. I guess he just wanted to be outside, I don't know. I went over and sat on the rocks beside him. I looked carefully at his face, his doe-colored skin so smooth and perfect, his eyes closed, the black lashes curling up, that tiny white ridge scar on his lip from where the bulls beat him. I didn't cry. I'd been crying all day and all night yesterday, I didn't have any tears left, I guess, and anyway, he just looked pure peaceful. I touched him, he was cold and hard like marble, and I knew that wasn't him in there, not his spirit, not Harlan. I kept my hand on him anyway. I touched his fingers, curled in just a little, frozen like that, like he was cupping his hands for a gift. After a while I realized Calm was gone, though I never heard when he left, but I knew he would be back later. He was just giving me and Harlan time to be alone, like he used to do when we stayed at his cabin that time.

So then I told Harlan everything, all that was in my heart, everything I was sorry for, everything I'd forgot to tell him in our time together because we were traveling so hard. I told him I was wrong about he never gave me anything in place of my family, I was sorry I'd held on to that. I told him about Ronnie. Well, I didn't say the name because I hadn't named him yet because I didn't know if he was a boy or a girl, but I told Harlan I was carrying his child. I told him we were going to keep this one, it was going to live this time, because at Mrs. Lambert's I was eating really good. I told him I could see what he meant about the patterns,

I could see how everything had to happen. I just couldn't see why.

At almost dark Calm came through the brush and sat over on the other side of the creek from us. When I looked up, he said, "I believe I could carry him on my back if you want to take him in to town." I said, "What town?" Calm kind of shrugged. I said, "I believed I'd just like to sit a while longer." Calm nodded and sat still, and I sat.

Later he got up and built a fire, because the night was getting cold, and I sat next to Harlan, silent then, touching him, but I was thinking to myself, What town? Harlan don't belong to any town, not to Sallisaw or Vardis, not Cookson, not even Marble City. This is all the home he knows. This creekbank here. He told me that one time. Those were his very words. And I thought, They'll just make a lie out of him. Those lawmen will strut around like he was some kind of desperate criminal, and folks in Cookson or Vardis or Sallisaw will start going around acting like they knew him, when they didn't. They didn't. They might even make a spectacle if we tried to bury him, the way they did Pretty Boy Floyd—all those thousands of people at Pretty Boy's funeral, the cars lined up for miles on the Sallisaw highway, that's what the papers said. And there won't be any way to clear his name, I thought. How am I going to make people understand that was just a pure accident? It was a mistake that boy died in McAlester. There's no way to let people know it was me that wanted to rob Mr. Teasley's bank, either. I mean, I knew I could tell it, but I didn't feel like it would do any good. When folks get their minds made up about somebody, you can't change them hardly. Most of all, more than anything, I didn't want them making Harlan out to be something he wasn't. Well, that's kind of funny, isn't it? Because by us burying Harlan how we did, that's probably what made people tell stories even worse. Because when daylight came I looked at Calm sitting yonder on the back side of the little fire, and I said, "I think we better just leave him here."

We didn't have a shovel to dig with, but I wasn't going to put him in the dark ground anyway, so we gathered stones from all up and down the creekbed, and some of them were kind of big, but a lot of them were round and small from all the years being tumbled in the water, and I wanted Harlan covered good, I didn't want any animals getting at him, I wanted that pile of rocks really high. So it took us a long time, nearly the whole day to cover him. When we were finished, Calm took a pouch out of his pocket and sprinkled some tobacco on top of the mound. The notion came to my mind to lash some sticks together to make a cross, but I told myself, no, if anybody ever does come through there, I don't want them to know this is a grave, they might mess with it, and then besides—

Oh, somehow I don't want to say it.

Well, I guess I'll just say it. I was scared Harlan wasn't really saved. I was scared I wasn't going to see him again in heaven. According to all I'd ever been taught, that would have to be so. But just to look at him, curled on his side like that, you could see he'd died peaceful. Seems to me like a person couldn't do that unless they were right with the Lord. Don't you think that has to be true? I just believe I'll see him in heaven, he'll probably be standing with the miners and farmers and working folks like he dreamed about. Or he might be over on the colored side making music. People still tell it that he was part colored, part Cherokee. Oh, they tell all kinds of things. They laid a bunch of bank robberies on Harlan that it's no possible way he could have committed because he was already dead. Well, they did the same thing to Pretty Boy. They did the same to Ned Christie—he was an old time Cherokee outlaw, or the papers called him an outlaw, and the lawmen did. He had to hide out in the hills just on account of they'd put a murder to his name that he never did commit. Same as Harlan, the same thing. But with Ned Christie and Pretty Boy Floyd and a bunch of others, everybody knows how the story ended. They know the law shot them to pieces, there were pictures in the papers to prove they were dead and how they died, but with Harlan, because me and Calm buried him and didn't tell anybody, well, to a lot of people's minds Harlan Singer just vanished into the hills. Nobody knows what went with him. Me and Calm and Mrs. Lambert are the only ones who ever did know, and now they're both gone. I would have told Ronnie when he got big enough, but he never got that big. So to this day there's nobody living who knows the true story, except me. Well, and now you. But it don't matter anymore. It don't matter. That's what I tell myself. It don't matter that the law never followed me and I probably could have just gone out to the creekbank as soon as I thought of it. I tell myself, Everything just went the way it went. You can't call it back, no matter how much you want to, no matter how your heart tries.

Ronnie was born at the end of August. He looked just like Harlan, he had Harlan's same doe coloring, that black curly hair. His eyes were brown though, like mine, and he was little like me, just really tiny. It's hard to know if he ever would have got any size to him, he was only nineteen months old when he died. All while he lived, though, and the whole time I carried him, even with how everything went, even so, that was the most peaceful time I can remember in my life.

Mrs. Lambert was so good to me, for one thing. And it was nice to be still awhile, just sit quiet in her front room in the rock house, nice to sleep every night in the same place. And I could feel Ronnie moving inside me, his life in there, and it was almost like having Harlan with me again. I kept the harp in my apron pocket. Sometimes I'd take it out and blow on it while I was trying to do a few chores. I couldn't play worth anything, of course, but I breathed in and out on it because Harlan breathed in and out on it and I wanted to believe some of his breath was still in there, hiding inside the square holes. The sound was still in there, that much I can promise. I'd suck in my breath sometimes, or blow out, my lips tight to the brass plate, and the sound that came out would be so sad and lonesome, so glorious, it was like Harlan was right in the room. I'd feel like my heart was going to just shatter. But then I'd slide the harp or move my mouth sideways, the next sound would be a terrible sour bleating, and I'd turn back to whatever I was supposed to be doing—rolling out dough for a cobbler, hemming a dishtowel for Mrs. Lambert, trying to sew a little newborn-size dress.

For a while Calm came to see us in Cookson about once a month. He'd walk into town with his dogs, always bringing some little gift for the baby, doeskin slippers one time, a tiny blanket. We'd sit on Mrs. Lambert's porch and talk. Well, probably I did most the talking, but he'd say a story every once in a while. He's the one told me how the kids at Marble City used to call Harlan that name, Pretty-Like-A-White-Boy. He said according to his mind, Harlan maybe wasn't even any Indian at all. I said, well, I always suspected that. Harlan just didn't look Indian. His hair was too curly. His eyes were so light, his features sharp. But the Cherokee kids at Marble City got it wrong, too, because my husband didn't look white either. He looked . . . foreign, more than anything. Like he belonged to some foreign tribe.

Then, just exactly a year after Harlan died, Calm came got me and took me back out to the creekbank. I wanted to bring Ronnie to see his daddy, but he was only seven months old and the walk was long and it was cold that day, the sun bright. I carried Harlan's harp in my pocket. Nobody had messed with his grave, I was real glad to see that. We didn't go down deep, just uncovered a few stones, and I blew one last long note on the harp, and then I handed it to Calm and he did the same, a real high-pitched pure note, like a bone whistle, and handed it back to me. I nestled it in there, in amongst the white stones. Oh, that harp shined pretty in the sun. I'd polished it really well. Calm sprinkled in some tobacco. Then we covered the stones back up and left.

And that's the last time I've been out there. I wouldn't know how to find it by myself, and Calm can't take me because somebody killed him not even a month later, or anyhow that's what I think. The fur trader found him in the clearing behind his cabin, next to the firepit. Calm and the yellow dog both, the one he called Wa'hyah, or Wolf, no sign of the black dog. They were swelled up and bloated, the trader said, the turkey vultures had been at them. That Fort Smith trader came to town telling that.

Folks said it was snakebite, they said likely a timber rattler had got the both of them, but I don't believe it. Calm Bledsoe was too good a hunter, his eyes were too sharp, and Wa'hyah the same, no timber rattler was going to surprise them. To my mind, it might have been a snake all right, but it was probably the human kind, because the trader also told it that every last one of Calm's winter pelts was gone from the cabin walls. Sometimes I ask myself—or really, what I'm doing, I'm asking Harlan, I'm whispering it to him, I can't help it, I'll ask, *How can you say that part went the way it was supposed to go? Somebody as good as Calm Bledsoe. A baby as innocent as our Ronnie. It's not right, you know it isn't.* I ask that over and over, but of course I don't ever get any answer.

The water's still rising. It's been rising a year nearly. I don't know when they expect it to quit. It took them four years to finish the dam, I guess it'll take a while to fill the valley. They moved Stratton's store up here to the high ground a long time ago, and a bunch of the houses. Not Mrs. Lambert's though, you can't move a rock house. Not my daddy's church either. They're both down there under Tenkiller Lake. I don't know if they expect it to back up along the creek where Harlan is, but I don't think so. I think that creekbank is too far in the hills, too deep in the timber. I just don't think the waters could reach that far. Or that's what I hope anyway.

in the silence, on the bed of white stones, the singer remembers

the illinois waters low, flowing slow around the bend below cookson

on the morning he stole her away from her family.

how he'd climbed down the bank and his leg slipped and he'd laughed to cover his shame.

how he'd picked up a small river stone, flat and smooth and pale, climbing back to her, how he touched it to her throat, an amulet, a jewel,

and still she would not smile, would not drink from the river.

how he made up promises and told them to her,

and would have given anything